Paul Finch is a former cop and journalist, now turned full-time writer. He cut his literary teeth penning episodes of the British TV crime drama, *The Bill*, and has written extensively in the field of children's animation. However, he is probably best known for his work in thrillers, dark fantasy and horror.

Paul lives in Lancashire, UK, with his wife Cathy and his children, Eleanor and Harry. His website can be found at: www.paulfinchauthor.com.

Sacrifice
PAUL FINCH

AVON

AVON
A division of HarperCollins*Publishers*
77–85 Fulham Palace Road,
London W6 8JB

www.harpercollins.co.uk

A Paperback Original 2013
1

Copyright © Paul Finch 2013

Paul Finch asserts the moral right to
be identified as the author of this work

A catalogue record for this book is
available from the British Library

ISBN 978-0-00-749231-2

Typeset in Sabon LT Std by Palimpsest Book Production Limited,
Falkirk, Stirlingshire
Printed and bound in Great Britain by
Clays Ltd, St Ives plc

MIX
Paper from
responsible sources
FSC
www.fsc.org
FSC˜ C007454

ACKNOWLEDGEMENTS

As with *Stalkers*, the first novel in this series, there are an awful lot of people I owe a debt of thanks to for this book. However, it is largely the same crowd, so it would seem a bit repetitive to namecheck them all again. In which case, perhaps you can allow me this opportunity to make a brief but rather personal acknowledgement.

My late father, Brian Finch, a very fine author in his own right, and a lifelong inspiration to me, departed this world in 2007 at the tragically young age of 70, having risen from very humble origins in our home town of Wigan, a sooty coal-mining borough back in those days, to embark on a career in television that, quite remarkably, would span almost four decades. He contributed numerous scripts to almost every popular TV show of the 1970s, 1980s, 1990s and 2000s, including such classic crime series as *Z Cars*, *Public Eye*, *Hunter's Walk*, *Shoestring*, *Juliet Bravo*, *The Gentle Touch*, *Bergerac* and *Saturday Night Thriller*, though his crowning glory was his loving adapation of Michelle Magorian's *Goodnight Mister Tom* for Carlton Television in 1998, which deservedly won a BAFTA.

All through this time, my dad was an invaluable source

of advice, encouragement and ultra-close friendship. I think he'd always harboured hopes that I would follow him into the writing game, but when I joined the Greater Manchester Police he was as supportive as ever. Many years later, when it became obvious that I too had a desire to put pen to paper, he was there at my shoulder again, a font of thoughts and enthusiasm. It was my dad's suggestion that I should write about what I knew best, police work. Of course, there was no shortage of cop stuff on the telly and an awful lot of authors wanted to participate, but my dad reckoned, correctly, that I would have an advantage over most of them in that I'd actually been out there and had done the job for real.

The rest, as they say, is history.

I have no doubt that my authentic police experience secured me my first script work on ITV's long-running police series, *The Bill*, and it was there, in one of the slickest script departments in modern television, where I learned my craft and honed my skill. And yet it remained the case until my dad's final days that he was always the first port of call whenever I had writing ideas to kick around, writing problems to resolve, or simply wanted a good old chinwag about the strange world we'd both bought into.

So there we go, Dad. You were the spark who lit the blue touch-paper and the warm breath who kept it burning during lean times. These books, which sadly you never saw, are the eventual outcome. It probably wouldn't be going too far to say that Mark Heckenburg, their central character, has many of your traits – an affable nature, a crafty street-wisdom and an indomitable spirit forged in the industrial north. What can I say but thanks a ton. I could never have done it without you.

For my lovely wife, Catherine, whose selfless and unswerving support has been the bedrock on which I've built my career

Chapter 1

The whole of Holbeck should be bombed.

That was Alan Ernshaw's view. Okay, he was a relatively new police officer – just ten months in the job – so if anyone overheard him make such a politically incorrect statement and complained, he'd have an excuse. But the gaffers still wouldn't be impressed. Holbeck, the old warehouse district located just south of Leeds city centre, might well consist mainly of buildings that were now empty shells, its Victorian terraced housing might now mostly be derelict, the few parts of it that were inhabited reduced to grotty concrete cul-de-sacs strewn with litter and covered in graffiti, but policemen didn't take these sorts of things personally anymore. Or at least, they weren't supposed to.

Ernshaw yawned and scratched the dried razor-cut on his otherwise smoothly shaven jaw.

Radio static crackled. '1762 *from Three?*'

Ernshaw yawned again. 'Go ahead.'

'*What are you and Keith doing, over?*'

'Well we're not sitting down for a turkey dinner, put it that way.'

'*Join the club. Listen, if you've nothing else on, can you get over to Kemp's Mill on Franklyn Road?*'

Ernshaw, who was from Harrogate, some fifteen miles to the north, and still didn't completely know his way around West Yorkshire's sprawling capital city, glanced to his right, where PC Keith Rodwell slouched behind the steering wheel.

Rodwell, a heavy-jowled veteran of twenty years, nodded. 'ETA . . . three.'

'Yeah, three minutes, over,' Ernshaw said into his radio.

'*Thanks for that.*'

'What's the job?'

'*It's a bit of an odd one actually. Anonymous phone call says we'll find something interesting there.*'

Rodwell didn't comment, just swung the van into a three-point turn.

'Nothing more?' Ernshaw asked, puzzled.

'*Like I say, it's an odd one. Came from a call-box in the city centre. No names, no further details.*'

'Sounds like a ball-acher, but hey, we've nothing else to do this Christmas morning.'

'*Much appreciated, over.*'

It wasn't just Christmas morning; it was a snowy Christmas morning. Even Holbeck looked picture-postcard perfect as they cruised along its narrow, silent streets. The rotted facades and rusted hulks of abandoned vehicles lay half-buried under deep, creamy pillows. Spears of ice hung glinting over gaping windows and bashed-in doors. The fresh layer muffling the roads and pavements was pristine, only occasionally marked by the grooves of tyres. There was almost no traffic and even fewer pedestrians, but it wasn't nine o'clock yet, and at that time on December 25 only fools like Ernshaw and Rodwell were likely to be up and about.

Or so they'd assumed.

'Something interesting . . .' Ernshaw mused. 'What do you think?'

Rodwell shrugged. He spoke in monosyllables at the best of times, and as he was now deep in thought there wasn't much chance even of that.

'Bunch of druggies or something?' Ernshaw added. 'Squatting? If that's it they'll all be dead by now. Must've been minus-ten last night, easily.'

Again, Rodwell shrugged.

Kemp's was a former flax-spinning mill, but it had been closed now for nearly two decades and was a forlorn reminder of prosperous times past. Its tall octagonal chimney was still intact, the square windows arrayed in uniform rows across its dingy frontage were largely unbroken, and most of its ground-floor entrances were supposedly chained shut, but, like so many of the derelict buildings around here, it wouldn't be difficult for determined intruders to force entry.

Snow crunched under their tyres as they slid to a halt on the mill's southward-facing lot. The gaunt structure loomed over them against the white winter sky. The red bricks with which it had been constructed were hidden beneath soot so thick it had become scabrous. Those pipes and gutterings that hadn't already collapsed sagged beneath alpine over-hangs of snow. At first glance there was no sign of life, but the place was enormous; not just a central block, which itself might have housed a thousand workers, but also all kinds of annexes and outbuildings. As the van eased forward at a snail's pace, it dawned on Ernshaw how long it might take them to locate 'something interesting' here.

He put his radio to his mouth. '1762 to Three?'

'*Go ahead, Alan.*'

'We're at Franklyn Road now. Everything looks okay so far. Any further on the complainant, over?'

'*That's negative, Alan. Could be some prat with nothing better to do, but probably best to check it out, over.*'

'Received,' he said, adding under his breath: 'Might take a while, mind.'

They drove in a wide circle around the aged edifice, their tyres sliding as they hit patches of sheet-ice. Ernshaw wound his window down. It was bitterly cold outside – the snow was still dry and crisp as powder – but even if they didn't see anything untoward, it was possible they might *hear* it.

That they didn't was vaguely disconcerting.

Christmas morning ought to be deeply quiet, restful, hushed by the freshly fallen snow, yet the silence around Kemp's Mill was somehow uncanny; it had a brittle edge, as if it could shatter at any moment.

They rounded corner after corner, gazing up sheer faces of windows and bricks, networks of ancient piping, and hanging, rusted fire-escapes. The van's wheels constantly skidded, dirty slush flying out behind. They trundled through an access-passage connecting with a row of empty garages, the corrugated plastic roof of which had fallen through after years of decay. On the other side of this they spotted an entrance.

Rodwell applied the brakes gently, but the van still skated several yards before coming to rest.

What looked like a service doorway was set into a recess at the top of three wide steps. There was no sign of the door itself – possibly it lay under the snow, but from the state of the doorjamb, which had perished to soggy splinters, this entry had been forced a long time ago. A pitch-black interior lay beyond it.

'2376 to Three?' Rodwell told his radio.

'Go *ahead, Keith.*'

'Yeah, we're still at Kemp's Mill. Evidence of a break, over.'

4

'*Do you want some help?*'

'That's negative at present. Looks like an old one.'

They climbed out, gloving up and zipping their padded anoraks. Ernshaw adjusted his hat while Rodwell locked the vehicle. They ventured up the steps, the blackness inside retreating under the intense beams of their torches. At the top, Ernshaw thought he heard something – laughter maybe, but it was very distant and very brief. He glanced at Rodwell, whose dour, pitted face registered that he'd heard nothing. Ernshaw was so unsure himself that he declined to mention it. He glanced behind them. This particular section of the property was enclosed by a high wall. The van was parked close alongside it, the entrance to the garage-passage just at its rear. Aside from the tracks the vehicle itself had made on entering the yard, the snowfall lay unbroken. Of course, flakes had been falling heavily until about two hours ago, so this didn't necessarily mean that no one had been here during the night.

They entered side-by-side, torchlight spearing ahead, and were immediately faced by three options: directly in front, a switchback stair ascended into opaque blackness; on the right, a passage led off down a long gallery zebra-striped by smudges of light intruding through the ground level windows; on the left lay a wide open area, presumably one of the old workshops. They ventured this way first, their torch-beams crisscrossing, revealing bare brick walls and a high plaster ceiling, much of which had rotted, exposing bone-like girders. Shredded cables hung like jungle creeper. The asphalt floor was scattered with planks and fragments of tiles. Here and there, the corroded stubs of machine fittings jutted dangerously upward. Despite the intense cold, there was a sour taint to the air, like mildew. The scuffling of their feet echoed through the vast building's distant reaches.

They halted to listen, hearing nothing.

'This is a wild goose chase,' Ernshaw finally said, his words smoking. 'You realise that, don't you?'

'Probably,' Rodwell replied, shining his torch into every corner. From the moment they'd received the call, Rodwell had seemed a little graver of purpose than usual, which was intriguing to Ernshaw. Keith Rodwell had been a copper for so long that he generally sized situations up instinctually. The way he was behaving now suggested that he genuinely believed something untoward was going on here.

'Okay, I give up,' Ernshaw said. 'What do you *think* we're going to find?'

'Keep it down. Even if this is someone taking the piss, let's catch 'em at it.'

'Keith . . . it's Christmas morning. Why would someone . . .'

'Shhh!'

But Ernshaw had also just heard the long, low creak from overhead. They regarded each other in the gloom, ears pricked.

'Take the front stair,' Rodwell said quietly, edging across the workshop. 'I'll go around the back . . . see if I can find another way up.'

Ernshaw retreated to the door they'd come in through. He glanced at the van out in the yard; as before, there was no sign of movement. He started to ascend, attempting to do it stealthily though his footsteps rang up the stairwell ahead of him. The first floor he came to comprised another huge workshop. Not all the windows up here were boarded, though their glass was so grimy that only a paltry winter light filtered through. Even so, it was enough to hint at an immense hangar-like space ranging far across the building, filled with stacked crates and workbenches, forested by steel pillars.

Ernshaw hesitated, gripping the hilt of his baton. This

time last year he'd been an innocent young student at the University of Hull, so he had no trouble admitting to himself that, while it was bad enough being made to work on Christmas Day – only the older, married guys tended to be spared that pain-in-the-arse duty – it was even worse having to spend it trawling through the guts of an eerie, frozen ruin like this.

A loud crackle from his radio made him jump.

The voice of Comms boomed out as it dispatched messages to patrols elsewhere on the subdivision. Irritated, he turned the volume down.

Ernshaw advanced as his eyes adjusted to the half-light. Directly ahead, about forty yards away, a doorway opened into what looked like an antechamber. For some reason, the rear brick wall of that chamber was lit by a greenish glow.

Green?

A coloured candle, maybe? A paper lantern?

Ernshaw halted as a figure flitted past the doorway on the other side.

'Hey,' he said under his breath. Then louder: '*Hey!*'

He dashed forward, with baton drawn and angled across his shoulder.

When he entered the chamber, nobody was there, but he saw that the odd-coloured light had been caused by a sheet of mouldy green canvas fastened over a window. A stairway – an indoor fire-escape, all rust and riveted steel – dropped down through a trapdoor; while a secondary stair rose up to the next level, though this was very narrow, scarcely broad enough for an average-sized man to climb it without turning sideways. He peered up, spying a ray of feeble daylight at the top. When he listened, he heard nothing, though it wasn't difficult to imagine that someone was lurking up there, listening back.

'Alan?' someone asked.

Half-shouting, Ernshaw spun around.

Rodwell gazed at him from the trapdoor, in particular at his drawn baton.

'Have you . . .?' Ernshaw glanced back up the stair, listening intently. 'Have you been up here once? I mean, have you been up already and gone back down for any reason?' Rodwell shook his head as he rose fully into view. 'Thought I saw someone, but . . .' The more Ernshaw considered it, the less substantial that 'figure' seemed. A shadow maybe, cast by his torch? 'Could've been mistaken, I suppose . . .'

Rodwell also glanced up the next stair. Without speaking, he ascended it, just about able to slide his big body between its encroaching walls.

Ernshaw followed, discomforted by the tightness of the passage. The floor at the top of this had been partitioned into small rooms and connecting corridors. Even fewer of the windows on this level were boarded, but there were less of them, so a sepulchral gloom pervaded.

Before they commenced exploring, Rodwell lifted a dust-caked Venetian blind and peered down into the yard below. It had occurred to them both, somewhat belatedly, that if this was some daft but elaborate ruse to create a diversion by which to steal a police vehicle, they'd be left with an omelette-sized egg on their faces. However, the van sat unmolested; the snow around it unmarked. From this height, they could see further afield into adjacent streets, or what remained of them. Most of the rows of terraced housing on the south side of Kemp's Mill had been demolished, but even with the recent snowfall, the parallel outlines of their old foundations were still visible.

There was no sign of anyone around. The nearest habitations were two blocks of 1970s flats about three hundred yards away, beyond a mountain of snow-covered scrap; only one or two lights – the garish neon of Christmas decorations – twinkled from their windows.

'2376 *from Three?*' the voice of Comms crackled from Rodwell's radio.

'Go ahead,' he said, dropping the blind back into place.

'*Anything from Franklyn Road yet?*'

'No offences revealed at this stage. Still searching, over.'

'*Message from Sergeant Roebuck, Keith. Don't waste too much time there. If it's just some kids messing around, leave it. There are other jobs piling up.*'

'Roger, received.'

'That it, then?' Ernshaw asked hopefully.

'No,' Rodwell replied.

They ventured along a central passage, peeking around the first door they came to, seeing what had presumably once been an office. In the middle of it, weak daylight illuminated a single filing cabinet from which a ton of paperwork had overflowed. Ernshaw entered, scooping up some of the documents: work rosters yellowed by age; dog-eared time-and-motion sheets. He tossed them away, moving through the next doorway into another identical office. Sometime in the past, vandals had scribbled slogans all over the walls in this one.

'Kids have been in here, alright,' he said. 'Dirty little buggers too. Seen this . . . "My little sister gave me my first blowjob. She'll do you too for a fiver." There's even a fucking phone number. "Every day I wank into my mum's knickers – now she's pregnant again. Oh shit."' Getting no response, he turned.

Rodwell had not come into the room with him.

Ernshaw went back to the door and glanced into the office with the filing cabinet; Rodwell wasn't in there either.

'Keith?' he said.

A footfall sounded behind him. He whirled around – to find that he was still alone. But on the far side of the room another door stood ajar.

Hadn't it been closed previously?

Ernshaw approached it, suddenly suspecting that someone was in the next room. Baton drawn again, he yanked the door open – entering yet another deserted corridor, the contents of more gutted offices spilling into it from adjoining doorways.

'Keith?'

Still there was no reply.

Ernshaw proceeded forward. At the extreme end there was another stairway, but when he reached this, it was only short and led up to a closed door, beyond which a crack of bright daylight was visible.

'Keith? You up there, mate?'

Again, nothing.

He ascended slowly, body half-turned so that he could watch both in front and behind. At the top, the door swung open easily and Ernshaw entered the most spacious office he'd seen to date – a good forty foot by thirty – the sort of palatial residence an MD might once have inhabited. It possessed several large windows, all intact, none covered by planking or sheets of green canvas. The walls were even papered, though the floor contained loose boards, several of which had warped and sprung. There was no furniture; just a scattering of broken bricks and, in one corner, rather curiously, a wheelbarrow rimmed with hardened cement, a pick and sledge-hammer standing against it.

But none of this captured Ernshaw's attention as much as the strange object on the farthest side of the room.

He walked forward.

It appeared to be a section of new wall; a seven-foot-wide rectangle rising almost floor to ceiling. The paper and plaster had recently been torn away, and the ancient stonework beneath demolished; new, yellowish bricks had been mortared into the resulting cavity. But what *really* caught his eye hung in the middle of this: a sheet of white paper with a message emblazoned on it in startling crimson. The paper was fresh and new; when Ernshaw took it from the wall it had been fixed there with Blu-Tack, which proved to be soft and obviously new as well.

The message had been printed by a modern desk-jet of some sort. It read:

Ho Ho Ho

Ernshaw's short-cropped hair prickled. This sign could easily be more empty-headed idiocy from the local scrotes. But there was something about it – probably the fact that it was clearly a recent addition to this neglected pile – that made him think it might be significant. He stepped backward, examining the wall again. It had definitely been constructed more recently than the rest of the building. At its base, two lumps of tapered black wood protruded through a tiny gap under the bricks; some builder's device, no doubt, to keep the whole thing level.

A hand tapped his shoulder.

Ernshaw spun around like a dervish. 'Fuck me!' he hissed.

'What's this?' Rodwell asked.

'Will you stop sneaking up on people!' Ernshaw handed him the notice. 'Dunno. Found it pinned to the wall.'

Rodwell stared at the wall first. 'This brickwork's new.'

'That's what I thought. Well . . . they'll have done all sorts of jobs over the years, to keep the place serviceable, won't they?'

'Not in the last twenty.' Rodwell glanced at the notice, then back at the wall again. 'This is a chimney breast. Or it was. Probably connected to one of the outer flues.'

'Okay, it's a chimney,' Ernshaw said. 'Bricking up an

old chimney isn't much of a criminal offence these days, is it?'

Rodwell read the notice a second time.

Ho Ho Ho

'Jesus . . . Christ,' he breathed slowly. 'Jesus Christ almighty!'

Moving faster than Ernshaw had ever seen him, Rodwell threw the paper aside and dropped to one knee to examine the two wooden stubs protruding below the brickwork. Ernshaw leaned down to look as well – and suddenly realised what he was actually seeing; the scuffed toes of a pair of boots.

Rodwell grabbed the pick and Ernshaw the hammer.

They went at the new wall as hard as they could, and at first it resisted their efforts – but they pounded fiercely, Rodwell stopping only to call for supervision and an ambulance, Ernshaw to unzip his anorak and throw off his hat. After several minutes grunting and sweating, mortar was bursting out with every impact – then they were loosening bricks, extricating them with their fingers, guarding their eyes against flying chips. Piece by piece, the wall came down, gradually exposing what stood behind it – though the aroma hit them first.

Ernshaw gagged, clamping a hand to his nose and mouth. Rodwell worked all the harder, smashing away the last vestiges of brickwork.

They stood back panting, wafting at the dust, retching at the stink.

'Good God!' Rodwell said as he focused on what they'd uncovered.

Though it stood upright, this was only because it had been suspended by the wrists from two manacles fixed above its head. It had reached that stage of early putrefaction where it

12

could either have been a shrivelled corpse or a wax dummy, its complexion somewhere between sickly yellow and maggoty green. It had once been an elderly man – that much was evident from the scraggly white beard on its skullish jaw, plus it was bone-thin, an impression only enhanced by its baggy, extremely dirty garb. This consisted of a red tunic hanging in foul-smelling folds, trimmed with dirt-grey fur, and red pantaloons, the front of them thick with frozen urine, their cuffs tucked into a pair of oversized wellingtons.

It was not an unusual experience, even for relatively new bobbies like Ernshaw, to discover corpses in a state of corruption. Not everyone handled it well, though Ernshaw usually had – until now.

He laughed. Bizarrely. It was almost a cackle.

'S-Santa,' he stuttered.

Rodwell glanced at him, distracted.

'Fucking Santa!' Ernshaw continued to cackle, though his glazed expression contained no mirth. 'Looks like there was no one nice waiting for him at the bottom of this chimney. Only naughty . . .'

Rodwell glanced back at the corpse as he recalled the words on the sign – *Ho Ho Ho*. He noticed that a red hood with a filthy fur trim had been pulled up over the wizened, hairless cranium.

'Christ save us,' he whispered. The corpse wore a tortured expression, its eyes bugging like marbles in a face twisted into a rigid, grimacing death-mask. 'This poor bastard was walled up in here alive.'

Chapter 2

If it was possible for a newsagent billboard to shriek, this one did.

Detective Sergeant Mark 'Heck' Heckenburg observed it through the driver's window of his Fiat while he waited at a traffic light. Homeward-bound commuters darted across the road in front of him, muffled against the February evening. Much of the heavy winter snow had cleared, but dirty, frozen lumps of it lingered in the gutters.

Heck eased his Fiat forward, glancing continually at his sat-nav. Milton Keynes was a big place; it comprised about two hundred thousand citizens, and like most of the so-called 'new towns' – purpose-built conurbation designed to accommodate the overspill population after World War II left so many British cities in smoking rubble – its suburbs seemed to drag on interminably. After half an hour, the entrance to

Wilberforce Drive appeared on his left. He rounded its corner and cruised along a quiet, middle-class street – though, in the current climate of terror, all these streets were quiet after nightfall, particularly in towns like Milton Keynes, so close to the M1 motorway.

The houses were semi-detached, nestling behind low brick walls or privet fences. All had front gardens and neatly paved driveways. In the majority of cases, cars were already parked there, curtains drawn. When he reached number eighteen, Heck halted on the opposite side of the road and turned his engine off.

Then he waited. It would soon get cold, so he zipped up his leather jacket and pulled on his gloves. Eighteen, Wilberforce Drive seemed almost impossibly innocent. A snug pink light issued through its downstairs window. A child's skateboard was propped against its garage door. There was even the relic of a snowman on its front lawn.

Heck took his notes from the glove-box and checked through them. Yes – eighteen, Wilberforce Drive, the home of Jordan Savage, thirty-three years old, a married man who managed the local garden centre for a living. The homely environs made it altogether less menacing a scene than Heck had expected. It would be easier than usual to walk up the path and rap on the door here – this wasn't the sort of place where cops normally got their teeth knocked out. But Heck was still nervous that he might be on the wrong track.

Not that he would ever know sitting behind his steering wheel. But before he could open the car door, another door opened – the front door to number eighteen. The man who stepped out could only be Jordan Savage: his solid build and six-foot-two inches made him unmistakable; likewise his shock of red, spiky hair. No doubt, up close, those penetrating blue eyes of his would be another give-away.

Savage was wearing jeans, a sweater and a heavy waxed

15

jacket. As Heck watched, he moved the skateboard aside, took a key from his pocket and opened the garage door. There was a vehicle inside; a green Mondeo Sport. The registration mark checked out as well. It was the same car the Traffic patrol had become suspicious of and had stopped that dank October night. The Mondeo's engine rumbled to life, its headlights snapped on and Savage eased it down the drive. If he noticed Heck seated in the car opposite, he gave no indication, but turned right along Wilberforce Drive, heading for the junction with the main road. When Savage was a hundred yards ahead, Heck switched his own engine on and followed.

Tailing a suspect was never easy, especially when you were doing it unofficially – but Heck had performed this task dozens of times. Once they were on the main road, he stayed about three cars behind – not too close to attract attention, but close enough to keep a careful eye on his target. Even so, after two and a half miles, when the Mondeo suddenly veered left onto what looked like another housing estate, he was taken by surprise.

This neighbourhood was less salubrious than the previous one. Its houses were council stock, some terraced with communal passages between them, some with front gates hanging from broken hinges. But its central artery was called Boroughbridge Avenue, and that rang a bell of familiarity. Heck didn't need to rifle through his notes this time to know that this was where Jason Savage, Jordan's twin brother, lived.

The Mondeo stopped outside a two-flat maisonette. Jordan Savage didn't get out, but sat there, his exhaust pumping winter fog. Heck slowed to a halt as well – just as a glint of light revealed that a door to the upstairs flat had opened and closed. A figure trotted down a narrow flight of cement steps.

Even from fifty yards away, the similarities between the

16

two men were startling. Jason Savage, who was a mechanic by trade, wore an old donkey jacket over what looked like black coveralls, but he too was about six-foot-two and had a thatch of bristly red hair. He climbed into the Mondeo's front passenger seat, and it drew away from the kerb. Heck remained where he was, wondering if they were about to make a three-point turn, though apparently there was another exit from this estate – the Mondeo drove on ahead until it rounded a bend and vanished.

Heck nosed forward. This was better than he'd hoped for, but it could also mean nothing. It wouldn't be the first time that two brothers had spent an evening playing darts together. That said, when he swung around the bend and found himself at a deserted T-junction, he briefly panicked.

Trusting to luck, he swung his car right and got his foot down. Leafless trees closed from either side as he passed through public woodland – this didn't look promising, but then it gave way to the high fencing of an industrial park, and about fifty yards ahead a red traffic light was showing, a lone vehicle waiting there. Heck accelerated and, to his relief, recognised the Mondeo. He'd be directly behind them now, but he couldn't afford to worry about that. His police instinct – the 'hunch' honed through so many criminal investigations (or alternatively, 'his imagination', as Detective Superintendent Gemma Piper called it), told him he was onto something.

The light turned to green as he pulled up behind the Mondeo, and it swung left. Heck followed, but decelerated a little. They were on another main road, with houses to either side, followed by shops and pubs. More and more vehicles joined the traffic flow. Heck slowed down further to allow a couple to push in front of him. Jordan Savage worked his way across the centre of Milton Keynes, negotiating roundabouts and one-way systems as if he could do it blindfolded. Heck, who wasn't a local and in fact had never even been to Milton Keynes until he'd arrived here as part of the enquiry team some six months earlier, found it more difficult, though thankfully that ultimate bugbear of the covert tail – a traffic light or stop-sign separating him from his target – never occurred. It *almost* did as they approached a bustling intersection, but Jordan Savage halted at the white line even though, if he'd floored his pedal, he could probably have made it through the break in traffic.

Heck was only one car behind Savage at this stage. He too slowed and stopped, by chance underneath a large Crimestoppers noticeboard. As well as various telephone numbers, including the hotline to the Main Incident Room at Milton Keynes Central, it carried a massive e-fit of the so-called 'M1 Maniac', a frightful figure with hunched, gorilla-like shoulders, wearing a black hood pulled down almost to his eyes, which in turn were half-covered by a fringe of lank hair, and a collar zipped up to his nose. It was impossible to tell in the yellowish glow of the streetlamps, but in normal daylight those eyes would be a startling blue and that fringe a vivid red. To emphasise this, the artist who'd constructed the e-fit had only colourised those sections; the rest of it was in black and white.

Heck followed as the Mondeo advanced through the inter-section. The vehicles between them peeled off left, but the Mondeo headed straight on, taking a narrow street between industrial units surrounded by high walls. Past these lay shabby apartment blocks: broken glass strewed their fore-courts, ramshackle cars cluttered the parking bays. Heck slowed to a crawl, but still managed to keep the Mondeo in sight. It was about a hundred yards ahead when it turned right, appearing to descend a ramp.

He cruised forward another fifty yards, then pulled up and stopped. He grabbed the radio from his dashboard, switched its volume down and shoved it under his jacket, before climbing out and walking the rest of the way.

The ramp swerved down beneath a monolithic tower block, which, from a rusted nameplate, was called Fairwood House. As Heck ventured down, he kept close to the wall on his right. When he reached the bottom, he halted, waiting until his eyes adjusted. A labyrinthine underground car park swam slowly into view. Unlit alleyways wound between concrete stanchions, or led off along narrow alleys between rows of padlocked timber doors. There was no immediate sign of the Mondeo.

Heck walked back up the ramp and climbed into his Fiat, releasing the handbrake. It was tempting to freewheel down there with his headlights off, but if he did encounter the Savage brothers, that would look suspicious in the extreme. Instead, he behaved as normally as possible, switching the engine on and driving down as if he was just looking for a parking space. Once below, he casually prowled, turning corner after corner. There were other exits, he noticed – some were caged off, others stood wide open. It occurred to him that his targets might have exited the place altogether; perhaps they'd sensed they were being followed and had used this car park as a diversion. But then, as he cruised another gallery between rows of padlocked garage doors, he saw orange, flickering light ahead.

Firelight?

He proceeded for forty yards, before parking and creeping the rest of the distance on foot. The firelight was reflecting on a wall beyond the next T-junction. When he edged forward the last few feet and peeked around to the right, he spied a parking bay in which a couple of ragged, elderly men were burning rubbish in an oil-drum. They were bearded and grizzled; one glanced around – his face was weasel-thin, his mouth a toothless maw.

19

Heck swore.

He went doggedly back to his Fiat. Somehow or other the bastards had eluded him. He slotted his key into the ignition – and bright illumination fell over him. In his rear-view mirror, two powerful headlamps approached from behind.

Heck sank down so low that he couldn't see the vehicle as it passed him slowly by. But when he peered after it, it was the Mondeo. It reached the end of the drag, turning left. Heck jumped out, running back to the T-junction. The Mondeo was now making a second left-hand turn. He chased after it, sweat stippling his brow. From the next corner he saw that it had stopped some thirty yards ahead, alongside another row of lock-ups. The Savage brothers climbed out, conversing quietly.

Heck flattened himself against the concrete wall to listen. He fancied he heard them use the word 'van', at which his hand unconsciously stole to his radio, though he managed to restrain himself from grabbing it. He risked another peek. Jason Savage clambered into the Mondeo's driving seat, switching its engine back on. Meanwhile, Jordan Savage approached the nearest lock-up, produced a key and, opening its narrow side-panel, stepped through into darkness.

Heck felt a massive tremor of anticipation.

It was several minutes before Jordan Savage reappeared, but when he did he had changed into black waterproof trousers and a black hooded anorak. He handed something to his brother through the window of the Mondeo – it looked like a pistol. Heck couldn't quite identify it, but a Ruger Mark II had been used in all eight killings to date.

Jordan Savage stepped back inside the lock-up and closed the side-panel behind him, while the Mondeo pulled forward about twenty yards. The lock-up's main door was then lifted laboriously from within. Headlamp beams shot out as a second vehicle emerged. Heck clutched the concrete corner with such force that it almost drew blood from his fingernails. When a white transit van rolled into view, he jerked backwards, retreating quickly, fishing his radio from his jacket and easing up its volume.

'DS Heckenburg on Taskforce, to Sierra Six . . . over?'

'*DS Heckenburg?*' came a chirpy response.

'Urgent message. Immediate support required. Underground car park at Fairwood House. Send as many units as possible, block off all exits . . . but silent approach. I also want a Trojan unit, over.'

'*Could you repeat the latter, sarge?*'

Heck tried to keep his voice low. 'Get me a Trojan unit pronto! And get me supervision . . . DI Hunter and Chief Superintendent Humphreys. I'm sitting on two targets I believe to be the M1 murderers, so I need that back-up ASAP, over and out!'

He turned the volume down again as the message went rapid-fire across the airwaves. Lurching back to his car, he unlocked the steering, knocked the handbrake off and pushed the vehicle forward. As he reached the end of the drag, he yanked the handbrake on and crept to the corner, where he risked another glance at the suspect vehicles.

The white van sat behind the Mondeo, both chugging fumes, while the two twins talked. Jason Savage had removed his donkey jacket and put on a similar black hooded anorak to his brother.

If they would just keep the conflab going until firearms support arrived . . .

'Any change today, sur?' someone asked loudly.

Heck twirled. One of the tramps had come stumbling around the corner and was standing out in the open with hand cupped. Grey locks hung in matted strands over his semi-glazed eyes.

Heck glanced back towards the Savage brothers, who were

21

suddenly staring in his direction. A piercing light sprang forward as one of them switched on a torch. Heck jumped back around the corner, but the tramp didn't move, except to shield his eyes.

No doubt the Savage boys knew there were human derelicts down here and had discerned there was no threat from them. But it was plainly obvious to anyone that this particular tramp was interacting with someone else.

'Just a little change, sur,' he said in fluting Irish, sticking an empty hand under Heck's nose. 'A couple of pounds wouldn't go amiss . . .'

Heck chanced another glance. One of the two brothers had opened the driver's door to the van and looked set to climb into it. The other was still frozen in place, still peering along the passage.

'Get down, you damn fool!' Heck hissed. 'Get on the floor now!'

'Just a little change, sur. An entry fee, if you loike. The price of visiting our little parlour . . .'

Heck lunged, grabbing the skeletal figure by the lapel of his coat and dragging him out of the torchlight, hurling him to the floor. At the same time he bellowed: 'Armed police! You're completely surrounded! Drop your weapons and get on the ground with your arms outspread!'

The response was two thundering gunshots, the first kicking a first-sized chunk from the concrete corner in front of Heck, the second whining past. There was an echo of slamming doors.

Heck slid forward to look. The transit van was already haring away down the passage, its tail-lights receding. The Mondeo sat unattended. Heck raced back to his Fiat, stepping around the groaning tramp.

''Tis a cruel thing to manhandle a fella so,' came a feeble voice.

Heck leapt behind the wheel, slammed his key into the ignition and hit the gas. The tramp, staggering back to his feet, gave a V-sign to the windscreen, only to be blinded by Heck's headlights. He toppled backwards as Heck wove the car around him, accelerating past the lock-ups, tyres screeching. Far ahead, the transit van rounded a corner at such speed that its bodywork drew sparks from the opposing wall. Heck took the corner tightly as well. The van was still far ahead; at the end of the next drag, it ascended another ramp into the sodium-yellow glow of the streets.

Heck thumbed the volume control on his radio and shouted at the top of his voice. 'DS Heckenburg chasing! Two suspects for M1 murders travelling in a white Ford van, leaving Fairwood House car park by what I believe is the east exit . . . no registration as yet! Urgent warning! At least one of the suspects is armed; shots already fired . . . no casualties, over!'

There was nothing more dangerous, nor more discouraged in the modern police, than high-speed pursuit of suspects through built-up areas, yet Heck knew he had no choice. For so many months they'd had nothing – no forensics, no CCTV footage, no crime scenes, no survivors (bar one, who was severely injured), no likely suspects at all – and now, suddenly, they had everything . . . just in front of him by a skinny fifty yards, yet moving at seventy miles per hour through a busy town centre.

Horns blared and pedestrians scattered, shrieking, as the white van mounted pavements to cut across junctions. Other vehicles swerved and skidded into shop-fronts, lampposts, or each other; panes of glass imploded, splinters of metal flew. Heck weaved frantically through the chaos. Reaching out of his offside window, he managed to throw his detachable beacon onto the roof of his Fiat. He shouted again into his radio, updating the Comms suite as best he could. By the approaching wail of sirens, other units were close by, but it still seemed likely that the target vehicle would escape. He lost sight of it completely when it sped through a stop-zone on red, other vehicles slewing sideways, one crunching head-long into the traffic light, buckling its pole and bringing the signal head down in a mass of dancing sparks. The cars in front of Heck shunted together, while others turned sharply to avoid the pile-up. Instinctively, Heck shot down a right-hand alleyway, trying to evade the snarled-up junction, only to see the van zip past the end of the alley, now headed in the opposite direction.

'DS Heckenburg to Sierra Six!' he bawled, swerving into pursuit. 'Target vehicle doubling back on itself, headed west along . . .' He scanned the buildings flicking by, trying to catch a street name. 'Heading west along Avebury Boulevard. The suspects are Jordan and Jason Savage, and they live at eighteen, Wilberforce Drive and fourteen, Boroughbridge Avenue respectively. I repeat they are armed and highly dangerous!'

Ahead, the van mounted a pedestrianised precinct, sending benches cartwheeling. Heck mounted the precinct as well, but the van slid to a halt about forty yards in front, smearing rubber as it pulled a handbrake turn. Heck only realised at the last second that he'd been lured into a side-on approach. He ducked as a gun-muzzle flashed from the driver's window, the projectile punching the top corner of his windscreen, spider-webbing it.

'Where's that firearms support!' he shouted, backhanding the Fiat into reverse, crashing through heaps of boxes.

A local police patrol, a Vauxhall Astra in yellow and blue Battenberg, came hurtling onto the precinct from the oppos-ite end, sirens whooping. The van lurched forward again, bolting down a side-street and veering left onto another main road. The patrol car made immediate pursuit, litter

24

swirling from its wheels. Heck went next, still shouting into his radio.

'Target headed north along Saxon Gate! Seventy-five plus!'

The van was all over the road as it hit speeds it had never been designed for, sideswiping a litter-bin through a shop window. The Astra kept pace from behind, only for the van's back doors to burst open and one of the Savage brothers to crouch there and take aim with his pistol. Over the howling engines, Heck barely heard the detonations, but the three rapid gun-flashes were clear enough. With windscreen peppered, the Astra crashed over the outer wall of a civic building with such explosive force, the footings tore out its front undercarriage, so that it finished standing on its nose in an ornamental pond.

'Police RTA on the entrance to Portway!' Heck shouted. 'Ambulance required!'

He wasn't sure that his instructions were even being heard. The airwaves were alive with frantic messages. In front, the van's rear doors slammed open and closed as it juddered from side to side. The gunman knelt just inside, slotting another magazine into place.

'Heading east along Portway!' Heck shouted. 'These guys are fucking packed! Get me that Trojan quick!'

Sirens could now be heard from all directions. A Thames Valley motorcyclist overtook Heck in a swirl of blues and twos. It tried to overtake the van as well, but the van swung right, sending the bike hurtling onto the pavement and glancing along a wrought-iron fence, from which it caromed back onto the blacktop, managing to right itself again – only to flip end-over-end when it struck the kerb of a traffic island, its rider somersaulting through the air.

Heck glimpsed this in his rear-view mirror as he blistered past. 'DS Heckenburg to Sierra Six! We now have two police

RTAs . . . one on Saxon Gate, one on Portway! At least two officers injured! Ambulances essential! Still pursuing!'

Ahead, flashing blue lights were clustered across a bridge. He hoped this meant that a stinger unit had been deployed underneath, but the white van rocketed through unhindered. Two more police vehicles, a Vectra and a Vivaro, came surging down the slip road; not soon enough to intercept the target, though they managed to block Heck's progress. He shouted and swore as he took evasive action.

The gunman opened fire again, concentrating first on the Vectra. Two holes the size of hubcaps were torn in its bonnet. A third slug missed, and ricocheted from the road surface, blasting Heck's offside mirror to shards.

The Vectra lost speed, pouring black smoke. Heck accelerated into the gap, he and the Vivaro running neck and neck. On an open, empty road there were manoeuvres they could attempt, boxing the van in, bringing it to a forced halt. But too many members of the public were around. A Royal Mail vehicle spun out of control as the target rear-ended it, trying to ram it out of the way. Heck swerved again to avoid a body-crumpling collision. The Vivaro wasn't so lucky: it slid across the opposing carriageway, hitting a row of bollards, jerking around on impact, steam boiling from its mangled radiator. The van accelerated again as it found open space, the gunman in the back falling left to right, unable to get a shot off at his one remaining pursuer, Heck.

The two vehicles tail-gated each other as they blazed across a flyover, beyond which signposts gave directions to the M1 motorway.

Heck swore volubly – there would be many, many more road-users on the motorway – and these guys had shown no interest in preserving innocent life.

Before they reached it they hit another roundabout. Here, more police patrols – Traffic unit Range-Rovers – were waiting at the turn-offs. They seemed more interested in holding back the public than in attempting to intercept the target, allowing it to roar away unimpeded, spewing black fumes. Possibly, Milton Keynes Comms were issuing orders for officers to stand off. But Heck had received no such instruction, so he continued the chase, bulleting along the slip road and down the access ramp.

The M1 southbound was busy at the best of times. Now, at the tail-end of rush hour, it was heaving. The average speed was still about sixty miles per hour, but it was a fast-moving log-jam. Despite this, the van forged ruthlessly ahead, ramming and shunting, ignoring the honking horns and shaking fists. Heck hit his own horn repeatedly, but had to swerve and skid as vehicles were sideswiped into his path.

The bastards were trying to *cause* a pile-up, he realised. Their plan was to create a barricade of car-wrecks. And on top of that, they were still armed. He glimpsed more flickering blue lights in his rear-view mirror, but they were far behind and nobody in the control room seemed to be answering his messages – at which point his quarry suddenly attempted the craziest manoeuvre Heck had ever seen.

There was a double-sided crash barrier down the motorway's central reservation. A fleeting gap appeared – and the van jack-knifed into it, attempting a U-turn.

A U-turn! At sixty miles an hour! On the motorway!

By instinct rather than logic, Heck did the same. The next junction was a good fifteen miles away, and he couldn't take the chance that the felons might escape.

But even though Heck jammed his brakes on as he turned, he lost control crossing the northbound carriageway, skidding on two wheels and slamming side-on into the grass embankment with such bone-shuddering force that his Fiat rolled uphill . . . before rolling back down again and landing on its roof, its chassis groaning, glass fragments tinkling over him. The white van had also lost control, but whereas Heck had lost it at thirty, the Savage brothers had lost it at sixty. Their vehicle didn't even manage to turn into the skid, but ploughed headlong across the carriageway – straight into the concrete buttress of a motorway bridge. The resulting impact boomed in Heck's ears.

That sound echoed for what seemed like seconds as Heck lay groggily on his side.

At length, in a daze akin to the worst hangover in history, he began to probe at his body with his fingertips. Everything seemed to be intact, though his neck and shoulders ached, suggesting whiplash. His left wrist was also hurting, though he had full movement in the joint. With an agonised grunt, Heck released the catch of his seatbelt, crawled gingerly across the ceiling of his car and tried to open the passenger door, only to find that it was buckled in its frame and immovable. For a second he was too stupored to work this out; then slowly, painfully, he shifted himself around and clambered feet-first through the shattered window.

When he finally stood up, he found himself gazing across the underside of his Fiat, which was gashed and dented and thick with tufts of grass and soil. Clouds of steam hissed from his busted radiator. Passing vehicles slowed down, the faces of drivers blurring white as they gawked at him. Multiple sirens approached from the near-distance.

Clamping a hand to his throbbing neck, he had to turn his entire body to gaze along the debris-strewn hard shoulder. Thirty yards away, the smouldering hulk of the white van was crushed against the concrete buttress, reduced to about a third of its original length. Heck hobbled towards it, but when he got within ten yards the stench of fuel and rubber and twisted, melted metal was enough to make him sick.

So was the sight of the Savage brothers.

Whichever one of them had fired the shots from out of the back had been catapulted clean across the van's interior, bursting through its windscreen, his head striking the buttress of the bridge and splurging several feet up the concrete in a deluge of blood, brain and bone splinters. The driver had been flung onto the steering wheel, and now lay across it like a bundle of limp rags. From the crimson rivers gurgling out underneath him, the central column had torn through his breastbone and punctured his cardiovascular system.

Heck tottered queasily away from the wreck.

Other police vehicles were now drawing in behind his Fiat. The first of their drivers, a young Motorway Division officer in a bright orange slicker, came running up. 'Is that him?' he asked. 'The Maniac?'

Heck slumped backwards onto the grass. 'Let's hope so,' he muttered. 'Bloody hell . . . let's hope so.'

Chapter 3

The 'M1 Maniac', to use the nickname the press had given him (or 'them', as it turned out), had terrorised southern England for the previous six months, primarily targeting teenage boys.

His hunting ground was confined to the vicinity of the M1 motorway, but this was not small. In geographic terms, his attacks ranged from Luton in the south to Northampton in the north; from Aylesbury in the west to Bedford in the east. He claimed nine victims, all older teenagers, all abducted from public places – usually when they were walking home from pubs or nightclubs. Eight of these were later found bound with wire, raped anally and orally, and killed by an execution-style gunshot to the back of the head. Their bodies had been dumped in ditches or roadside culverts.

The victim who survived was fourth in terms of the running order. His name was Lewis Pettigrew, and he was a nineteen-year-old Oxford University student who was on a visit to his parents' home in Milton Keynes. Like the others, he was found bound, badly assaulted and with a bullet-wound to the back of the head, but in his case, possibly because of the angle at which it was fired, the bullet had lodged in his skull rather than penetrating his brain. Pettigrew, though he'd lost the power of speech, was able to write and thus informed the police that he had been standing at a bus stop just around midnight when a white van pulled up alongside him. The hooded driver climbed out and produced a handgun, forcing the boy into the back, where his wrists and ankles were tied with wire which was pulled so tight that he feared it had cut off his blood supply.

The van was then driven around for an estimated half-hour or so. When it finally stopped, the abductor climbed from the driving cab and re-entered the vehicle through its rear doors, still armed with his pistol, at which point he forced Pettigrew to perform fellatio on him. When this was over, the abductor climbed out of the van, only to climb back in again a few minutes later and sodomise the prisoner. When this second sex act was complete, the van's rear doors were opened again, Pettigrew was forced to kneel up, facing outwards – into what looked like isolated woodland – and was shot in the back of the head. It was a miracle he survived, but an entire day passed before a woman walking her dog discovered him; like the others, he had been dragged into a ditch and covered with branches and moss.

This was a major break for the police, because it explained the M1 Maniac's *modus operandi*. There was no DNA, just as there never was with any of the other cases, because the killer always wore protection, but at least Pettigrew was able to describe the van and the assailant, even if this latter description amounted to little more than a man with blue eyes and red hair, wearing a black anorak hood.

Unfortunately, none of this did much to make the public less frightened, because the murders continued. The fact that it was red-blooded young men who were the object of the viciousness made it all the more disturbing. There were athletes among them; one had even been a junior boxing champion. Additionally terrifying, the Maniac's victims had been grabbed off the street while going about their everyday business. A criminal psychologist on the radio exacerbated the situation when he voiced a theory that the perpetrator was probably not gay; that in fact he was straight and that his sexual sadism was simply a means to assert his dominance. Women could be next, he said.

Needless to say, others were less sure about this, and as the panic rose the public order situation deteriorated: anti-gay graffiti appeared, gay nightspots were stoned. Vigilante justice became ever more brutal and indiscriminate – a prominent gay spokesman was dragged from a podium and beaten while attempting to address a public meeting.

In the midst of all this, the police came under mounting criticism. It was noted in the popular press that speed-cameras had assisted in the prosecution of thousands of motorists in the time since the reign of terror had begun, but that they seemed incapable of playing any role in the apprehension of this 'real criminal', even though road-use was integral to his method.

Such an incendiary atmosphere was soon going to explode. It looked increasingly unlikely that the hunt for the M1 Maniac would end in anything less than a disaster.

Though perhaps no one realised how much of a disaster, Heck thought, as he sat in A&E, trying not to wince while an orthopaedic collar was carefully fitted around his neck. Even now, the bodies of the Savage brothers were being brought to the mortuary here at the Milton Keynes Hospital. He grunted his thanks as the nurse told him he was done and moved away. As well as the neck-brace, his left arm had been strapped and fixed in a sling; a doctor had checked it earlier and concluded that it was only sprained but that it needed rest – which was always easier said than done. Heck shuffled to the lavatory. When he'd finished his ablutions, a surprisingly complex procedure with one hand, he regarded himself in the mirror over the washbasin. He'd looked better. His black hair was a sweaty mop, his lean, rugged features cut and bruised. He was thirty-eight later this year and still in reasonable nick, but time waited for no man, and whenever he got a little beaten-up these days, it seemed to take that much longer to recover.

When he went back into A&E, two other officers from the Serial Crimes Unit were waiting for him.

Detective Constable Shawna McCluskey was of short stature, in her mid-thirties, and of shapely, athletic build – 'a neat little package', as she'd written on a file for the personnel department when asked to describe herself. She was pretty, but in tough, tomboyish fashion, with a dusting of freckles on her turned-up nose, hazel eyes and lush, dark hair which she nearly always wore up. A broad Manchester accent, which she'd never moderated despite working in the south for several years, revealed solid blue-collar origins. Detective Constable Gary Quinnell was formerly of the South Wales Police. He was six-foot-three, barrel-chested and broad-shouldered. He'd have been handsome in a wholesome 'family man' sort of way, had a few too many Rugby Union forwards not kept breaking his nose for him. Despite being younger than Shawna, he was already thinning on top, so kept his reddish hair cropped very close. Had he realised that this combined with his cauliflower ears to give him a vaguely criminal aspect, he'd have been more upset than he could say.

Both had been into A&E once already, firstly to check that Heck was okay and then to congratulate him, which Shawna did by hugging him and Quinnell did by slapping his shoulder hard – the latter causing Heck to yelp in pain.

'Press are gathering outside,' Shawna said.

'Shit,' Heck groaned. 'How did *they* find out?'

Quinnell chuckled. 'How do you think? Half of Milton Keynes just got trashed.'

'No supervision here yet?'

'No one,' Shawna said. 'You sure you're alright?'

Heck nodded.

'Your Fiat's a write-off,' Quinnell observed.

'Something good came from this then.'

'And the word is they've found the gun,' Shawna added.

Heck glanced up. 'Yeah?'

'In the back of the van.'

'Thank Christ for that!'

Quinnell laughed again. 'So even if they're not the murderers, at least we could have done them for using you and Thames Valley for target practice, eh?'

Heck was about to respond when Shawna nodded past him. He turned. Detective Inspector Bob Hunter was approaching.

Hunter was in his mid-forties but hadn't yet gone to seed. His short blond hair was running to grey and he'd thickened around the middle, but he was bull-necked, square-jawed, and his grey eyes brooked no nonsense. His jacket and tie were uncharacteristically dishevelled, though that wasn't a surprise. He'd been off-duty this evening – it was his first evening off in months; apparently they'd traced him to a local health club, where he'd been in the process of having a swim and a sauna.

'Sir,' Heck said.

Hunter glanced at the other two. 'Security are having problems with the press . . . why don't you give 'em a hand?' They nodded and left. 'Sit down, Heck,' Hunter said.

Heck pulled up the chair in the treatment bay and lowered himself into it. Hunter half-drew the curtain before getting straight to the point.

'What made you think there were two of them?' he asked.

'It was just a thought,' Heck replied. 'It struck me as odd the perp was always able to perform sex twice so quickly in succession.'

'Some blokes can.'

'Like I say, sir, it was just a thought.'

'And *that* led you to the Savage twins?'

'Not straight away.' Heck adjusted his position. It seemed that every part of his body had taken a beating during the crash. 'Given we both agreed the investigation was stagnating . . . I took it on myself to go back through the case notes to see if we'd missed anything.'

He had to be careful how he worded this; he didn't want to imply that Hunter had handled things incompetently. Hunter had not been the official boss of the enquiry, but once the Serial Crimes Unit had been brought in – and that had been at a relatively early stage – he'd taken over the whole show.

'You'll recall that Jordan Savage was one of several persons formerly of interest to us but later dismissed,' Heck said.

Hunter shrugged. 'Don't even remember him.'

'Well . . . it seems Savage was interviewed last October because he was stopped driving late at night on the outskirts of Leighton Buzzard, where, as you know, two of the early murders took place. The patrol that stopped him felt his description matched the suspect – blue eyes, red hair. Anyway, a stop-and-search was performed. When he was found to be in possession of burglary tools, he was arrested for going equipped, though as this was his first offence and there was nothing else to link him to the murders, he got cautioned and bailed.'

'What motor was he in when he was stopped?'

'A green Mondeo, not a white van. That was the problem.'

'Okay . . . go on.'

'I assessed that stop-and-search again, sir. That was when

35

I observed that Jordan Savage was actually going equipped with a pair of pliers.'

Hunter looked puzzled. 'Pliers?'

'If you remember, the medical examiner told us the wire bonds on the victims had been drawn so tight that it might have been done with a tool. I got thinking . . . pliers.'

Hunter pondered this.

'That's why I looked at Savage more closely,' Heck said. 'When I found out that he had a twin brother, Jason, I started wondering . . . did the two of them trawl the streets *together* but maybe in separate vehicles? Suppose the one in the van actually secured the victim and performed the oral rape? The second one then arrived a short time later – in the green Mondeo – to perform the anal? That would have explained the Maniac's apparent virility.'

'And this is what led you to Jordan Savage's door?'

'It was a theory, sir. I had nothing that wasn't circumstantial. So I was only planning to speak to him, tell him we had a couple of things to clear up about the stop-and-search, and see how he reacted to learning that he was still a suspect . . .'

'And that was when you caught them going on the prowl?'

'That was a stroke of luck.'

'"Give me lucky generals," said Napoleon,' Hunter mused. Then smiled, which was alarming because it didn't happen very often. 'That was excellent work, Heck. On-the-hoof, but still bloody excellent.'

Heck acknowledged the compliment, but couldn't help thinking that it should not have come to 'on the hoof'. As only one of dozens of junior and mid-ranking detectives attached to the Maniac taskforce, Heck couldn't possibly be blamed that this vital clue about Jordan Savage had slipped through the net at an early stage, but Bob Hunter could. As deputy SIO, it was his job to keep everything under review.

That Hunter had made this error in the first place was worrying, but his apparent unawareness of it was more worrying still.

'Two of the worst bits of scum the Home Counties ever saw have been taken off the streets,' Hunter said in a satisfied tone.

'We need to be sure it's them,' Heck cautioned.

'Don't worry, we're sure. The van's been towed off for forensic – but I've already had word that its interior matches the description of the vehicle in which Pettigrew was abducted. On top of that, they've found rolls of wire in there, spent bullet-casings, and the not insignificant matter of the gun.'

'I thought they'd have tossed the gun at the first opportunity.'

'Wanted to go down fighting, didn't they?'

'That chase was a bit Wild West, boss. Sorry about that. Didn't plan it.'

'Bollocks. You had more than enough justification. There'd likely be a ton of physical evidence in that van. What if they'd torched it?'

'That's what I was thinking.'

'How you feeling anyway?'

'Stiff, but that's all.'

'Well you've done a cracking job.' Hunter stood up. 'We're all in your debt.' He turned as Quinnell came ambling back across A&E.

'Going like a chippie out there, sir,' the big Welshman said.

'No sign of Humphreys?' Hunter asked.

'Not yet.'

Hunter snorted, as if this was no more than he'd expect. 'Hang fire, Heck,' he said over his shoulder as he headed out. 'But don't dash off.'

'I won't, sir.'

When Hunter had gone, Quinnell grinned. 'Did I hear that right? He reckons he's in your debt? He can't have said that to many people.'

'It was a general term, not him in particular.'

'He's chuffed to buggery, I'll bet.'

Heck sat forward. 'It's a result, but it would have been nice to know a bit more about them, eh – the Savage brothers? I mean why they did the things they did.'

Shawna reappeared. 'Heck – the boss wants you out front.'

'Why?'

'He's decided he's making a statement to the press.'

Heck felt vaguely alarmed. 'What about? We don't know anything yet . . . not for sure.'

'He's got to say something. There's a whole raft of journos.'

'What about Chief Superintendent Humphreys?'

'Won't surprise you to know he's still not available.'

'What's Bob saying?'

'If you come out, like he's asked you to, you'll know?' Shawna said.

Heck allowed her to hustle him to his feet and steer him out of A&E to the front of the hospital steps, where DI Hunter was standing in front of a bank of mikes, Dictaphones and video cameras. Flash-bulbs went off constantly. At least fifty journalists were present, with more streaming across the car park to join the throng.

Heck stood nervously to Hunter's rear. Shawna and Quinnell stood even further back.

'So you're attached to the Maniac taskforce, sir?' one of the journos shouted.

'Correct . . . I'm with the Serial Crimes Unit at Scotland Yard,' Hunter replied. 'As you're probably aware, we regularly get seconded to regional forces in the event of major crimes like this.'

It was rare the DI allowed himself any displays of emotion

while on duty, but as a clear indication of the immense pressure that had been removed from his shoulders, he was beaming like the Cheshire Cat – though maybe it went a little further than that. Heck wondered if Hunter had perhaps finished his sauna and had been in the health club bar when the team had reached him.

'Can you identify the two fatalities?' another journalist asked.

'Not at this stage, no.'

'Is there *anything* you can tell us?'

'You must understand, these events have only just occurred. We're still assessing the situation, gathering evidence and so forth, but I will say this . . . we're very happy.'

'When you say "we", DI Hunter . . . do you mean the Serial Crimes Unit or the Maniac taskforce?'

'All of us. There *has* been a double fatality and that's always a tragedy, but I must reiterate . . . we are very pleased with developments to date. Ah . . .' He noticed Heck lurking at the rear, and ushered him forward. 'Here's one of the officers who attended the scene. This is Detective Sergeant Heckenburg, also from the Serial Crimes Unit. As you can see, he's had a tough evening, but let me assure you this is one top-notch officer who has more than done his job today.'

'Were you involved in the pursuit, Sergeant Heckenburg?' a reporter shouted.

Heck hesitated before replying. He didn't have the first idea how much Hunter had revealed about the car chase, though given the severity of it, it was likely the press had already discovered an awful lot.

'I was in one of the cars pursuing the suspect vehicle,' he admitted.

'Can you tell us what happened?'

'As I've told you,' Hunter interrupted, 'we can't say any more about that at present.'

'Were you in the vehicle that rode the two suspects off the motorway, DS Heckenburg?' a different voice asked.

'There were a number of police units involved,' Heck replied.

'When was it that you realised you were chasing the M1 Maniac?'

'I've told you, we can't say anything yet,' Hunter answered for him.

'Did you know from the beginning there were two murderers?'

'Please gentlemen!' Hunter said. 'We've told you all we can.'

'And that would be that you're very happy two men have died in a car crash, sir?'

Hunter's smile tightened, but he retained his cool. 'I think you know what I mean . . .'

'Sir,' Heck whispered, 'we've probably said enough.'

Hunter raised his voice one final time. 'All you need tell the public at present is that there's been a major development in the M1 Maniac enquiry – a *major* development – and that we are very, very encouraged by it.'

He and Heck turned and walked back into the hospital, ignoring all further questions. Once they were safe in A&E, Hunter dabbed sweat from his brow with a handkerchief but still looked satisfied. 'That gave them something to chew on at least.'

Heck didn't say what he was thinking: *Yes, sir . . . your arse.*

Chapter 4

Todd really liked Cheryl, and Cheryl really liked Todd. In fact, if they were honest, it went a lot further than that. The first time Todd had told Cheryl he loved her it had been just before Christmas, while they were walking Monty, her parents' pet Labrador, over the snowy ridges of Rivington Moor. She'd simply replied: 'I know.'

Which had thrown him a little.

Todd could only muster small-talk all the way back to the car park. But once Cheryl had installed Monty on the blanket in the back of her boyfriend's periwinkle-blue Volkswagen Polo, and had climbed into the front passenger seat alongside him, she kissed him on the cheek. Not just any old kiss, not just a peck; it was long and moist and warm. He turned to face her, and their lips entwined and their tongues snaked together, and there'd been no going back really from that point on.

They hadn't told anybody yet, especially not their respective parents, but they planned to marry in about two years' time, depending on their ability to save up for a mortgage. Of course they were only nineteen and twenty, so they weren't rushing anything.

Even so, they were electric together.

That was what Cheryl told her girlfriends: 'We're electric.' If Todd so much as touched her hand, a warm jolt passed through her. And in one of their more intimate moments, he confessed the same about her.

They couldn't wait to see each other that Valentine's Eve.

As always, Todd arrived at Cheryl's parents' house bang on time, looking spick and span in his dark jeans, his bold striped sport shirt and well-pressed blazer. His gleaming, newly-washed Polo waited at the end of the drive – her chariot. That was one thing Cheryl's parents really liked about Todd. He nearly always drove, so he rarely drank, which was a good thing in itself and in addition meant their lovely daughter was always assured of getting home safely.

It was Cheryl's mum, Marlene, who answered the door. She was a bit of a looker herself, and she too was going out somewhere that evening, so she looked sexy, her voluptuous curves wrapped in chiffon and black lace, her blood-red toenails peeking out of patent black stilettos. But it was Cheryl who was the star of the show in a metallic-blue sequin dress with gloss tights and sky-high heels. Presenting Cheryl with ten red Valentine's roses, Todd didn't know what to say, except what he always said, which was that he was the luckiest man alive.

By seven-thirty they'd hit the road. After stopping for a bite to eat at their favourite pizzeria, they drove to a pub they knew, where they met up with two other couples they were friendly with. After a few drinks, the girls already getting tipsy on the landlady's special Valentine's cocktail, they headed off to Manchester together to hit one of the expensive, glitzy nightclubs.

It was a cracking event.

City centre clubs could get a bit crowded, a bit sweaty, a bit noisy – but the atmosphere in this one was just right.

The music was ultra schmaltzy, but Cheryl really didn't care because tonight was all about love, and she had Todd. There was lots of dancing and lots and lots of kissing. Subsequently, by two o'clock in the morning, their intense affection for each other had become unmanageably passionate. So they said their goodbyes and hurried outside hand-in-hand, giggling.

It was another very cold night, their breath steaming, and the light sweat on their foreheads prickling like ice. As they made their way down the back alley to the car park, its cobblestones were rimed with frost.

The moment they got into the car and closed the doors, Todd put a hungry hand on Cheryl's nylon-clad thigh.

'Not here,' she said, pouting.

Todd glanced around. She was probably right. People would be coming and going for a little while yet. 'Usual place?' he asked with an impish grin.

'It's a lot quieter there,' she said.

So Todd drove them back out of Manchester along the M61 motorway. Their home town, Bolton, was only about eight or nine miles away, but before they reached it, they diverted along the A675 onto the West Pennine Moors. En route, Cheryl lifted the hem of her dress to reveal that she wasn't wearing shiny tights at all, but shiny stockings fastened to pretty white suspender straps. She wiggled her bottom as she drew a pair of panties down her shapely legs.

'Watch the road,' she said sternly as Todd kept glancing down, his eyes popping.

There were few other cars around at this time of night, especially here on the West Pennine Moors, though these weren't wild moors as such – more like open countryside alternating with reservoirs and dense tracts of woodland. But only one or two main roads led through this area, with few streetlamps.

Todd eventually decided he couldn't wait any longer and pulled up in a lay-by – only for Cheryl to glance around, discomforted. 'Here?' she said. 'We're still on the road.'

'There's no one out at this hour,' he replied, loosening his seatbelt.

'I thought we were going to the usual place?'

'That's another five minutes off . . .'

'Yeah, but it's more sheltered than this.' She pouted. 'Please.'

Sighing, he switched the engine back on. Two miles further along, they swung left down a short access way and into a small car park, which was used during the day by walkers and picnickers but at night was nearly always deserted. At present it was pitch-black, huddled beneath a roof of branches so interlaced that only faint beams of frosty moonlight penetrated. Even so, Todd drove down to its farthest end, about a hundred yards from the entrance. He pulled up, applied the handbrake and switched off his headlights.

Beside them stood a wall of leafless thickets, but these were only vaguely distinguishable in the gloom. Beyond those lay a blackness in which nothing stirred, at least nothing they could see. At normal times they might have been a little oppressed by this sense of isolation, but now the twosome were hot for each other, breathless with anticipation.

At first only Cheryl reacted to the brief, shrill cry, which sounded from somewhere close by.

'What was that?' she said, sitting bolt upright.

'Does it matter?' Todd fumbled eagerly with the button of his jeans.

'No Todd, seriously . . . what was it?'

'I don't know . . . a bird probably.'

'In the middle of the night?'

'Mating call. How appropriate.' He leaned over, planted

his mouth on Cheryl's perfumed neck and tried to worm a mischievous hand between her thighs – but she kept them clamped together and pushed him away.

'Stop it . . . that didn't sound like a bird to me.'

Realising that she wasn't just being coy, Todd straightened up. 'What's the matter now?'

Cheryl stared through the windows, beyond which tendrils of icy mist ebbed amid meshed, naked twigs. 'What . . . what if it's someone messing around?'

'All the way out here?'

She pondered that, inwardly agreeing that it seemed unlikely, but still discomforted. 'Look, I definitely heard something . . .'

'There *are* night birds, you know.'

'In February?'

He shrugged. 'Maybe. Hey . . . if someone's here, and . . . I dunno, if they want to watch us, would they give themselves away by making daft noises?'

'Watch us?' She looked dismayed by the mere thought. 'You mean like doggers?'

'Well . . . yeah. But what are the chances of that at this hour?'

Even as he said this Cheryl thought she glimpsed movement: a black shadow flitting out of sight behind the even blacker pillar of a tree-trunk. She squealed and grabbed Todd's hand. 'There's someone out there, I know it!'

'Cheryl, there's no one. It's three in the morning!'

She peered into the encircling darkness, and he could tell that she was genuinely frightened.

'What did you think you saw?' he asked quietly.

'I don't know. It could have been a trick of the light . . .'

'There is no light.'

Todd opened the car door and jumped out, his smoky breath wreathed around him as he scanned the nearby trees.

Fleetingly, he too felt vulnerable. In darkness this opaque someone could be very near and he wouldn't necessarily see them. But it was ridiculous, surely? No one would be all the way . . .

Something flickered at the corner of his vision. He spun in that direction; a low bough on the car park's edge was quivering, as if someone had just brushed past it.

'Hey!' he called, striding quickly over there. 'Hey, you fucking pervert!'

'Todd, don't!' Cheryl hissed.

'Why don't you go back to the internet and knock a quick one off over some underagers, eh?'

'Todd!'

He halted at the edge of the undergrowth, right next to the quivering bough. 'There's nothing here for you tonight . . . you got it?' His eyes slowly attuned as he peered into the foliage, though it diminished quickly into a foggy gloom.

In truth, he'd only half heard the keening cry that had distracted Cheryl. But now that he pondered it, there *had* been something vaguely fake about it, as if – how had Cheryl put it? – someone was messing around. Again, Todd scanned the murky woodland, his ears pricked. It was so still, so quiet, as though the roots, the branches, the bark were listening back to him. He hung on there for several more seconds, defying someone to respond.

'What do you think you're playing at?' Cheryl said, coming up behind, heels clattering the tarmac.

He shrugged. 'Just a precaution.'

'You'll make them angry.'

'Cheryl, there's no one here, okay? I shouted on the off chance, but it's a bit late at night for someone to be creeping around.'

She took his arm in a tight grip. 'Right, fine . . . enough showing off, alright?'

'I'm not showing off.'

She led him back to the car. 'You don't have to do stuff like that to impress me . . .'

Her words tailed off as they stumbled to a standstill.

An electric light was visible about seventy yards away, in the farthest corner of the car park. It was a single, feebly glowing bulb, only just managing to illuminate the narrow doorway underneath it, which they knew gave access to a small public lavatory. But this was the first time either of them had noticed it.

'When did that get switched on?' Cheryl asked quietly.

Todd mused. 'Must've been on all the time.'

'I didn't see it when we first arrived.'

'Were you looking?'

'No, but surely we'd have spotted it?'

Todd started towards it, slowly at first but then with purpose.

'What are we doing now?' Cheryl asked, following, still clutching his arm.

'Just seeing if there's anyone there.'

'Er . . . why?'

'Because like you say, we don't want spectators!'

'But you said there'd be no one here at this hour.'

Todd had no immediate answer to that. It was possible they'd simply driven in here and hadn't observed that the lavatory's exterior light was on, but he doubted it. The clicking of their footfalls echoed eerily as they approached the tiny structure, its simple square dimensions slowly coming into view. They were about thirty yards away when its light winked off – they froze mid-stride – and then winked on again.

'Not working properly,' Todd stated. The exterior light flickered several times more, finally went off again, and then stayed off. 'Just wait here . . . I'll go and check.'

Cheryl remained where she was while Todd ventured forward over the last few yards, one eye on the lavatory's half-open door behind which lay dank blackness, the other on the deep, dim undergrowth at the building's rear. That too lay thick, motionless and impenetrable.

The lavatory was little more in size than a suburban outhouse. It was built from red brick and when seen in daylight, written all over with obscene slogans. Inside, it comprised a single narrow passage with a broken washbasin at the far end, and two cubicles that, when he'd gone in there once before to take a leak, were as dirty and smelly as animal stalls. Todd poked his head around the door first and fumbled along the jamb for a switch. He encountered two, and when he threw the first the interior bulb flickered to life, revealing an unwashed tile floor and damp plaster walls. He glanced into both cubicles. The first was empty and the toilet lid closed, but in the second the lid was open and someone had daubed the bowl's fecal contents all over the surrounding woodwork in broad smears, at one point attempting to write something with it. Not surprisingly, the stench in there was appalling, and Todd was grateful to beat a hasty retreat. As he exited, the internal light also began flickering and buzzing loudly.

'Loose connections,' he said, rejoining Cheryl outside. 'Probably been going on and off all day.'

'But why would it be on in the first place?' she asked as he walked her back across the car park.

'Someone left it on . . . it's no big deal.'

'Listen, Todd . . .' She glanced again at the encircling wood-land, clotted with night-mist. 'I think we should just go home.'

They'd now reached the Polo, and he gazed at her across its roof, hugely disappointed. 'Oh . . . come on, Cheryl!'

She regarded him carefully. Todd was every inch the gentleman – he'd been so quick to protect her honour then, even against foes that were possibly imaginary – but he was a man too, and they hadn't got frisky with each other for over a week. No wonder he looked so dejected.

'Well at least get close to the road,' she said, 'so we can make a quick getaway if we need to.'

'Whatever you say.'

They climbed in together. Todd twisted the key, put the Polo back in gear, and nosed it around in a three-point turn. Finger-like twigs groped at the windscreen and then at the side windows as the vehicle manoeuvred. As they drove back across the car park, Cheryl glanced towards the lavatory block. Both its internal and external lights had now gone off.

'Even if there is someone around,' Todd said cheerfully, 'they won't see much in this darkness.'

'Dirty old men,' she replied with disgust.

'Dogging's a popular sport these days. You get codgers, you get husky athletic types. All sorts.'

'You seem to know a lot about it?'

'Hey, I'm a man of the world.' Todd was making light of the situation, though he couldn't help glancing over his shoulder again, eyes roving the empty, moon-dappled tarmac behind them. It was funny how once you'd told yourself you weren't alone in a dark and lonely place, it was difficult to get the idea out of your head. Not that it was easy to be distracted by this for long, the way Cheryl was now moistening her lips with the tip of her tongue.

'I hope you're going to show me how much of a man you are in a minute,' she said.

He grinned as he drove.

This time they parked at the foot of the access lane, about thirty yards from the car park entrance. Even though a slice of grey, moonlit ribbon was visible where the main road passed by, deep, skeletal thickets blotted out the rest. Todd hurriedly unzipped his flies and pulled his trousers to his knees, pushing his underpants down after them. As his engorged penis sprang to life, Cheryl climbed over the gearstick to face him, straddling his lap. He entered her easily and quickly.

She grunted gently as she rode him, wrapping her arms around his neck, bending her head down to greedily kiss at his lips, their tongues lashing. Cheryl screwed her eyes shut to suffer no other distractions, to maximise every millisecond of bliss. And then, for some reason unknown to her, she opened them again.

Only briefly, fleetingly – but that was when she realised they had company.

At first she thought the tall figure with the glowing green eyes was standing in the car park directly behind them – only to realise that this was a reflection on the inside of the rear window. The figure was actually standing in front of the car.

As if telepathically connected, Todd realised someone was there too. His eyes snapped open and he stared past Cheryl's suddenly rigid shoulder, focusing on the figure about twenty yards in front. He couldn't distinguish anything about it except that it was taut, as though twisted partly around. In the very same second Todd realised why this was. The figure was straining on some complex, hi-tech instrument; he appeared to have drawn a heavy cord back to his shoulder.

Todd gasped, choked . . .

It was a bow and arrow.

There was a muffled twang.

And the windscreen shattered.

Chapter 5

When Detective Superintendent Gemma Piper gave you a bollocking, you knew you'd been bollocked. They didn't call her 'the Lioness' for nothing. When Gemma roared, the corridors at New Scotland Yard shook. And she was articulate with it, so it wasn't just uncontrolled rage you were exposed to; her choice of words could be so scathing that even if delivered in terms of friendly banter, they could make an eavesdropper wince.

And this wasn't friendly banter.

Heck sat alone outside her office as he listened to the racket within. Because of his rank, Bob Hunter had been summoned in to see the superintendent first. That had been a good thirty minutes ago, and Gemma was still tearing strips off him, the whipcrack voice penetrating the closed door and ringing down the central corridor of the Serial Crimes Unit. By the sounds of it, she'd now moved from criticising Hunter's handling of the enquiry, primarily the way he'd allowed it to 'crash and burn', to something more akin to common abuse. Phrases like 'swaggering overconfidence', 'buffoonish disregard for protocol', and 'off-the-scale ineptitude' sounded decidedly non-specific.

In one respect, it all seemed a little unfair, given that the M1 murders had officially been solved. The evidence found in the wrecked van, including the pistol used in all the killings, had strongly indicated that the Savage twins were the culprits. What was more, two days ago, the inquest into their deaths, which had delayed the team returning to base from Milton Keynes, had returned a verdict of death by misadventure, so there ought to be no further questions regarding the double fatality.

The problem was that even though the case of the M1 Maniac was now firmly closed, the press, who had fed on it for months in a shark-like frenzy, weren't content to leave it there. With the inquest over, the finer details of the enquiry had been made public, and fascinated journalists had pored over them, determined to find mistakes. It almost seemed as if the actions of two cold-blooded serial killers had provided insufficient explanation for the deaths of eight teenage boys. Any errors made by those charged with catching the deranged duo had to be immediately and ruthlessly exposed, as though these constituted sins as reprehensible as the homicides themselves.

Heck wouldn't ordinarily dispute that viewpoint – it was the job of the police to catch killers, and if they couldn't do it, they ought to be asked why. But the hunt for the M1 Maniac had stirred widespread panic across southern England and put intolerable pressure on the investigating team. There'd been massive interference at all levels, both judicial and political; everyone from the Prime Minister down to the average petty criminal had stridently demanded a resolution. Exhaustion had set in, mental and physical, so it was no wonder errors were made by the team: failure to follow up leads, failure to update computer files, innocent suspects suffering heavy-handed treatment from overworked officers, and so forth.

Now, after the revelation that Jordan Savage had been spoken to at an early stage of the investigation but then disregarded, resulting in he and his brother going on to commit a further five murders – the press were having an absolute field day.

'Keystone Cops,' one headline proclaimed over a photograph of the Yard's famous revolving signpost. 'Police 2, Bad Guys 9,' another said. Its strapline added: 'So how dare they claim victory'. It was enough to make even Heck cringe with guilt, and he was the one who had broken the case.

He wasn't sure where to look when the door to Gemma's office opened and Bob Hunter came stiffly out. The DI winked, but the only colour registering in his chastened face were two dots of bright pink, one on either cheekbone. He stuck a thumb over his shoulder at the half-closed door, turned and perambulated down the corridor, his gait slow and delicate.

Heck stood up and brushed his hair with his hand, before knocking.

'Yes?' came an irritable voice.

Heck walked in, closing the door behind him.

'Ah-hah . . . the arresting officer!' Gemma said. 'Or something to that effect.'

Her personal office was always fastidiously neat – and rather bare, in fact some would say 'spartan' – and yet surprisingly small, given her high rank. Of course, this made it all the easier for it to be filled by her towering personality.

Detective Superintendent Gemma Piper was formidable; a force of nature. Her beauty helped her in this regard. It was fierce, leonine (hence the nickname) – she had wild, ash-blonde hair, blue eyes, red lips, flawless features – all the usual accoutrements of fine femininity, yet somehow it combined to create a warrior rather than a princess. In addition she was tall and athletically built, and she dressed to enhance this; men could be reduced to jelly in Gemma's presence for all kinds of reasons. Heck knew this better than anyone, because at one time, many years ago now, he'd shared her life and her bed.

'Morning, ma'am,' he said.

She pointed to the chair in front of her desk. He sat.

'You know why I want to see you?' She leaned forward, fingers steepled. She was pale in the cheek, but her anger seemed to have abated a little, presumably because she'd vented most of it on Bob Hunter – though there was still a menacing snap in her tone.

'Yes, ma'am.'

'Because this . . .' and she dropped a file related to the M1 enquiry on the desk; it landed like a paving stone, '. . . should have "Cowboys and Indians" written on it. Particularly the bit at the end. You know, the bit where the damage runs into hundreds of thousands of pounds . . . caused by a frantic car-chase, which *you* instigated. The bit where the two perpetrators suffered horrific, life-ending injuries. I mean, killing the two chief suspects, Heck . . . that kind of *faux pas* knocks everything else that went wrong on this enquiry into a cocked hat.'

'Ma'am . . .' Heck shrugged helplessly. 'These guys had a lot to lose. They were never going to come quietly.'

'I understand that, but we still have to be accountable for our actions.'

'If we have to account to Joe Public, we've no worries. He's fine with it.'

'Joe Public is an arsehole!' she replied, her voice sharpening again. 'Joe Public will turn on us viciously the first time we do the slightest thing he doesn't agree with. Don't pretend Joe Public is our mate, Heck, because he isn't.'

'Ma'am . . .' Heck tried his most earnest tone. 'You can surely see I had no choice but to pursue the suspects?'

'Even though they were armed and you weren't?'

'Well . . . yes. I knew it was a risk, but it was less of a risk for me than it would have been a risk for the general public if those two were allowed to remain at liberty. For what it's worth, if I'd been going there to make an arrest, I'd have taken armed support with me, but it didn't happen that way.'

Gemma pondered this. There was no doubt she was torn. If Heck's actions leading to the fatal accident were reckless, he'd also showed exceptional bravery, which was something she valued in her officers.

'Even if the suspects had got away, ma'am, I couldn't afford to lose that van,' he added. 'It was chock full of physical evidence.'

'Celebrating its capture hardly seemed appropriate, given that two men had died.'

'I know that.'

She sat back. 'It won't surprise you to learn that Max Humphreys has distanced himself – by some margin – from the comments Bob Hunter made on the hospital steps.'

'No, that doesn't surprise me.'

Detective Chief Superintendent Max Humphreys of the Thames Valley Police, nominal SIO in the M1 Maniac enquiry, had struck Heck from the outset as an uninspiring leader; too old and tired, too disorganised, and alarmingly prone to avoiding responsibility. For all that, Bob Hunter's triumphalist attitude in front of the press had been very ill-advised, given the errors that would later emerge.

'Now in actual fact,' Gemma said, 'I'm not too concerned that *you* were involved in that extremely injudicious press conference. I know you were acting under Hunter's orders, and I've already had it verbatim from DCs Quinnell and McCluskey that you were against the idea. But I'm very concerned at the way this investigation ended overall. What should have been a feather in our cap has brought ridicule on us. The press are ripping us a new one.'

Heck snorted. 'To be fair, ma'am, the press did their own bit to turn the M1 Maniac into a monster. *They* created the name, *they* caused the anti-gay panic. In fact, the whole thing's ended too quickly for them. They wanted more and more – a show-trial, exemplary sentences, maybe a protracted appeals process. And now they can't have it, and they're looking for scapegoats . . .'

'Have you finished?' she asked, eyebrows arched. 'Because anyone would think *you* believe the investigation was handled well!'

He shook his head. 'Ma'am, Chief Superintendent Humphreys . . .'

'I'm well aware of Max Humphreys' shortcomings. He'll be getting exactly the same bollocking up at Thames Valley that you lot are getting now. But Max Humphreys is a carrot cruncher, whereas *we're* supposed to be experts. We were advising him, leading the enquiry, and by the looks of it, missing stuff that was right under our noses.'

Heck nodded, unable to disagree. 'That's why I spent three days going back through the files. I'd never known any case before where we just weren't getting anywhere.'

'And it was good initiative. So congratulations. And I mean that, Heck.' She sighed, the annoyance finally sapped out of her. 'If you hadn't done what you did, God alone knows how this thing would have ended. But . . . and I appreciate it may not seem very important after how close you came to getting killed, this is not the way the brass want the Serial Crimes Unit portrayed. Like some redneck posse charging around. Especially not after the investigation was botched. Needless to say, the Savage family is pushing for a public enquiry. The coroner exonerated us of any wrongdoing, the case is officially closed and it's in no one's interest to rake over it again, so I'm sure we'll be spared *that* . . . thank God. But at the end of the day it's about professionalism. We need to keep the mayhem to a minimum.'

'Has anyone told the criminals that?'

She arched an eyebrow again. 'Are you trying to be clever?'

'No, ma'am . . . but, it's not an irrelevant point.'

'One way or another, the criminals will go down. My concern is that SCU may go down with them.'

'How so? We stopped the M1 killers . . .'

'We also stopped the Nice Guys Club, and look at the bad publicity that caused.'

'That was Laycock.'

'And he paid the price,' she said. 'Which should be a salutary lesson to all of us.'

Heck pursed his lips, nodding. There was no question that she was right on that score. The Nice Guys enquiry, in which he had played an integral role, had led to several deaths on both sides of the law, and an embarrassing internal investigation, which eventually saw National Crime Group Commander Jim Laycock demoted in rank and removed from his post for gross negligence. If Heck had got his own way, Laycock would have been investigated for criminal activity, but there hadn't been sufficient evidence of that.

'The point is that attention is now focused on *us*,' Gemma said. 'On SCU. We're a key facet of the National Crime Group. We're part of the bright new future for British law enforcement. Or at least we were, until we started initiating cock-ups on a regular basis.'

'I wouldn't call it regular . . .'

'One is too many, Heck! Two is a total clusterfuck.'

That was a sure proof of how upset she was: Gemma almost never swore. She took another moment to compose herself. 'So the first thing I'm going to do is appoint a full-time Media Liaison Officer.' He raised a quizzical eyebrow.

'Just for us,' she added. 'A civvie . . . a real pro. Someone who can give us a far more professional face.'

'Does the budget extend to that?'

'It wouldn't do normally, but as you know, Des Palliser's retiring at the end of next month. If I don't replace him we can manage it.'

'You're going to replace an operational DI with a civvie?'

'He's hardly operational. He's been acting duty-officer for the last eighteen months, which means filing paperwork and manning phones. I'm sure we can live without him.'

'Someone'll have to do that job.'

She eyed him carefully. 'Bob Hunter.'

Heck thought he'd misheard. 'You're taking Hunter off the streets?'

Gemma shuffled the paperwork on her desk. 'Bob's better days are behind him. Milton Keynes wasn't the first time he's shown a lack of judgment recently.'

'But we're already under-strength, ma'am.'

'Bob Hunter's grounded for the foreseeable, and that's all there is to it. We *are* under-strength, I agree . . . but the last thing I need at present is a loose cannon out in the field. Now let's get back to work. We're all busy.' Heck stood up. Gemma was already engrossed in checking another report. He headed for the door. 'Well done on the case,' she said to his back. He glanced around, but she didn't look up. 'I said I meant that, and I do. But none of us smell of roses right now. And I have to take any action necessary to put that right.'

Heck nodded and left.

Chapter 6

If nothing else, Kate was glad it was spring.

Okay, some parts of Liverpool didn't look great at any time of year, and Toxteth was undoubtedly one of them, especially when rainy as today. But just standing outside the front of the shop this evening and not having to wrap up like an Eskimo was a boon.

To call the winter that had just passed 'bitter' would have been a big understatement. An arctic air-stream had caused record lows and persistent whiteouts across the whole of the UK from mid-December until well into February. Great fun, of course, for the kiddies, whose schools were repeatedly closed. But there were an awful lot of people for whom those conditions were a living hell. The flotsam of the city – the lonely, the homeless, the sick, the drug-addled – did well to get through their average day and keep warm, dry and fed, but rotting cardboard boxes, piss-stained sleeping bags and windy concrete underpasses offered scant protection when the ice and snow bit with that much savagery.

Kate chuffed on her cig, and considered it a miracle that any of her charges had survived this last winter at all – and they weren't totally out of the woods yet. It was seven o'clock now and today's inclement weather appeared to be clearing at last, though it still felt dank and chilly.

She was in the process of closing up, loading bundles of plastic-wrapped second-hand clothing, all cleaned and pressed, into the boot of her battered old Ford Fiesta. The backstreet on which the charity shop was located, which was unused by any other businesses, became a deep, dark canyon once night fell. Only a single yellow lamp glowed at the far end, and as the street was narrow and the industrial buildings running down either side of it were tall, gloomy and mostly windowless, no more than a thin slice of sky was visible overhead. Kate shivered as she loaded the last bundle into the boot. She would get all this lot down to the Whitechapel Centre on Langsdale Street and then hang around to see if they needed a spare volunteer for the evening. She'd put in a lot of hours recently, but she didn't care. She wouldn't sleep easily tonight knowing there were people out of doors who'd be neither warm nor dry.

She stubbed her cigarette out, pulled her Afghan coat on, wove a scarf around her neck and was about to switch the lights off inside, when she heard a loud, metallic *clank* from somewhere to the rear of the shop. She stopped what she was doing to listen. No additional sound followed. Assuming something in the kitchen had fallen over, she wandered into the shop to check, remembering that she needed to empty the bin while she was at it – but nothing looked to have been disturbed. Her knife, fork and dinner plate were stacked on the draining board, where she'd left them that lunchtime. Her coffee cup was in its usual place alongside the kettle, which was safely unplugged, its cable wound around it. The doors to the fridge and microwave were both closed; the dishcloth and sponge were in the washing-up bowl, the Fairy Liquid on the windowsill.

Shrugging, Kate lugged the bulging plastic sack from out of the bin, tying its neck in a knot, and opened the back door – and only then did it occur to her that perhaps the sound she'd heard had come from outside. That wouldn't be unusual, even though she worked here alone; this was a city, people did things at all hours, there were loud noises. And yet, fleetingly, she was hesitant to go and investigate the murky yard. The only light out there came from the interior of the shop via its grimy window and narrow back door. There was a faint ambient glow in the sky – the residue of surrounding street lighting, though no lamps shone directly down on the yard.

Kate hovered on the step. From what she could see, everything looked to be in place: the wheelie-bin, the bucket and mop, the row of empty plant-pots. There was nothing suspicious here.

Except that the back gate was open.

That wasn't a big thing in itself, though Kate was sure she'd closed it earlier. Was that the sound she'd heard? Had someone climbed over the gate to case the place, and had they then opened it to get away again?

Good luck to them, she thought; it wasn't like there was much here worth stealing.

Her eyes had now adapted to the dimness, and she could see that she was alone. There was no dilapidated shed for someone to hide behind, no concealed corner where they might crouch unseen. Deciding she was being daft, she went boldly forward, throwing the rubbish sack into the bin and walking over to the gate. She even stepped outside it. The cobbled alley beyond wasn't too salubrious, but they never were in this part of town. There were no other vehicles of course; no one was packing or unpacking goods. But at least that meant she could see clear down to either end of the alley. On the left it ran forty litter-strewn yards before halting at a wall of sheer bricks. On the right it ran further, eighty yards or more, and then opened into an adjacent road. Even down there, the street lighting was restricted to a narrow gap, where a caul of mist was slowly twisting.

That was spooky for sure, but it wasn't unusual either – even if Kate did stare at it for several seconds, as though mesmerised. They were very near the river. And it was only April, as she kept reminding herself. The main thing was that there was no one skulking about. She went back into the yard, this time ensuring to close and bolt the gate, then re-entered the building, locking the back door behind her, before turning the lights off and leaving the shop.

Her car was years old, so it would take an age for the radiator to warm up. Kate pulled her mittens on, twisted the key in the ignition and steered the chugging old motor along the street. That sound she'd heard would have been nothing, but it was strange how even though you'd worked in the heart of the city for so many years, its dreary facades and bleak, empty passages could occasionally menace you. Perhaps it was the way the light leached into its stones, the way shadows seemed to clot at its every nook and corner. You were surrounded by people in the inner city, yet it was the easiest place in the world to feel isolated and threatened. How much worse it must be, of course, for those who roamed it endlessly with no place to call their own.

In perfect sync with these thoughts, and before Kate had even reached the next junction, her headlights swept over another pathetic specimen of humanity huddled in a trash-filled doorway. All she saw at first was a dingy quilted blanket, frayed around its edges and odiously stained. The shape curled up beneath was visibly shuddering.

She pulled up at the kerb and applied the handbrake, but left the engine running to try and warm the vehicle's interior. She climbed out amid clouds of exhaust made thick and pungent by the dampness. The poor sod must have known she was there, but made no effort to look up.

'Hi,' Kate said, approaching cautiously. Even someone with experience had to be a little bit careful – some of these cases were so damaged that they were almost animalistic in their reaction when frightened or disturbed. 'Can I help?'

There was no response. The shrouded form continued to shudder. God alone knew how long the miserable creature had been out here.

'My name's Kate. I run the outreach shop at the end of the road there. Look . . . there's nothing to be scared of. I'm sure I can assist.' Kate hunkered down. 'I'm on my way to one of the shelters in the centre of town right now. Why don't you hop in and I'll give you a lift? In half an hour you'll be drinking hot soup and have a proper bed to sleep in. You can have a wash, a change of clothes . . .' Whoever was under there stopped shuddering, as if they were suddenly listening. 'Here,' Kate said, encouraged. She reached forward to peel the ragged blanket away. 'Let me help you . . .'

The figure sprang.

Kate never saw this – before she knew it, *she* was the one swathed in filthy material. The pavement hit her in the back. She gasped with shock, but could barely draw a breath as the blanket was wrapped tightly around her – as if she was being quickly and efficiently packaged. Something cinched her waist – a rope or belt – binding her arms tightly to her sides. Effortlessly, she was scooped into someone's arms.

Kate made muffled screams, even though she knew no one could hear her. She was flung into the back seat of her own vehicle, where what felt like further straps were fixed in place and another blanket was tossed over her. A split second later someone climbed into the driving seat, closed the door and put the car in gear.

She screamed again, futilely. The traitorous vehicle rumbled on along the narrow street as though the brief, terrifying interlude had never occurred.

Chapter 7

'Get stuffed, Heck!' Shawna McCluskey said. 'That wasn't me.'

'It was,' Heck assured the bunch of detectives crammed around them in the pub vault. 'I drive round the back to try and cut these idiots off. I look up, and there's two uniforms coming down the other side of the pub. One of them's Shawna. These two lads they're chasing see me in the panda car, and cut across this patch of grass. Shawna veers over it to intercept. Best rugby tackle you've ever seen. She took this big bastard right out, almost killed him.'

There was laughter.

'That wasn't me,' Shawna informed everyone for the umpteenth time.

'And what had he done again?' Des Palliser asked.

'He'd only bitten some bugger's nose and ear off in a fight in the pub,' Heck said. 'The other one had kicked the shit out of the landlord when he objected. Anyway, she takes out Jaws, and then wallops the other one as well. Puts him down with one punch.'

There was more laughter.

'That wasn't me either,' Shawna said tartly. 'It was Ian

Kershaw. "Dreadnought", we used to call him. He didn't want the lock-up because it was ten minutes to finishing time and it was his sister's wedding the next day. I took the prisoners for him.'

'What did the two scrotes say?' Gary Quinnell asked.

'Nothing,' Heck replied. 'They were out cold. They didn't know *who'd* hit them.'

There were further roars of laughter.

The Chop House was located under the arches on the edge of Borough Market, and was redolent with Victoriana: leaded windows, etched mirrors, elegant hardwood décor, and an open fire. Its various rooms were packed with off-duty police and police civilian staff, the booze was flowing and there was an atmosphere of bonhomie.

Shawna shook her head as though tolerating the boyishness around her, and handed Heck her empty glass. 'For that, it's *your* round.'

Heck nodded and threaded his way through to the bar, taking a rash of orders en route. Bob Hunter was leaning there, a treble scotch in his hand. He looked rumpled and sour-faced; his tie hung in a limp knot.

'Everyone's having a good time, I see,' he said as Heck put the order in.

'Gotta give Des a send-off, haven't we?' Heck replied.

'No sign of the Lioness yet?'

Heck looked around. 'Thought she'd be in by now.'

It was possible that Gemma was in one of the other rooms – she always had a lot of flesh to press at police functions – but the bulk of SCU were squashed into this one, so he'd have expected her to come in here first, probably to buy Des Palliser a drink.

'Second round of interviews this afternoon for the Media Liaison job, wasn't it?' Hunter said.

'Oh yeah, that.'

'Yeah . . . *that*. What a fucking joke, eh? This is the way they repay us for taking nutjobs off the street.'

Heck shrugged. 'Won't interfere with our work, will it?'

'Says who? *I've* been demoted to fucking duty-officer!'

'It's only temporary.'

'How temporary is temporary, Heck?' Hunter barely acknowledged the double scotch that Heck placed in front of him. 'Fucking Lioness wants me out, I can tell.'

'She doesn't,' Heck said.

'Why, has she told you that?'

'No, but . . .'

'Exactly . . . no.' Hunter swallowed whisky. 'Suddenly the way I work doesn't suit her anymore. I wonder why that is? I'd say it was because some over-decorated twat on the top floor had her by the gonads . . . but as a bird she hasn't got any, has she?'

'Bob . . . it was a fuck-up. We should never have spoken to the press.'

'Alright, I accept that.' Hunter looked surprisingly contrite. 'But it was a spur-of-the-moment decision. Christ's sake, Heck . . . we'd just topped and tailed the fucking M1 Maniacs. Some kind of result, that. No wonder we were all a bit excited. I'll tell you, I'm fed up with this fucking job.'

Heck had heard such a sentiment before, of course; he'd expressed it himself.

'You may as well know, I'm putting my papers in for a transfer,' Hunter added.

'Where to?'

'I don't know. Anywhere out of NCG.' Hunter wrinkled his nose, as though the whole thing literally stank. 'Could've been the best gig in town, this, but now it's going like everything else. It's all politics these days. I mean, you of all people ought to be pissed off by that.'

Heck was; he'd had his share of reprimands over the years,

and when in his cups he too was inclined to make such comments, though in reality he kept soldiering on.

'Just don't do anything hasty, Bob,' he said. 'We don't know how long this duty-officer thing'll last. At least you're working nine-till-five again.'

'Why should that appeal to me? I've nothing to go home to. Sal took the kids yonks ago.' Hunter shook his head as if that was someone else's fault too. 'Fucking Lioness! Sorry, Heck, I know you and her were an item.'

'That was a while ago.'

'But when she bites . . .'

'She's *here*,' Heck said, spotting that Gemma had entered the pub in company with a slim young woman in a smart skirt-suit. 'Keep it down, eh?'

Hunter took another big swallow. 'Don't worry, pal. I'm not stupid enough to give her any more ammo than she needs . . .'

'Drink ma'am?' Heck said, stepping away from the bar to hand out the rest of the round he'd just bought.

'Perrier please, Heck,' Gemma said, taking her raincoat off. She turned to the woman beside her. 'Claire?'

The young woman, who was girlishly pretty – her black hair was cut to shoulder-length in a cute 'pageboy' bob, she had a fresh complexion and startling peppermint-green eyes – smiled nervously. 'Same for me please,' she said.

Gemma nodded. 'This is Detective Sergeant Heckenburg, by the way. Heck, this is Claire Moody, our new Media Liaison.'

Heck was caught by surprise. He hadn't expected a candidate to be selected so quickly. 'Oh . . . you got the job then?'

Claire seemed equally amazed. 'Looks like it.'

'Congratulations.'

She nodded her thanks.

'I thought this'd be a good opportunity for Claire to meet the rest of the team,' Gemma said, eyeing the raucous crowd gathered around Des Palliser, who was sniffing at an exotic-looking cocktail someone had just bought for him. 'But I'm not so sure now.'

'We are what we are, ma'am,' Heck said, adopting his best blokish air.

'And she must take you or leave you, eh?' Gemma said.

'Something like that.'

She turned back to her new employee. 'DS Heckenburg is one of our more . . . *persuasive* officers. He could sell STD ointment in a nunnery, if you'll pardon the crude terminology. So long as you remember to believe only five per cent of everything he tells you, you'll get along with him fine.'

'Ouch!' Heck said, which Claire seemed to find amusing.

Gemma sighed. 'Well . . . might as well try and get everyone's attention while they're not totally bladdered. Come on, Claire. I'll introduce you.'

The two women moved away, Gemma clearing a path through the mob.

'Cute little thing anyway,' Hunter remarked. 'Looks like butter wouldn't melt.' He snickered. 'I give her a month at the most.'

Heck said nothing.

Hunter remained for another half-hour, before downing his drink and sloping away without saying goodbye. Claire Moody, rather to Heck's surprise, lasted a little longer, which in some ways was admirable given that she didn't really know anyone here. She stuck fairly close to Gemma, probably because most of the rest of the team had moved in on her in predatory fashion, alternately trying to flirt or wind her up, though he later saw her being led to one side and getting her ear bent by Shawna McCluskey.

'Heck . . . hey Heck!' Shawna shouted. 'Come over here a sec!'

He drifted over. Everyone was now well-oiled. Deafening

laughter boomed; beer was sloshing. Shawna was on her way to getting drunk too.

'Claire . . . you met Heck yet?' she shouted, gesturing with a lager bottle.

Claire smiled awkwardly. 'Sort of.'

'Heck's our ace thief-taker. Me and him were in GMP together when we were whippersnappers.'

Claire frowned. 'GMP . . . that's Greater Manchester Police?'

Shawna laughed. 'Bang on. The pride of the northwest.'

'And you both ended up in London?'

'We didn't come down together,' Shawna replied, burping. 'Sorry. Heck transferred to the Met while he was still in uniform. It was a few years later with me. I joined CID in Manchester, then the Major Crimes Squad. When I heard SCU had a vacancy, I jumped at it. I arrived here and stone me, Heck's on the next desk . . . a bloody DS! Mind you, I shouldn't have been surprised. When he was in uniform he did more locking-up than the rest of the relief put together. If he fell over a wall he'd find two tea-leaves on the other side waiting to do a job.'

'Yeah, I'm so lucky I passed my inspector's exam fourteen years ago, and I've never had a sniff of an interview,' Heck replied.

Shawna slapped his shoulder. 'Too gobby, pal, that's your trouble. Always too gobby.' She turned to Claire. 'He's not like me – I'm not gobby. I'm just crap. Not be a mo . . . gotta pee.'

Shawna blundered away, leaving her half-drunk bottle in Claire's hand.

'She's not actually,' Heck said. 'She's a pretty good detective. She wouldn't be in SCU otherwise.'

'I was a bit intimidated about that,' Claire admitted; her accent was refined South Coast, which was rather fetching.

'I mean, you chaps are not just any old police unit are you? I heard you've cracked some really big cases.'

'Well, things haven't gone totally swimmingly for us in recent times.'

'I heard about that too. And . . . I'm hoping that's something I can help you with.'

'Claire!' someone else shouted. Gary Quinnell, minus jacket and tie, lurched towards her. Beefy red faces grinned behind him. 'Can we have you over here?'

'Sure,' she replied, handing Shawna's bottle to Heck, giving him a nervous glance.

'There's something you need to know about if you're going to work with us,' the burly Welshman said, leading her away. 'But it isn't covered in any manual.'

'Okay . . .?' She still sounded nervous.

'It's called the Ways And Means Act . . .'

'I'm going to miss all this,' Des Palliser said, appearing at Heck's shoulder.

'Don't beat yourself up too much,' Heck replied. 'It's not like we roll out the barrel every week.'

'We should. Reminds everyone what life's really about.'

Briefly, Palliser looked pensive. He was a grizzled oldster with a lean frame and a scraggy grey beard. A knowledgeable detective with good political acumen, he knew how to play the game but, with such long service in, he'd had little personal ambition left and thus had become something of a 'father-figure' in SCU; a font of wisdom and reliable advice for those junior officers he regarded as his protégés.

'What I meant was I'm going to miss you lot,' he said. 'Bunch of scruffy urchins. Who's going to knock you into shape if I'm not there?'

'Enough, thank you!' Gemma's voice carried across the pub. In one corner, Detective Constable Charlie Finnegan was standing on a table with his trousers around his ankles.

70

'Remember who we are and where we are, please!' Finnegan got down, abashed.

'Who do you think?' Heck said.

Palliser smiled fondly. 'Taught her everything she knows.'

'I always knew we had to thank you for something.'

'I'm glad you could come, pal.'

Heck glanced around at him. 'No one had to drag us here, Des. You'll be missed too.'

'I want you to do something for me.'

'Name it.'

'Be careful, okay?' Palliser regarded him gravely. His face was a nest of wrinkles, his teeth gnarly and yellowed by decades of smoking, yet all of this served to give him character. 'No more go-it-alone heroics like we saw during the Nice Guys enquiry. No job's worth putting your life on the line for.'

Heck smiled. 'It's not something I plan to make a habit of.'

'And that M1 Maniac thing was almost as bad. You got some kind of death-wish?'

'Just the way the cards fell, Des.'

'Doesn't matter.' Palliser put a hand on his shoulder. 'Heck, you've got a good boss in Gemma. Make use of that. Try and forget you and her once had a thing going. Unless of course, well . . .' he almost sounded hopeful, 'unless you feel like going there again?'

Heck glanced towards Claire, who, though she was besieged by shouting, guffawing coppers, was also laughing. Gary Quinnell made some jibe, but she responded sharply and they fell about again.

'I don't think so,' Heck said slowly.

Palliser followed his gaze. 'Something more interesting on the horizon?'

'Who's to say?'

'Well . . . if it gives you a reason to go home at night, all to the good.'

71

'Who are we kidding, Des? She's probably got a boyfriend with a Ferrari.'

'Just remember what I said, eh? Do what you do, Heck . . . you're bloody good at it. But be sensible and be safe.'

Heck nodded, surprised by the depth of feeling in his colleague's voice.

'Anyway, what're you having?' Palliser lurched away to the bar.

'Bitter please,' Heck said to his retreating back. 'Pint of.'

Gemma strode up. She looked as cool and unruffled as ever, despite the heat and noise. She glanced after Palliser. 'He sorry to be going?'

'Thinks SCU will fall apart without him,' Heck replied.

'The perceptiveness of old age.'

Heck nodded towards Claire. 'Our new recruit looks comfy already.'

'Good.' Gemma sipped her mineral water. 'Because there's no point us handling her with kid gloves. This'll be a testing job.'

'Presumably she's well qualified for it?'

'Worked for a major financial house in the City and at least two government departments.'

'When does she start?'

'Tomorrow morning.'

'That soon?'

'She might as well get her feet under the table while things seem to be fairly quiet.'

Heck pondered that, wondering if they were challenging fate. He wasn't superstitious, but one thing he'd learned during his seventeen years as a police officer was that you didn't make any decisions based on an assumption that nothing tumultuously crap was about to happen. Because, almost invariably, it was.

Chapter 8

'Look . . . whatever happened to you in your past, whatever it is that's making you do this, I beg you to reconsider.'

Kate wasn't sure how much her abductor could hear. He hadn't actually gagged her, so, although she was swathed in this dirty old blanket which stank of sweat and stale urine, there was nothing to prevent her trying to project words. No doubt they'd be muffled, while the ongoing rumble of the engine and the vibration of the tyres on the road might blot them out altogether. But given that she was still bound and that no matter how much she wriggled, she remained tightly trussed, she had no option but to keep trying.

'Please listen to me,' she begged. It had been two hours at least, and at no stage had she received a single reply. 'I understand that someone was once cruel to you. Maybe they tortured you – over months, perhaps years. But what you're doing now is in no way going to make up for that. You won't be getting even with them, you won't be punishing them. You'll just be hurting an ordinary person who bears you no ill will, doing exactly the same thing as was done to you . . .'

She was more terrified than she'd ever been in her life.

The revolting stench inside the blanket would only get worse as her own sweat of fear mingled with it; it was highly possible she'd add her own urine to it, maybe her own vomit, and the temperature didn't help. The heater in the car had activated some time ago and now was at its stultifying worst, but she couldn't afford to let it fog her reason – not yet. The only weapon available to her was her intellect – so she had to continue with this, trying to appeal to his better nature, if he had one.

It was appalling to think that anyone could be reduced to such a state that they'd do this sort of thing. She'd heard stories of course: about street people who'd had petrol poured on them and been set alight while they were sleeping rough, about stabbings and clubbings, about their being made to fight each other with chains and bottles while someone filmed it. Yet none of these abhorrent things had seemed real – not even to Kate, who worked with the victims – until now, when it was apparently happening to her.

'Listen . . . please!' It took an immense effort of will to reduce the quake in her voice, to make her sound less like a frightened little girl. 'Please . . . this hatred you're demonstrating. It's not a natural state for a human being to exist in. Don't you see that? Animals don't live that way, not even animals that have been scarred by illness or injury. They just accept it and get on with life. Don't let the person who abused you win by watching you become a mirror-image of him. Remember what it was like when . . .'

She'd wanted to talk about the days when he himself was a young child, but no . . . that could be a horrendous mistake. Some of these poor creatures' earliest memories comprised nothing but pain.

'Remember your humanity. Try to think how *you* like to be treated. I know that's something that was denied to you. But try to picture yourself on a normal morning, setting out

74

with no intention of doing harm to anyone, just hoping to get through the day in a simple, dignified manner. Isn't that how you feel most of the time? There's no pleasure to be found in what you're doing now. You understand that, I know you do.'

She halted, not just to get her breath – which was increasingly difficult in the sweltering confines of the blanket, but to listen in case there was any response from whoever was driving. There wasn't. But if nothing else he *had* to be listening. He hadn't put the radio on to drown her out.

'I'm making one last appeal to you,' Kate said. 'Whatever you think you'll gain from this, you're wrong. I know that sounds arrogant and presumptuous of me. But I honestly know about this. I work every day with people who have suffered the most dreadful misfortune. Most of them are deeply miserable and deeply angry. But in almost all cases – when you sit down and counsel them, try to get through to the person who was there before – they are ordinary men and women, and they realise that giving in to their baser instincts will achieve nothing . . .'

Her words petered out as she realised the vehicle was jolting and bouncing, as if traversing rough ground. The terror of this took her breath away. She imagined wasteland somewhere, far from prying eyes.

There was a change of tone from the engine. The Fiesta was slowing down.

With a clunk, the gearstick shifted, then the handbrake was applied. When the engine was switched off, the silence was ear-pummelling. Despite the kiln-like heat, the sweat coating Kate's body was ice-cold. A seatbelt was unfastened; a car door was flung open. Horrifyingly, there was no sound of night-traffic from beyond. Wherever he'd brought her to, it was far, far from civilisation.

Kate's whimpers became helpless wails as a door was

opened next to her head, and brute hands yanked the straps aside, grabbed her and threw her over a brawny shoulder. The effect of this was to nauseate her, a sensation that grew worse as she was carried through the darkness. Heavy feet crunched what sounded like soil and leaf debris, and then clumped on hollow wood, the impacts of which began to echo – she was inside a building. Different smells assailed her: sawdust, fresh paint. When she was dumped onto the floor, she felt rugged planking, nail-heads. Old hinges squealed and a foul smell arose. Kate felt a new sense of paralysing horror.

A trapdoor had been opened alongside her.

Those hands gripped her again and lifted her. Before they dropped her down into the void, a hoarse voice whispered in her ear: 'You have a good heart and an eloquent tongue. That makes you more than worthy.'

Chapter 9

'Morning!' came a bright, cheery voice.

Heck, who wasn't suffering from a hangover, but who was slightly muzzy-headed, glanced up from his desk. Claire Moody was standing in the doorway to the Detectives' Office, or DO, as they called it. 'Oh, erm . . . hello,' he said awkwardly.

She stripped off her overcoat as she glanced at the empty desks and unmanned computers. It was just past seven in the morning. Heck was the only one in, but perhaps Claire hadn't expected to find anyone. 'You're bright and early,' she said.

'Well . . . so are you.'

'I didn't have anything to celebrate last night.'

'None of us did, if only we'd realised it. Des is a good guy. Look, don't stand out there on ceremony, come in.'

Claire entered, coat folded over her arm. 'Des obviously has a lot of friends.'

'Yeah, got a bit crazy in there, didn't it? Your office up and running now?'

'Hardly . . . I don't know where anything is yet.'

As far as Heck was aware, a room had been set aside for

the new Media Management suite just along the main corridor, and though a carpentry team and then the techie guys had been in it during the last few days, he hadn't got the impression it was anywhere near ready for use. But he remembered what Gemma had said about easing Claire in as quickly as possible.

He stood up. 'Erm . . . I can give you the tour, if you'd like.'

'No please, it's okay. Don't let me interrupt you. I think your work's a bit more important than mine.'

In broad daylight, viewed through the eyes of sobriety, Claire was even more attractive than he'd first realised. She wasn't just pretty, she was gracious, well-spoken, innately pleasant . . . almost genteel. He had a worrying feeling that what Bob Hunter had said might turn out to be true, and that Claire would prove to be too nice for this environment.

'If nothing else, I can offer you a brew,' he said. 'I'm guessing you haven't got your own tea-making stuff yet?'

'I hadn't even thought about it. Thanks, I'd love one.'

He produced a key, unlocked a cupboard near his desk, and took a kettle out, along with a big bottle of water, two mugs, a jar of teabags, a cup of sugar and a sachet of powdered milk. 'Here's a tip. Keep this kind of gear secured, because round here it'll walk . . . usually upstairs to Organised Crime.'

'You can't trust police officers, eh?'

'Definitely not.' He filled the kettle and plugged it in. 'Don't be scared of us, though; we don't really bite. Speaking of which, the boss will be in soon. I suppose she'll brief you on everything you need to know.'

'She's fire and brimstone, isn't she?'

'See . . . you know her already.'

Claire glanced around again at the sprawling, open-plan

office. Despite its size, the DO bore the usual police hallmarks of organised chaos. There might be nobody else in at present, but desks were strewn with documents, in-trays overloaded, paperwork and photographs hanging in disorderly wads, not just from noticeboards but from those few patches of wall that weren't already covered with maps, timetables and flow-charts.

'I was a bit unsure I was doing the right thing when I actually got the job,' Claire said. 'I mean, I've been in PR all my working life, but this is something totally new.'

'It'll probably amount to the same thing you had at the Department of Utilities.'

She looked surprised. 'You know I was at Utilities?'

'Not to mention the Ministry for Cultural Affairs,' he added. 'Don't worry . . . nothing stays quiet round here for long.'

'Obviously not.'

'Just do what you did there. Fob the public off with any old crap.'

She gazed at him, uncertain whether to take him seriously.

'Do that and you'll fit right in,' he said mischievously.

'You're Detective Sergeant Heckenburg, aren't you?'

'Call me "Heck". How many sugars, by the way?'

'None please, just milk. If I remember, Superintendent Piper said I should only believe five per cent of anything you told me.'

Heck handed her a steaming mug. 'That was a bit mean of her. Ten per cent at least. While you're still a newbie.'

She looked thoughtful as she sipped. 'Seriously, do we often get crimes where . . . well, where we have to be economical with the truth?'

'Seriously? . . . I couldn't comment. All I do is investigate them.'

'Superintendent Piper seems to think you're very good at that.'

'Even though I'm a bare-faced liar?'

'She thinks you're too opinionated as well. And sometimes pig-headed, and that you try to do everything yourself because you think – wrongly – that you know better than anyone else in the whole police force.'

'You two had a chat about me, eh?' Heck feigned suspicion, but inwardly was pleased. He'd just revealed to Claire that he'd researched her, and she was now revealing that she'd researched him. *Touché*.

'She also thinks that you enjoy much more leeway in the job than is good for you, or her,' Claire added. 'And that you don't know how lucky you are to have her for a boss.'

He arched an eyebrow. 'Are you pulling my leg?'

'She's still glad you work for her though.'

'That proves it. If you're not pulling my leg, she was definitely pulling yours.'

Claire chuckled. 'So what's on the agenda for today?'

He indicated the documents and photos on his desk. 'Well, for me . . . these.'

Claire glanced down – and almost dropped her tea. 'Oh my God!' She promptly turned a milky shade of grey. 'Are these . . . real crime scenes?'

Heck eyed her curiously. 'Well, we don't deal in movie-stills.'

The first of the two photos displayed a youngish man, possibly in his late twenties, stripped to his underpants and hanging by the hands from a tree branch. His limbs and torso were black and purple as though from a savage and sustained beating – but perhaps the most disturbing thing was his face, which had been painted with clown make-up: a white base, rouged cheeks, a red nose, black cream liner around his glazed, bloodshot eyes. The second picture showed a naked woman

80

lying in a bath; she too had been brutalised, her body battered beyond belief, splintered bones protruding through the pulped, shredded flesh – and she too was wearing clown make-up, the lips green, the eyes and mouth thickly outlined in white, forming a ghoulish smile.

Claire had physically backed away; it had been an involuntary motion, but there was more to it than a nervous flinch.

'You alright?' Heck asked.

She nodded, her eyes riveted on the photographic horrors. 'I will be, yeah. Sorry . . . that's the first time I've ever seen a real murder.'

'That's something you're going to have to get used to, I'm afraid.'

'Yes, yes . . . I realise that, of course. Oh my God, these are awful . . .'

Heck flipped the photos into a buff folder. 'Probably a bit much for your first morning.'

'Probably, but . . .' She seemed to steel herself, planting her tea on the desk. 'As you say, it's something I've got to deal with. So, why don't you tell me about it?'

'This case, you mean?'

She nodded.

He regarded her warily. 'If you're sure?'

She nodded again, determinedly.

'Okay . . .' He sat down and reopened the folder. 'The murders of this man and woman occurred last month, about two weeks apart – in Gillingham and Maidstone respectively. The Murder Squad in Kent sent them along for our assessment as a matter of course.' He glanced up at her. Claire was doing her damnedest to focus on the two images and at the same time maintain a cool, professional demeanour. 'They obviously look similar,' Heck said. 'But my impression is that they aren't connected.'

'They aren't?'

'Given his own criminal record, I suspect the male was the victim of a gangland vendetta. The brutality is quite excessive, so it may have been a punishment.'

'They were making an example, you mean?'

'Correct. My gut feeling about the woman is that she died during a domestic incident. The perp is probably her husband.'

Claire looked at him askance. 'Are you serious?'

Heck shrugged. 'He reads about the first homicide in the papers, and he thinks it's so wild and whacky that it can only be a matter of time before a lunatic capable of doing that will strike again. So he decides here's his chance to knock off his nagging missus and make it look like someone else. Of course, he doesn't realise that the first killing is down to organised crime . . . which illustrates the advantage we gain from only telling the press as much as we have to.'

'But how can you be sure this is domestic?'

'I'm not absolutely sure. But my advice to the Murder Squad in Kent will be to look a bit closer to home first, and the other facts support this. This woman was murdered in her own bathtub early evening – to be specific between seven-thirty and eight-fifteen. The timing of that incident alone would make it unusual for a home-invasion by a stranger. In addition, the window of opportunity is too small. The husband, who found her, would have us believe that he'd driven off to the local golf club to pay his annual subs. He'd also have us believe that in this brief time, some head-case happened to walk up to an ordinary suburban home, ascertained that the female occupant was alone, forced entry, did the dirty deed, painted a clown face on her, and then vanished without anyone seeing or hearing a thing.'

'It seems unlikely, but *could* that be what happened?'

'We don't close the door on any possibility – the perp

may have scoped the house out beforehand and lain in wait. But the husband didn't leave the premises as part of a regular routine. So that makes it improbable. On top of all that, the first victim was a male in his late twenties, the second a female in her early forties. There was no sexual assault in either case. Okay, it could be some complete madman who just gets off on drawing clown faces. But that's not the sort of guy you'd expect to have kept his light under a bushel up till now.'

'So . . . what happens next?'

Heck sat back. 'I send it to Gemma with my report. I don't recommend that we get involved because I don't see any need. Our main responsibility is to identify patterns, series and clusters that may indicate a repeat-offender, and then respond accordingly.'

'What if Gemma disagrees with you on this?'

'If she disagrees, some of us – almost certainly me, as I copped for the job in the first place – will be off to Kent, which would be great because that'd take me out of the office. But I can tell you now she won't. Most likely she'll just send our official observations.'

Claire glanced further along the desk. There was another pile of similar folders awaiting his attention. Other desks in the room were equally weighed down. 'Are all these files the same kind of thing?'

'We get copied in on a lot of stuff,' Heck said. 'But most of it is what we call "slush".'

'Slush?'

'Not relevant to our remit. Various types of crimes are automatically sent for our assessment. All stranger-murders of children, for example. All murders of prostitutes. All murders of runaways. All murders committed during burglary or rape. All murders involving exceptional violence, sadism or depravity. All murders where there are ritual or theatrical elements. All murders where there's evidence of bizarre post-death behaviour – mutilation, dismemberment, necrophilia. All murders where the perpetrator has apparently tried to contact the police or press . . . left clues, cryptic messages, that kind of thing. All murders which may not satisfy any of these criteria but where there is reasonable suspicion that it's part of a series. And basically any murder at all that we request to look at. No police force in England and Wales has the right to refuse us.'

Claire glanced around the room again. In another corner, two more crime scene blow-ups were mounted on a notice-board amid masses of scribbled notations. One was a close-up glossy of a middle-aged black woman. She looked to have been propped against a wall in a house or flat. Her grin stretched from ear to ear – literally, because someone had slashed her cheeks with a razor blade and had fixed a stick vertically in her mouth. The other had been taken in a bedroom, which looked like it had been wrecked by a hurricane. The bed occupied the centre of the image. A figure lay in it hidden by a sheet, though so much blood had soaked through this that a clear outline of the body was visible. On the wall above it, bloody handwriting proclaimed: 'Hey Mum, he fucked me first!'

'And this you call "slush"?' Claire said, unable to conceal her revulsion.

'It's just a turn of phrase. Every one of these files represents a life lost. You can't hide from that. But it's an odd fact that by far the highest percentage of homicides committed in the industrialised West, however they may initially appear, are the work of family members or other so-called loved ones. Either that, or they're one-off events committed by people who will probably never break the law again. The result of anger, greed, jealousy . . . course, we need to establish that before we send them back. Oh crap, your tea's gone cold.'

'Doesn't matter.'

'I'll make you another.' He attended to it. 'If there's one thing I'm supposedly good at round here, it's brewing up.'

Claire pulled a chair and sat down. She hoped Heck didn't notice that she *needed* to.

'The upside to all this,' he said, as he handed her a fresh mug, 'is that there's no better feeling than getting justice for these people.'

'It'll make a change,' she said. 'Doing a job that feels worthwhile.'

He sat down too. 'You must have done *some* useful stuff in your previous jobs.'

'No, you were right before. Telling lies to cover ministerial incompetence, massaging figures to make inaccurate departmental forecasts look good, putting out endless spin to save someone their one-forty-K-a-year salary . . . that doesn't always make you feel like a useful member of society.'

'There you are then,' Heck replied. 'You're in the right place with SCU. No one ever screws up here.'

She caught his sidelong glance, and couldn't help but chuckle. Heck smiled – and almost on cue Gemma appeared in the doorway, peeling off her raincoat. She made a good job of disguising her double-take at the sight of them cosied up together.

'Morning,' Claire said, standing.

'Morning Claire. Heck.'

Heck stood up too. 'Ma'am.'

'None of the other sleeping beauties checked in yet?'

'I'm sure they're on their way.'

Gemma glanced at her watch. 'They've got forty-five minutes. If no one's shown by then, start making phone calls. And don't shy from using harsh language.' She moved back out into the main corridor, but then reappeared. 'Heck, you haven't seen Joe Wullerton this morning, have you?'

'Not so far, ma'am.'

'I've got a note to go up and see him.'

'Can't help you with that.'

'Okay.' She breezed away.

Heck turned to Claire. 'Forty-five minutes. Enough time for breakfast?'

'Breakfast?'

'There's a smashing little deli round the corner. They do a nice egg sandwich.'

Claire glanced again at the photo of the woman with the stick in her mouth. 'I'm not sure I can eat, but . . . hey, the fresh air can't hurt.'

Gemma watched from the other end of the corridor as they headed off together.

For a thirty-year-old, Claire Moody was already very experienced. Her references had been among the best Gemma had ever seen, and she'd interviewed excellently. The girl's good looks and lively personality were another bonus – the bulk of the detectives in SCU were men, and if that would make them more deferential around her, all the better; at least until she'd found her feet. It was no surprise that Claire was being hit on of course, though it took Gemma aback a little to see Heck's interest.

Not that she could afford to worry about that now. She let herself into her office, dumping her coat and brolly and thinking again about Joe Wullerton.

She hadn't known him very long – he'd only been in his post about half a year, having replaced the disgraced Jim Laycock, and from the beginning had set his stall out to be an affable, approachable boss with an even temper and easy manner. On first arrival, he'd voluntarily changed his official title, replacing the macho Metropolitan Police-style 'Commander' of the National Crime Group with the more neutral 'Director', which she fully approved of. But she wasn't naïve enough to think it would be warm and fuzzy all the way. Wullerton had transferred in from the Hampshire Constabulary's Critical Incident Cadre, which he'd run effectively for fifteen years, so he was clearly a sharp bloke who knew his job, and probably a toughie as well. And he would need to be for the new position he occupied: as well as the Serial Crimes Unit, NCG also comprised the Organised Crime Division and the Kidnap Squad, and that little lot would take some managing.

She glanced again at the memo to go and see him. Rather than being emailed to her, it had been handed to her – in fact *shoved* into her grasp – the moment she'd entered the building.

Somehow that seemed ominous.

Chapter 10

Kate wasn't sure how long she'd lain in the darkness.

It was difficult to work out how far she'd fallen when he'd dropped her down into this pitch-black hole – ten feet, twelve, maybe more. But the impact at the bottom, though slightly cushioned by what felt like straw, had knocked her unconscious for a time.

Sick and dazed, Kate now lay balled up in a crumpled heap. The blanket had been ripped away as she'd descended, but wherever she now was, it smelled equally disgusting.

That was when she realised that she wasn't alone.

Movement sounded somewhere to her left; she detected a dull, hoarse breathing.

Kate jerked upright onto her knees.

Her late father, who'd been a coal miner, had often used the phrase 'it's as black as the pit', meaning there were no chinks of light at all. That was the situation now. Impenetrable blackness veiled Kate on all sides. Yet she knew there was somebody else there. She could hear them – shuffling about, and not too far away. She groped into the pocket of her Afghan, where mercifully her cigarette lighter was still in place. She held it in front of her as she struck it, as though to ward off a blow.

The sudden flame, though weak and wavering, was initially like a burst of lightning in the pitch blackness. She had to shield her eyes, but when they finally adjusted, she didn't know which to be more horrified by: the sight of the cell she'd been imprisoned in or the sight of her two cell-mates.

The former resembled the bottom of a well. Its geometry was circular, its walls constructed from damp, mildewed brick and rising into opaque shadow. There were no windows and no apparent handholds or footholds by which she could climb out. Its floor was hard-packed earth covered in straw. She also saw where the stench came from: one side of the cell – and it was close at hand, because the entire place was probably only ten feet in diameter – had been used as a toilet. Numerous human droppings were scattered there, indicating the length of time her fellow prisoners had been confined. One of these sat against the opposite wall, his knees drawn up to his chest; the other was kneeling about three yards away on her left.

Kate quickly backed away, though both were scrawny and dirty, and pop-eyed in the unexpected light; they looked as fazed by her arrival as she was.

The one on the left wore a grubby white vest and khaki pants, a military-training-type ensemble, which somehow contrived to make him look even more emaciated than his bony frame actually was, as did his tattoos – of which he had plenty, though all looked cheap and homemade. His face was rodent-thin, his hair a greasy, ginger mat. The one against the wall wore a light blue shell-suit, though this too was ragged and exceedingly dirty. His hair was an unwashed mop, Like his mate, he had gaunt, pock-marked features, and was hollow-eyed with fear and pain.

Fearing that her lighter fuel would run out, Kate flicked it off, plunging them into blackness again. She stayed where she was, back firmly to the wall. 'Who are you?' she asked. 'Where am I?'

'I'm Carl,' said a voice on her left; that was the guy in the khaki pants.

'And I'm Lee,' said another voice.

They were flat-toned, whiney. Kate was reassured that she was not in imminent danger, though she still had to struggle to contain her emotions.

'Okay . . . Carl, Lee. Why are we here? What is this place?'

'We're underground,' Carl said.

'I think I realise that!' she replied, more sharply than she'd intended. 'Just . . . what's going on?'

'Dunno.' That was Lee. 'Bastard just grabbed us and chucked us down here.'

'We don't know why,' Carl added. 'We don't know who.'

Their accents were thin, nasal. By the sounds of it, they came from Manchester, but one of the poorer districts.

'Where are you from, Carl?' Kate asked, sensing that he was the less beaten-down of the two.

'Salford,' he said, confirming her suspicion.

'Me too,' came Lee's voice.

'You were together when this happened?'

'Never met each other before last week.'

She shuddered. 'You've been in here a whole week?'

'Seems like it,' Carl said. 'Difficult keeping track. Can you put your lighter on again?'

'I'd better not. We should save it. But you think it's been a whole week? Seriously?'

'Could be longer.'

'What actually happened?'

Carl hesitated before saying: 'I was screwing cars on the Weaste.'

'You mean stealing?'

'Riding round in them.' He sounded briefly defensive. 'I

always left them after. The owners got them back, or got the insurance. No one ever got hurt.' He sniffed. 'I wasn't looking for anything in particular. Just summat I could take for a spin, you know. Maybe whip the CD and sat-nav as well. I'd fixed on this Renault Scenic in a side-street, when this big bleeder stands up in front of me – right in front of me, like he's been crouching down, waiting – and punches my fucking lights out. I woke up in here. Thought maybe it was his cellar, or something. Then, a couple of days later, he drops Lee down as well. It's like he's collecting people.'

'Who is he?' she asked.

'Didn't see him properly. Too dark.'

'I didn't see him either,' Lee said. 'I'd been doing houses up Clifton . . . I know that sounds bad. But I've got a habit, haven't I? I've got to get money somehow. It's not like I want to do it . . .'

'Oh, can it for fuck's sake!' Carl blurted. 'Just admit you're a thieving little scrote. Maybe if this bastard's listening, that's what he's waiting for. Maybe he'll let us out when we finally 'fess up to all the fucking shit we cause.'

'Did you get a look at him, Lee?' Kate asked.

'Nah. It was half-one in the morning. Pitch black. I'd just gone over this back wall. Next thing I know, this big fucker's waiting on the other side. At first I thought it was a copper. I was going to go quietly – bed for the night, you know, square meal. Even if it *did* mean I'd be strung out in the morning . . .'

'Did he say anything?' she interrupted.

'Nothing. Cracked my head on the bricks. Don't remember anything after that.'

'He wouldn't keep feeding us if he wanted to kill us, would he?' Carl said, sounding faintly hopeful.

'He feeds us, does he?' Kate didn't know whether to be encouraged by that revelation, or even more worried.

91

'Every so often he drops a few slices of bread down,' Carl said. She heard the scrunch of wrapping paper, and pictured him licking at it, trying to mop up every minuscule crumb. 'Couple of chocolate biscuits as well, only a couple of them mind.'

'What do you reckon, missus?' Lee said.

'If he's feeding us, it means that he wants us alive,' Kate agreed. She didn't bother to add: *for the time being*. You didn't kidnap someone and keep them in an underground cell with no light and no running water because you had something pleasant in mind.

Chapter 11

According to the piles of documentation they'd each been provided with, all bound in special folders and stencilled: 'Operation Festival', the withered corpse walled into the base of the old factory chimney had been a homeless man called Ernest Shapiro.

'He was sixty-eight years old and so far down the pecking order that he was never even reported missing,' Gemma told the thirty-five SCU personnel gathered in the DO.

They gazed at the big screen in fascinated silence.

'In case you were wondering, this was done to him while he was still alive,' she added, 'as evidenced by the loss of tissue from his wrists where he'd attempted to wriggle free of his manacles. The cause of death was slow dehydration – in other words, thirst – which meant he'd been imprisoned in his brick coffin at least a week before the lads in Yorkshire found him.'

There was a similar astonished silence when she brought up images of the second crime; a double homicide in this case, a young male and female facing each other in the front seat of a parked motor vehicle, the female seated on the male's lap. His head had slumped to the right, hers to the left. They were covered front and back with thickly clotted blood.

'Todd Burling and Cheryl Mayers,' Gemma said, 'twenty and nineteen respectively – killed a month and a half after Shapiro, on February 14, Valentine's Day. Believe it or not, they were transfixed together through their hearts by an arrow while having sex in Burling's parked car.'

'The Father Christmas victim was found on December 25?' Shawna McCluskey asked. 'And *this* happened on Valentine's Day?'

'Correct.'

'Someone has a sense of humour,' Charlie Finnegan snorted.

'It gets funnier.' Gemma hit her remote control and brought various images of a third murder scene to their attention. These were the most graphic so far. They portrayed an elongated, only vaguely human form, blackened almost to a crisp and lying on leaf-strewn grass. 'This was Barry Butterfield,' she explained. 'Male, aged forty-three, and a registered alcoholic. His body was found last autumn, late on the evening of November 5, on the outskirts of Preston, Lancashire.'

'Not burning on a bonfire by any chance?' Detective Inspector Ben Kane wondered.

He was one of Gemma's more bookish officers, a stout, bespectacled man of about forty, with neat, prematurely greying hair and a neat line in corduroy jackets, checked shirts and dickie-bows.

'However did you guess?' she said, hitting the remote control several times more, presenting a number of grisly close-ups.

Some fragments of clothing still adhered to the burnt carcass, but charred musculature and even bones were exposed. The face had melted beyond recognition – it

94

resembled a wax mannequin after blowtorch treatment, yet somehow its look of horrific agony was still discernible.

'It wasn't initially treated as suspicious,' Gemma added. 'Apparently Butterfield went off on solo pub-crawls every night. The first assumption was that he'd got thoroughly intoxicated and found his way to some unofficial bonfire on wasteland outside the town, probably looking for more booze. Whether there were other people there at the time, or it was after everyone else had gone, there was no obvious indication . . . but it seemed possible that in his inebriated state he passed out and fell into the flames.'

'So the cause of death was burning?' Shawna asked.

'That's the problem. The coroner ordered a post-mortem, which then revealed that Butterfield had died before he was put into the fire . . . as a result of neurogenic shock caused by massive internal tissue damage. Almost every joint in his body was either torn or dislocated.'

'It was like he'd been stretched out on a rack.' This came from Detective Chief Inspector Mike Garrickson, who had recently been seconded to the unit to act as Gemma's DSIO and up until now had been sitting quietly to one side.

'And if you remember your school history,' Gemma said, 'Guy Fawkes was stretched on a rack before he was executed. And we celebrate the anniversary of this event on November 5 by burning his effigy on bonfires.'

'We're dealing with some kind of calendar killer?' Gary Quinnell said. He almost sounded amused by the notion, but the expression on his face told a different story – even to hardened homicide detectives like the Serial Crimes Unit, the graphic images of Barry Butterfield were stomach-turning.

'It would seem that way,' Gemma replied. 'And he's now struck three times.'

'I take it there are no other connected homicides or assaults that we're aware of?' DI Kane asked.

'Not according to the National Crime Faculty,' Garrickson said.

Standing in one of the corners, Heck pondered the documentation they'd been given, glancing again at the file from Lancashire and noting the Lancashire FME's thesis that Barry Butterfield had been 'racked' by being stretched between a moving vehicle and some stationary object, like a tree or gatepost. That small detail ran his blood cold.

'Worrying, isn't it?' Garrickson said. 'That there's a worse maniac out there than the M1 murderers.'

Heck eyed him carefully, wondering if there'd been a hidden barb there.

With Gemma's two most experienced DIs unavailable – Des Palliser retired and Bob Hunter grounded – Garrickson had been brought in as her deputy for the duration of this enquiry. Whether Gemma was pleased about it, or irritated, nobody had dared ask, though they all knew that she'd been summoned upstairs the previous day, ostensibly for a meeting with NCG Director Joe Wullerton, only to find herself confronted by the entire Association of Chief Police Officers Crime Committee. As well as being allocated this case in its entirety – SCU were to provide the bulk of the investigation team – she was also given Garrickson . . . but as her number two or as her watchdog?

Heck had seen Garrickson around the Yard, but had never spoken to him and, in truth, hadn't known much about him except that he was one of those smooth operators from the Organised Crime Division; well-dressed, swaggering, supremely confident that the importance of his position meant he could spend any amount of time drinking with villains in shady London pubs and never be questioned about it. His brutish physique perfectly complemented this 'diamond geezer' attitude. He was of squat, powerful build, had broad cheekbones, a square jaw and mean eyes; his hair was a stiff red thatch. Even wearing his best Savile Row suit with a purple silk handkerchief poking from the breast pocket, he looked like a cheap gangster.

'But what kind of motivation are we looking at here?' Ben Kane asked. A naturally studious type, he was always the first in SCU to hit the analysis button.

'He wants to create a sensation,' someone suggested. 'That's all it can be . . . a macabre sensation.'

'Yeah, he's putting on a show,' another voice agreed. 'A big, sick show.'

'There's got to be more to it than that,' Shawna said. 'Are there hidden meanings behind these special days?'

Gemma glanced towards Detective Sergeant Eric Fisher, who, as their main intelligence man, tended to be a mine of information on numerous subjects.

Fisher shrugged his big shoulders. 'Christmas and Valentine's Day are complicated . . . at least their origins are. They're not nearly as straightforward as the average bloke on the street may imagine.'

'They were pagan festivals once, weren't they?' Gemma said.

'In the dim and distant past, yeah. What're you suggesting, ma'am? Human sacrifices?'

'I don't know,' she replied. 'We obviously need to investigate the backgrounds of these events. See if there are any links.'

'There are no *obvious* rituals here,' Gary Quinnell pointed out. He was the only one among them who regularly attended Church services, so his opinion on this was likely to be valid. 'These deaths look more like nasty jokes to me, ma'am. But if there is a kind of quasi-religious thing going on . . . could it be, I dunno, a satanic cult?'

Garrickson snorted. 'I can just hear the reaction of the trendy left if we start hassling Satanists. Even that lot have rights these days, you know.'

'I reckon it's just shock and awe,' Charlie Finnegan said. He was a lean, efficient-looking character, always well suited, but with black, slicked-back hair and crafty, vaguely untrustworthy good looks. One positive aspect of his scornful personality was that he called things the way he saw them. 'We got it right the first time. He's just trying to blow our minds with the weirdness of it.'

'Presumably lines of enquiry have already been generated, ma'am?' Kane asked.

'Several persons of interest were fingered before we realised these cases were linked,' Gemma replied. 'For various reasons all were eventually disregarded by the original investigation teams. However, DCI Garrickson and I will personally be re-evaluating each one of them. We'll also be going through all existing witness statements with a fine-tooth comb. We have a few other possibilities – not exactly MLOEs, but half-formed leads, which we'll need to assess carefully before they go into the policy file.'

'Physical evidence?' Finnegan asked.

'Not so far,' Gemma replied.

'CCTV?' Kane suggested.

'There, we may have lucked in,' she said. 'It's pretty apparent that at least two of the victims – the young couple murdered on the West Pennine Moors – were stalked beforehand. Maybe all of them were. I don't believe Ernest Shapiro and Barry Butterfield were simply jumped on because they happened to be in the wrong place at the wrong time. While they may have been targets of convenience – a homeless tramp, a wino looking for a drink – I think they were selected first and then lured. The original investigation teams thought the same and were in the process of attempting to plot all the APs' final movements with footage from various cameras – nightclubs, pubs, street-corners, bus shelters. Nothing obvious has come to light so far, but there's still quite a bit to go through.'

'And there's absolutely no link between any of the APs?' Gary Quinnell asked.

'None that we've been able to establish to date,' Garrickson said, climbing down from the table where he'd been perched. 'And before we waste any more time visiting ground that's already covered in the briefing notes, local informants have provided us with no leads as yet and no suspects have been identified purely on the basis of *modus operandi*, though that's an area we can keep looking at as we widen the net. Likewise, there's nothing to suggest these offences have been disguised as something they aren't. In no case is there indication of robbery or indecent assault . . .'

'No, they're thrill-kills,' Heck said.

Garrickson, perhaps not used to being interrupted, gave him a long, measured glance.

'This is not routine criminality,' Heck added. 'Far from it. For some reason unknown, the perp is gaining immense satisfaction from staging these . . . elaborate celebrations.'

'Celebrations?' Shawna said.

'That's what he's doing . . . he's celebrating feast days. But he's going to an awful lot of trouble to do it. In my opinion, the event is the main thing. The victims are almost incidental. From what we're seeing so far, status is unimportant, age is unimportant, gender is unimportant. It's like they're just . . . well, stage-props.'

Garrickson looked sceptical. 'The centre-piece of each of these "events" . . . as you call them, sergeant, is a cold, premeditated murder. I think we can assume these victims mean a bit more to him than stage-props.'

'Don't get me wrong, sir,' Heck replied. 'It's important to him that they bleed and scream. But there's more going on here than cruelty for its own sake.'

'Okay . . .' Gemma put in. 'We can theorise as much as we want in due course. In the meantime, let's discuss practicalities.

We have three separate murder scenes, so I propose to set up three Incident Rooms with the MIR at Bolton Police Station, as that's our most central location. The other two will be at Preston and Leeds City Centre, though obviously we'll stay in touch through video-conference and MIRWeb. Gold Command will operate from here at the Yard . . .'

There were cheers. No one wanted some pompous OIOC with ivory tower notions about 'budgetary constraints' or 'community trust' getting in the way.

'Silver Command,' Gemma added, 'that's me and DCI Garrickson, will be based at the MIR and will focus initially on the double murder in Bolton. DCI Garrickson will also action-manage the enquiry overall. We're all going to have to double-hat on this one, ladies and gents. Bronze Command is comprised as follows: DI Kane – DSIO Leeds; DI Brunwick – DSIO Preston. Most of you haven't met her yet, but Claire Moody is now our Media Liaison Officer.'

Claire, who was standing to one side, nodded as everyone focused on her.

'Claire hasn't had time to assemble her department yet, so for the time being she'll be working with me to devise a full media strategy,' Gemma said. 'The rest of you, primary responsibilities are outlined in the briefing notes, and are as follows . . .'

There was a slow bustle in the room as, one by one, the team members were assigned their roles and duties; laptops snapped shut, documents were stuffed into briefcases. When Gemma received a call on her mobile, she stepped through into a side office, and the meeting broke up properly, everyone relaxing and chatting loudly.

Heck sat at his desk and began to sort his paperwork. Some of it he'd need to take north with him – pending jobs which simply wouldn't wait. He lifted one more item from his drawer and placed it with the stuff to go. It was a thick, leather-bound ledger, so old and well-thumbed that sticky tape had been used to bind its fraying edges. When he opened it, it was half-filled with photographs of faces – some new, others old and creased. Four more were now added: the headshots of the victims in the Operation Festival brief. He slipped them into the back of the scrapbook rather than gumming them in place. There was no possibility he could classify these as permanent additions yet.

'Hi,' said a voice.

Heck glanced up, seeing that Claire had appeared at his shoulder. She peeked curiously at the scrapbook, which he promptly closed.

'So,' she added. 'I guess this is the real deal?' Given the seriousness of the task ahead, she looked amazingly bright-eyed and bushy-tailed.

'And you thought you were in at the deep end yesterday,' he replied. 'How do you feel now?'

'Well . . . it's exciting.'

Heck was surprised by that, though perhaps he shouldn't have been. During breakfast the previous day, Claire had cheered up considerably, taking notice when he'd advised her that she would from this point on be an integral part of major criminal investigations, and as such to view herself as a soldier in the war between good and evil. She'd smiled at that, and he'd smiled too, saying that he wasn't being totally serious with that latter comment, but that it sometimes helped if you regarded these victims of crime as the reason why you did your job, as the impetus behind your work.

'These are the people we go the extra mile for,' he'd said. 'And others like them . . . who may, because of our efforts, avoid the same fate.'

She'd smiled again at that, liking what she'd heard. Afterwards she'd discussed the murders in Kent with him, keenly, professionally.

'I hope I didn't seem too wimpish yesterday,' Claire now said. 'The way I reacted to those crime scene photos.'

'There's nothing wimpish about being upset by murder.'

'That egg sarnie you bought me . . . just what the doctor ordered, as it turned out.'

'It's not normally an antidote for a queasy stomach, but whatever works. So . . . you're happy?'

'Well . . . I'm clearly on a learning curve. A steep one.'

He shrugged. 'Hell, so are the rest of us.'

'Yeah, but I think you guys have a bit of a head start. I mean . . .' She flipped through the briefing notes. 'I've got an idea what an Exhibits Officer does, but Disclosure Officer? H-2-H Co-ordinator?'

'Don't worry, you'll pick it all up as you go along.'

'According to this, you are "Minister Without Portfolio"?' She raised a querying eyebrow.

Heck smiled. 'That's a kind of unofficial title. Means I haven't got a specified role . . . more a roving commission. I keep a working knowledge of the enquiry overall and fill in where I'm needed. Not every SIO would go for it, but Gemma seems to think it works.'

'Okay everyone, listen up!' Gemma shouted as she came back in.

The room fell silent again.

'As you all know, we've lost the Golden Hour advantage. But let's not regard this as a problem. It may give us the opportunity to create some slow time, allow us to take stock rather than go at this thing like a bull at a gate. For this reason, while I expect you all to make your own way to your designated command posts, the Easter weekend is about to commence, so that gives us a couple of days to get our crap together. But we start officially on Bank Holiday Monday morning, when I want everyone reporting in by seven sharp. Am I clear?'

There were mumbles in the affirmative.

'Any further questions?' she said.

'I've got one, ma'am,' Shawna spoke up. 'Why has this case been assigned exclusively to SCU?'

The team listened with interest. It was a rare event these days when they were all sent out together.

Gemma half-smiled, as if she'd anticipated this query and had not been looking forward to it. 'Owing to the disparate geographic locations, this enquiry can't fall under any single force's jurisdiction. Which makes it ideal for the Serial Crimes Unit. But . . .' and she sighed, 'in reality, it's a case of the fewer officers involved, the better. The brass were quite clear. They want this kept in-house. So far, the public and press aren't aware that we've got another series to deal with. And that's the way we want it to stay.'

'We'll obviously be using some local troops when we get out into the sticks,' Garrickson added. 'But we've got to keep a tight bloody rein on it. We can't have horror stories running the length of the country. We can't have panic in the streets and public disorder. Not again. The M1 enquiry was a disaster in that regard. Made SCU look the biggest idiots since Charley Farley and Piggy Malone.'

Gemma didn't flinch when Garrickson said this, but Heck couldn't imagine she wouldn't be irked to hear such statements from an outsider.

'In this respect, Operation Festival is under a news blackout,' she said. 'That means every aspect of it is embargoed. I'm serious, people. You don't talk to *anyone* about this. Neither friends nor loved ones. And all contacts with the press – *all* of them – are to be conducted through Claire Moody. Look . . . we might as well face facts. Police cuts are the in-thing at present, and the Home Office is watching SCU. Units like ours cost a lot of money, and after the M1 enquiry people are wondering if that investment's been worth it. Joe Wullerton reckons the best way we can prove we are is to get out into the field as a self-contained unit and take down some bad guys. And I agree with him. It's in all our interests to make this work.'

She paused to let that sink in.

'There's one other thing.' Her tone now changed; softened, yet at the same time seemed to intensify. Briefly, her penetrating blue eyes fixed on each and every one of them. 'I want you to put all sensational aspects of this case out of your mind. Let's remember that, no matter how grotesquely the assailant has dressed it up, each one of these homicides is a human tragedy, which has had and will continue to have devastating repercussions for countless people above and beyond those whose lives have actually been taken. I'll say what I always say at times like this . . . we can't bring these victims back or undo the torture they suffered. But as the investigating police team we are morally and professionally obliged to put the one responsible for this in front of a court. There is no greater duty. No one in the world at this moment has a more vital job when it comes to the safety and security of families, communities, the country where we live as a whole. You all know what you have to do, ladies and gents – so get out there and do it.'

Chapter 12

Kate wasn't sure how long the racket from overhead had been going on for, but it seemed like a day at least: the relentless hammering, the grinding shriek of wood-saws. It echoed in the deep, narrow dungeon, beating the three prisoners down like a fist.

But this was only a new torture to lay alongside those others they'd already been suffering. The heat in the cramped cell had become stifling, and with it the stench. Three people having to defecate in the same place over and over created a reek so overpowering that they could almost taste it.

And then there was the thirst.

Every so often a cable was lowered from the blackness overhead – it was a coaxial cable with a dim bulb located halfway up it to allow them to see, and a bucket suspended at its end. Sometimes this bucket contained a few scraps of bread, a few rashers of bacon, a raw carrot or two, but though Carl said that at other times it was filled with water, there hadn't been anything to drink all the time Kate had been held here, and they were now parched.

Carl and Lee's answer to this was to lie groaning, though the latter's suffering was worse as he was also going through cold turkey. Kate understood this to an extent; her own cravings for a cigarette were nagging at her, though they couldn't be half as painful as Lee's. She'd tried to assist, but her lighter had long ago exhausted its supply of fuel and in the pitch-dark she'd been unable to do anything useful with his trembling, sweat-soaked form. Carl, who'd initially appeared to be the stronger of the two, hadn't turned out to be much of a cellmate either. On this last day in particular, he'd collapsed as though having a breakdown, whimpering about the noise, about his throat being dry as shoe-leather. But even before then, when she'd attempted to talk to him about a possible escape, he'd been spectacularly useless.

'Look . . . I couldn't have dropped too far,' she'd said quietly, fearful that their captor might be listening to them. 'Otherwise I'd have broken something. That means if one of us climbs on the other's shoulders, he might be able to reach the trapdoor.'

'What the fuck are you talking about?' Carl had replied in a voice of disbelief.

She'd imagined his weasel face elongated with shock at the mere suggestion he do something physical, those jaundiced bug-eyes ready to plop from their sockets like poached eggs.

'I know we're not gymnasts,' she'd persisted. 'But how hard can it be when our lives may depend on it? Look, you try climbing onto my shoulders first.'

'You've got to be kidding!'

'For Christ's sake, Carl . . . you might be able to get out of here! Then you can go and get help.'

'*Me* . . . go to the pigs?' He'd sounded outraged by the mere notion.

'Who else do you think is going to come and save us? The House-Breakers Union? Car Thieves Incorporated?'

'I'll never fucking make it,' he'd whined.

'We'll never make it if we stay down here. At least Lee won't. He needs to be in hospital.'

'That's his fucking problem. He's the junkie. Do you think *I* haven't wanted to do drugs? Think I haven't had a shit life I'd like to forget from time to time . . .'

She'd sighed, rubbing her aching forehead. 'Maybe I can get on your shoulders then.'

'Yeah, right,' he'd scoffed.

'Christ, you're fucking spineless!' It was a rare occasion when Kate lost her temper. Apart from anything else, it generally served no purpose. She'd learned from experience that people who faced abuse every day tended to stop responding to it. The same thing had happened now.

'Whatever,' he'd said, uninterested.

'You can at least try,' she'd pleaded. 'If we don't try, we'll be stuck here.'

'We won't be stuck here. He'll let us out at some point. He must do. Why would he be keeping us alive?'

That question again – increasingly one Kate had no desire to ponder.

And then they'd heard movement overhead, and any hope that they might climb acrobatically out of here was gone, because the hammering and sawing had started. At first Kate had shouted, trying to be heard above the ear-pummelling dirge.

'For God's sake give us a break, won't you! Isn't it enough that we're turning blind down here? Isn't it enough we're choking to death on our own stink? For Christ's sake show some pity! We're human beings, not animals! You bastard . . . you sodding, heartless bastard, we're dying down here!'

Of course, even she at length had slumped down, broken and sobbing, though she knew that was unwise as it would expend even more vital moisture from her body.

Uncountable hours later it seemed, the bedlam above ended

107

as it had begun – abruptly, without warning. A roaring silence followed.

Kate gazed weakly up into the blackness. As always, not even a glint of light was visible. Carl was moaning to himself again, muttering incoherently. There was no sound from Lee, which was some kind of small mercy. Slowly and exhaustedly, Kate rose to her feet. She crooked her neck back to shout again. 'Please . . . pleeeaaase . . . give us something! If nothing else, we need water!'

She was so unused to getting any response that her surprise when a hatch creaked open almost knocked her flat. She peered upward, fascinated, at a square of dim light. She heard a dull clank and realised that the metal bucket was being lowered. Droplets of cold water scattered over her as it slopped during its descent.

It was the same pattern as before. The electric bulb, fixed about seven feet above the bucket, was activated when it was almost within reach. The drear brick walls of the cylindrical prison sprang into blinding relief. Carl came scuttling from his corner, a begrimed stick-insect, his red-rimmed eyes goggling, but Kate got hold of the bucket first. Only a few days ago it would have been inconceivable that she'd take any food or drink from a receptacle like this. It was dirty, dented, its rim rusted, its broken handle fastened with duct-tape. But at this moment it might have been a crystal goblet. What was more, it was brimming with fresh, clean water.

She took several deep draughts before Carl snatched it away and began to guzzle. There was only a quarter of the bucket left when it occurred to Kate that Lee would need some as well. She grabbed the bucket back and carried it over to their semi-comatose companion, managing to dribble some water into his gaping mouth. At first it overflowed and ran down his chin, but then he coughed and choked and even though he didn't open his eyes, he began to swallow

– swallowing and swallowing until there was no water left.

Immediately the bucket ascended, swaying out of Kate's reach. She glanced up, wondering if she might see their captor's head in the aperture, but there was nothing.

'Hey!' she shouted. 'Hey, you've not gone too far yet! We're all still alive down here, no thanks to you! Look . . . why don't you let us go before this turns into something much worse? I don't care how you do it . . . blindfold us, gag us, take us and dump us on a motorway somewhere. But we're not dead yet, so you need to get real!'

Carl muttered something. It sounded like: 'Can't feel my feet . . .'

She glanced around at him. The light from the bulb was extinguished as the bucket was lifted from view overhead, but the dim pillar of radiance descending from the hatch was still sufficient to show Carl standing against the wall. He leaned on the bricks with one hand but had doubled forward. He shook his head groggily, and his free hand groped at his brow, which shone with sweat. As he sank slowly to his knees, Kate felt a growing lethargy and heaviness in her limbs, which went way beyond anything she'd known up to now. Suddenly she too was groggy – she tried to shake it off, but she was turning nauseous as well. Her vision fogged over and she slumped down onto her side. The last thing she saw before unconsciousness overwhelmed her was a rope-ladder unravelling into the pit, and a figure descending with what looked like several bundles of cable over its brawny shoulder.

Chapter 13

Even for officers in SCU, messages arriving before six in the morning were so rare that they tended to mean bad news. Heck wasn't aware what time it was when the mobile, which he always left on his bedside cabinet at night, began bleeping in the darkness. Before his groping hand managed to locate the offending article, he focused across the room on the digital clock, whose glowing numerals read 5.58 a.m.

He put the phone to his ear, at the same time yanking the pull-cord on the bedside lamp. 'Yeah, Heckenburg?'

'Heck!' It was Shawna McCluskey. 'Are you online?'

'I'm in bloody bed. What's going on?'

'You'd better get online quickly.'

Heck cradled the phone under his chin as he blundered down the darkened passage to the small, cold room he used as his office.

When he got online, he found that Gemma had just circulated an MPEG.

'That's crime scene footage . . . shot about an hour ago by Merseyside Police,' Shawna said.

Heck's matted hair stiffened as he gazed at the pixellating image.

'Well?' she asked. 'What do you think?'

'What do I think?' he said. 'I think someone's just cancelled the Easter break.'

Bad as it had appeared on film, the crime scene was even more terrible in reality.

Though most of the team was able to cut short their weekend break early, the Bank Holiday traffic was flowing thickly by mid-morning, so it had taken them several hours to flog their way up the M1 and M6 motorways, and then join the M62, where it ran west from Greater Manchester into Liverpool. The weather was fine, remarkably sunny for an early day in April, so that made the going all the heavier.

The slagheap in question, a great barren hummock of spoil-land on the north side of the motorway, had once been part of the Sutton Manor colliery complex, the rest of which was now long vanished. It stood maybe fifty metres at its apex, so its upper ridge was visible from the M62 even though Merseyside Police had managed to screen off its lower section with tall curtains of canvas and steel, which they'd borrowed from a festival staging company and had deployed along the motorway's hard shoulder, having first closed that stretch of the nearside lane and turned it into a temporary car park. Gemma's team left their vehicles here because in this first instance they themselves were not permitted access to the slagheap. An unmade road led onto it from the rear, but for the time being that, and much else of the open land on the other side, had been closed off for finger-tip inspection by Merseyside crime scene examiners.

'Good God!' Mike Garrickson said, peering up the motorway embankment. 'Good God in heaven!'

'Well he isn't down here, I'll tell you that, boss,' Gary Quinnell replied in a daze. 'Not today.'

'They wouldn't like that in Chapel, Gaz,' Shawna McCluskey replied.

The big Welshman made no further response. His mouth had sagged open. Heck understood why. For everything they'd experienced thus far in this specialist murder squad, none of them had ever seen anything like this. In fact, it was likely that no one had seen anything like this for several centuries or more.

'Someone tell me this isn't real,' Charlie Finnegan said.

'This is the most real Good Friday you're ever likely to experience,' Garrickson replied.

Mid-way up the slagheap slope, three heavy crosses had been set up in a row. They had been constructed from new, freshly-sawn timber, and were all roughly the same size: their uprights stood to about eight feet; their crossbars, which had been bolted into squared-off grooves cut specifically to accommodate them, spanned about six feet each. At first glance, the symmetry of the display was amazing, even down to the naked bodies spread-eagled on each frame. Those to left and right were white males of as yet undetermined age, but in rank-poor physical condition – spindly, undernourished, covered with old scars and jailhouse ink. Their legs were mottled purple by post-mortem bruising, their lifeless faces fixed in contortions of agony. The one in the centre was a white female; she was in a slightly better state – if it was possible to use those terms to describe someone who had died by crucifixion. Her fair hair hung down over her face in a stringy mat, covering it, but her body was hourglass shaped, only wrinkled here and there, which suggested she'd been no more than thirty years old. She was white as porcelain, though, like the others, her lower limbs were tinged purple where the blood had settled after death.

The only movement came from the early-season flies crawling on the bodies, and the two Merseyside medical staff

112

in Tyvek coveralls, taking measurements and writing on clipboards. Further out, beyond the inner cordon of tape, officers from the Merseyside photography unit were packing up their gear.

There were ongoing gasps as more SCU arrived, crowding into the narrow space behind the screens. It occurred to Heck that Claire would turn up at any moment. She'd presumably set off at roughly the same time as all the rest, but she'd be driving her own car and was unlikely to be as gung-ho about getting here as the others. It was tempting to go around to the other side and wait for her, to advise her to gird herself for what she was about to see, but there was no time. Heck was already assessing the scene, trying to bring a professional eye to bear, and immediately noticing oddities.

Whoever the three victims were, they had been transfixed to their crosses in the traditional way, by nails or spikes. No other bindings were visible – no ropes, no chains. But there was a variation from the norm – at least the norm as it appeared in Church artwork. The victims' hands were all hidden from sight, because they had been nailed to the back of the crossbar, the steel driven in from behind. Likewise, they had not been nailed through the front of the feet, but through the ankles, one to either side of the upright. So four nails had been used per victim, instead of three. Heck wondered if this could be a mistake, though so far the killer had been very meticulous. If he had consciously altered the method that everyone else believed had been used when Christ had been crucified that first Good Friday two millennia ago, then something told Heck that everyone else was wrong.

'When in Rome,' he said under his breath, 'do as the Romans do . . .'

Quinnell glanced around at him. 'What's that?'

Heck turned to Gemma. 'Ma'am, this guy knows what he's doing . . . to the absolute letter.'

'Gotta be more than one guy,' Shawna said. 'To pull off something like this.'

Heck nodded. 'I thought that when I saw the shots from Yorkshire – there were two implements used to break open that chimney breast; a pick and a hammer. That meant two assailants. Now I think there are more even than that. Maybe more than three.'

'More than three?' Shawna looked astonished.

'This was put on as a show for motorway users on Good Friday morning. Must have been erected during the hours of darkness last night, that's what . . . eleven hours? Knock a couple off either side to allow for twilight. Say seven hours of pitch-darkness. Not long enough for anything less than a whole gang of them.'

Quinnell turned to Gemma. 'What do *you* think, ma'am?'

'I think we need more men,' she said, white-faced. 'A lot more.'

Chapter 14

'There is no question that this is a despicable crime,' Claire said. She looked cool and composed, oblivious to the camera-flashes on all sides of her. 'We are as shocked as the public by this incident, but all that will do is reinforce our determination to bring the person responsible to justice.'

'Do you have any leads yet?' a local reporter asked.

'At present we're considering an organised crime connection – possibly with Liverpool. But that's all I can say at the moment, for reasons which I'm sure you'll understand.'

'Have you identified the three victims?' came another question.

'We have but I'm not at liberty to disclose any of those details until the next of kin have been informed.'

'Have you located the next of kin yet?'

Before Claire could reply, another journalist asked: 'Are the victims members of a Church group?' The query had come from a brassy-looking woman with peroxide-blonde hair pulled in an unattractively tight bun. She'd elbowed her way to the front of the press pack on the forecourt at Manor Hill Police Station, and now offered a Dictaphone for Claire's response. 'What I mean is, could this be some kind of revenge attack . . . is it perhaps connected with a child abuse enquiry, or something similar?'

'There's no evidence to suggest anything of that nature,' Claire replied.

'No evidence?' The brassy blonde laughed. 'You've got three bodies nailed to crosses on Good Friday. If that's not an attack on the Church, I don't know what is.'

'All I'd say is that things aren't always as they appear.'

'Good answer,' Gemma said.

She, Garrickson and Heck were watching Claire's performance on live television in Gemma's office, though this was little more than a partitioned area of the Major Incident Room. Given recent events, it would have been a crass decision to continue with the plan to locate the MIR twenty-five miles away in Bolton. Gemma had thus latched onto nearby Manor Hill, an old-fashioned Merseyside nick, which rather fortuitously had a one-storey prefab annexe to its rear, formerly used for admin but now defunct. With the assistance of the local chief super, she'd commandeered this to house the MIR and use as her official HQ. There was still plenty of installation work to be done. Tech guys carried computer terminals in and laid cables and phone-lines along skirting-boards; sparkeys checked light fittings; Merseyside bobbies, stripped to their shirt-sleeves, helped SCU officers bring in desks, tables, filing cabinets and so forth. However, most of the team was already hard at work, their phones trilling, their keyboards rattling.

'That won't reassure the locals, miss,' another reporter called. 'Whoever's done this . . . is there a chance they may strike again?'

Heck watched Claire intently. She had been badly shaken on arrival at the crime scene, but now was handling herself with aplomb.

'There's nothing to suggest that either,' she said.

116

'Have there been any other murders like this?' someone else asked.

'At this stage, there is no reason to assume the perpetrators of this crime have committed similar offences elsewhere.'

'*Perpetrators!*' the brassy woman said. 'So you think there's more than one?'

This revelation prompted a dirge of renewed shouting, which briefly seemed to leave Claire fazed. She could only mumble her first response, apparently struggling with the realisation that she'd made an error.

'That was a slip and a half,' Garrickson said.

Gemma shrugged. 'It ties in with the mob cover-story.'

'We must consider all possibilities,' Claire replied on screen.

'How many perpetrators are you looking for?' the brassy woman asked.

'We can't put a number on it yet,' Claire said.

'But three people were nailed to crosses!'

'Yes, we picked that up.'

'Tetchy,' Gary Quinnell said, having just come in.

'Is there anyone the public should be looking out for?' another reporter queried.

'We've no suspects as yet. But assistance from the public is always welcome. If there is any information anyone wishes to impart to us, the phone-lines are now open – the numbers are detailed on the press release and with Crimestoppers.'

Another reporter came forward. He was older and bespectacled, with thick, sandy hair which simply had to be a toupee. He had the air of a time-served hack. 'Miss Moody?' he said, his accent strong Scouse. He too offered her a microphone. 'If this is a one-off incident related to underworld activity, or if that's what you suspect it is, why is it not being handled by the Merseyside Murder Squad? In fact, why is it being handled by the Serial Crimes Unit, not Merseyside Police?'

'Fuck!' Garrickson said. 'Didn't take them long to find that out.'

'Merseyside Police are still involved in this investigation,' Claire countered.

'Yeah, but only as junior partners.'

'We can't keep these things quiet,' Gemma said resignedly. 'Every cop on Merseyside knows we've taken charge of this case.'

On the TV screen, Claire was looking progressively less comfortable telling such blatant lies. 'As a three-victim murder, this incident falls well within the Serial Crimes Unit's remit . . .'

The old hack seemed unimpressed. 'But most of the time you hunt serial killers. Can you categorically assure us that isn't what you're doing here?'

'As I said before, there is no evidence that this trio of homicides is connected to any others currently under investigation in the United Kingdom.'

'Is the Serial Crimes Unit going to make as big a foul-up of this as they did the M1 Maniac murders?' someone else asked.

'I'm sorry, that's all I'm able to tell you at the moment.'

There was another clamour of questions, but Claire merely turned and re-entered the building. Gemma switched the TV off and sat down.

'That went well,' Garrickson opined. 'Don't know why she didn't just give them the policy log.'

'I'm not sure what else she could have done,' Heck said.

'How about stick to the official line? How about "we don't know anything yet . . . thanks for your interest"?'

'In that case why bother having a press conference at all?' Quinnell wondered.

'What do you want, Gary?' Gemma said, finally noticing he was there.

'Oh . . .' He consulted his pocket book. 'More info on the deceased, ma'am. Seems Kate Rickman was reported missing midday on April 4th, when she failed to open her charity shop in Toxteth to receive some deliveries of second-hand clothing. Merseyside began looking for her seriously the next day when her burned-out car was found on wasteland near the old Burtonwood brewery, which is not that far from here. The other two are Carl Croxton and Lee Cavendish. Both Salford boys, both had form as long as your arm. Croxton was reported missing by his common-law wife . . . would you believe forty-eight hours after he failed to return home from one of his nightly jaunts. That was on March 30. Lee Cavendish was never reported missing at all – just happened a member of Merseyside CID, who'd recently transferred in from GMP, recognised him.'

'All formally identified?'

'Correct. Common-law wife in Croxton's case, mother in Cavendish's case, and Kate Rickman by her ex-husband.'

'Two thieves and a charity worker,' Heck mused. He glanced at the fistful of print-outs he was carrying; most depicted artistic renditions of Christ's crucifixion. 'He's following the script so far . . .'

Shawna McCluskey stuck her head in. 'Ma'am, Professor Fillingham's here.'

'Show him in please.' Gemma stood up. 'Gary, can you give us a minute?'

Quinnell nodded and withdrew, just as a rather dapper chap entered, short in stature and thinning on top, but possessed of a neat salt-and-pepper beard and moustache, and wearing a tweed suit and bright pink bow-tie. Professor Donald Fillingham was senior forensic pathologist at the Royal Liverpool University Hospital. At Gemma's request, he had performed the post-mortem examinations on the three victims earlier that evening. As they'd only spoken on the phone so far, Gemma shook hands with him, introduced herself, then DCI Garrickson and DS Heckenburg.

Professor Fillingham's blue eyes twinkled as he appraised Heck. 'Heckenburg? . . . weren't you the one who raised a question regarding the crucifixion method? The way the bodies were nailed?'

'Oh . . . yeah.' Heck was surprised. He knew that Gemma had sent along some preliminary crime scene observations, but he hadn't thought she was paying much attention when he'd gabbled to her about the correct way to fix someone to a cross.

Professor Fillingham was clearly a man who believed in getting down to business. 'Perhaps you could elaborate on that?' he said.

'Erm . . . sure.' Heck laid his print-outs on the desk. 'According to some research I did – and it was only quick, I must admit – the way we've always assumed Jesus Christ died might be incorrect.'

He held up one particular sketch. It was crude, just a line-drawing, but it illustrated a figure bound to a wooden cross, his ankles nailed to the sides of the upright and his arms spread, but his hands pinioned to the back of the crossbeam rather than the front.

'This apparently is the way Middle Eastern archaeologists now think it used to be done,' Heck said. 'Apparently they've found some skeletal remains – bones with bits of rusty nails stuck through them. But it's a fairly new theory. Which . . . well, if it's correct, means that our boy is bang up-to-date.'

The pathologist assessed the sketch, and then flipped through one or two other documents, all of which displayed more traditional images of Christ's death. 'It would make sense,' he said. 'May I sit?'

Garrickson pulled him up a chair, and they sat around the desk together.

Fillingham pored through the images again, before adding: 'You see . . . crucifixion actually poses quite a few problems for the crucifiers. If someone was nailed to the cross in the way we normally assume Jesus was . . . with one nail through his feet and one through the palm of each hand, the weight of his body just wouldn't have been supported. Especially as the victim became weaker. The hands would simply have torn away from the nails, and the weight of the body falling down would have done the same with the feet. Even if the nails penetrated the wrists, and were lodged in place between the radial bone and the ulna, the weight of an average human body, particularly at the point of death, would have made it fall forward . . . the wrists would have torn free again, and so the feet. But with both ankles nailed securely to either side of the central post, and the arms pinned to the rear of the crossbar, the weight of the body is then very evenly distributed, even in death. It couldn't simply fall off the cross. Not until it had turned to carrion.'

They listened to this dispassionate explanation with as much detachment as they could. When the corpses had been taken down late that afternoon, the process had so closely resembled movies they'd seen about the life and death of Jesus – the limp bodies being lowered in slings, forlorn figures waiting at the foot of each cross to receive them – that it had touched feelings many of them hadn't known since childhood.

'How does someone actually die on the cross?' Gemma asked.

'Well . . .' The pathologist gave a wry smile. 'This may be the good news.'

The three cops glanced at each other.

'First of all, we need to understand that crucifixion is normally one of the most terrible forms of death imaginable. In the Ancient World, it was reserved for the lowest of the low – slaves, outcasts and rebels. The victim was transfixed to a cross, suspended by nails which would cause him to suffer prolonged and extreme agony. But he would only finally expire from exposure, dehydration or hypovolaemic shock. Jesus is believed to have died relatively quickly – within three hours – because he'd suffered massive blood-loss from the Roman scourging. Healthier specimens could linger for days . . .'

'And that's the good news?' Garrickson said in a distant voice.

'The good news is that our three victims had been dosed beforehand with flunitrazepam.'

'The date-rape drug?' Heck said.

The pathologist nodded. 'That's one of its uses, yes. On this occasion it served the dual purpose of making it easier to crucify the victims and preventing them crying out or shouting for help once they'd been suspended. But the net-result was that all three were likely already unconscious when they were actually crucified. Their whole bodyweight was thus supported by their outstretched arms, which caused hyperextension of the chest-muscles and subsequent asphyxiation.'

'So they died quickly?' Gemma said.

'Mercifully so, yes.'

'Bit of a downer for our killers,' Garrickson observed.

'They gave up the perk of crucifying their victims in private and watching them die slowly, because for them it's more about making a public spectacle,' Heck replied.

'Well they've certainly achieved that,' Shawna said from the doorway. ''Scuse me, ma'am.' She laid an evening newspaper on the desk top. Its front page headline read:

Bad Friday!

Almost the entire rest of the page was occupied by a massive, full-colour photo, no doubt shot by a passing motorist. The three crucified figures had been blurred out, though their outlines were visible, framed against the rutted ridge of the slagheap.

'If it was hard keeping this thing quiet before, it's going to be hell on earth now,' Garrickson said.

Heck found Claire alone in the MIR's kitchenette. She was seated at the table, both hands cupping a mug of coffee which, by the skin on its surface, was only lukewarm. She gave him a wan smile.

'And as good days go, how does this one rate?' he asked.

'I'm alright.'

'Yeah?'

'Well . . . it's nothing six months of leave wouldn't fix.'

He leaned against the sink. 'You've hardly arrived and you want to go on leave already!'

She tried to match his chuckle, but it was forced and flat.

'Honestly,' he said, 'you did very well out there.'

'Honestly . . . I don't remember a thing I said. Any old crap could come back to haunt us after that.'

'Nah, you did good.'

'Well . . .' She sighed. 'I suppose the occasional bit of gibberish can be forgiven, seeing as I'd just witnessed my first live crucifixion.'

'*Anyone's* first live crucifixion. I've never seen one before either.'

She took a sip of coffee and pulled a disgusted face. 'Were they alive when they were nailed to those crosses?'

'Yes . . . but probably unconscious. We don't think they lasted very long.'

'Thank God for that at least.' She lifted the mug to her lips again, only to realise what she was doing and shove it away with a grimace.

Heck picked the kettle up. 'Want me to make you a fresh one?'

'No thanks. I'll have enough trouble sleeping tonight. Isn't like you see on the films, is it?'

'What's that?'

'Dead bodies on crosses. They hang there like dummies. Everything just goes floppy. Don't look like real people at all.'

'Maybe it's best if that's how you think of them. Might take a bit of the hurt away.'

'Oh come on . . .' She eyed him sceptically. '*You* don't do that. Not with that scrapbook of faces you always keep with you. Shawna McCluskey told me about it. She said those are all the victims of violent crime who you've managed to get some kind of justice for. And that you . . .' her voice trembled, as if about to break, 'you check it every day.'

Heck regarded her for several moments, before pulling up a chair and sitting down. 'Okay, yes . . . that book's a record of the reasons why *I* do this job.'

'The good versus evil thing again?'

'Sorry?'

She sniffled, unconsciously knuckling away a tear. 'That's what you said the other day, isn't it? About good versus evil.'

He shrugged. 'If you believe in good and evil, then yes. But my philosophy's actually more selfish than that.' He lowered his voice in case someone was earwigging out in the corridor. 'Whenever someone gets murdered on my watch, Claire – or raped, or tortured – I take it very, very personally. I have to. So that I don't become institutionalised. So that I never get to the stage where I accept whatever this job throws at me as another i that needs dotting, or another t that needs crossing. It's too easy to forget, or at least pretend you've forgotten, the human cost of crime. I look at those faces every day to ensure I never make that mistake.'

Another tear trickled down her cheek as she listened to him.

'Here . . .' He handed her a napkin. 'But that's just me. Everyone has to find their own way to deal with this tragedy. It's not something we can coach.'

'It's a real battle, isn't it?' She dabbed at her eyes. 'With real casualties.'

'Absolutely. It ain't for the faint-hearted. But to be honest, that's why *you're* here. Because *you* fit the bill.'

'If you say so.' She half-smiled, dabbing at her eyes again, only belatedly realising what she was doing. 'This is nothing, by the way. Delayed shock . . . that's all.'

'Course.'

'Look, you'd better get on.' She gestured brusquely at the door. 'You've got work to do, and so have I.'

'You're sure?'

'Yes, I'm sure. Stay in here and people will think there's something wrong, and there's *nothing* wrong. I'm okay.'

Heck stood and moved away, turning back once. 'Claire . . . seriously, you did very well. This is your first case and it's like the Devil himself is at work. But you've dealt with it. You'll be fine. I can feel it in my bones.'

She nodded and smiled, as though amply reassured by his trust. Once he'd left the room, she finished her coffee, drinking it in slow but determined swallows, unconcerned by how foul or tepid it was. Yet even then, another tear stole treacherously down her cheek.

Chapter 15

The crime scene on the slagheap had been covered by a vast tent, which Gemma had hired from a firm in Cheshire who normally catered for celebrity weddings, and divided up with strips of tape into no-go zones still awaiting forensic examination, though official access ways now led between them.

Heck, clad neck to toe in Tyvek, stood alone in the centremost passage, gazing up at the three empty crosses, particularly at the middle one, on which Kate Rickman had died, a woman who – though she had once been married and worked as a dental nurse, living, to all intents and purposes, a normal middle-class life – had one day experienced a kind of epiphany, giving it all up to help the outcast and destitute. That fact, more than any other, illustrated a degree of forward-planning that put this current set of felons on a different level from most criminal organisations – which was not encouraging.

Heck relayed all this into his Dictaphone, making additional notes on his clipboard. The cross had always been a brutal symbol of course, but his proximity to this particular example brought it home how much. It was a well-made object: it had been precisely measured, intricately squared-off; the upright and the crosspiece had been fitted together by someone who knew their joinery, and yet inevitably it was a heavy, ugly thing – sharp around its edges, coarse-grained. In addition it was spattered with congealed blood, mainly around the holes made by the nails, which, when they'd finally been extracted, were each as thick as a man's forefinger and at least ten inches long – so long in fact that they'd protruded through the front of the crossbar. The holes left there were only pinpricks, but even so a single droplet of blood had run down from each one of them. At the lower end of the upright, where the victim's ankles had been fixed, there was more than mere blood: strands of sticky tissue hung from the nails' entry points – threads of human flesh and muscle.

'DS Heckenburg?' a voice carried across the interior of the tent. Another figure in Tyvek was approaching down one of the designated pathways.

Heck swore under his breath.

He'd argued with Gemma about this only that morning. Apparently, to assuage Merseyside's annoyance that this multiple homicide was being taken off them before they'd even had a shot at it, but also because Gemma had decided she needed extra staff, she had requested and had been granted the assistance of a number of Merseyside detectives. On the age-old basis that two sets of eyes were better than one, everyone had since been informed that, from this point on, they'd be working in pairs. When Heck had asked who he was being teamed up with, he was told it was a promising young local officer, Detective Constable Andy Gregson.

'Young?' Heck had said.

'Young,' Gemma had replied, distracted – she was in the process of assembling notes for her morning video-conference.

'How long has this lad been in CID?' Heck had then asked.

'Eight months, I think . . .'

'Bloody brilliant!'

She'd glanced up at him. 'He's just a spare limb, Heck! What do you want . . . someone who'll do their own thing? Someone who won't listen to you?'

'He's a Scouser and I'm a Manc. What makes you think he'll listen to me anyway?'

'Let him know you're in charge,' she'd said, her voice snapping with impatience. 'Tell him you're in charge of this whole case! Christ's sake, everyone else around here thinks you are!'

'Andy Gregson, sarge,' the young officer said, offering his hand. He was somewhere in his early twenties, of average height but lean build. His hair, which was shaved down to the bristles, was carroty-red in colour, roughly the same tinge as the freckles that dusted his youthful features, to either side of which hung a pair of unfortunately overlarge ears. His accent was strong Liverpudlian. 'Pleased to meet you.'

'Yeah . . . same,' Heck said, trying not to sound too insincere. 'Look, I can't waste time breaking you in. You've been fully appraised about Operation Festival's remit?'

Gregson nodded. 'Yeah . . . bit of a shock to be honest. Didn't realise it covered the whole of the north.'

'You know to keep *schtum*?'

'Had that drummed into me.'

'Good. Because if anything leaks to the press from us and the brass get wind of it, we'll have to *post* our resignations.'

Gregson nodded again, but remained blank-faced and unemotional.

'So . . . what do you know about the mechanics of crucifixion, DC Gregson?'

Gregson shrugged. 'Only what I've seen on the telly.'

'On telly the effects people make it look easier than it is.'

Heck indicated the three crosses. 'Try to imagine how difficult it would be in real life.'

'Big buggers, aren't they?'

'Bigger than most people think,' Heck replied. 'We estimate they're standing in pits that are at least two feet deep . . . which would have been dug beforehand of course; a job in itself on compacted slag. That means the central posts, which are solid oak, could be more than ten feet long.'

'Heavy,' Gregson observed.

'Very heavy. Very awkward.'

'And all this was done during the hours of darkness?'

'Hard to believe, isn't it?' Heck said. 'The killers would need to be team-handed at the very least to erect this lot in one night.'

'Street-gang maybe?'

'That's something we're considering, but I'm not convinced and I've made that point to the gaffers. Hardly a gangbanger thing, crucifixion. We're talking numbers, though. Even if you silence the APs with drugs, hanging people on crosses is a messy business. Bringing three prisoners and three disassembled crosses to this slagheap would have been too risky, too time-consuming, especially in the dark. So I reckon the poor sods were crucified first. Brought here when they were already nailed, which would have required a bit more than a delivery van.'

Gregson nodded. 'I heard we're looking for an HGV.'

'Possibly an artic,' Heck said. 'Let me bring you up to speed on everything else . . .' They tramped away, following another designated route up and over the ridge of the slagheap. 'We now know that the Father Christmas costume Ernest Shapiro was bricked up in was not his. It was either homemade or might have been purchased from a fancy dress shop. Both of those options are being looked into. Likewise, the bricks were all new – so a full check is being made on thefts from sites, builders' yards, wholesalers and such. Best of all, seems they've now found human hair beneath two of Shapiro's fingernails. It's possible we might get some DNA.'

The news had only come through that morning, and everyone was excited about it, though a blob of DNA could only help convict someone if the perpetrator's DNA was already on file, which wasn't always the case.

'The old geezer put up a fight, eh?' Gregson said.

Heck nodded. 'With regard to the Valentine's Day killings in Bolton, the arrow has been thoroughly swabbed, but it's clean. It's not unique – it's one of an aluminium brand widely used at archery clubs around England. They're all being investigated as we speak. We've also brought a criminologist in from Liverpool John Moores. He's created a geographic profile. There are only four known crime scenes, so it's not a totally reliable pattern yet in my opinion, but the anchor point is starting to look like Manchester. In the meantime, these crucifixion murders are *our* priority. "Ours" as in me, you and everyone else currently based at Manor Hill.'

They left the tent and headed down the other side of the slagheap, a distance of about fifty yards, to a point where the broken surface of the heap gave way to a rough, single-track road running west to east. Beyond this lay more spoil-land covered with clinker and tufts of thorn.

'We've located one recent tyre track on this access road big enough to indicate an HGV,' Heck said. He walked thirty yards east to a point where another canopy had been set up, cordon tape fluttering around it. He indicated a patch of mashed-flat mud bearing what looked like a lorry's tyre tread. 'We've had a cast taken, obviously.'

Gregson seemed unimpressed. 'This is industrial land, sarge. Any number of HGVs, dumper-trucks, whatever, could have been up here in the last few days.'

'True enough.' They continued along the road to the outer cordon, which was now manned by two uniformed bobbies. 'I'll admit it's a long-shot,' Heck said. 'But that tyre mark's the only clear impression we've got . . . which means it's probably the most recent, so we've got to run with it.'

They stepped under the tape, entering a lay-by where various police vehicles were parked, their own included, and began stripping off their coveralls, gloves and boots. Underneath, Heck was in his usual slacks, shirt and tie. Gregson was the same, but his top button was fastened, his tie-knot neat and sharp, his trousers pressed to a razor's edge.

'How long you been in the job anyway?' Heck asked.

'Three years, three weeks and two days, sarge.'

'Married?'

'Two years, eight months, three weeks.'

'Keep an exact account of everything, do you?'

'Always came in useful when I was on the beat.'

'Suppose it must have.' Heck tossed his Dictaphone and notepad through the open rear window of his metallic-blue Peugeot 306. 'Least I won't need this lot anymore. Manor Hill still under siege?'

Gregson nodded. 'Turning into a bit of a circus, isn't it?'

'The world of *Grand Guignol,* DC Gregson.'

'Come again?'

'*Grand Guignol*. It's a French term. It was a theatre of the macabre in the early twentieth century. Freaks, gore, gothic horror.' Heck pulled his jacket on. 'Exactly what our perps are trying to create, in my opinion.'

'What . . . put on a show? They'd do all this just to shock people?'

'I reckon it's a kind of artistic thing.' Heck pondered. 'A bunch of thickie criminals, the sort we normally deal with – there's nothing in this for them. They nearly always want

131

the obvious. Cash, drugs, sex. By contrast, these murders have been crafted, choreographed. It's like there's some kind of crazy aesthetic going on . . . that's only my theory, of course. The bosses aren't totally convinced.'

Before he could explain further, his mobile began bleeping. When he put it to his ear, Jen Weeks, Operation Festival's Head of Civilian Admin Support, was on the line.

'DS Heckenburg!' she said urgently. 'HGV reported on fire. Witness says it's been dumped on wasteland and deliberately set alight.'

'Where?'

'Place called Ingley Nook. Six miles from the crucifixion site.'

Heck signalled to Gregson, who was about to climb into his Ford Galaxy.

'I'll take my own motor, sarge,' Gregson replied.

'Do you know this area?'

'Well, yeah . . . my first beat was round here.'

'In that case you're riding with me.'

Ingley Nook turned out to be a row of terraced former pit-cottages sitting alongside an unmade road, which wound across yet more spoil-land covered with ash.

'Bloody undercarriage!' Heck swore, as they jolted and bounced on the pot-holes.

'One drawback of bringing a decent motor,' Gregson replied.

'You might have warned me.'

'It's worse than I remember . . . but I've not been round here for a while.'

They travelled another two miles, all habitation falling out of sight into the smudged, dingy distance, before they finally sighted smoke and the flashing blue lights of two fire engines. When they got close, they saw that the lorry – which was articulated – had been driven off the track and down a shallow slope onto open ground, where it appeared to have crashed into the concrete foundations of a former colliery outbuilding.

Heck parked up and watched as jets of water arced over the wreck. The rear section was still partly in flames, clouds of black oily smoke pulsing across the landscape, driven by a strong westerly breeze. The make and model was not immediately recognisable, while the rear registration plate had already gone, but the fire-fighters had it under control and it wouldn't be long before the cops were allowed to make an inspection. In fact, the local station-officer was already trudging back up the slope, lifting his visor, loosening his heavy, flame-retardant tunic.

Heck climbed from the car and flashed his ID. 'Arson?'

'No question.'

'Accelerant?'

'Probably petrol. Some genius chucked it all over the trailer section, inside and out, but not the cab. Good job. If the engine had caught there'd be nothing left.'

'They made a mistake there,' Gregson said.

'We *think*,' Heck replied. 'Could this fire have been burning all last night?'

The station-officer nodded. 'Possibly. It's a long way out – wouldn't have been noticed straight away. Could have taken quite a while so long as the petrol tank didn't blow.' He moved off, barking orders at his men.

Heck and Gregson started down the slope. The lorry was now a hissing, blackened skeleton. While the fire-fighters reeled in their hoses and gathered their equipment, Heck fished out his mobile and placed a call to Jen Weeks.

'Jen, it's me!' he said. 'This burning HGV . . . who reported it?'

'Don't know,' came the reply. 'Call came through St Helens central control.'

'Try to get some details, yeah. And have a word with DCI Garrickson . . . we'll need a house-to-house on Ingley Nook. That lot may have seen something.'

From the angle of the burnt lorry, not to mention the swerving tyre tracks left behind on the slope, it had been driven off the road at speed. They peered into its interior as they circled around to the front; it had been completely gutted – every inner surface charred to a crisp. If anyone nailed to a cross had been transported in there, there'd be no trace of it now – no matter how much blood had been shed. Even more frustrating, the wheels had also been torched, each tyre so melted that the treads were unrecognisable.

The lorry had struck the foundations full-on, as though driven at them deliberately. Its radiator grille was smashed, mechanical innards poking through, leaking steam, while its front two axles had been ripped away; it had come to a rest tilting downward, its front fender at ground level. The impact had crumpled the bodywork of the cab – its roof had buckled and split wide-open, and most of its windows had warped in their frames and shattered, though the fragments remained in place. As the station-officer had said, the fire had not consumed this frontal section, though the paintwork on the cab was scorched and blistered by heat. However, though the front offside wheel was again a smoking, crispy remnant, the nearside wheel was missing.

Heck searched around for it, and located it several yards away, lying alongside the vehicle's registration plate, which had broken into several pieces. He put the number through for a PNC check, and while he waited, crouched to examine the wheel. Unfortunately, this one had also suffered fire damage, though not as extensively as the others. It wasn't possible to say for sure that its tread pattern was a match for the marks at the slagheap – again the rubber was melted and distorted, but there were some similarities.

134

'*PNC to DS Heckenburg*,' came a tinny voice.

'Go ahead.'

'*Checks out as a Scania R470 heavy goods vehicle, sarge. Reported stolen from a lorry park in Longsight, Manchester, on January 18 this year.*'

'Thanks for that.' As Heck shoved the radio back into his pocket, his phone rang. The caller's number indicated that it was Gemma. 'Ma'am?' he said.

'What's the story with this truck?' she asked.

'It could be ours, but there's no obvious link yet. The tread patterns are damaged, so it's hard to say for sure . . . but they're not a world away from the ones we found at the scene.'

'How much did the fire leave?'

'Enough for us to go at. It needs covering up ASAP – we'll probably want another of those wedding tents.'

'Okay.' She paused before asking: 'Any gut feelings?'

He glanced overhead. The sky was largely blue, but streamers of cloud were blowing in from the west. 'The only real one is we'd better get the lab rats down here quickly. The scene's already deteriorated badly, and we could get rain before the end of today.'

'No problem.' She rang off.

'Have a look round,' Heck told Gregson. 'Search for any containers that might have been used to carry petrol. Also any suspect footprints. Bear in mind the fire brigade wear hobnailed boots, so we're looking for trainer patterns, leather-soled shoes and the like.'

Gregson moved away and Heck climbed onto the running-board to glance through the Scania's driver door, though it was difficult seeing anything through the cracked, smoke-blackened glass. He took a pair of latex gloves from his pocket, pulling them on and snapping them into place around his wrists. Making the minimum possible contact, he

135

depressed the button on the door handle. With a *clunk*, it opened; thanks to the cab's tilted angle, the door swung outwards and he was able to peer inside.

It was a typical motorised hovel. Maps and dog-eared vehicle documents were crammed into an open glove-compartment. Empty crisp packets and coffee-stained paper cups had been crushed into a side-pocket. A tatty little teddy bear and a set of rosary beads hung in front of the wind-shield. In sharp contrast, girlie posters – lithe, golden-tanned models in high heels and string bikinis – adorned the rear wall. But one thing in particular caught Heck's eye – a book of matches, half used, lay in the middle of the passenger foot-well. He regarded it thoughtfully, before glancing up at the broken ceiling.

He didn't want to interfere with this crime scene so soon, but the elements weren't on their side. If it rained, the interior of the cab could be washed out. Deciding he had no choice, he reached down and, taking a pair of tweezers from his pocket, gripped the book by one edge, and lifted it up to take a closer look.

'Bingo,' he whispered.

Right in the middle of the matchbook's shiny cover sat a large, oily thumbprint.

Chapter 16

Claire's phone hadn't stopped ringing all day. If it wasn't journalists from the dailies it was the Press Association, if it wasn't the Press Association it was Reuters. Her jaw was stiff and her throat dry from trotting out the party line, and no amount of coffee seemed able to put that right, though it did its bit to scramble her nerves.

At length, she decided enough was enough, put all calls on hold and went out into the main area of the MIR, to stretch her legs. A few minutes earlier, she'd seen Gemma, Garrickson and several others coating up as they left the building. Hopefully that meant ground was being gained somewhere, but she knew she shouldn't count on it. Herds of detectives came and went in this office like shoppers on a sales day. The atmosphere wasn't exactly frantic, but it wasn't relaxed either: everyone else's phone seemed to ring as often as her own did; keyboards were relentlessly hammered.

However, none of this caught Claire's attention now as much as the three large display boards that Eric Fisher was working on. She already knew about the middle one, which documented the various crime scenes, while the one on the left was covered with more mundane imagery: rural life in old England, by the looks of it; trees and bushes woven with ribbons, village fetes, hordes of people in fancy dress. But Fisher was now in the process of adorning the board on the right, and in this case with material of a very different nature. They were mainly sketches or drawings, even a painting or two; thankfully there were no photographs.

The first depicted a naked man bound face-first to a wooden frame. Two figures stood one to either side; both were hairy and brutish, clad in chain-mail and helmets. One was armed with a dagger, the other with a hammer and chisel. The victim's back had been split open lengthways, and his spinal column was exposed; the ribs on one side had been chopped away from it like sticks of celery.

'The Viking Blood-Eagle,' Fisher said, when he saw what she was looking at. 'A sacrifice to Odin designed to win his favour in war. The prisoner's back was carved open, his ribs cut apart and the lungs pulled out to resemble the wings of an eagle. It was practised by conquering Viking armies, but not widely – the only captives deemed worthy of this death were kings or great war-leaders. Believe it or not, it was an honour.'

'An honour,' Claire said in disbelief.

'Amazing, eh?' Detective Sergeant Eric Fisher was a bit like a Viking, himself. He was in his late fifties and a huge, heavyweight chap, his monumental gut hanging down past the front of his waistband. He had beetle brows and half his craggy face was buried under a dense, red-grey beard. So out of shape was he that, no matter what he wore – and it was usually the required shirt and tie – it seemed scruffy on him. He wheezed when he walked and smelled constantly of sweat and cigarette smoke, but Claire knew that in SCU's experience, as a researcher and analyst, Eric Fisher was unsurpassed.

She glanced at the next image along. This one was a

138

painting, probably from the classical era; it portrayed two men being burned at the stake. However, wood hadn't been piled around them. Instead, they stood on a heap of red-hot coals. The implication was obvious – the fire would burn torturously slowly. Though the victims were still alive, their eyes raised to heaven, their legs and feet had been reduced to naked bones.

'The executions of Jacques Molay and Geoffrey de Charney in 1314,' Fisher explained. 'Two Templar knights burned for heresy. The idea was to drag out the immolation for as long as possible, so that all debts would be paid before they met their maker – gave them a better chance of avoiding hell.'

'What are all these?' Claire asked.

'Religious killings,' he replied. 'Rituals, sacrifices . . . the purpose to achieve redemption through pain.'

Religious . . . redemption . . .

'Or to impose one's belief system over another,' Fisher added chattily. 'What better way to show your god is top dog than by offering him the next god's biggest supporters? And what better time to do it on than some special occasion that's sacred to your faith – a feast day or what-not! How chuffed would your deity be?'

Claire tried to look away, but even glimpsing some of the other imagery was enough to turn her stomach: blood streaming down the steps of a sunbaked ziggurat, at the apex of which a feather-wearing priest had just used a clawlike metal tool to tear the heart from the breast of a body spread on a slab; a huge idol smeared with gore, a mound of flayed corpses draped in its extended grasp, while around it priests and acolytes danced nude, except that, no . . . they weren't nude, they were wearing the skins of the sacrificial victims. Claire swore she could hear a demonic drumbeat accompanying that last one.

What a stupid child you are, she thought as she walked stiffly back to her office. *Disturbed by a few drawings*. But then it wasn't the drawings so much as what they imparted. People had done these terrible things everywhere and since time immemorial. Compared to that appalling truth, what a cosseted world *she* had grown up in – where the most shocking thing that would happen during the average week was her father murmuring 'shit' after snipping his finger while pruning the prize roses in the garden of their middle-class Bournemouth home. How far removed she'd been from all this, and yet now, in the blink of an eye, she was right in the belly of the beast.

It was difficult to believe, but yesterday – *only yesterday*! – she had witnessed a live crucifixion. She'd tried not to show it at the time, but that had knocked her for six. Heck had expressed similar revulsion – of course he had, but he was back out there, working, unaffected; in the rest of the office, people gabbled as they got on with stuff, ribbed each other, sniggered at idle jokes. Only now did it really strike Claire just how brave she was going to have to be – braver than she'd ever been in her life – to remain part of this team.

'I can do it . . . I know I can!'

And she meant it; she did, in all seriousness . . . though she still hoped no one had overheard her. Because though she'd uttered the words with such determination they had almost brought a sob from her throat, they still didn't sound convincing.

Not even to her own ears.

Chapter 17

Heck made his way back to the car and placed his fingerprint sample in a sterile container in the boot, before pulling his gloves off. Below him, Andy Gregson was working his way around the burnt lorry in steadily wider circles. Heck glanced along the road. There was no sign of any support yet, but they shouldn't be long . . .

A glint of light caught his eye.

He straightened up, gazing past the lorry and across the spoil-land, which, thanks to his elevated position, now lay before him in a wide, arid plain.

The light glinted again. It was very distant – maybe half a mile away, and it appeared to be located on a low ridge-line covered with scrub vegetation. When the light glinted a third time, Heck moved from suspecting that someone was watching them with binoculars, to a near-certainty that they were.

Fleetingly, he was undecided what to do. It could be a completely blameless action. People wandered the countryside carrying binoculars for all sorts of innocent reasons.

Yeah, right . . .

He leapt behind the Peugeot's wheel and shoved his key

into the ignition, the 2.0 turbo diesel engine throbbing to life.

As he roared down the unmade slope, he saw Andy Gregson emerge from around the blackened wreckage, staring at him with mouth open, but there was no time to stop and explain. The underside of Heck's Peugeot took another battering as he gunned it forward over the rocky, undulating waste, wheels skidding, chassis jolting. He swerved sideways at one point, losing grip on the broken surface; with a sickening crunch, what sounded like his exhaust pipe fractured, his engine thundering in response.

'Shit!' Heck snapped.

The ridge drew closer, but only slowly – distances out here were apparently deceptive. He hit troughs and dips, which threw him every which way as he crashed into and over them. Wiry thorns tangled around his wheels; an oil drum clattered away as he clouted it with his nearside headlight, which duly shattered. Despite all, his eyes remained locked on the approaching ridge. He hadn't seen another flicker of light since he'd jumped into the car, but that was hardly surprising – they'd have spotted him coming, which was why speed was more important than stealth.

With a grinding of axles and squealing of gears, he covered the last fifty yards along a shallow gully, bouncing over heaps of broken masonry and house bricks. A section of sewer pipe made from solid concrete jutted out at one side; only by swift, deft manoeuvres was he able to swerve around it without flaying paint from his flanks. The rutted slope of the ridge, a solid mass of compacted rubble, loomed directly ahead. He hit the brakes, again slewing sideways before staggering to a halt, jumped out and began scrambling uphill as much on all-fours as two feet. It was steeper than he'd expected, but the top couldn't be far overhead. He fished his phone from his pocket as he climbed.

'Andy!'

'What's going on?' came the startled reply.

'Someone's watching us . . .'

'What . . . who?'

'Dunno.'

'That motor of yours'll be a write-off.'

'NCG can have the bill. Just stay where you are . . . Gemma's en route.'

Heck shoved the phone away. The sweat was dripping off him by the time he reached the top. He stood there, panting, scanning the level ground ahead. It was covered with spoil-land vegetation, twisted, stunted trees for the most part, meshed in clumps, and though it was only spring, knee-deep in brambles and thick green shoots of Idle Jack. There was no sound, not even a twitter of birds – which seemed ominous.

He proceeded warily, seeing only narrow, sun-dappled dells. After a few yards, he glanced behind, realising that he was already losing sight of the open ground he'd driven across; the straggling undergrowth had closed to his rear like a pair of curtains. A voice then came from his right: somewhere in the near-distance, calling to someone.

Heck halted in his tracks, listening hard.

He moved a couple of yards in that direction, pushing aside branches and weeds, still seeing nothing. The voice sounded again. Distinctly deep, distinctly male. As before, it was calling a name, but the name was unrecognisable, and why had it this time sounded as if it was coming from a different direction? Was it the acoustics of this place, or – and this was an eerie notion – was there more than one individual here? Were they hiding out, making sport of him? He fingered at the phone in his pocket, but that would be little or no use – no one else was going to drive over that waste-tip. They'd have to come on foot, and that would take

143

ages. A better plan might be to withdraw, but at what cost? What if the perps were *here* . . . and he just walked away?

He heard another shout, this one further afield, carrying an echo. Despite his better judgment, Heck ventured forward again, pushing more branches aside, following the path as it zigzagged, still seeing no one, though, as the gradient began to slope downward again, the scrub vegetation thinned out, replacing itself with larger, healthier trees like oaks and sycamores. Beyond these, the ground fell away steeply and suddenly he found himself gazing down into open space, on possibly the last thing he'd expected.

A graveyard . . . but a graveyard of trains.

Heck was left speechless. Lines of carriages, and even the odd locomotive or two, were drawn up against rusty old buffers, and standing seven or eight in a row on railway tracks thickly overgrown with weeds. Their windows were frosted and filled with jagged black holes where rocks had been thrown. Spray-paint ran over them in arterial red and blue veins; their bodywork was dented, streaked with moss.

At least this explains the echo, he thought vaguely.

The old siding, which was probably connected in some way to the Liverpool-to-Manchester line, was a good sixty feet below him, lying in a natural valley. The path led down to it via a perilous gradient – so perilous in fact that he might not have bothered trying to descend, until he spied movement down there. What looked like a figure in a hooded, green waterproof had just stepped out of sight behind one of the derelict hulks.

Heck hovered where he was, but the figure did not reappear. He fished his phone from his pocket, but because he was on lower ground than previously, the bulk of the spoil heap reared behind him, blocking out reception. He tried his radio, but the same problem affected it. He shoved the gadgets back into his pockets, making sure to turn down the volume on the radio first – it would be typical of a police PR that it had apparently died on you, only for it to buzz with static just as you were sneaking up on a felon.

He started downhill, walking side-footed to avoid falling, all the time watching the rows of disused rolling-stock. At the foot of the slope, the path veered sharp-right and ran alongside a tall wire-mesh fence, but this was loose in many sections, and Heck had no trouble sliding underneath it. He stood up again, beating the dirt from his hands, listening intently. If people *had* been calling to each other, they weren't doing it anymore. Was that because he was onto them? He ventured forward, stepping carefully amid thistles and rotted sleepers, peering down the narrow gaps between the vast, silent vehicles, where the shadows were deepest and the foliage grew neck-high. Doors hung open on either side, rank darkness lurking in the gutted interiors behind. There was still no sound. Only as he passed the fifth of these alleys did he spy movement at its far end: a fleeting glint of green. As before, someone had just lurched out of sight. Heck halted, holding his breath, and then an impulse made him spin around. If there was more than one of them, an unseen assailant could be stealing up from behind – but there was no one, just more open space, more rubble.

A row of squarish, yellow frontages faced him from some thirty yards away: abandoned diesels; dented, grimy, daubed with spray-painted obscenities. On the other side of those, corroded rails dwindled off along a canyon filled with under-brush. He turned back to the narrow passage. There was no movement down there now. He glanced up the slope; there was no movement among the trees at the top either. If Gemma had arrived at the suspect lorry, she clearly wasn't concerned to discover why he'd suddenly dropped off the air. Not yet.

A loud *clang* diverted his attention back down the alley.

It reverberated for several seconds, but still there was no sign of movement.

Heck moved on to the next alley. This one was longer than any of those previous, the two trains between which it had formed consisting of four or five carriages each, instead of one or two. But it was the figure at the far end that most caught his notice.

He jumped backwards, flattening himself out of sight – until he realised that the figure's back was turned. Again, he saw a heavy green waterproof, its hood pulled up to a goblin-like peak. But the figure, which was broad across the shoulders – to the point of being foursquare, almost like a rugby prop forward – remained perfectly still.

Inviting him to approach.

Oh, I will . . . but not the way you want me to, pal.

Stealthily as he could, Heck clambered up through an open doorway into the hulk on his left, and found himself looking down an arched gangway littered with glass, over-turned tables and the guts of slashed or fire-blackened seats. Aside from the odd jammed-open door, he could see a consid-erable distance in both directions. By his feet lay a mass of crinkly, yellow newspaper. It looked like the *Daily Mail*; its front page lead expressed horror at the death of Diana, Princess of Wales. Heck stepped over it, advancing quickly and quietly. At the end of the first carriage, in a boarding area filled with more shattered glass and several half-bricks, he paused to listen. There was no sound from outside, but some indefinable concern made him linger. And then he heard it – a plasticky *crackling* from just behind him.

He twirled, to see a toilet door standing ajar by half a foot or so. Impenetrable green shadow lay on the other side. That crackling again; louder this time. He pictured a heavy waterproof jacket, its wearer shifting position. Was he staring at Heck right now through that open slice of doorway?

146

Heck had no choice; he charged forward, throwing his shoulder at the door. It barely shifted under his weight; and for a second he completely and absolutely believed that someone was braced against the other side.

And then he saw the truth.

The tiny toilet cubicle had been crammed with plastic rubbish bags. And the intrepid squirrel who'd been investigating them leapt for the broken, moss-covered window and vanished through it in an ash-grey blur.

Heck remained in the doorway for several seconds; head drooped, trying to regain his composure. Then he continued along the train at speed, glancing through one smashed window after another, catching ephemeral glimpses of the eroded bodywork flanking him on either side. He slowed again as he approached what had to be the front of the vehicle, advancing with the lightest footfalls possible. Directly ahead stood the open door to the driver's compartment. First, Heck sidled to his right, glancing down into the alley. The figure he'd seen ought to be standing just to the front of this pos-ition, but now no one was in sight – just an empty gap between the two locomotives.

Swearing under his breath, Heck pushed his way into the driver's cab. Where once there'd been a bank of controls, all that remained were tufts of oily wiring and rusty rivets where the two seats had been positioned. He slid through the open door and clambered down to the ground, glancing back along the alley, which was still deserted. Only when he advanced into the open did he see the figure again.

It stood thirty yards to his right; as before, its back was turned, but now its left arm hung motionless by its side. The figure appeared to be staring at a half-collapsed siding shed. This time as Heck advanced, he made no attempt at stealth, his feet crunching loudly on gravel. Despite the noise, the hooded figure remained static, refusing to look around – which

147

was faintly unnerving, as was its size. Up close, it looked big enough to break an opponent in half. Heck had a crazy idea about landing a rabbit punch between the burly shoulder-blades, just at the base of the neck, putting the guy out of action before the fight even started, but he didn't.

'Police officer!' he shouted, grabbing the figure's left wrist, twisting it up and behind the back in a sharp-angled goose-neck.

The figure went down surprisingly easily, gasping with pain, hood flopping sideways.

And Heck saw several things at once: firstly, that though he was big across the shoulders, this guy was late middle-aged and pot-bellied, with a thick growth of grey fuzz on his podgy, florid face; secondly, that he hadn't heard Heck approach because he was wearing a pair of earphones attached to an iPod; thirdly, he hadn't moved because he'd been concentrating on an object mounted in front of him on a flimsy tripod – it was an optical level, and it had now fallen over, snapping apart; and finally, the stencilled lettering on the right lapel of his waterproof, which read: *DAYNTON HOMES Ltd.*

Heck heard a similar shout to those he'd heard before, though now more intelligible.

'Mal! You got them flaming earphones on again?'

A second figure, also wearing a green waterproof, perambulated into Heck's peripheral vision. This one was younger, clean shaved and of much slighter build, but his jacket too was emblazoned with the Daynton Homes logo and he was carrying his own levelling instrument at his shoulder. He stopped dead.

'Oi! What's your bloody game!'

'Alright . . . easy,' Heck said, releasing his prisoner. 'Simple mistake, yeah?'

'Who are you? This is private land . . . it belongs to Daynton Homes.'

'I realise that now.' Heck dug his warrant card from his pocket. 'I'm a copper.'

The bearded guy had rolled over onto his backside and was gingerly cradling his arm. 'What'd you attack me for? I didn't do anything to you . . .'

'I didn't mean . . . look, I'm sorry. I thought you were . . . someone else.'

The younger guy had now deemed it safe enough to come forward and assist his overweight chum to his feet. 'Fucking idiot.'

'Relax, pal.'

'I'm not your pal!'

'Just answer me this . . . were you lot up on that ridge overlooking the open ground running to Ingley Nook?'

'Who else? We're building all the way to the pit cottages. Four phases in the next two years.'

'Awww,' the bearded guy moaned, picking up the remnants of his hi-tech measuring device. 'He's broken my sodding level!'

'Gonna cost you, this,' the younger guy warned. 'Big time.'

Heck nodded glumly. It looked like his exhaust and head-lights would be coming out of his own pocket after all.

Chapter 18

Gracie was wearing her regulation satin hot-pants, her leather thigh boots and a clingy halter-top – the really flimsy one that always enhanced her overly generous 38E bust. She'd applied tasteful make-up and wore her auburn hair in a thick braid, which she'd coiled at the back. It might be spring but it was still cold and damp at night, so she was also wearing a fleecy jacket, which she of course kept zipped down so that her best assets remained in the open.

Chantelle, her junior by twenty years, wore a denim mini-skirt which barely concealed her black stocking tops and suspender straps. Her boobs were smaller than Gracie's but firmer (she liked to boast), so she generally didn't bother with a bra. Tonight she only had a string vest under her open leather coat, through which you could see her nipples protruding; the chill helped a lot in that respect. Chantelle's shoulder-length hair was blonde, but only because it was bleached – in fact she'd bleached it so many times now that it was dry and straw-like; so to conceal this she wore it in bunches. She had a feline beauty, she'd once been told, so she tried to accentuate this with heavy make-up: black eye-liner, green eye-shadow, deeply powdered cheeks, and a slash of vermilion on her lips. In addition she was tall – statuesque, she always felt – five-eleven compared to Gracie's five-five; her usual killer heels added to this.

But the pair might have made a more striking picture of sexually empowered womanhood had they not been regulars on the Bradford meat-rack. No matter how saucy the attire, it was always difficult to maintain an aura of *real* glamour when you'd been raped, ripped off and slapped around as often as Gracie and Chantelle had.

Gracie's curves were the most eye-catching thing about her, especially when you glimpsed her in the blinking blue and pink strobes of the sex-for-sale district, but when you got close there was no hiding the ashen pallor or the sagging flesh. And you could never conceal the truth about your hands with make-up, the way you could with your face; Gracie's were so shrivelled they looked more like claws – the long nails and crimson polish she favoured only boosted this illusion.

In Chantelle's case, even the facial make-up didn't work. She thought it made her look like a cat, but in fact it made her look like a cadaver. She wasn't statuesque either, she was gangling – an emaciated beanpole whose sexy clothes would have looked more alluring on a wire-framed mannequin. And it wasn't as if Butch – who liked to call himself their 'manager' – ever offered much advice in this regard, at least none that was friendly, and it went without saying that he offered them zero protection. He kept them in just enough cash to keep vodka in their bellies, speed up their noses and nicotine in their lungs. But if they ever got so stoned that they brought home wages of the Mickey Mouse variety, out came his leather belt with the brass lion's head buckle, and he'd more thoroughly chasten their flesh than the kinkiest punter ever had.

It was perhaps no surprise that the two girls had thus

devised their own strategies to ensure at least a modicum of security. They always worked together now – never apart. That didn't mean they went off with johns together. There was always that spine-freezing moment when, despite every molecule in your body telling you it was a bad idea, you got into a car belonging to someone you didn't know and were driven away, watching your friend's face in the rear-view mirror as it receded into the distance. But they always did their best to vet a punter beforehand and would refuse anyone they didn't like the look of. It didn't matter if Butch was vexed when they got home (so long as he never found out they'd deliberately turned a punter away of course); it was better to be safe than sorry.

Another thing they did – and this was Gracie's innovation – was carry paper and pencils in their handbags. Neither would now ride off with a customer unless the other one had taken a note of his registration mark first, and they always made sure the customer knew this. When she'd first come up with the idea, Gracie had been very pleased with herself. She'd almost thought it a perfect plan. Only an idiot would try something nasty once the girls had got his number.

Or a lunatic, of course – and that wasn't reassuring.

Because there was no shortage of lunatics around; not when the night came down on Britain's old industrial cities. This one for example, Bradford, had once been a hunting ground for Peter Sutcliffe, the infamous Yorkshire Ripper. What a terror tale that had been. Despite frenetic police activity, when the indigo sky turned black and these old terraced side-streets ran red with bloody light, Sutcliffe had gone prowling, taking girl after girl, reducing them to lifeless, butchered husks. That had been before their time. The last Ripper victim had died in 1980, while Gracie was at junior school, eight years before Chantelle was even born. But take this cobbled pitch they walked on now, with decayed

Victorian arches overhead, a derelict, boarded-up factory to their front and a cavernous, trash-filled gloom behind them, the distant outlines of tramps huddled around piles of burning rags, the flames of which cast crimson phantoms on the aged crumbling brickwork: girls had disappeared from this very spot, and not just during the Ripper's reign – or so the story told.

Of course, at the end of the day it was needs must. Neither of them was here voluntarily. Not in truth. It was just that they couldn't get anything else. Chantelle always told people that she wasn't a bad girl at heart, but that she'd made a lot of mistakes in her life, which now prevented her from getting a real career or looking after her two children, who were in the care of her mother. By contrast, Gracie had held various jobs; she'd been a barmaid, a coat-check girl at a nightclub; she'd once loaded shelves in a supermarket. Alright, she'd been a lap-dancer and a photographic model as well. No doubt the moral majority would have sneered at those two occupations, but at least there hadn't been any physical contact between her and the customers – not in those early days. It was difficult now, gazing back through the haze of drugs and booze, to work out exactly when that 'no touch' rule had been ditched. But what they were doing now was still an earner, even if it was a bit distasteful.

Not that either of the two girls had earned much over the last few months. It was April, but the after effects of a very hard winter were only just wearing off. Snow, ice and fog were never good for business, and the likes of Chantelle had become increasingly desperate. The last few nights she'd driven off with blokes she probably shouldn't have: a shifty-eyed porcine individual with a thick, spittle-filled beard and bloodstained clothes, driving a grimy old butcher's van; a more respectable-looking sort, who'd promptly ruined the illusion by telling her before they struck a deal that she had to agree to be cuffed and blindfolded – and had laughed like a hyena as he drove her away.

It was almost inevitable that when they saw the first vehicle this evening, Chantelle straightened up and squeaked with excitement. It was a Jaguar, and it drove slowly along the street, kerb-crawling but barely breaking speed as it passed them by. Gracie tried to scan its occupants, though all she saw were two vague figures, one driving and one in the front passenger seat, and then it vanished round a corner.

'He'll be back,' Chantelle said confidently.

'There were two of them,' Gracie replied, vaguely discomforted.

'Even better. One for each of us.'

'They've gone anyway.'

'Nah . . . they'll be back.'

The Jaguar *was* back, three minutes later, cruising down the street in the same direction. As before, it drove slowly – perhaps a little more slowly this time. Chantelle ensured she was at the edge of the pavement, head high, hand on hip, such bust as she had thrust outward. Once again, the car passed them. More by instinct than design, Gracie took a scruffy slip of paper from her fleece pocket and a stub of pencil, and scribbled down its registration mark.

The car again vanished around the corner. This wasn't unusual. Some johns, especially first-timers, were nervous about picking up girls – it took them a while to pluck up the courage. But that knowledge didn't put Gracie at ease. She folded the paper and slid it into her left thigh boot. When the vehicle appeared a third time, now travelling in the opposite direction, it stopped – but not directly alongside them; on the other side of the road, against the wall of the dilapidated factory.

'Listen, Chant,' Gracie said under her breath. 'Posh gits don't come down here. You've got to be sensible, yeah?'

'I need to score, Grace,' Chantelle said from the side of her smile-curved mouth. 'Maybe you can afford to have scruples. At the moment I fucking can't, alright?'

But they were both surprised when the figure that had ridden in the Jaguar's front passenger seat climbed out and came around the car, crossing the road towards them – because it was a female. Quite young, seventeen or eighteen at the most, exceedingly pretty in a fresh-faced schoolgirl sort of way. Her platinum-blonde hair was wild and straggly, and hung almost to her waist. She was very slim, but also shapely – like a dancer. She wore a short black dress, a black cardigan, black tights and white plimsolls. Her arms were folded as she walked quickly but prettily across the road towards them.

'Hi,' she said, smiling brightly, which made her look prettier still. 'You guys working tonight?'

'We could be,' Chantelle replied.

'Good, 'cause I've got a proposition for you.'

'We don't do kids,' Gracie said in a flat tone.

The girl chuckled – a delightful sound, which implied that the idea amused her but was also wide of the mark. 'We need a couple of extras for one of our movies.'

'Movies?' Chantelle said.

'Yeah . . . look, my boyfriend and me, we make porn movies. You know, at our home, and we post them on our website. I say "extras" . . . but you won't really be extras. You'll be working, if you know what I mean.' She chuckled again – provocatively.

'You and your boyfriend?' Gracie said warily. 'Is that him over there in the car?'

'Yeah, he's a bit shy.'

'But he's not too shy to post videos of himself online?'

'That's different, isn't it? He can't see the audience then.'

'How much?' Chantelle asked, as if she'd already heard enough to know this was a good idea.

The girl was about to reply when something briefly distracted her – movement in the dark recess behind them. They glanced around: a grizzled, ferrety face had just peeked out from a cardboard box, the sagging walls of which had been reinforced with sheets of urine-yellow newspaper. His eyes were glazed and rheumy; he muttered something incoherent and then reached up a twisted paw to pull more newspaper down over the entrance as he withdrew inside.

'Don't worry about him, he's harmless,' Chantelle said. 'How much?'

'Oh . . .' The girl smiled. 'How does two hundred sound? Per hour? Each?'

Even Gracie was taken aback by that.

'You've got a deal, darling,' Chantelle replied.

'Wait a minute,' Gracie said. 'We need a look at this bloke of yours first. If he's the Hunchback of Notre Dame, it's gonna cost you a lot more.'

The girl nodded. 'Fair enough. I'll see if I can talk him into showing his pretty face.' She walked back across the road.

'Have you gone mental?' Chantelle hissed. 'This'll be a piece of piss. Two bits of kids and big cash.'

'Two bits of kids driving a forty-grand car?' Gracie said suspiciously.

'Alright, so they're rich kids. Doesn't mean they're going to be trouble. Come on love, this is easy money. Plus we'll be together, and it'll probably be a nice pad – warm, cosy. Might get a couple of drinks out of it as well.'

In all honesty, Gracie couldn't think of a reason why she didn't want to do this. Everything her friend said was correct: this was a dream job – easy work in a pleasant environment, with two non-threatening customers. So why did she still feel uneasy?

'Suppose it seems a bit too good to be true, that's all.'

'Hey!' Chantelle tapped her arm. 'Good things *do* happen sometimes, you know.'

'I don't know, Chant . . .'

'Listen . . .' Chantelle lowered her voice confidentially. 'Are you seriously telling me you don't want a taste of that young, blonde pussy?'

'She looks underage to me.'

'She looks borderline, and who cares? They came to us first. Look, they post films of themselves online. They must be covered legally to do that.'

'Ladies!' came the girl's voice.

They glanced across the cobbled street. The driver had climbed out and was standing alongside the car, one arm linked with hers. He waved at them sheepishly, almost shyly. From what Gracie and Chantelle could see, there was nothing about him that put either of them off. In fact, quite the opposite.

'Don't look the type, do they?' Chantelle said as they crossed the road together, their spike heels clacking in the night air.

'Kids grow up too quickly these days,' Gracie replied. 'Fucking internet.'

'Don't knock it. We might get regular work out of this. Safe work too.'

'Like you say . . . good things do sometimes happen.'

The interior of the Jaguar was plush and warm, fragrant of leather and felt. Low music was playing: something croony and melodic from the Big Band era.

'Very nice,' Chantelle said, making herself comfortable in the back. 'What're your names then?'

'I'm Jasmine,' the blonde girl said, turning round from the front passenger seat. 'This is Gareth.'

Gareth was now behind the wheel. He said nothing as the engine purred to life.

'How far have we got to go?' Gracie asked.

'Just out of town. It's not too far, and we'll bring you back here when we're done. Or we can take you both home.'

'Back here'll be just fine, thank you,' Gracie said.

'What's your poison, ladies?' Jasmine asked.

Chantelle tittered. 'You planning on taking us for a drink first?'

'I wasn't planning to, but here . . .' She opened a leather zip-lock bag and lifted out two plastic goblets, which she handed over, one to each. She unscrewed the top from a bottle. 'It's no problem to stretch to a drop of Chablis . . . on the house of course.'

'Ta,' Chantelle said, licking her lips as the goblets were filled.

'What exactly do we have to do in this movie of yours?' Gracie wondered.

'Just the usual stuff. Nothing too weird, I promise you.'

There was nothing particularly weird that Gracie and Chantelle hadn't already experienced, but it was always reassuring to hear that a punter wanted it straight.

'I hope *you're* performing with us?' Chantelle said.

'I've got my part to play, don't worry.' Jasmine turned back to the front.

Chantelle winked at Gracie, and they sipped their wine together as the Jaguar pulled away from the kerb. Neither of them noticed the blonde girl glance out through her window and across the road into the gloom beneath the railway arch. Neither saw the hooded figure, which had waited for them to depart, now slink out of the clustered shadows.

'Whaaa . . . what the fu . . .' the ferrety-faced tramp shouted as the cardboard roof was torn away from over his head. But his words choked off when he saw the hooded shape standing over him, in particular when he saw it hefting a huge, flat stone in its gloved hands – by the looks of it, at least half a paving slab.

He tried to scream, but it was too late – the stranger had already raised the slab on high and now swung it down with all his considerable might. It struck the tramp's skull with a crunching impact. A second blow followed, then a third, a fourth and a fifth. The heavy, meaty echoes resounded through the aged archways.

Chapter 19

'These are the upcoming dates we may need to be concerned about,' Eric Fisher said.

Heck and Andy Gregson regarded the picture boards that Fisher had assembled in the MIR. Previously they'd only glimpsed them, but now, having come in early this morning, they were able to assess them properly. The one on the right had been distracting enough, layered as it was with images of ritual slayings from throughout the historical past, but the one on the left was of more immediate importance.

Photos of church parades, children formed in choirs and Morris Men dancing had all been added to the pictures of the walking-days, fetes on village greens and so forth. Each had a label attached to it, and a date, alongside a typed-out précis of the event itself and the circumstances surrounding it. Despite the jollity on view, none of it made for easy reading. April alone boasted eighteen entries, such mystifying dates as Hocktide and Low Sunday figuring alongside the more traditional Easter and St George's Day. There were similar treats in May: everyone knew about May Day, Empire Day and Whitsun, but who knew anything about Helston Flora or Royal Oak Day?

'Never heard of half of these,' Gregson commented.

'That's because we're not a spiritual nation anymore,' Fisher replied, handing out printed sheets to the various detectives who'd gathered around them. 'When I was a lad, anything to do with the Church, we'd have a day off school for it. Used to call them "holy days of obligation". Most folk have never heard of that now. But this is only scratching the surface, if I'm honest. There are local events – things they go big on in some parts of the country, which are ignored in others. Different kinds of celebrations. Some vary from parish to parish, never mind county to county. But religion is the underlying theme. All these special days once meant a lot more to people than they do now.'

'What's religious about Bonfire Night?' Charlie Finnegan asked.

'Nothing now,' Heck replied, 'but the original Gunpowder Plot was supposed to signal a Catholic uprising. Least that's what I was always taught at school.'

'Correct,' Fisher said. 'I've scrutinised these festivals a bit more carefully since we've been here. November 5 is an old Protestant celebration. It's not seen that way now, except in places like Lewes in East Sussex, where papal effigies get burned. But that was its start point.'

'Simplifies things, at least,' Finnegan said. 'We're after a bunch of religious freaks.'

Heck looked doubtful. 'Possibly, but *which* religion? Eric, didn't we decide that some of these festivals were once pagan?'

Fisher nodded. 'Christmas was the ancient Germanic Yuletide; Valentine's Day was the Roman feast of Lupercalia. And that's the story almost across the board. The things we do on these occasions now are just remnants of older, more elaborate ceremonies.'

'And were they marked with human sacrifices?' Shawna McCluskey asked.

Fisher pulled a face. 'Some of them were, sometimes . . .'

'It doesn't pan out,' Gary Quinnell argued. 'Celebrating Christian feasts with vicious murders, even celebrating pagan feasts with murder – that was centuries and centuries ago. Modern Wiccans are like us; they don't believe in shedding blood. On top of that, these special days are all different. Most of them have no connection with each other in terms of origin or activity. There's no recognisable theology under-lying any of this. None that makes sense to me.'

'Well, whoever they are, with so many special days to pick from, they could strike at any time,' Fisher said.

'They have to plan though, don't they?' Shawna replied. 'They can't just pick dates off a calendar at random.'

'They've planned this whole thing already,' Heck said. 'Months ago, maybe years.'

They all pondered that – and were demoralised by it. The patience required to hatch and evolve such a complex scheme suggested a mindset that was not just cold, calculating and patient – *infinitely* patient – but obsessive to the point of madness. As Heck stared at the joyful images – top-hatted 'tuttimen' carrying poles decorated with spring flowers, a foliage-covered Jack-in-the-Green parading through a village square with hordes of laughing children in pursuit – it was still difficult to imagine that this whole thing was nothing more than a ghoulish but ultimately meaningless game.

'Suppose they're not *celebrating* these feast days,' Shawna suddenly said. 'Suppose they're *desecrating* them.'

Everyone glanced around at her.

'Don't you think?' she added, looking amazed that she'd come up with such an idea. 'They're not just mocking them, they're ruining them forever.'

'You mean like . . . an anti-religious group?' Quinnell said. 'Like a bunch of, I dunno . . . militant atheists, or something?'

Finnegan chuckled. 'Who was it mentioned upsetting the trendy left?'

'Mockery,' Heck said thoughtfully. 'Is all this just a massive piss-take?'

'Whatever these nutters' motivations, they are bloody well organised,' Fisher said. 'The way they're selecting victims, luring them into traps, nabbing them. They're so well organised it wouldn't surprise me if they aren't following the investigation in order to improvise . . . in case we get too close.'

'Useful stuff,' came Gemma's voice. She'd approached from her office and was standing close by, pen in hand. 'And sound advice. Even more of a reason not to tell tales out of school. In the meantime, Heck . . . a word please.'

Heck followed her into her office, dragging off his jacket. DCI Garrickson was already in there, stripped to his shirt-sleeves and leafing through a pile of reports. He barely grunted as Heck said 'Morning' to him. Gemma slid back behind her desk, nodding at Heck to pull up a chair. He did so.

'Nothing useful from the gang-intervention units, I'm afraid,' she said. 'I've been in touch with Merseyside, GMP and West Yorkshire. None of them seem to think these types of crimes are a fit for any of the groups they monitor.'

Heck shrugged. 'No surprise really. This whole case reveals an extreme level of deviancy . . . I've said all along this isn't the work of everyday criminals.'

Garrickson groaned. 'Not this psycho-babble again. Look . . . if we're not looking for criminals, who are we looking for?'

'All I can tell you, sir, is that this is something very different from the norm. And very difficult to explain, especially as there's no obvious gain for those involved.'

'This thrill-kill business?' Garrickson sounded unimpressed. 'This showmanship thing?'

Heck nodded. 'That's one explanation. Religious fanaticism might be another, but personally I doubt that one. Shawna's come up with a neat idea. She thinks we're looking at deliberate desecrations. You know, vicious acts designed to hurt and upset the maximum number of people. That would certainly match the narcissist profile.'

'A narcissist thrill-killer,' Gemma mused. 'They tend to be individuals.'

'One individual could be controlling the others,' Heck replied. 'A master manipulator, who's surrounded himself with misfits, outcasts . . . naïve types who'll follow any orders.'

'As in a cult?' she wondered.

'The more I think about it, the more that seems possible,' Heck said. 'I'm not sure it's a very big group, though. Can't be more than a handful of members.'

Garrickson regarded him with fascination. 'You've really hit the speculation button, haven't you?'

'Well, the more heinous the crime, sir, the harder it is to get people to participate . . .'

'I'm perfectly aware of that. I just don't know how we've got from not knowing anything to putting APBs out on the Manson family . . .'

Shawna barged in. 'Sorry, ma'am. But you'll want to see this email.'

Gemma took a couple of print-outs from her and read them carefully – not once but twice. Then she placed them on the desk and glanced up. 'The lab has managed to lift a DNA profile from the hair found under Ernest Shapiro's fingernails. What's more, we've got a positive hit on it. It belongs to a certain Cameron Boyd of Longsight, Manchester . . . thirty-three years old and well known. Boyd has form for robbery, car-jacking, GBH and rape.'

'They used to call him "Cam the Spike",' Shawna said. 'Because his weapon of choice was a sharpened screwdriver.'

Garrickson looked delighted. 'That's what I call a lead! We should pick him up now, give him the third degree!'

Heck took one of the print-outs from the desk.

'Known associates?' Gemma asked Shawna.

'Take your pick, ma'am. He's into everything . . .'

'Serial murder?' Heck wondered.

'Well . . . not up till now,' Shawna replied. 'But he's a player. Surely you can see that?'

'Course . . . but it's all commonplace stuff. Car-jacking, robbery.'

'Rape?' Shawna said.

Heck tapped the print-out. 'According to this, he was convicted of raping his girlfriend. Doesn't make him a nice guy, but it doesn't make him a night-stalker either.'

'What are you suggesting?' Garrickson asked.

'I don't know.' Heck focused on Gemma. 'It's a development, I'm not denying it . . . it needs checking. But ma'am, if we were chasing run-of-the-mill offenders, wouldn't our grasses have tipped us some kind of wink by now? Look at Boyd's sheet – he left school at sixteen, having spent most of his time there excluded. He's not just a scrote; he's as thick as pigshit. Would he have the first idea how to affect a proper crucifixion?'

'All he'd have to do is watch a movie,' Garrickson said.

'Not according to Professor Fillingham.'

'Could he not just be an assistant?' Shawna said. 'Hired muscle maybe?'

Heck blew out a long breath. 'Could be, I suppose . . .'

Garrickson chuckled. 'You suppose? That's big of you.'

Heck turned back to Gemma. 'Ma'am, it's only a gut feeling, but I thought we'd be looking for more educated suspects. I know it seems unlikely, but a writer, a historian . . .'

'Heck,' she said, 'are you seriously saying you want me to ignore a DNA lead?'

'No . . .' Belatedly, Heck realised that he was asking her to accept the impossible. Not only that, he was asking it of himself. You couldn't really argue with DNA. Cameron Boyd *had* to be involved in this at some level. Possibly, like Shawna suggested, as an enforcer. But still there was that element of doubt. 'Look, ma'am . . . while you lot are fixed on Boyd, why not let me make a sweep of all the college faculties in the Merseyside and Greater Manchester areas? Sixth form and up? See if I uncover anything.'

'On your own?' Gemma said. 'You know how many that's likely to be?'

'I'll have Andy Gregson with me.'

Garrickson pushed himself back from the desk and stood up. 'So first it was Charles Manson, and now it's the Nutty Professor . . . is that right?'

'Not specifically,' Heck said.

Garrickson rounded on Gemma. 'This is bullshit, ma'am. Your Minister Without Portfolio wants to go off on his own again. We'll end up with as big a body count as we had during the Nice Guys enquiry.'

Heck was about to respond to that by telling the DCI where he could shove his flash suits and prissy silk hand-kerchiefs, but Gemma cut him off.

'Heck!' she warned. Heck glanced at her and shut his mouth. 'I'm sorry,' she said. 'I can see you've given this a lot of thought, but I agree with Mike. We can't spare you, let alone you and Gregson. We're working under a time-limit. It could only be a day or so before these maniacs strike again. So for the moment we need to concentrate on hard evidence, not theory.'

'Or wild fantasy,' Garrickson added.

Heck knew that he'd lost the argument, and probably with good reason. They were still under-strength; that was a fact. And anyway, as soon as DNA leads came in, rival theories became insignificant. At the end of the day, all he'd offered was conjecture – meanwhile, the killers' clock was ticking. They needed to prioritise.

There was a knock at the door and Gary Quinnell entered. 'Sorry to interrupt, ma'am . . . but we've just had a call from SOCO. The print lifted from the book of matches in the burned wagon has been identified.' He checked the paperwork in his ham-fist before handing it over. 'Belongs to one Terry Mullany . . . from Manchester.'

Shawna half-gasped. 'Ma'am . . . Mullany's another Longsight criminal! He's on the list as a known associate of Cameron Boyd!'

Garrickson slapped the desk. 'That settles it.'

'Possibly.' Gemma maintained her cool. 'But we're not moving on them yet.' She called out: 'DS Fisher . . . can I have you in here please!'

Eric Fisher ambled in. 'Ma'am.'

'Two things,' she said. 'First of all, anything on the CCTV from the lorry park in Longsight where the burned Scania was stolen?'

'No useable images, ma'am. But other footage from cameras between Longsight and Manor Hill is still being examined.'

'Okay, good. Secondly, what's the next special day coming up?'

'Well . . . there's all sorts, ma'am. The Queen's birthday might be worth thinking about.'

'What date is that?' Garrickson asked.

'April 21,' Fisher replied. 'It's not got any underlying religious significance of course, but it's well known.'

'It's not that big a deal surely?' Quinnell said.

'Does it need to be?' Shawna wondered.

'We don't know,' Gemma said. 'Not enough to make assumptions either way.' She stood up. 'Okay, here's the plan . . . Mike, draw up a rota. I want two-man teams working around the clock, obbing every move these two bastards make, up until and if necessary beyond April 21.'

Garrickson nodded. 'Ma'am.'

'Eric . . . pull off everything you can on these two.' She handed over the paperwork for Boyd and Mullany. 'They're now our prime suspects. I want to know where they've been living, what they've been up to, who they've been seen with . . . the works!'

Fisher grabbed the documents and withdrew.

Gemma circled her desk with the air of someone who at last had a target to aim for. 'Heck . . . that print was an excellent spot. Well done.'

He nodded.

'Shawna, come with me. Did you have dealings with Boyd and Mullany when you were up in Manchester?'

'No . . . after my time, ma'am. But I can speak to some of the lads up there who will have done . . .' Shawna's voice faded as she and Quinnell followed Gemma outside.

Heck went out after them, but diverted to the vending machine in the corner. Claire was already in attendance there, blowing the froth off a beaker of steaming cappuccino.

'Kitchen kettle kaput?' he asked.

'Oh, hi,' she replied. 'No it isn't, but that instant stuff in there is so vile. Not that I'm sure this'll be much better.' She risked a sip and promptly pulled a face.

Heck smiled and got himself a tea.

'I've just seen your car,' she said. 'What happened?'

'Ah, that . . .' He tried to laugh. 'On-the-job wear and tear.'

'Is it drivable?'

'Not legally. Least, Gemma won't let me take it out. Borrowed another from the local CID pool. Volkswagen

Golf. About a thousand years old. No matter what, I always end up driving a shed. How are you bearing up, anyway?'

'No problem,' she said with a wry smile. 'Certainly being kept on my toes. I got in this morning to find eighty-five messages on the answering machine. One of them was from a TV documentary maker. He was wondering how close we are to wrapping this thing, as he's planning a new film about torture-killers, and he'd like to include "the Crucifier" – his choice of name, not mine – at the top of the show.'

Heck snorted. 'Murder groupies. That's something else you'll need to get used to.'

'I doubt they'd be so keen if we stuck them face-to-face with the real thing.'

'I'm not so sure, to be honest.' Heck swigged his tea, and tossed the empty beaker into the nearest bin. 'Look, I've gotta go . . . we've got some new leads.'

'Heck,' she said, as he moved away. 'Thanks.'

He glanced back. 'What for?'

'Everything . . . being a mate, trying to gee me up.'

'We all need a slap on the back now and then.'

She nodded and smiled, but he couldn't help noticing that she already looked sallow-faced, tired – and it wasn't yet mid-morning.

Chapter 20

When Gracie and Chantelle came round together in the pitch-darkness, all they could do was hold each other and weep.

It hadn't taken long for the grogginess caused by the drug to wear off, and the full horror of their predicament to seep through them. They were in an underground dungeon; they could tell that from the dankness and the stink – sewage of some sort was close by.

'This must be a game,' Chantelle stammered. 'Some kind of cruel, spiteful game.'

'I don't think this is a game, Chant,' Gracie replied.

'So why they doing this?'

'Can't help you there, darling.' Gracie didn't know where she was finding it inside herself to be the stronger one, even though she too was shivering with terror.

Some of the stories she'd heard in the past were so horrible that she didn't want to think about them: not just the girls who'd been murdered – murders were ten-a-penny; they were almost a relief after some other things she'd been told: girls who'd been held prisoner for years in wardrobes with only

170

tiny holes through which to breathe; girls who'd been found with their eyelids fastened down by superglue, their pussy lips stapled together; girls who'd been chained up in cellars and used as baby factories.

God alone knew what awaited them down here. Gracie had already decided that she would kill Chantelle before she let anything like that happen to her, and then she'd kill herself. She didn't know how she'd do it, but death by almost any means seemed preferable to prolonged torture and abuse. But whatever their predicament eventually demanded of her, all she knew at present was that she had to be strong for her childlike friend. So she stifled her own sobs, and wiped away her tears and the mucus running from her nose, and squeezed Chantelle all the harder, the younger girl's head resting on her shoulder. Gracie kissed the dry, ropy hair and brushed it down.

'Why do they do these things to us, Grace?' Chantelle wept. 'Why do they hate us so much? We don't hurt anyone.'

'I don't know, pet . . . I just don't.'

'All we do is offer a service. We're the ones who take all the risk, we're the ones who have to deal with the dirt . . . and we don't get much for it. A few quid, that's all.'

'I know, pet.'

'Remember two years ago when that bastard beat me up, lashed me with his belt until I could hardly walk? Called me a pox-ridden whore?'

'Yes I do.'

Gracie could hardly have forgotten; it was a Saturday night in high summer and she was the one who'd half-carried Chantelle to hospital, and had then stood alongside her in A&E, propping her up because there was nowhere to sit down. They'd waited there nearly three hours, being virtually ignored by the staff, who'd assumed from their tarty garb and smeary make-up that they were just another pair of slatternly girls who'd got too drunk in the city centre.

'Why would he do that?' Chantelle gabbled. 'I go for health checks all the time. I wouldn't go on the street if there was something wrong with me, you know that.'

'I know . . .'

'And that pretty little blonde girl. What's in this for her?'

'Who knows, pet. Maybe she's a prisoner too?'

'I don't think so . . .'

'No.' Gracie didn't think so either.

In retrospect, there'd been something altogether too confident about that platinum-haired totty-maude. A slip of a seventeen-year-old – she couldn't have been more than that, Gracie decided – approaching two street-walkers as casually as you like, not batting an eyelid at the squalid environment where she found them. How had a forty-four-year-old like Gracie not seen through it? It had been a well-rehearsed routine, she realised: telling them lies about porno films, offering silly money, providing a plush ride. It was like she did it all the time. Gracie couldn't conceal a whimper of her own at *that* thought.

'*What?*' Chantelle asked.

'It's nothing . . . it's nothing, pet.'

'*What . . . tell me?*'

'I hope you're happy, you little bitch!' Gracie bellowed into the darkness overhead. When she'd first woken up down here, she'd probed her way around the encompassing wall. There'd been no entrance, which meant they'd been dropped down from above – they were in a pit of some sort. 'You hear me?' she shouted, her voice so shrill it became a screech. 'You bitch! You nasty little bitch! This how you get your kicks is it, imprisoning people who've never done you no wrong?'

'Shhh!' Chantelle mumbled, pressing snot-stained fingers to Gracie's lips. 'You'll make them angry.'

Who cares? Gracie nearly said. *What can they do to us that they aren't already planning?* But she didn't say that. Instead, she pulled her friend close again and wrapped her arms around her. This time they sobbed together.

Chapter 21

After learning about Cameron Boyd and Terry Mullany, Mike Garrickson organised two sets of four teams whose brief was to spend the next few days pursuing round-the-clock surveillance on them.

In Longsight, Manchester – a shabby district by any standards – Heck, Gregson and three other pairs of detectives were to alternate eight-hour shifts, which they'd mainly spend sitting in cars across the road from Boyd's council flat, or idling along the dingy streets, dressed in scruffs, covertly following his every move, taking note of whomever he spoke to and keeping in touch by a reserved radio channel. Several miles away in Rusholme, an identical operation was being run with Terry Mullany.

If they hadn't known beforehand that Cameron Boyd was a criminal, it would be easy to deduce it. He was about six feet tall and well built, but there was a feral look about him: he was lean-faced, narrow-eyed and permanently unshaved. His hair was a greasy mouse-brown thatch, his cheeks pitted and scarred. His hands and neck bore the usual plethora of tasteless tattoos; his wardrobe consisted mainly of oily denims, old leather and army surplus. When he walked, he strutted, shoulders hunched and head thrust forward like a wolf. His mean-spirited attitude was evident just from his daily activities, though ironically he never did very much. The surveillance team rarely saw him before lunchtime, but usually around then they would tail him from his flat to the local fish-and-chip shop, or to the bookies, or to the newsagents where he'd buy himself a newspaper, some cigs and a carton of milk. Occasionally, he'd call in at the off-licence and reappear with a plastic bag filled with tins of lager. Everywhere, people stepped out of his way. He didn't open doors for the elderly or for mothers with kids; he casually flicked his butts onto the floor, and scrunched and tossed his beer cans and chip wrappers without looking for a bin. In the evenings, he made rounds of all the pubs and socialised with other rodent-like individuals, only emerging after midnight to totter home, usually stopping at least once to piss on someone's gatepost.

Even wearing his professional head, Heck found it difficult not to be depressed by the banal routine of Boyd's lifestyle: the empty days, the casual bone-idleness, the endless leeching off the state, the cosy acceptance that not a penny of this money was being put to good use. Heck was aware that he was being judgmental. But so what? That was part of his job description. Of course the one thing they didn't observe while they were tailing Cameron Boyd was crime. And this was the real crux of their frustration. While Heck still wasn't convinced that Boyd was the mastermind behind these murders, he was clearly linked to the case in some capacity – though that in itself, given the target's history of *routine* criminal offending, was a baffling mystery – and the desire to solve it had become a nagging imperative. If nothing else, Heck had assumed that if they sat on Boyd twenty-four-seven they'd eventually catch him doing something illegal, which would give them a way to get to him. But that hadn't happened. They were also interested in any lock-ups he might lead them to, as these could conceivably have been where the crucifixion murders had occurred. But Boyd apparently had access to no such premises, and neither, from what Heck was told by Shawna McCluskey, did Terry Mullany.

The ninth day of this tedious stakeout was the Queen's birthday, which, aside from brief news items concerning gun salutes in Hyde Park and at the Tower of London, generated minimal excitement. Cameron Boyd didn't interrupt his humdrum existence to celebrate it either. Or desecrate it. But as there were further special events coming up, a decision was taken to persist with the surveillance.

The day after the Queen's birthday saw Heck and Gregson spending more uneventful hours in yet another unmarked vehicle close to Boyd's flat. This time they were ensconced in the driving cab of a grubby old Bedford van parked about twenty yards down the street, rather than on the open waste-ground opposite. The new position required them to keep watch through the wing-mirrors and rear-view mirror, which seemed to demand extra concentration and was even more tiresome than normal. The van's interior was pretty odious too – grimy and damp, reeking of cigarettes and vinegar from the fish-and-chips the last team had scoffed. Not that this kept hunger at bay now that the end of the afternoon was approaching.

'Whose turn is it to get tea?' Heck asked.

'Mine, I suppose.' Gregson thumbed at his eyes to remove any last vestige of the forty winks Heck had allowed him earlier on. 'Usual?'

Heck grunted in the affirmative. 'Usual' could either mean a burger and fries from the McDonald's on the nearby precinct, a couple of greasy sausage rolls from the baker's shop just beyond it, or a bacon and ketchup bap from the deli on the next corner. He'd reached the stage where he wasn't bothered which.

Gregson, looking suitably like a workman in boots, jeans and a donkey jacket, slid out of the van and wandered idly away.

Heck continued to watch the rear-view mirrors, again wondering if it was possible they were on completely the wrong track. Could it be that his initial gut feeling had been correct, and that this case was nothing at all to do with Boyd and Mullany? The burning lorry in which the latter's thumb-print had been found could be a coincidence; the melted tyre treads hadn't definitively proved that it was the same vehicle that had been on the slagheap. But no; the discovery of Boyd's DNA was undeniable – that was something they *had* to find an explanation for.

Heck brooded on this for several more minutes, while outside the van the wind sent litter skittering down the street. This was Norfolk Avenue, which in an odd way sounded quite pleasant. Just as Suffolk Avenue – which was the next one along – did, and Cumbria Road beyond that, and then Hampshire Street and Derbyshire Walk. Pity they were all run-down crapholes with rusty, ramshackle cars along their kerbs, broken-down fences and gardens filled with festering heaps of household trash.

The door suddenly thudded open and Andy Gregson climbed back in, in more of a rush than usual. He handed Heck a bag containing a pasty and a can of Coke, and then thrust an evening paper at him. 'Check that out,' he said.

Noting the uncharacteristic flush to Gregson's cheeks, Heck shoved his food onto the dashboard, and unfolded the paper.

Its main image, which filled almost the entire front page, had been recycled from the numerous internet pictures taken of the crucifixion scene by passers-by on the motorway, though now the victims were less blurred than they had been. But that wasn't the worst of it. The gigantic headline read:

DESECRATION DAY!

Above it, there was a smaller strap:

Cops in desperate hunt for serial killer dubbed 'Desecrator'

Heck's hair briefly prickled as he read the opening two paragraphs:

With the blood still drying on the motorway bridge where twin mass murderers Jordan and Jason Savage were killed during a police chase, and the dust still settling after the furore caused by the crucial errors made in that enquiry, the Herald *can exclusively reveal that a new maniac is on the loose. This latest madman, who has claimed seven lives in a brutal six-month murder spree, is being referred to by the taskforce charged with catching him as 'the Desecrator' because he appears to be following a 'feast day' cycle.*

Despite taking great care to publicise himself, and using disgusting methods designed to desecrate our most beloved holidays and festivals, the unknown assailant has to date been murdering with impunity, the police apparently helpless to stop him.

The recent triple crucifixion on Merseyside, which so appalled the nation, is only a small part of this horrendous chain of events . . .

'They've got everything,' Gregson said. 'They've linked each case. They're even calling him "the Desecrator". How the hell did they get that detail?'

The name 'Desecrator', as unintentionally coined by Shawna McCluskey, had stuck. Nicknames tended to be adopted through force of habit in serial murder cases. In this case especially, with an unknown number of subjects, it had seemed easier for the team to simply refer to 'the Desecrator' rather than 'the perpetrators' or 'those responsible'. All along though, given the sensitivity of this investigation, Heck had thought it unwise to create so sensationalist a hook. Now he'd apparently been vindicated.

'One of your lot probably,' he said.

Gregson's cheeks coloured even more. 'You're saying someone in Merseyside's blabbed?'

'Or someone in SCU. What does it matter? Someone always blabs in the end. The press make it too worth their while. We were never going to keep this quiet for long.'

He laid the newspaper down, only able to imagine the anger on the top floor at Scotland Yard, and wincing at the thought of the phone calls that were now going to bombard Gemma's office. She got paid a lot more for undertaking such responsibilities of course, and maybe that was some consolation . . . but he was still glad he wasn't in her shoes at present.

'There'll be an enquiry,' Gregson warned.

'So there should be.' Heck sat up. 'Not our problem though. On the subject of which, what's the next big occasion to look forward to?'

Gregson consulted his notebook. 'St George's Day . . . that's tomorrow.'

Heck mulled it over. St George's Day. For some reason, that didn't bode well.

'The day after that is St Mark's Eve,' Gregson added. 'Don't know much about that one.'

'Supposed to be a good day for reading the future.'

'Great. Maybe they'll club someone to death with a crystal ball. The real biggie's in eight days' time according to Eric Fisher. April 30 . . . Beltane. Eric reckons it's a full-blown pagan Sabbath, *whoaaa . . . Boyd's on the move!*'

179

'Can't see him,' Heck replied, checking his own mirror. 'He's coming this way.'

Heck snatched the newspaper open again and slid down a few inches, so that it concealed him. Gregson bent into the foot-well as if to rummage through an imaginary tool-bag. Boyd sauntered past. They watched him warily as he receded down the road.

'You walked last time, my turn today,' Heck said, opening the door, then rolling the paper and stuffing it into his back pocket. 'Give me five, then bring the van. Don't call me, I'll call you.'

Gregson nodded and Heck slipped out. Fifty yards ahead, Boyd crossed the street and vanished down a ginnel. Heck followed as casually as he was able.

Initially, the pursuit took its usual desultory course through the endless warren of flats and maisonettes. But this time, instead of entering the local bookies or off-licence, Boyd pressed on through Longsight into West Gorton, where he entered a small corner shop café. Heck waited at the bus stop opposite, still reading his paper, watching covertly as Boyd sat in the window and wolfed down egg, chips and buttered bread. He used his mobile to summon Gregson, who appeared a few minutes later and parked the van in a side-street.

It was seven o'clock by the time Boyd shifted again, and daylight was waning. Two buses, now with headlights switched on, had passed Heck's stop without him climbing aboard. To keep up appearances, he'd jumped onto the third, getting off again at the next stop, and jogging back. He approached the café again, just as Boyd stepped out onto the pavement. Heck darted into a doorway, but Boyd headed in the opposite direction, hands jammed into pockets. A second passed before Heck continued the pursuit, calling Gregson and informing him.

Dusk was now turning to darkness; one by one, streetlights flickered to life. Some thirty yards ahead, Boyd entered a pub called The Hayrick. The name evoked an image of rural idyll; a cottage-style inn with a black-beamed exterior and thatched roof. But in fact it was a squalid-looking building, half redbrick and half grey plaster, with grubby windows and a rusted iron bar where the pub sign had once hung.

'Andy?' Heck said into his mobile. 'Where are you?'

'Hyde Road,' Gregson replied. 'Where are you?'

'The Hayrick on Gorton Lane. I'll go in and buy a round . . . like I'm meeting someone. Show up in ten?'

'Got it.'

The Hayrick's interior matched its exterior. It was filled with a dull, brownish light; its upholstery looked worn; and even though the smoking ban had been in force for a number of years, there were yellowish marks on the walls and ceiling, indicating how long it was since the place had last been decorated. The sparse clientele suited their environment. A bent old man with stringy, grey/green hair was seated at one end of the bar, nursing a large scotch. Halfway along it sat a middle-aged woman, overweight and wearing too much lipstick; her tight denim miniskirt exposed podgy white thighs encased in fishnet. Two lads, who couldn't have been a day over seventeen, their hair cut very short and shaved into fanciful patterns at the rear, accosted the fruit machine, arguing and swilling beer as they fed in coin after coin. Seated next to them was a bored-looking girl: again overly made-up, again in a miniskirt and high heels, though she couldn't have been much more than sixteen, despite the pram she had alongside her. Boyd sat alone in a corner, a lager on the table in front of him.

'Two bitters please,' Heck said. 'Pints of.'

The barman, who was twenty stone at least, with a beaten-up face and long, straggling red hair, served him without comment. Heck glanced sideways at the woman in fishnets. She smiled. It was a pleasant smile actually, warm and friendly; under all that slap she might once have been a looker. But Heck didn't bother speaking to her. He took the two drinks away, walking past Boyd's table – the criminal didn't even glance at him – and through an open door to the pool room, which was currently empty.

Heck chose a berth diagonal to the entrance, so that he could keep an eye on his quarry and, to maintain appearances, set the pool-table up. Five minutes later, Andy Gregson ambled in. During the time they'd been shadowing Boyd, he'd used a variety of watering holes. They hadn't followed him into this one before, though all were pretty interchangeable in terms of how depressing they were.

'Really knows how to live, this fella, doesn't he?' Gregson said, lowering his voice as they commenced a leisurely game of pool.

'Want my take?' Heck replied. 'He's laying low between jobs.'

'Yeah?'

'No one leads a life this uneventful. Apparently it's the same with Mullany. Pissed at night, lies in bed all morning, greasy spoon for his lunch, bookies in the afternoon, on the piss again . . . sees a few people, chats, goes home. Too easy, that. Him and Mullany are best mates. But they haven't seen each other in a fortnight. That's suspicious too.'

'Who's sitting on Mullany this evening?' Gregson wondered.

'Gaz and Shawna.' Heck downed a stripe. 'We'll get a conflab with those two tomorrow, and see what we know. Assuming nothing of interest happens tonight.'

Chapter 22

Though a Manchester cop for seven years before transferring to SCU in London, Shawna McCluskey had never worked on the E-Division, which was South Manchester. She'd been located five miles away in Salford, the F-Division, so only knew Cameron Boyd and Terry Mullany by reputation. She'd never dealt with them personally, nor any of the other criminals in this neck of the woods. As such, it had seemed a reasonable option to put her on a plainclothes stakeout here.

It was pure bad luck that Theo Taylor, a gangbanger, otherwise known as 'Mr Ed' because he had a mouthful of protruding yellow horse-teeth, should have turned up at this very moment. Over in Salford, Shawna had arrested him three times – once for burglary, once for having an offensive weapon and once for robbery. The latter of those charges ought to have sent him to prison for a couple of years at least, but his barrister had performed intellectual gymnastics over some legal technicality, which the judge had been swayed by, and Mr Ed had walked out a free man. Shawna and everybody else in Salford CID had felt cheated at the time, but the law was the law even if it was sometimes an ass. And ultimately it hadn't mattered much, because Mr Ed had dropped out of sight shortly afterwards, apparently having moved on, which they were all mightily glad about.

The problem was that he'd moved here, to Rusholme.

'DC McCluskey, isn't it?' Mr Ed shouted. 'I fucking knew it!'

They were in a supermarket at the time. It was unusual for Terry Mullany to do any shopping. Both Shawna McCluskey and Gary Quinnell had been caught on the hop by it, even if it did transpire that all he was popping into the store for was a case of beer. But it was seriously bad luck that they'd met Mr Ed in there as well.

'What're you going to try and fit me up with this week, detective?' he shouted.

Shawna stared down the aisle at him in disbelief. He was wearing a long yellow coat and a snazzy purple running-suit, an ensemble which looked vaguely ridiculous over his tall, gawky frame. He still hadn't had his teeth fixed – they were a mismatched bunch of yellow pegs – but he was laughing loudly as he approached, arms outstretched, a bunch of his idiot pals sniggering behind him.

'What's it to be?' he shouted. 'Shoplifting? Fuck, I haven't chosen anything yet . . . but hey, give it a go. I'll enjoy watching them rip the shit out of you in court again!'

Shawna was less concerned about Mr Ed than she was about Terry Mullany. She gazed the other way along the aisle in the direction of the tills. Mullany was at the rear of the queue with his case of beer, but he, like the other shoppers gathered there, had heard the fracas and glanced around. He fixed on her intently, perhaps finally thinking it odd that he'd glimpsed her, or someone like her, once or twice in the last few days – and suddenly broke from the base of the queue, chucking his goods and running towards her with heavy, clumping steps.

Shawna went rigid, not sure what he intended, but then

realising from his thousand-yard stare that he was actually looking *past* her. He was seeking to escape, not attack.

Mullany was a slobbish, toad-like individual, with a wide mouth, a broad, flat nose and eyes buried in pallid flesh. But he was at least six feet tall, and must have held a seven-stone advantage on her. However, Shawna had been raised in the GMP school of thought that the only excuse you could ever offer for letting a scrote escape was if he beat the living crap out of you.

So she stepped into his path.

Mullany kept coming.

She attempted to crouch, throwing her arms out, hoping to rugby tackle him around his legs. But all she caught was his denim-clad knee full in her face. Pain lanced through her head, along with a crackle of cartilage.

And then she was down on her back, the side of her skull smacking the floor.

'Hey!' she heard someone shout.

It was that buffoon, Mr Ed; probably bewildered – and not a little upset – that none of this was about him. Blood bubbled into the back of her throat as she craned her head around to look. Mr Ed and his cronies jumped to one side as Mullany's big frame barged past them, his left shoulder catching Ed in the chest, catapulting him backwards through a neatly-stacked pyramid of spaghetti tins.

'G– Gary,' she stammered into her radio. 'I've been clocked. The bastard's coming out the back . . .'

Mullany tore through the supermarket stock room, kicking boxes out of his path, cannoning into staff members and sending them flying. He ran outside via a goods door at the rear, jumping down from the concrete platform into a loading bay, fishing the mobile phone from his pocket. An engine roared and tyres shrieked as a dented Volvo swerved into view around the nearest corner.

The call was answered. Mullany didn't wait to hear his mate's voice; he just began jabbering. 'Leg it! They're onto us! Dunno where you are, just go, fucking go!'

When Gary Quinnell jumped out of the Volvo in front of him he looked so big that for a split second Mullany had trouble rationalising how he'd ever fitted into it in the first place. The cop wasn't just tall; he was as broad as an ox, with a neck as thick as a telegraph pole.

'Give it up, boyo,' Gary Quinnell said menacingly.

Mullany hurled his phone over the nearest wall, hoping to Christ that it would land somewhere like a river or sewer from where it couldn't be retrieved, and then tried to run again. Quinnell ballooned into his path. Mullany tried to change direction. But Quinnell blocked his way yet again.

The rugby tackle the big cop now put in was somewhat more successful than the one his female colleague had attempted. The brawny shoulder that smashed into Mullany's capacious gut felt as though it had cut him in half. The fugitive was flung down on the concrete with so much force that the air *whooshed* out of his lungs. Quinnell landed on top of him, eighteen stone of bone and muscle, his ham shank forearm crushing Mullany's windpipe.

'You're locked up, you little bastard!'

In The Hayrick, Cameron Boyd only heard the start of this commotion. He stood bolt-upright in shock, the phone clamped to his ear. White-faced, he pivoted around, gazing across the pub interior. There was nobody immediately, obviously suspicious. That slapper at the bar? No fucking way. The barman himself? That was a non-starter as well. He'd seen that fat bastard in here a dozen times. The kids in the corner were too young.

Then Boyd heard another phone ringing.

He peered left through the entrance to the pool room.

There were two blokes in there, weren't there? One of them had red hair, freckles and ludicrous ears. But it was the other one who Boyd saw answer the call – the lean, dark-haired fella – *he* now stood there with phone to ear, cue in hand. A rough-looking customer, but he seemed agitated. Then the one with the ears stepped back into view and gazed out into the main bar – his eyes locked with Boyd's.

And he knew.

Both of them knew.

Chapter 23

'Sorry Heck, I got clocked,' Shawna said into Heck's ear. She sounded half-dazed. 'Some fucking clown from years ago. We've had to lock Mullany up.'

With a crash, a table was upended as Gregson dashed from the pool room.

Heck spun around – just in time to see Boyd sprinting across the pub interior, glasses rolling in his wake, and vanishing through the door that led to the toilets. Gregson vanished through the door after him. Heck gave chase too. Both officers came under attack in the narrow, darkened passage. Boyd had hung on to his own pint glass and now flung it at them; it struck the wall and glass exploded, causing both to duck. Boyd ran on, leaving the pub by a rear exit.

'You alright?' Heck shouted.

'Yeah!'

'The bastard's running . . . you know what that means, don't you?'

'Pretty good idea, sarge!'

'Whatever happens . . . whatever, don't let him get away!'

Behind the pub there was a small car park. Its entrance was a rutted drive, which cut left around the side of the building to the main road. But a small alley branched away in the opposite direction. Of Boyd there was no sign. Heck and Gregson halted, breathless.

'Check the front,' Heck said, lurching to the alley mouth. 'If you don't see him, grab the van.'

Gregson nodded and galloped away. Heck was twenty yards along the alley, which veered downhill between sheer brick walls, when he heard a tin can clattering ahead.

'DS Heckenburg, SCU . . . to Echo Control?' he shouted, switching channels on his radio.

'*SCU?*' came the reply.

'Chasing a suspect for the Desecrator murders – down the alley behind The Hayrick pub! I need support fast, over!'

'*Received, sarge. We'll get someone there, over!*'

The alley's slope steepened. Heck passed a point where an empty can was rolling. Someone had just clouted it as they'd hammered past. The mobile bleeped in his pocket. He slammed it to his ear. 'Heckenburg!'

'Sarge, it's me!' Gregson shouted. By the rumbling engine, he was back in the van. 'Where are you?'

'Dunno . . . tell you in a minute. Try and get round to the back of the pub.'

He emerged from the alley on level ground. To his right a street led away between terraced houses, but directly ahead stood a one-storey, flat-roofed building, which looked like a working man's club. Beyond this lay open rough ground with a few parked cars dotted across it. Past those stood the tall, monolithic shapes of tower blocks. A distant figure was fleeing towards them.

'Got him,' Heck shouted into his radio. 'He's running past St Mary Magdalen social club, heading towards the flats, over.' He could hear sirens in the distance, but a long way off. The radio crackled in response, as messages were dispatched back and forth.

'Sarge?' Gregson bellowed down the phone. 'Can't find you!'

'This is the blind leading the blind, Andy! Follow the radio chat.'

Some distance ahead, Boyd vaulted over a metal crash-barrier, scrambled down a paved embankment and vanished into an underpass. Heck leapt over the crash-barrier as well and almost turned an ankle as he side-scampered down the flags. He staggered at the bottom and fell, only just avoiding scatters of broken glass. When he regained his feet, Boyd was already about eighty yards away, running full pelt.

'DS Heckenburg, *we need your precise location, over!*' came the voice of Comms.

Heck gave it as he ran, even though he knew his message would break up with so much concrete and steel above and around him. 'Target is Cameron Boyd!' he added. 'White male, thirty-three years old, strong build. Well known to your lot, I'd imagine. Wearing a black canvas jacket, white t-shirt, khaki pants!'

Boyd swerved left at the end of the underpass and disappeared. Heck skidded around the corner a few seconds later, and saw him racing across a kiddies' playground. The night was now filled with sirens. He spotted spinning blue beacons in his lateral vision, but they were still far away – hurtling over bridges in the wrong direction, or parked on flyovers, attempting to locate him. Meanwhile, Boyd ducked through a wire-mesh gate at the far side of the playground. Heck ran on, chasing him down the next street. Terraced houses stood down either side, and a row of concrete bollards sat at the far end, but just as Boyd reached these, a pair of headlamp beams slashed across him and a vehicle screeched into view on the far side. It was the Bedford van. The driver's door burst open and Andy Gregson jumped out.

Boyd came to a sliding halt. He whirled around, spotted Heck . . . and darted left towards a fence made from front doors nailed together. With the athleticism of the truly desperate, he sprang up, catching the top of this rickety construction with both hands, and in a single smooth movement, threw himself up and over.

'Back in the van!' Heck shouted to Gregson. 'Keep trying to head him off!'

The younger cop nodded and doubled back.

Drenched with sweat, lungs aching from the exertion, Heck scrambled up the fence and levered himself over – into a shadow-filled yard, where a small, bullet-like shape came at him, snarling. It was a pit-bull, but thankfully it was chained. Heck edged around it and stepped out through an open gate, beyond which a narrow entry cut left to the foot of a flight of steps. At the top of these, a single bulb glowed over an arched brick entrance. There was a clamour of splintering wood.

Heck galloped up there, three treads at a time. The entrance opened into a passage connecting various council flats. The first door on the left had been reduced to a mass of shattered softboard. Heck shouldered his way through. On the other side, a heavy, middle-aged man had clearly been seated in an armchair watching the small television in the corner; he was now on his knees, one hand cupping his nose, from which blood was flowing copiously. He regarded Heck with dazed eyes, and pointed through an open door.

'What address is this?' Heck asked.

'G– Gornall Rise,' the man stammered.

Heck relayed the details via radio as he raced through into a small bedroom, the window of which hung open. Beyond this lay a sloping roof. Heck climbed out, jumped down and hurried forward, rubber soles sliding on the rain-slick slates; on the far side he found an eight-foot gap between this roof and the next, from where a fire-escape zigzagged down twenty feet or so into a dismal alley. Boyd was already down there, dashing around a corner, scattering a clutch of wheelie-bins.

Heck backtracked a few yards, then sprinted forward and dived for the fire-escape. His body smashed against it hard and he just managed to catch hold, dangling there by one hand – rusty iron burning his twisted fingers – before he got to grips with it properly, and scrambled down. He charged around the corner, only to find himself peering over a steel fence into a vast canyon-like abyss. Below, traffic sped by in both directions. About fifty yards to his right, Boyd was making his way across an arching steel bridge. He reached the far side and disappeared up another entry.

Heck followed wearily. The entry became a tiled tunnel. Heck ran through it, to deafening vibrations from overhead. It sounded like a train, and indeed, a few seconds later, he bounded up another flight of stairs and came out onto the westbound platform of Ashburys station. As he'd heard, a train had just pulled in and was now idling there. It was a local connection, four compartments only. From what he could see through its grubby windows, quite a few passengers were travelling. He glanced along the platform. An elderly lady and two children were boarding at the train's farthest end. A young guy with a backpack was getting on closer at hand. There was nobody else in sight but the train doors had been open for at least a minute – Boyd could have got on board before Heck arrived. He loitered there, torn with indecision. A sharp electronic bleeping, warning that the train doors were about to close, jerked him to life. He threw himself forward, entering the nearest compartment. The doors hissed closed and the train jolted into motion. He'd moved so quickly that he almost overbalanced. But no sooner had he steadied himself than a figure seated not five yards away with back turned, jumped to its feet and spun around.

It was Boyd. He was ghost-white and gleaming with sweat, his hair a tangled, oily mop. 'Pig bastard!' he spat, spittle seething through rotted brown teeth. 'Had to fucking push it, didn't you!' He stuck his right fist under his left armpit and pulled out a long screwdriver, maybe twelve inches, its handle bound with duct-tape, its blade sharpened to a needle point.

Heck braced himself, but Boyd didn't charge. Instead, he retreated along the aisle. The passengers had finally realised something was happening. They froze or shrank away, terrified by the sight of the drawn steel. One of them was close on Boyd's right: a girl, about eighteen – a Goth, with fancy make-up, piercings and spiked, sprayed-green hair. She shrieked as Boyd grabbed her by the collar of her heavy black coat and hauled her to her feet, the point of his spike pressed against her throat.

'Pig bastard!' Boyd hissed again.

'Everyone relax!' Heck shouted. 'I'm a police officer, and there's no need for anyone else to get involved.'

'Yeah . . . let 'em know who you are, you fucking pig bastard!' Boyd laughed. 'You'll get this tart killed, and the rest of 'em. I'm fucking warning you . . . back off!'

'You'd better think this through, Cameron.' Heck advanced warily. 'You're in deep shit and you've got nowhere to go.'

The girl whimpered. The point was jammed so hard against her white throat that beads of blood were appearing.

'I'm warning you, I'll kill this bitch!'

'And I'll shove that thing so far up your arse you'll be picking your teeth with it!'

Neither saw the compartment door behind Boyd swing open as the conductor, a tall West Indian guy, came through. Even Heck, who was facing that way, only saw him when it was too late. At first the conductor looked startled by what was going on, but then his expression hardened – perhaps people had been mugged on his train before. He approached, lifting the strap of his ticket-machine over his head, only for Boyd to sense him at the last second. He planted a foot in his captive's backside and propelled her forward into Heck, before whirling around. The conductor swung a right, but Boyd blocked it with his left, and struck with his spike, not stabbing, but smashing it downward like a club, cracking the conductor on the bridge of his nose, splitting it crosswise.

The conductor tottered backwards and fell over a seat.

Somewhere between being thrown at Heck and colliding with him, the girl had fainted. Heck had to catch her and lower her to the floor. He looked up – just in time to see Boyd spinning the ticket-machine by its strap and hurling it. It was a heavy piece of steel and it came at him hard; he ducked, but it struck him a glancing blow on his temple, which sent him to his knees.

Hot fluid streamed down the side of Heck's face as he looked up again, trying to refocus – he glimpsed Boyd vanishing through the door at the end. Groggy, Heck blundered in pursuit, stopping briefly to check on the conductor, who still lay on the seat. The conductor, his handsome ebony face a mangled, gory mess, was dazed but conscious.

'Look after this guy!' Heck yelled to the other passengers, continuing along the aisle and at the same time shouting directions into his radio. When he entered the next compartment, the train was pulling into another station. The doors hissed open. Passengers who hadn't realised what was going on got up to disembark, blocking his passage. 'Out of the way! Police!' He tried to push past them.

At the far end, Boyd jumped out onto the platform. Heck swore as he shoved sideways, exiting through a nearer door.

People were crammed around him and he had to shoulder them aside, attempting to identify himself as he did. He looked up and glimpsed Boyd already crossing the narrow footbridge towards the station exit, which he would reach in a few seconds.

Heck glanced around and behind him.

Ardwick station was elevated over another busy road. Some forty yards away from him, across the westbound tracks, there was a chest-high stone balustrade. Two rusty iron hoops revealed an emergency ladder dropping down the other side. It would mean crossing two railway lines, but it would be quicker than trying to push his way over the crowded footbridge in pursuit. Heck didn't hang around to ponder the wisdom of this, just leapt down from the platform, and after checking the way was clear, sprinted over the tracks and vaulted on to the balustrade – only to discover that it was more of a drop to the road than he'd reckoned with. Some forty feet below, rivers of traffic shunted back and forth, engines echoing in the tunnels under the bridge. The ladder should have alighted on the pavement far below, though from this precipitous angle it didn't look as if it reached all the way.

Heck didn't have time to be concerned; he swung around and began to climb down, his ears ringing. The ladder was discomfortingly narrow; he could only descend it by placing hand directly below hand, foot directly below foot. When he reached halfway, he saw that it had been built in sections which slid over the top of each other. His weight automatically disengaged the first one, and he rode down for ten feet or so, juddering to a halt, the force of which almost dislodged him, though the impact of this then disengaged the third and final section as well – and he descended all the way to the ground. His grip slipped en route, and he plummeted the last five feet, but landed upright. He rounded the corner onto a cobbled side street – just in time to confront Cameron Boyd running towards him from the station exit.

The look on Boyd's sweat-soaked face was priceless; it would have been funny had Heck not been equally exhausted.

The felon veered sideways across the main road, threading between the honking vehicles, hurdling over bonnets. Heck followed, more horns blaring, more cars skidding to avoid hitting him. He had no breath left with which to respond to the shouts of abuse. Police sirens could be heard over the hubbub, but no blues and twos were visible yet. Boyd made it to the far side, and took a passage between two dingy shops. Heck bawled into his radio. 'Ardwick station! Crossing a main road . . . think it's Devonshire Street!'

At the end of the passage there was a tall, barred gate – but it stood open. Boyd had already passed through it and was now headed across a small, brick-strewn lot. Heck clumped after him. Just ahead, a chain-link fence separated the lot from an area of railway sidings, where cement-mixers, portakabins and parked-up JCBs indicated that building work was in progress. Boyd halted to pick up a length of rusty chain, and flung it. It struck Heck like a bolas, wrapping around his legs, and tripping him. This bought Boyd a little extra time, but now headlights came spearing through the portakabins and the plastic-covered piles of building materials. The Bedford van swerved into view.

'Good lad, Andy!' Heck shouted, extricating himself from the chain. He got up and staggered into the sidings.

Boyd blundered towards the railway line, though the tall mesh fence would prevent him going further than that. Hearing the van screech to a halt just behind him, he attempted to curve back between mountainous stacks of house-bricks. The one in front of him was only about four feet high. He climbed up on top of it, lurching across and trying to jump up onto the next, which was a couple of feet higher.

Heck was still about fifty yards away, but he saw what was happening. He also saw Andy Gregson climbing in pursuit.

'Where do you think you're going!' Gregson shouted. 'Fucking idiot! Give it up!'

Boyd continued up onto the next pile of bricks and the next one after that. Gregson was much the fresher of the two, not to mention younger and fitter. As they ascended from one level to the next, loose bricks shifting beneath their feet, he gained steadily. Boyd was about fifteen feet up and shinning his way to the top of the highest stack, when the first brick was dislodged beneath his sliding foot.

It was an accident – that much was plain; Heck saw it clearly as he ran forward. But the brick still fell six or seven feet before it struck Gregson in the face. The second fell a similar distance, as did the third, the one that caught him in the middle of his cranium. This particular stack had been poorly made. It comprised individual towers balanced against each other, rather than carefully-aligned layers. So when one of these now teetered over, another followed, and then another. As the entire structure fell chaotically apart, Boyd crashed to earth on the far side, gasping as the wind was driven out of him, but sufficiently aware of his peril to roll and roll until he was out of the way.

Andy Gregson was less fortunate. He'd already been clobbered by the first three bricks, and slumped half-senseless as the avalanche descended on him.

'*ANDY!*' Heck bellowed, his voice almost drowned by the clattering, cacophonous rumble. After several seconds wafting through a choking cloud of brick-dust, he found the young cop jackknifed backwards, half buried in broken bricks. His head and torso were completely hidden, but he was moving slightly.

'DS Heckenburg to Echo Control!' Heck shouted into his radio. 'Urgent message! DC Gregson down and seriously injured. Get an ambulance to the railway sidings off Devonshire Street now! Do it now! And get me some back-up for Christ's sake!' Frantically, he heaved lumps of shattered rubble aside. 'Andy?'

He uncovered a shirt thick with grime and blood, and then a severely battered face, both its eye-sockets and cheekbones busted at a guess, its nose flattened, multiple lacerations extending far above the hairline, from which fresh blood was throbbing. Heck placed two fingers to Gregson's neck to check his carotid; it was still pulsing – but the kid was losing his life-fluid at a rate of knots. Heck could hear sirens, but they still sounded far, far away.

'Get someone here *NOW!*' he bellowed into his radio. 'Casualty has a severe head trauma, and multiple other injuries . . .'

'I'm alright . . . sarge,' Gregson mumbled. 'Alright . . .'

'You're going to be okay,' Heck said. 'Ambulance'll be here in no time . . .'

A rattling of chain-links distracted him. He glanced up: not thirty yards away, beyond the fallen mound of bricks, Cameron Boyd was attempting to climb the mesh fence. Heck could barely conceal the snarl in his voice.

'I'll be back in one minute, pal,' he said into Gregson's ear. 'One minute, tops.'

Boyd, who looked too weary to climb further, had only made it to about five feet in the air; clearly his body was a deadweight. It should have been no problem for Heck to grab him from behind and haul him down. But again, with that jungle animal instinct, Boyd detected an enemy's approach. He turned and jumped down; his knees buckled and he was so tired that he couldn't evade the first haymaker Heck swung at him. It took him full on the left side of his face, sending him sprawling into the dirt.

'You don't have to say anything,' Heck said. Boyd tried

to crawl away on all fours. Heck kicked his backside. 'But it may harm your defence . . .' Boyd went into a forward roll, this time getting to his feet and reaching under his jacket, pulling out his spike; Heck grinned crookedly – now he could claim self-defence, '. . . if you fail to mention something you may later rely on in court.'

Boyd charged, spike raised. Heck met him in the throat with a forearm smash.

'But anything you do say . . .' Boyd lost his spike as he went gargling to the floor. Heck grabbed him by the sweat-soaked collar, and lifted him about a foot from the ground so that his next right hook would rocket straight to the jaw, '. . . may be given in evidence!'

Chapter 24

'I ought to inform you that we've photographed my client's injuries, and that we intend to make a full and official complaint,' the solicitor said.

His name was Snodgrass; he was immaculately suited, as they always were, but also tall and weak-chinned, with short sandy hair and pale, watery-blue eyes.

'Do so,' Heck replied as they walked down the custody suite corridor at Longsight Police Station. 'Both DC Gregson and I will happily tell any enquiry that we saw your client fall off a fifteen-foot pile of bricks.'

'He should be in hospital, not here.'

'The Greater Manchester medical officer has passed him fit for interview. That's good enough for me.'

'Your attitude is most unhelpful, Sergeant Heckenburg.'

Heck rounded on him. 'No, what's unhelpful, Mr Snodgrass, is your insistence on representing *both* of these . . . suspects.'

The doors to two separate interview rooms faced each other across the corridor. Gary Quinnell stood by the one on the left, Shawna McCluskey, who had almost as big a plaster across her nose as Heck had on his left temple, on the right. Terry Mullany was inside the room Quinnell was guarding; Cameron Boyd was in the other.

Snodgrass merely shrugged. 'As both my clients are being held on suspicion of committing the same offences, namely a series of heinous murders, it seems entirely reasonable.'

'It's not remotely reasonable,' Heck retorted. 'It's the oldest delaying tactic in the book, and it won't wash! You know it means we can only question our suspects one at a time. You're deliberately running the clock down.'

It wasn't normally his practice to be so bullish with legal reps. These guys were only here doing a job, despite the public's instinctive dislike of them; their serpentine skills were something many an embattled police officer had been glad of in the past. But while they were chatting, Gemma was at the Longsight Royal Infirmary, where Andy Gregson was undergoing life-saving surgery.

'You realise you're going to get torn apart in court, don't you?' Boyd grinned across the interview room table. It wasn't a pretty sight; his brown teeth were ugly enough, but now several were missing. Bloodstains were still visible around his swollen mouth.

'For what, Cameron?' Heck asked.

Boyd threw a cocksure glance at Snodgrass, who was making notes alongside him. 'For what, he says! Well, how about kicking my fucking face in while you were locking me up?'

'You resisted arrest, Cameron . . . very violently indeed. In fact you came at me with a deadly weapon.' Heck produced a sealed plastic package containing Boyd's so-called spike. 'For the tape, I'm showing Cameron Boyd Exhibit MH1, which is an industrial screwdriver, the tip of which appears to have been sharpened to a point. This is yours, isn't it, Cameron?'

'Never seen it before in my fucking life.'

'It hasn't been checked yet, but I'm pretty sure it'll have your fingerprints all over it, given that you were wielding it like a knife when you attacked me.'

'You planted them. Wrapped my hand around it while I was out for the count.'

'You also used it against a young girl called Sally Baines. She was on the train tonight travelling from Glossop to Manchester Piccadilly, the same train you boarded at Ashburys station at roughly nine-forty p.m. You may remember . . . you put her into an arm lock and pushed the spike against her throat. You actually drew blood, Cameron, you wounded her. And all she was doing was sitting there, reading a magazine.'

Boyd gave a nonchalant shrug. 'I'm sorry for this tart, but it wasn't me.'

'As well as Sally Baines, there was Martin Ruckworth. He was the conductor on the same train. Remember him? You smashed the spike across the top of his nose, causing him severe facial injuries. I'm sure you recollect that.'

'Same reply. Wasn't me.'

'Then there were all the other people on the train who also saw you,' Shawna McCluskey said.

Boyd glanced at her and shrugged. 'They'll have seen someone. I'm sorry this bad thing happened, but like I say, it wasn't me.'

'If that's true,' Heck said, 'after I confronted you at the exit of Ardwick station, why did you run off onto the railway sidings?'

'Now we're getting to the truth.' Boyd examined his chewed, dirty fingernails. 'I wasn't on that train, but I *was* at Ardwick. I was checking train times on the noticeboard. I'm off to see my mum tomorrow in Hadfield. I come away, walk around the corner, and there's you. Just jumped off this ladder. I didn't have a fucking clue who you were, but you look like a right thug, you must admit. You came straight at me, spooked me, I ran. When you started chasing, that's when I really legged it. What else am I supposed to do?'

'So you're claiming mistaken identity?' Shawna asked him. 'DS Heckenburg and DC Gregson were chasing someone else and somehow you got mixed up with that person?'

'Telling me that couldn't happen?' Boyd said. 'At night? The way this fella was going at it? Like a fucking madman, he was. Eyes rolling, sweat pouring.'

She smiled. 'It's an interesting story, Cameron. But the chase actually started when you ran out of The Hayrick pub in Gorton, where DS Heckenburg and DC Gregson had been observing you earlier in the evening.'

'Observing someone maybe. Wasn't me.'

'What we're really interested to know, Cameron, is why you actually ran out of The Hayrick in the first place,' Heck said. 'We've got your phone so we know it happened as soon as you received a call from an associate of yours, Terry Mullany.'

'Terry's a mate. Rings me from time to time. Doesn't mean anything.'

'So you admit you were in The Hayrick pub when you received that call?'

'What does it fucking matter? I haven't done anything wrong.'

'So why did you run like the clappers?' Shawna asked. 'Why were you so desperate to get away that you injured three innocent civilians, one of them severely?'

'Deny the incident on the train all you want, Cameron,' Heck said. 'But we've got your prints on the weapon and we've got witness statements coming out of our back pockets. All we need to do is put you in front of an ID parade, and all the people you assaulted, not to mention everyone else on that train, will pick you out with no difficulty at all. And that's before we even look at the CCTV footage.'

'Put-up job,' Boyd sneered. His demeanour was still that of someone who had nothing to worry about, but a trickle of sweat down his left cheek suggested otherwise. 'Always the same.'

'Let's try something else,' Heck said. 'Where were you on Bonfire Night last year?'

Boyd feigned amusement. 'Wait, don't tell me . . . you're trying to frame me for those Desecrator murders?'

'Where were you?' Shawna asked.

'Probably in some pub, watching fireworks I didn't pay for . . . like every other fucker with any sense.'

'Get over to Preston much, do you?'

'Never been there in my fucking life.'

'How about Yorkshire?' Heck asked. 'Get over there much?'

'As little as fucking possible.'

'Were you over there last December . . . specifically around Christmas?'

'No. I like to spend Christmas at home.'

Heck leaned back in his chair. 'We have a witness who says different. We have a witness who can't just place you in Yorkshire, but in Leeds, at the actual scene of the second murder.'

Boyd snorted. 'What fucking witness?'

'*You*, Cameron,' Shawna said. '*You're* the witness.'

Snodgrass glanced curiously up from his paperwork. Boyd was briefly speechless.

'You look a bit surprised,' Heck said.

'You're talking shite, that's why.'

'Is your DNA talking shite too?'

Boyd stiffened. Snodgrass laid his paperwork down. Heck

watched with interest. The criminal's taut body language registered fear rather than guilt.

'L– look!' he stammered. 'I don't know what you think you've got, but me and Terry never killed anyone.'

'You and Terry, eh?' Heck said. 'So you're at least acknowledging that you and Terry are in this together.'

'We're in nothing together!' Boyd raised his voice. 'You got that, you fucking pig!' Snodgrass placed a hand on his arm, but Boyd shook it off angrily.

Heck remained studiedly calm. 'So why did you both leg it when you realised we were onto you?'

'That was nothing to do with this.'

'What was it to do with?'

'You're not fitting me up for these fucking murders!'

'I'm giving you a chance to tell your side of the story.'

'You've got Terry in here too, haven't you?'

'He's in the next room,' Shawna confirmed.

'He'll be saying exactly the same. We had nothing to do with this Desecrator shit.'

'A denial is the very least the court will expect,' Heck replied. 'But so far it's *your* word against the forensics lab. The odds aren't looking too good, pal.'

'Excuse me, sergeant,' Snodgrass intervened. 'May I speak with my client in private?'

Heck glanced from one to the other – Boyd suddenly wild-eyed and nervous, Snodgrass unruffled as ever. 'Sure,' he said. 'Interview suspended, ten thirty-eight p.m.'

A few minutes later he and Shawna were out in the corridor, sipping tea.

'What do you think?' she asked quietly.

Heck shook his head. 'I think it's a load of bloody bollocks.'

'What do you mean?'

'Boyd's not a serial killer. He's a scrote who actually thought he was being clever in there by denying the blatantly obvious. A brainless idiot who thinks it's a victory to waste time in the interview room.'

'He's got a track record of violence that goes back to being a juvenile.'

Heck chucked his beaker in the nearest bin. 'What's in it for him? You've seen his form . . . he's a thief and a drunk.'

'Come on, Heck . . . we've got his DNA. It's got to be him.'

'I don't think so, Shawna . . . I really don't.'

Before they could say more, the door to the interview room opened and Snodgrass stepped out. 'Sergeant . . . my client would like another chat.'

'Oh, he would?'

'He'd like to confess.'

At first Heck thought he'd misheard. 'He's putting his hand up?'

Snodgrass replied with guarded confidence. 'Not to these murders, no.'

'A string of burglaries?' Gemma said, looking every bit as harassed as Heck had expected when he'd gone out into the police station car park to meet her.

As if the big development of the day – the Desecrator story going public – hadn't been stressful enough, he'd now had to hit her with this bad news.

'*Aggravated* burglaries,' he said. 'Pretty serious stuff.'

She slammed her car door closed. 'Him and Mullany?'

'Yeah. They've coughed to three.'

'Whereabouts?'

'Levenshulme, Fallowfield and Stockport.'

'Who's dealing?'

'GMP Major Crimes. They're on their way over. They obviously want to talk to us.'

206

'So this is why Boyd and Mullany ran?' Gemma said.

'Makes sense. They suspected the law might be onto them. It was, only for different reasons . . . course, they didn't know that.'

'And Boyd expects us to take his word for it? When the DNA tells us something completely different?'

'I'm afraid there's a bit more to it than that, ma'am.' Heck tried not to look as glum as he felt. 'We've just learned something else, having looked through his antecedents. Seems he's been inside recently.'

They were now entering the station. Shawna met them in the entry passage. She took up the story. 'He did twenty-eight days for assaulting a nightclub doorman, ma'am.'

'When?' Gemma asked.

'November 24 last year,' Shawna said. 'Until December 21.'

'Ernest Shapiro was walled into that chimney in Leeds no later than December 17,' Heck added. 'While Boyd was serving time.'

'So why didn't Boyd tell us that when we first arrested him, instead of 'fessing up to other jobs?'

'Because he didn't know Shapiro had been in that chimney for well over a week,' Shawna replied. 'He thought it happened around Christmas itself, when *he* was back on the streets and a viable suspect.'

Gemma stood silent, face white with disbelief.

'Ma'am,' Heck said gently, 'Cameron Boyd *can't* be the Desecrator.'

'So the evidence we found at the Christmas murder scene was a plant?'

He nodded. 'An attempt by the real killers to fit Boyd up for the crime. The burned lorry was also a decoy. That's why they didn't burn the actual driving cab, because that was where Mullany's fingerprint had been left for us to find. That was a decoy too.'

'That fire could still have reached the cab,' Gemma said. 'They took a big risk.'

'There was less chance of that if the fire was only lit shortly before we got tipped off. And the truth is we don't know when the fire was lit. In retrospect, it seems unlikely it could have burned all night.' Heck shook his head. 'I should have sussed that thumbprint at least . . . it was too perfect. Plus, it was *inside* the cab. Why would someone *really* trying to cover their tracks have gone back inside once the fire was started? If the arsonist was careless enough to drop his book of matches, he'd have done it outside. But they couldn't risk that in case it pissed down, soaked the thing and rendered the thumbprint useless to us. Someone's been playing us like a fiddle . . . but we haven't helped ourselves by missing the bleeding obvious.'

Chapter 25

'So who have you pissed off, Cameron?' Gemma wondered.

Boyd sat across the interview table, again showing his brown Halloween grin. He wasn't exactly happy with the turn of events, but he seemed pleased to have regained what he considered to be the upper hand. 'Dunno. How far afield are we going?'

'You're taking it very well that someone tried to frame you for a series of murders,' Heck said.

Boyd shrugged. 'It's only what you lot thought you were going to do . . . till you found out you couldn't.'

'Can you think of anyone in particular?' Gemma asked.

'Now you want my *help*? Are you fucking serious?'

'It's *you* this maniac has got his sights on,' Heck reminded him. 'Not us.'

Boyd snickered. 'What do you want me to say? I'm a fucking criminal. I make enemies both sides of the fence, and I always have.'

'Try thinking about it, Cameron,' Heck persisted. 'This person's a cut above the normal gutter trash you associate with. The matchbook with the fingerprint on it would be easy enough to obtain . . . probably taken from a dustbin at the back of Terry's house. But how the hell did your DNA end up on the Christmas victim? I mean, you being such a smart guy and all, I'm sure you'd have noticed if someone yanked out a lump of your hair.'

Boyd shrugged. 'Beats the crap out of me . . . oh, sorry, you've already done that, haven't you? Don't worry.' He grinned again. 'My brief's taken pictures. We're still going to rip you apart in court.'

The ICU, though quieter than it would be during the day, was still busier than most other hospital departments at this late hour. Soft-soled shoes whispered on polished floors as personnel busied themselves between the rooms, checking notes and providing medication to patients. Andy Gregson was in a special bay at the far end of the main corridor. Heck appraised him through an observation window.

The kid lay unmoving on a raised bed, his head invisible under layers of post-surgical wrappings and various feeding and breathing tubes. Cables connected him to a bank of bleeping monitors. He was also on a drip, which a young male nurse in blue scrubs was in the process of changing. Next to the bed, a very young woman – little more than a girl – was curled up on an armchair, asleep. No doubt this was Gregson's wife, Marnie. Her make-up was smeared and sweaty, her shoulder-length auburn hair in disarray. Some thoughtful member of staff had laid a blanket over her.

'Can I help?' someone asked in a Glaswegian accent.

Heck turned and found a stocky, red-haired woman alongside him. She too was in scrubs; the tab on her collar indicated that she was Mavis Malone, Head Nurse.

'Sorry,' he said, showing his warrant card. 'Detective Sergeant Heckenburg. DC Gregson's partner.'

She gave him a business-like frown, and he realised that

210

she was assessing his own state of health. 'You look like you've taken a battering yourself.'

'It's been a rough night.'

'Can I fix that dressing for you?'

'It's okay.'

'I think it probably needs it.'

Heck reached for his temple, and found only a sticky twist remaining of the plaster applied earlier. When his fingers came away, their tips were smeared red. 'Erm . . . maybe . . . yeah.' She smiled and led him to a side-desk. 'How's Andy doing?' he asked.

'He'll be okay.' She cleaned his cut, then carefully and delicately covered it with a fresh dressing. 'He suffered a depressed skull fracture, which the neurosurgeon managed to elevate without any complications. We also evacuated the extradural haematoma underneath. The CT scan would have revealed if there was bleeding elsewhere, but there wasn't. He's now on Mannitol . . . it'll help keep the swelling down.'

'No disrespect, but that's double-Dutch to me. Will he be properly okay? Will he be fit to work again?'

'If his recovery stays on track, he'll be perfectly fine.'

Heck moved back to the window, wondering why he didn't feel more relieved – probably because his senses were too dulled by fatigue. Beyond the glass, the young couple lay motionless; Marnie curled in her armchair, Gregson comatose in bed. They made a picture of damaged innocence. As a murder detective, that was something you saw often, but it always cut deeper when it was one of your own.

Heck trudged tiredly back through the ICU, attempting briefly, but unsuccessfully, to wipe all concerns from his mind. With the DNA and fingerprint evidence gone, the enquiry had reached another dead-end. Where they went from here, he truly didn't know.

'Don't worry, he'll be fine,' Nurse Malone said, smiling as he passed her desk.

Heck nodded in appreciation of the thought, but it was difficult to smile back.

Outside, the car park, which would be bursting at the seams during daytime, was now largely empty – apart from Gemma's BMW, which had just pulled up in the next bay along from Heck's borrowed Volkswagen.

'Do I want to go back in there?' Gemma said, getting out of the car and gazing reluctantly up at the huge, impersonal building, most of whose lights were now either turned off or dimmed.

Heck shrugged. 'Up to you, ma'am. But he's out for the count.'

'How's he doing?'

'Apparently he'll be okay.'

'And how are you?'

'Well that depends . . .' Heck sniffed and shoved his hands into his pockets. 'I'm tired . . . but I'm also wired. If that makes sense. Not sure I'll be able to sleep tonight.'

'You'd be as well trying. Here . . .' Gemma took a flask from her coat pocket; when she unscrewed the cap, there was an aroma of coffee laced with something else – Irish whiskey. She filled the plastic beaker and offered it to him. 'Not saying this'll help you sleep, but it's always a good anaesthetic.'

He took a couple of sips, before handing it back. 'What did you think of Boyd?'

'I don't think I've ever met anyone as stupid in my entire life.'

'He's looking to his own interests.'

'What . . . and he won't help us find someone who so hates him they'd fit him up for a series of torture-murders?'

'Like he said, there're loads of people who hate him. While

he's on remand he's protected. His problem now is how to wriggle out of three aggravated burglaries.'

She chuckled without humour. 'Good luck to him on that. Did you speak to Marnie Gregson?'

'She was asleep.'

'Pity. She might have welcomed a few words of comfort from the partner her husband's been bigging up to her.'

'He's been bigging me up?' Heck was bewildered. What the hell had he done to merit that? Had he impressed the young detective with his world weary air? How about his irreverent attitude and reckless self-confidence? That Gregson was so much a rookie he failed to recognise all this as insecure bullshit made him somehow even more endearing, and his injury infinitely more painful. 'I wouldn't have had many words of comfort to give her, would I?' Heck finally said. 'I couldn't even tell her Andy fell in a good cause.'

Gemma didn't reply to that. Instead, she glanced up at the sky. 'Feels like rain . . .' She hit her fob and the BMW unlocked itself. Once they were inside, she topped up the beaker and handed it over. Heck sipped again, glumly.

'You know, Mark . . .' Her tone became tentative; it was a rare occasion when she called him by his first name. 'It's been a soul-destroying day. But it's not all bad. No one else is going to say this to you, so I will. What you did tonight . . . that was an amazing bit of coppering.'

'Hey, I'm an amazing kind of copper.' But he didn't sound as if he believed it. He handed the beaker back.

'I just want you to know how glad I am that you're on the team.'

'So is this the carrot as opposed to the stick?' he wondered.

'You can be an obnoxious prat sometimes, but . . . can't we all?'

He watched glassy-eyed as an ambulance screeched to a halt in front of the double-doors to Casualty. An emergency team spilled outside as the paramedics eased a stretchered form from the rear, one of them carrying a saline drip.

'Me and you should have stayed together all those years ago,' he said slowly. 'We should have tried to stick it through.'

She sipped at the fortified coffee. 'Yeah, because that would make this mess go away.'

'Then we wouldn't have to do this in hospital car parks at three o'clock in the morning.'

'Excuse me . . .?' She glanced around. 'We're not doing anything.'

'Maybe that's the trouble.'

She gazed out front again. 'Don't view the past through rose-tinted specs, Heck. That way you never learn from your mistakes.'

'Mistakes?' Heck was vaguely aware that he wasn't really thinking straight; that he was dizzied by fatigue, but sometimes you saw things more clearly that way, didn't you? And now when he remembered he and Gemma's mutual past – when they'd both been hotshot young DCs working out of Bethnal Green together, under exactly the same stresses and strains, keeping similar frantic schedules, similar exhausting hours, and thus able to fall into each other's arms at the end of the day and get straight to the nitty-gritty without preamble – it didn't seem like it had been particularly ill-fated. Even with the advantage of hindsight. Neither phone calls in the middle of the night nor alarm bells at the crack of dawn had posed much threat to that relationship.

'Too much of a distraction all that stuff, Heck,' Gemma said, almost indifferently. 'We'd never have got on with our lives.'

'Well there's getting on and getting on, isn't there?' he retorted. '*You* may have managed it. But look at me. Look where I am.'

She glanced at him, half-amused. 'And you wouldn't have it any other way. Or so you never cease to tell people. What

214

was all that working-class hero claptrap you used to spout: "I'm an investigator, not an administrator. I'm a detective, not a suit." Yeah, yeah, very noble of you. But don't start giving me bloody sob stories . . .'

'Oh, put a sock in it!'

'*I beg your pardon?*'

'You heard.'

'*Bloody right I heard! Don't tell me to put a sock in it! I'm your supervisory officer, or had you forgotten?*'

'Yeah, must have.' He gazed at the ambulance again. 'You make that so easy.'

They relapsed into somnolent silence.

'Listen to us two,' Gemma finally said. 'Like an old married couple.'

'But without the good stuff.'

'Jesus Christ, lighten up. The last thing I need now is *you* flipping out.'

'Sorry, it's just that . . .' He sighed. 'Well . . . the truth is, I get lonely.'

'Make a move on Claire. You seem matey enough with her.'

'We're *just* mates, that's all. Anyway, Claire's struggling . . .'

'You don't say.'

'Don't get me wrong, she's sexy, she's pretty . . . but every time I see Claire, I see a scared little girl. And I don't want a little girl . . . I want a woman.' He glanced round at her again. 'Who I can make love to all night, as energetically and imaginatively as possible. Who'll snarl in my ear. Who, when I bite her, will bite me back. In short, I want a lioness . . .'

When Gemma eyed him this time, it was almost reproachfully. 'You're a real swine, you know that, Heck? *You're* the one who dumped me!'

'You think I need reminding?'

'I don't care.'

'I think you do.' And he leaned forward and kissed her. Full on the mouth, attempting to probe past her lips with his tongue – but she kept them firmly together. At last he relented and drew back.

'Feel better?' she asked coolly.

'Damn it, Gemma . . .'

She turned her ignition key; the engine rumbled to life. 'You're stressed, Heck. And worn out. You need some sleep. We all do.'

'You want me back. I know it.'

'Even if I did, would you want *me*?' She gave him a frank stare. 'Truly? Genuinely? And I mean for more than just a good screw? Be honest now. Because that would be a very big issue for both of us in the morning.'

'Okay.' He tried to wave the logic aside. 'It's just . . . times like this, you know?'

'Oh, I know, Heck. Except that times are not always like this, are they? Even in *our* world, it isn't every day when a bit of no-strings nookie can take your mind off the crap that's going on around you.'

'I really miss you,' he said.

She put the car in gear. 'You see me every day.'

'No I don't. I see a caricature. I see a front that you put on.'

'Yeah, course . . . I'm a suit.'

'I've never meant that about you . . .'

'Go to bed, Heck. Before you say something you *really* regret.'

He climbed sullenly out, closing the door behind him – only to get spattered by icy raindrops. She'd been right about that at least. In truth, she'd probably been right about the other stuff too. He tapped on the passenger window. She powered it down.

'Sorry,' he mouthed.

'That word's almost foreign to you,' she said. 'You sure you know what it means?'

'Not for saying I want to take you to bed . . . for calling you a caricature.'

'That was a new one, I must admit. Now step away from the car, sergeant. I'll see you in the morning.'

She drove from the car park in a swirl of exhaust, leaving Heck to soak in the deluge.

'That went well,' he told himself.

Though by the standards of the day, it probably had.

Chapter 26

'So the incident at Longsight was actually nothing to do with the Desecrator murders?' the first reporter asked.

'That's correct,' Claire replied.

'But it's true that a Merseyside detective assisting with this enquiry was hurt?'

'As you'll have seen in the official press statement, Detective Constable Andrew Gregson, who is normally attached to St Helens CID, last night underwent neurosurgery at Longsight Royal Infirmary. However, the operation was a success and he's already showing good signs of recovery.'

'How did it happen?'

'All that information is in the press statement.'

Claire was doing her best not to sound irate, but she'd slept poorly the night before. The last thing she really wanted now – at seven in the morning – was yet another confrontation on the station steps. On first rising, she'd taken one look at the slate-grey sky and drizzling rain, and had assumed it would put some of them off, but apparently not. Here they all were again, clustered together under brollies and anorak hoods, like a bunch of scraggy, scavenging vultures.

'I understand the two suspects are being held in connection with a series of violent burglaries that the Greater Manchester Police were investigating,' asked the peroxide-blonde. 'Are those burglaries definitely unconnected to the Desecrator crimes?'

'As far as we can tell,' Claire said.

'So why . . .?'

'Different police units do sometimes assist each other. It's not unusual.'

'With regard to the murders your people are *supposed* to be investigating,' said the seasoned Scouse hack in the toupee, 'can you be certain that only seven have been committed so far?'

Claire nodded. 'We're working on that basis.'

'But it wasn't so long ago when you were certain there were only three? At least . . . that's what you told us.'

'Does the name Tara Greenwood mean anything to you?' Miss Peroxide asked.

'I'm sorry?' Claire said.

'How about Lorna Arkwright? Those are the victims of unsolved murders dating from 2009 and 2010 respectively. April Fool's Day and Remembrance Sunday.'

Claire hadn't the faintest clue what the woman was talking about. She could do no more than ineffectually shrug. 'I'm sure . . . if you go back through the annals of unsolved crime, you'll find an unfortunate number of cases that coincide with special dates.'

'Yeah, but are *you* going back through these dates?' someone else asked. 'The public are very frightened, not least because the police team charged with catching these lunatics is the same team who ignored vital evidence and allowed the M1 Maniacs to claim five more victims.'

'The same police who arrested the wrong suspects in Manchester last night,' added the hack with the wig.

'The public have a right to know how much danger they're in,' Miss Peroxide said.

That was when Heck butted in. He'd been on his way to the MIR at the rear, but the sight of that pushing, shoving gaggle demanding to be 'allowed to do their job', was more than he could take.

'On the subject of the public and how much they have a right to know,' Heck said, appearing on the steps alongside Claire, 'Tara Greenwood was bludgeoned to death on April Fool's Day, 2009, in Lincolnshire . . .'

'Erm, who are you?' Miss Peroxide asked, bewildered by the sudden appearance of this rugged, intense-looking man with his cut, bruised features.

'DS Heckenburg,' he replied. 'You may recollect that the main suspect for the murder of Tara Greenwood was her live-in boyfriend Johnny Repton. He was charged but later acquitted after a number of witnesses drawn from his wide circle of friends came forward offering statements, which, though highly questionable in many cases, gave him an adequate alibi. Lorna Arkwright was raped and strangled in Humberside on Remembrance Sunday, 2010, after being grabbed walking home from a nightclub. The chief suspect in that case was Wayne Hubbard, an escaped convict who had been serving time for three other rapes. Hubbard remains the chief suspect to this day because he was never apprehended – he was smuggled abroad by friends after having first been given refuge in various different houses on his home estate. It was while he was hiding there that he is believed to have committed the attack on Lorna Arkwright, who, for the record, was only thirteen years old. So, on the subject of the public and how much they need to know, perhaps the question you should be asking is how much do they already know?'

He treated the silenced crowd to a frank stare. 'Sometimes it's more than you may think. That's all for this morning.'

He turned and steered Claire back inside. There was a renewed clamour of questions behind them, but he closed the station door.

'I . . . I have some more updates to give them . . .' she stammered.

'Never mind.' He led her through the personnel door, then through the police station to the rear, where they crossed the car park.

'Christ,' she said, as the full import of what he'd just done dawned on her. 'I can see the headline now – "Public to blame for Desecrator killings!"'

'Ultimately they are, aren't they? Who creates these monsters if not society?'

'Those kinds of headlines aren't what Operation Festival needs at this moment . . .'

'They're headlines, Claire. They have the lifespan of a day. We can live with them.'

They'd reached the annexe, but Claire stopped. She didn't want to go inside in her current state. Angry tears sprang to her eyes. 'For God's sake, Heck! It's alright for you . . . but they're going to come back at me about those unsolved murders, and maybe other ones. I don't know anything about them!'

'Speak to Eric Fisher,' he said, handing her a tissue. '*He* does.'

'What do you mean?'

'Claire, we weren't born yesterday. We've already pulled off every unsolved murder that coincides with one of these special dates, going back five years. None of them are a match. In nearly all cases there were viable suspects who avoided getting jailed by the skin of their teeth. Talk to Eric. He'll bring you up to speed.'

'Someone should have told me that before,' she said, her voice sharpening even more.

'You're right. They should.'

'I felt a complete fool out there . . .'

He wanted to respond that she was part of this enquiry too, so the onus was on her to do some research of her own. He knew she rarely had a minute to spare from her other duties, though it wouldn't have hurt if she'd at least raised the question. But Claire was currently undergoing a baptism of fire, and Heck was already beginning to suspect that she wouldn't emerge from it unscathed. Or that any of them would, for that matter. He himself wasn't going to enjoy meeting Gemma today; not after the way they'd parted last night.

Typically, Gemma was the first person he saw on entering the MIR. She was walking straight towards him, in company with Mike Garrickson. Both had coats on.

'There's been another one,' she said before he could ask.

Heck halted in mid-stride. In all the excitement, he'd completely forgotten that today was St George's Day. He glanced at Shawna McCluskey, who was seated at a desk to one side. She looked physically sick.

'Be a piece of cake finding anything in here, won't it?' Charlie Finnegan complained from the back seat of Heck's Volkswagen when they pulled up on the car park at the front of Horwich Zoo. 'How many punters must pass through this place every day? A thousand, two . . .'

'Give it a rest, Charlie,' Shawna said. 'We all know this is going to be a bag of shit.'

They climbed out and stood on the rain-wet car park.

'Plenty of CCTV anyway,' Gary Quinnell remarked, glancing along the zoo's perimeter wall, which was about fifteen feet tall and sported security cameras every fifty yards or so.

'I've stopped putting my trust in technology,' Shawna replied. 'It hasn't helped us once yet.'

Heck said nothing. It was now almost noon, but there was a chill in the air and the skies had darkened; the drizzle persisted, smudges of blue light flickering across the soaked tarmac. GMP officers stood in quiet huddles, rain glinting from their fluorescent slickers. A few yards away, Gemma climbed from her BMW, shrugging into her raincoat. Garrickson climbed out after her. Claire was also in Gemma's car, but she made no move to get out; presumably she was under instructions to wait behind. She regarded Heck through the window with no visible emotion. He tried to smile, but she didn't smile back. If he was honest, his own effort didn't amount to much.

'Make sure we stick to the public areas please,' Gemma said, leading them through the zoo's main entrance. 'Obviously avoid any zones that have been taped off for examination.'

'Yet more cameras,' Quinnell observed as they passed into an assembly area with toilets on one side and souvenir shops on the other, all closed. 'What about security guards?'

'There were two security guards,' Garrickson said. 'Two old boys. Clock-watchers waiting to retire. They were the ones who raised the alarm this morning.'

'They didn't see anything at the time?'

'Not likely. They were out cold on flunitrazepam.'

Quinnell glanced around. 'That's the same drug that was used on the crucifixion victims.'

'Correct.'

'How'd they get dosed?' Shawna asked.

'Seems one of them was in the habit of going out for a smoke . . . so he used to leave the emergency door open at the back of their office. That door also connected with the kitchenette where they kept their tea-making stuff.'

Quinnell looked impressed. 'Perps did their homework.'

'I think there's more to it than that,' Heck said. 'But we'll know for sure when we check the security footage. If they know their way around this place *too* well . . .'

'What do you mean?' Shawna asked. 'Inside job?'

He shrugged. 'The public only get to see a quarter of what happens in places like this. If the perps know this zoo like the backs of their hands, it's something to consider.'

Gemma had now consulted the large map-board in the centre of the assembly area, and strode on without speaking. The others followed.

Horwich Zoo, one of the oldest in England, having been opened in the 1930s, had a viewing area covering a hundred acres, but a total land-holding of about three hundred. It was a hugely popular attraction, and, according to *Forbes*, consistently figured among the best zoological gardens in the world. It was constructed in that typical family-friendly way, tarmac paths snaking between manicured profusions of jungle-like vegetation, branching repeatedly, ascending onto walk-overs, descending into foot-tunnels, in all cases giving maximum vantage on the numerous animal enclosures, most of which – this being the start of the summer season – were occupied: the big cats prowled their cages; giraffes tore at the overhanging leafage; chimpanzees sat in rain-damp huddles on their moated islands, watching quietly, as if aware that something out-of-the-ordinary was happening. There were also picnic areas filled with tables and chairs made from bamboo, and playpens containing climbing frames and swings. All were empty, save for the occasional GMP bobby, clad neck to toe in fluorescent green and glistening with rain.

They approached the Reptile House along a looping side-path stencilled with images of serpents and lizards. The exterior of the building had a look of faux Victoriana, with a spired roof, green terracotta tiles on the walls, and tall, narrow stained-glass windows depicting tropical flora. They halted only briefly, to gaze up at a security camera on the building's southeast corner, the lens of which had been punctured by an aluminium arrow.

'How close would you have to be to make a shot like that?' Shawna wondered.

'A normal human wouldn't even be guaranteed to make it from here,' Quinnell said.

'This *is* a normal human,' Garrickson countered. 'Let's not get carried away.'

No one argued with him. But no one agreed with him either.

The killers had apparently entered the Reptile House through a service door at the rear, which they'd smashed down with sledge-hammers after first deactivating the alarms by clipping the outside cables with wire-cutters; further proof in Heck's mind that they were intimately familiar with this place. Inside, a grim-faced uniform introduced himself as Inspector Perkins from Bolton Central, and said he'd take them up to one of the viewing galleries where the intruders had not been. Rain drummed on the roof tiles as they ascended, streaking down the outside of the stained-glass windows, filling the dim stairwell with trickling shadows.

They at last came to a steel railing, where various cameras and powerful halogen lights were already in position, and gazed down through a slanted Perspex roof into a pit some ten feet deep and about thirty feet by twenty in circumference. At least two thirds of it was filled with greenish water, though now a red scum floated on the surface. Lush, equatorial vegetation grew around its fringes.

Its usual occupant, a twenty-foot-long male crocodile, had been removed to a containment area in a different part of the building, while two medical examiners, wearing waders as well as the usual Tyvek coveralls, made investigations around what remained of its last meal.

'St George's Day,' Eric Fisher said, somewhat unnecessarily. 'We should have seen this one coming.'

'No one could have seen this coming,' Garrickson replied. Even he had been jarred by what he was now viewing.

That the victim had once been human was evident, but only because it still had a torso, and four partial limbs, all of which were gruesomely mutilated, the skin entirely torn away, the flesh and musculature pulled from the bones. Its internal organs had been rent out in a mass of glistening, slimy ravels, and though a head was still attached to the neck, it had been crushed into something non-identifiable, shards of white bone glinting through the flaps of ravaged flesh and tufts of thick, blood-sticky hair. The face no longer existed. The single length of chain with which the victim had been bound was still in evidence, still padlocked in place in fact, while rags of gore-soaked clothing were scattered in the vegetation. One pink high-heeled sandal, containing a severed foot complete with green toenail polish, lay on a mud-bank at the edge of the pool, revealing that the victim had been female.

'Apparently Congo just worried at her,' Inspector Perkins said in a dull voice. 'Or else there'd be nothing left at all.'

Garrickson glanced sidelong at him. 'Congo?'

'The croc that did it.'

'What do you mean "worried at her"?' Gemma asked.

Perkins shrugged. 'The animals here are well fed. So he wasn't hungry.'

It was Heck who eventually gave voice to the numbing horror they all felt. 'You mean he just . . . played with her.'

Perkins nodded and swallowed. He couldn't take his eyes off the butchered horror lying below; his face was white as a bowl of curdled milk. 'All night, they reckon. He was still at it at six this morning, when the security lads arrived.'

'Jesus, Mary and Joseph,' Shawna breathed.

She hadn't intended it as a prayer, but Gary Quinnell continued it in that vein: 'Have mercy on us all . . . and this poor soul, who died here alone and in such pain.'

None of the others held religious beliefs, but none of them objected.

Chapter 27

Overnight, Horwich Zoo became the biggest crime scene in British history, but as Charlie Finnegan had said, it was a nightmare gleaning any useful information from it. Despite the preponderance of cameras at the site, there was surprisingly little security footage that they were able to use, which appeared to reinforce Heck's suspicion that the perpetrators had been on familiar ground.

In an observational report, he wrote:

The intruders at the zoo either had an accurate floor-plan, or already knew the procedures in minute detail. Evidence of this can be found in their highly efficient assault on the zoo's security staff – which, owing to the complete lack of physical evidence in the security cabin's kitchen area, was most likely achieved by a single infiltrator – and the speed with which the rest of the team moved so unerringly from their point of entry, the wall at the zoo's northeast corner (only 8ft high and overlooking a stretch of unoccupied wasteland known locally as Red Moss), to the Reptile House, a journey of nearly 500 yards. In both cases these separate journeys were made in complete darkness and without use of electric torches.

It is also noteworthy that, in both cases, the intruders managed to avoid all the zoo's main CCTV points. We know this because the route they chose to the Reptile House was not the most direct one. They circled south around the lion and tiger enclosures, but could have halved their journey time by cutting these out altogether. Of course, if they had done that it would have taken them past the Nocturnal Forest attraction, where there are two camera stanchions facing east and west. They also circled around the rhino and camel enclosures instead of taking a shorter route past Lemur Island. In both cases they would have been forced to pass a camera, but the camera next to Lemur Island, which they avoided, is functional, while the camera at the junction of the camel and rhino pens, which they chanced, is not.

Another clue can be found in the camera overlooking the southern approach to the Reptile House. This one was also operational, and the intruders would have had no choice but to pass directly beneath it in order to enter. Thus, the target arrow that shattered its lens and put it out of action, does not just indicate that the archer responsible is highly skilled and proficient (as also proven in the two deaths on the West Pennine Moors in February), it also proves that the perpetrators were fully conversant with the threat posed by this particular camera, and had made plans beforehand to deal with it.

All of this suggests knowledge of the zoo's security arrangements, which goes far beyond the norm. It is my strong recommendation that every member of staff at Horwich Zoo be assessed and interviewed rigorously.

For all this, the killers hadn't completely avoided visual detection. From some distance away, a camera perched on the roof of the aviary had captured a snippet of them proceeding along the walkway past the rhino enclosure just after two o'clock in the morning. There were five or six of them – the exact number wasn't totally clear. All were clad in dark clothing, including hoods and masks, and were bundled with rucksacks. Chillingly, two of the figures had carried a struggling shape between them, which looked as if it had been swathed in a bed-sheet. They had clearly entered the complex from its northeast corner because, though the ladders they'd used to scale the wall had been removed, there were imprints in the ground next to the wall's footing, plus a strand of barbed wire at the top had been freshly cut away.

As with the other murders, it seemed to take a painfully long time just for these meagre details to come to light. The team flogged through hours and hours of footage before finding what they wanted. Forensic examination of the route the killers had taken would drag on for another day at least, and so far had uncovered nothing.

Meanwhile, the world outside the besieged sanctuary that was the MIR at Manor Hill appeared to be falling apart. On every news channel there was uproar; the dailies were going crazy. Claire's face was constantly on TV, looking ever more tired, ever more harassed. The other morning, her first reaction on seeing photographs of the obliterated corpse had been to stagger to the toilet and vomit. To be fair, she wasn't the only one.

Thanks to the mangled state of the as-yet-unidentified victim, it was the best part of a very stressful week before a full pathology report was available. Gemma assembled everyone she could in the MIR when she finally received the information.

'The victim is a white female, aged somewhere in her mid-to-late twenties,' she announced. 'You'll be relieved to know . . . *possibly* you'll be relieved to know, that most of the damage inflicted on her body was post-mortem. The actual cause of death was cardiac aneurysm. The AP, whoever she was, already had a damaged heart, probably as a result of alcohol or substance abuse. In this weakened state, it was unable to withstand the extreme anxiety she suffered when she was lowered . . .' Briefly, Gemma had trouble forming the relevant words; for an alarming second, Heck thought she was going to burst into tears. 'When . . . she was lowered into the crocodile pool. In other words, ladies and gentlemen, she died of fright.'

No one replied as the awfulness of such a thing washed over them. Certainly no one felt in any way relieved. Okay, it was perhaps marginally preferable to being systematically dismembered by a giant bull-crocodile over a period of several hours, but just trying to imagine the extent of terror that must have struck the poor woman was almost impossible. Just how frightened did you have to be to self-induce death?

Heck met Claire's gaze from across the room. Her face was grey, her eyes tearful.

Gemma placed the document on a table, where everyone could read it for themselves. 'There are firsts in everyone's career,' she said in an oddly conversational fashion. 'But I don't think I've ever experienced quite so many in one particular enquiry.'

'And we've absolutely no idea who she was?' Shawna McCluskey asked.

'We're running her DNA obviously,' Gemma replied. 'No hits as yet.'

'Alcoholic?' Eric Fisher said. 'Druggie? Surely we'll have her on file.'

'Maybe, maybe not . . . we don't round toms up like we used to.'

'We sure she was a prozzie, ma'am?' someone else asked.

'What's left of her clothing would seem to indicate that.'

Visuals of the AP's clothing – ribbons of black nylon stocking, ripped fragments of black string vest and of course that pink high-heeled sandal – were already up on screen behind her. Heck observed them carefully. Sometimes in modern Britain, it was difficult to tell girls on the game from girls out binge-drinking – both from their behaviour and their scanty clothing – but there was something tawdry and lived-in about these shredded articles, suggesting that they weren't just Saturday night attire.

'In which case we need to start looking at missing persons reports,' he said. 'Focusing on prostitutes and drug addicts.'

Gemma nodded vaguely. It would take forever of course. Britain's sex-workers were a transient population at the best of times. That said, any lead was a lead, and it wasn't as if they hadn't picked up other leads from the zoo as well. The chain that had bound the victim was being meticulously examined. Polished metal was always a good bet with the forensics boys. It preserved prints nicely, and in addition, if it was hinged, jointed or articulated, like a chain, there was a good chance that body traces would be retained: skin might have been pinched or hair snagged. Officers had also been dispatched to collate footage from the speed and traffic cameras in the area, and there were plenty of those.

This was all good stuff, and yet Gemma didn't respond positively, at least not immediately. Heck watched her bodylanguage; he'd never seen her look so dispirited.

'We also need to consider that it's two days to Beltane,' she added. 'When Eric first drew up his list, he reckoned that was the most likely date this month to be marked with a . . . sacrifice, desecration, whatever you want to call it.'

'Could they really mount another so soon after the last one?' Charlie Finnegan asked.

Gemma shrugged. 'We don't know. We don't know anything. But think about it, people . . . April 30. Beltane, or Walpurgis Night as it's known in parts of Europe, is one of the biggest festivals in the occult calendar. We're talking witches, druids, demonology.'

'It's tailor-made for something bad to happen,' Gary Quinnell said.

'Agreed . . . but as we don't know where or even what form this bad thing will take, there isn't much we can do to prepare.' Gemma shrugged again. 'All I can say is be aware of it. Keep your eyes to the ground, and your ears open. That's it for now.'

The team jolted back into life; Heck continued to watch Gemma, concerned at how lost she looked in the midst of the bustle. It only lasted for seconds and then she was back to her efficient self – raising her voice to issue commands, berating everyone for their tardiness – but Heck hadn't liked what he'd just seen. Gemma had always been the cool head, the pillar of strength, the supreme organiser – but perhaps for the first time the weight of an operation that was expanding unmanageably in almost every direction was getting too much.

Ten minutes later, she called him into her office and had him close the door. She sat behind her desk, from where she appraised him carefully. 'It's probably a bit late in the day to ask you this, but I don't suppose you've ever encountered anything similar to this?'

Heck shook his head. 'I've never even heard of anything similar to this.'

She knuckled at her brow. 'Of course, it's just a murder

enquiry like any other. We mustn't let the ghoulish elements distract us. It needs to be dealt with in the same time-honoured fashion.'

But the tone with which she said this alarmed him, because he could tell she wasn't attempting to instruct him as much as herself. She looked tired, stressed and – though he wouldn't exactly have said 'vulnerable'; 'Gemma' and 'vulnerable' were two words that could never appear in the same sentence – there was an unguarded weariness about her, as if she was briefly off her game and didn't mind people knowing about it. Or at least didn't mind *him* knowing about it. He wondered in what capacity she'd asked him in here: underling, colleague, friend . . . or something else?

'So we've got to focus, Heck. You especially. Not that you haven't been so far . . .' She gave him a look that was almost a plea. 'But I need my best fighters in absolute peak form . . . or I'm worried these bastards are going to beat us.'

'They won't,' he said. 'I guarantee it.'

'They'll have beaten us if they do it one more time. Never mind a hundred more, and at present they seem to be going for the record.'

'We'll get them.'

She stood up and pulled on her suit jacket. 'Well hold that thought. We're off to Strangeways Prison.'

'Strangeways?'

'The remand wing. Apparently Cameron Boyd would like a chat. Don't worry . . . I'm not asking you along to hold my hand. He specifically requested to speak to *both* of us.'

When they headed out into the MIR, it felt more cramped, crowded and noisy than ever. Despite the expense, Gold Command had been in no position to ignore Gemma's requests for increased manpower. This meant that extra desks had needed to be crammed into minuscule spaces, and more computer terminals and phones added, all of which contributed to the general clamour. In the heart of all this, Heck came face to face with Claire, who was rooted in front of a display board plastered with images from the crime scene at the zoo.

For once she hadn't bothered to do anything with her hair or make-up. Her cheeks were pale as ash. Even her peppermint eyes had lost their lustre.

'You look terrible,' he said, startled.

She nodded at the images in front of her. 'I could be worse.'

'Why don't you go out and get some air?'

'Yeah, and be mauled to death by the press pack. Again.'

'Claire . . .'

'There used to be a phrase, didn't there? The banality of evil.' Her voice was almost tearful, and yet she remained distracted by the crime scene photographs, fixated on the grotesque imagery as if trying to find some sense in it. 'It means the most wicked deeds are often committed by little people who otherwise don't matter. But the people who've done this matter, don't they, Heck? There is nothing banal about this!'

'Claire, listen . . .'

She shook her head. 'This is beyond anything I ever imagined. I'm not naïve, I knew I'd be seeing gory, upsetting stuff. I was nervous, but I thought I could deal with it. But I'll be absolutely honest with you . . . I'm not sure I can. I really don't think I'm up to *this*.'

Heck glanced towards the door. Gemma had already gone outside to the car.

'Claire, we're all affected by . . .'

'Don't give me that, Mark. You're not. Not *you*.' It was a tone of near-accusation. 'You're in your element here. You might say you hate it, and on the surface you probably do. But this is what you're good at. It's what you live for. Some people would be impressed by that, but I . . . I can't even comprehend it.'

She turned and headed back to her own office, in which the telephone, yet again, was insistently ringing.

'We'll talk later,' he said after her.

She waved without looking back.

Outside, Heck volunteered to drive and Gemma accepted, which was a rare event. However, once they were on the road, she seemed to get herself together, glancing into her compact mirror and cringing at what she saw. She took a brush from her handbag, combing out her unruly ash-blonde locks, and then applied some fresh lipstick and eye-liner. Gemma was not the sort to over-emphasise her looks, but she knew that she was handsome and never hesitated to put this front forward – anything that added strength was to be embraced.

'Good idea,' Heck said.

'What is?'

'Licking yourself into shape. The troops'll appreciate it.'

'Yeah, because we can't have them taking orders from some bird who isn't hot to trot.'

'You know what I mean. If they see *you're* cracking up, they'll go the same way.'

'I know.' She snapped her compact closed. 'But . . . Christ, Heck, I'm dreading what may happen in two days. I mean . . . Beltane. Used to mean nothing. Was a word I heard occasionally on devil-worshipper movies. Now . . .?' She shook her head.

'If it was that simple, all we'd have to do is stake out the nearest deconsecrated church,' he replied.

'Tell me again about this theory of yours . . . that some twisted intellectual is behind these killings.'

'Well . . .' he began. 'There's an educated mind at work here, even if it is pretty warped . . . but I'd be kidding myself

236

if I didn't admit that things have got so weird that even I'm not sure what's going on. Someone's either trying to mock these ancient festivals, or draw attention to them . . . and at the same time take vengeance on a world that doesn't appreciate him. That's the usual motivation for these self-obsessed psychopaths.'

Gemma considered. 'The general consensus is that ignorance and disadvantage breed hate. Those who've managed to better themselves by education rarely have issues they need to work out of their systems through violence.'

'There are always aberrations,' he replied. 'Look at Harold Shipman. Whatever's going on here, someone is playing a massive, elaborate game – and is hugely enjoying the distress that it's causing. Either way, we're not dealing with everyday criminality. This whole thing is too artful.'

'Like you said . . . a circus show of the macabre.'

He nodded. 'And guess who the bloody clowns are.'

Chapter 28

Cameron Boyd sauntered into the prison interview room with the air of a man who knew he had the upper hand. The steel door slammed closed, and he slumped into the seat on the opposite side of the table from Gemma and Heck.

'Smashing to see you again.' He displayed his orange bib. 'How do you like my new gear?'

'Suits you,' Heck replied.

'It's not very stylish.'

'You'll get used to it.'

Boyd grinned his brown-toothed grin. 'I'm not so sure, actually.'

'Cut the bollocks, Boyd,' Gemma said. 'You've dragged us off an important investigation so please don't waste any more of our time than is necessary.'

Boyd eyed her as though amused. 'You like to go at stuff fast, don't you, Miss Piper? I thought you'd have learned to be a bit more cautious after last time – when you nabbed the wrong bloke.'

'You know, Cameron,' Gemma said, 'this "what a clever villain am I" act would be more convincing if you weren't facing a long stretch inside.'

'Funny you should mention that. Because that's what I want to talk to you both about.' He leaned forward, still grinning. 'You two think you've taken me off the streets for quite some time, don't you? But I'm not the one you really want.'

'You're right,' Heck said. 'You've been a distraction, nothing more.'

'In that case, you can put in a good word for me.'

'Excuse me?' Gemma said.

Still Boyd grinned. 'The last time we spoke, you asked if I could remember when someone might have grabbed a handful of my hair. Well guess what . . . I now have.'

'Who?'

'Ah-ah . . .' He wagged a finger. 'There's no such thing in life as a free lunch. Well, there is in here, I suppose. It's fucking shit, but it always tastes better when the taxpayer's footing the bill. Anyway . . . I can tell you exactly who pulled my hair out, and exactly when it happened. But you're going to have to do me a favour.'

'Go on,' Gemma said.

'As you know, me and Tezza Mullany are going to stand trial for three aggravated burglaries. We haven't got a cat in hell's chance. We'll get fifteen years each, easy.'

'That'll be a shame,' Heck chuckled.

'Be a shame for you too, you pig bastard!' Boyd snapped.

'Keep this friendly, Cameron,' Gemma warned him. 'Or we'll walk and you'll get no kind of deal.'

'I want the charges reduced. Knock 'em down to ordinary everyday burglaries – take out the "aggravated" bit – and I'll tell you what you want to know.'

'You've got to be kidding.'

'Do I look like I am?'

'You tied people up in their own homes,' Gemma said. 'You held sharpened objects to their throats, to their eyeballs.'

'They'll get over it. Look, I'll still go down . . . only difference is it'll be three or four years, tops.'

'Some kind of justice, that,' Heck said.

Boyd sat back. 'That's the price of my intel.'

'It's too high,' Gemma said. 'I dealt with the paperwork for those home-invasions you and Terry Mullany committed. I liaised with the Manchester detectives who were investigating them. They were among the worst I've ever seen. As far as I'm concerned, fifteen years would be too short. You and Mullany should be going down for life.'

'In which case this interview is finished.' Boyd stood up. 'You sure you don't want to think this over first?'

'There's nothing to think about,' she said firmly.

He grinned again, and banged on the door. 'Your loss.'

The rain had stopped outside, but it was still cloudy and cold. Gemma didn't immediately climb into Heck's Volkswagen, but stood thinking. She glanced back at the soulless mountain of brick that was Strangeways Prison.

'Boyd's a major bullshit artist, you realise that?' Heck said.

'Well . . . now I don't suppose we'll ever know.'

'Have you considered giving him what he wants?'

'Are you serious?'

'Just because he's charged with burglary doesn't mean the judge won't be made conversant with the facts. He'll hand down a stiff sentence.'

'It'll still go a lot easier for him than it should.'

'Agreed, but it seems pretty simple to me.' Heck loosened his tie. 'Whoever obtained Boyd's DNA is a link to the Desecrator. They could lead us straight to him.'

Gemma shook her head. 'I don't think I could get those charges reduced even if I wanted to. I wasn't kidding in there . . . those aggravated burglaries were bloody serious. GMP would be all over us like a rash if we tried. And they'd be right to. Sorry Heck, but there's got to be such a thing in this job as principle. Boyd and Mullany need to be kept off the streets for as long as possible. I'm not going to prevent that happening, whatever I stand to gain from it.'

'Even if it means other lives may be saved?'

She gave him a haggard stare, but before she could reply her mobile began bleeping. Her face fell even more when she spied the number of the caller. 'Hello, sir,' she said.

Heck waited patiently while Gemma nodded repeatedly, occasionally getting a word or two in: 'Yes sir . . . of course . . . tomorrow, yes.'

'Tomorrow then, eh?' Heck said when she'd hung up.

'First thing in the afternoon . . . Joe's office.'

'You're at the Old Bailey later this week, aren't you?'

'I am, as it happens. Cooper v Regina. Joe says come down a day early. We can kill two birds with one stone.' Gemma gave him a wan smile. 'Was nice knowing you.'

'It'll just be a progress report.'

'And look how much I've got to show him.'

'Going to mention Boyd's offer?'

'Am I bloody hell! I know what his response would be – I'm a high-ranking, highly trusted police officer. I should be catching criminals, not bribing them. And if I can't do that, someone else will.'

'There's no harm in telling him that Boyd made the offer. Least that'll take the burden off your shoulders.'

She gave him another frank stare. 'Do I look like I need the burden taking off?'

'Do you want the truth?'

'Just get in the car.'

They drove the twenty-five miles back to Merseyside in almost complete silence, not even commenting on the heavy early-evening traffic. Halfway there the rain returned, grey

241

pulses of it sweeping the bleak, post-industrial landscape. Still Gemma said nothing, just sat there, gazing past the thudding windscreen wipers.

They pulled into the car park of their motel, and gazed up at the unimposing structure. It looked faceless, functional. Little wonder, on the first day, they'd christened it the 'Motel-With-No-Name'.

'We don't need to go in, you know,' Heck said. 'We could go for a drink somewhere. Just to unwind. Can't hurt . . . we're both wrecked.'

'No.' She gave him a studied sidelong glance. 'I don't think that would be smart. Because if we go for a drink together, the way I'm feeling right now . . . this time it's me who might jump on you. And like I said before, that wouldn't be good for either of us.'

She climbed from the car and closed the door.

'Speak for yourself,' Heck said under his breath.

Chapter 29

'Heck!' Garrickson yelled across the MIR.

The DCI was seated in Gemma's chair, but he didn't look especially comfortable; if anything he looked harassed. His tie was uncharacteristically loose and his jacket had been tossed into a corner; his attention was divided between various forms splattered across the desk and his open laptop.

'What've you got in your diary for today?' he asked without glancing up.

'We're working our way through the staff at the zoo,' Heck replied. 'I thought it might help to draw up a list of ex-staff too. Anyone who's been and gone recently.'

'Good idea. Stick it in the log and give it to someone else. I've just had a call from DI Kane in the Leeds Incident Room.'

'Okay?' Heck didn't like the sound of this.

'He's got another corpse for us.'

'Oh, Jesus . . .'

'But personally, I'm not sold on this one.' Garrickson swung his laptop around.

Heck stared down at more grainy crime scene footage, this time with a West Yorkshire Police insignia in its top right-hand corner. The quality was so poor that at first it was difficult to see what exactly was going on. The harsh glare of lights didn't help, while water was dripping from some gantry overhead. By the looks of it, a ragged figure lay huddled in foetal fashion amid a mass of crumpled, rain-soaked cardboard. Its head resembled a soggy shoebox squashed out of shape, but the blood that drenched it had turned black.

'This was shot in Manningham, Bradford, about two hours ago,' Garrickson said. 'Some tramp's had his head bashed in with a stone.'

'Doesn't sound like one of ours,' Heck replied.

'My thoughts too. But local plod have told Kane they think this might be the place where the Jane Doe in the crocodile pool got abducted from. Seems the clothing we circulated is very similar . . .' he glanced at a notebook, 'to that worn by a local tom called Chantelle Richards. She went missing from her normal pitch with a mate called Gracie Allen the best part of a month ago.'

'And this is the pitch?'

'Sounds like it. I suppose it's possible this poor sod saw whoever took the two girls and got his head caved in as a result . . .'

Heck nodded. This was worth looking into. 'Good job Ben Kane's on the spot.'

Garrickson switched his computer off. 'Ben Kane's taken charge on our behalf. I've scanned him over the dental X-rays we took from the crocodile girl. He's taken them to a local clinic where this Chantelle Richards used to go for health check-ups. But Kane's already DSIO on the Father Christmas murder. So he can't do it all himself.'

Heck knew what was coming next. 'I'm guessing you want me over there?'

Garrickson sat back. 'Why not? You're our Mr Roving Commission . . . or so everyone keeps telling me.' He scooped up the documents on the table – Heck recognised them as fax sheets – and shoved them across in no particular order. 'Here's the necessary paperwork. Chop fucking chop, sergeant . . . we've got some killers to catch!'

Though Bradford wasn't far away in real terms, about fifty miles – and the M62 motorway ran straight over there, rising and falling like a rollercoaster as it breasted the high Pennine moors – the traffic was sluggish, and it got worse. As Heck crossed Rockingstone Moss in snail-like fashion, a thunderstorm broke. Clouds so pregnant with rain they were bruised a livid green and purple, split open amid blistering flashes of lightning, and a cataclysmic downpour commenced, drumming on vehicle roofs, thrashing on windscreens. The tussocky moorland grass lay flat beneath its onslaught; soon there was several inches of surface-water on the road.

Heck finally entered West Yorkshire's second largest city several hours after he should have done, in early afternoon. Still the rain teemed down, drenched pedestrians dashing across the gridlocked streets, sheltering beneath brollies or briefcases. Heck's sat-nav at least was unaffected by the elements, and finally brought him to the correct coordinates, a decrepit district of empty lots and condemned properties. But so many local police vehicles, both uniform and CID, were already crammed into the narrow side-streets here that he had to park about half a mile away. He zipped himself into his anorak, pulled up the hood and headed along an alley running between two rows of boarded-up terraced houses. In the near-distance blue lights flickered on the underside of a decayed railway viaduct.

DI Ben Kane's usual 'lecture hall' garb was hidden beneath an all-enveloping sou'wester. He was waiting at the crime scene's outer cordon, on a cobbled backstreet jammed between a derelict mill and the viaduct, the extensive area beneath which was a forest of rain-sodden trash: dumped fridges, car wrecks, broken furniture, and rotted, mould-covered mattresses.

'Where's everyone else?' Kane said, seeing that Heck was alone.

'Who else were you expecting?' Heck replied, glancing over the tape; thanks to the big arc-lights West Yorkshire had set up under the gantry, the tramp's motionless body was visible even from a distance of thirty yards.

'You're kidding me, right?' Kane said. He indicated various men and women, presumably West Yorkshire officers, some in Tyvek, others hatted and coated, standing in watchful silence under any bit of shelter they could find. 'This lot already think we're a bunch of fucking idiots.'

'They've been reading the newspapers too, have they?' Heck said.

'They hardly need to. They're waiting to find out whether we want this or not, so they can process the scene. I don't think they were expecting to wait all day.'

Heck nodded at the corpse. 'He's in no rush, is he?'

'Very funny. The point is we still can't pronounce whether it's ours or theirs five hours on. And when I ask for some assistance, I get one man.'

'We have a few other victims,' Heck reminded him. 'Time of death?'

'Doctor reckons around twenty days ago.'

'Same night this Chantelle Richards went missing?'

'There or thereabouts.'

'Anything back on the X-rays?'

'Not yet. The medical centre where I sent them . . . it's a kind of walk-in place. A lot of street people get fixed up there. Going like a chippie twenty-four-seven.'

'Well we can't make living patients wait for dead ones.' Heck glanced around. 'I can see this is the arsehole of

Bradford, but it shouldn't have taken someone three weeks to find this poor bastard.'

'He was wrapped up in that box,' Kane said. 'Could have been there a lot longer, but West Yorkshire turned up here when two local toms spotted a Crimestoppers flyer concerning the crocodile pool girl, and thought they recognised the clothing. They decided they hadn't seen these two mates of theirs, Chantelle Richards and Gracie Allen, for quite some time and reported it.' He handed over two documents in clear plastic envelopes. 'Here are their witness statements. Apparently, this was Richards' and Allen's regular pitch, so West Yorkshire came and had a poke around, and lo and behold . . .'

Heck glanced across the waste-ground beneath the railway. 'What about the other dossers? Did no one else see anything – the girls being abducted, this fella getting his head smacked in?'

'Fuck's sake, Heck! I only found out about this a couple of hours ago, and I'm supposed to be running the Incident Room in Leeds. I haven't got the time or the men to go scouring the streets for homeless lowlives who may know something. That's why I'd hoped her ladyship might have sent a team over.'

'Do either of the missing women have families?'

Kane again consulted his notes. 'Chantelle Richards does. She's got two kids, but she doesn't live with them. They're officially in the care of her mother.'

'Have they been shown pictures of the clothing?'

'I don't know.'

'Do they even know she's been reported missing?'

'Course they do. Well, the mother does. She's probably worried sick.'

'Gee, do you think . . .'

'Look, I know what you're getting at.' Kane's voice became

a harsh whisper. 'You reckon someone should get down there. Well, I'll tell you now, if you think I'm going to be the one who tells some sweet old grandma and two tiny tots that their beloved mum may – *may*, Heck! – have been torn to pieces by a fucking crocodile, you can forget it!'

Heck could hardly upbraid him for that. It wasn't the kind of duty any police officer would volunteer for. 'What about Family Liaison?'

'We haven't got anyone on this side of the Pennines . . . the only victim we've got to date over here is Ernest Shapiro and he had no family.'

'Can't West Yorkshire help us?'

'I can ask, I suppose.'

'You haven't already?'

'Don't even think about judging me, Heck! I'm up to my eyes as it is. Anyway, we need to wait for the results from the medical centre. With luck they'll tell us it's not Richards. Then we can hand this whole mess back to West Yorkshire and get on with what we're supposed to be doing.'

'Whether or not it turns out Chantelle Richards is the croc girl, the mere fact that she *may* be is a development. We can't just not tell them anything because we'd rather someone else did it.'

Kane shoved his hands into his anorak pockets. 'In that case, DS Heckenburg . . .' his expression was bleak, '*you're* the guy from head-office.'

Heck opted not to wait for the results from the medical centre, partly because it was only right that the family be updated, and partly because something else now nagged at him.

Above the city's tower blocks and old, industrial roof-tops, thunder still boomed in a prematurely darkened sky. Rain fell in sheets as he tried to negotiate a chaos of late-afternoon traffic, his headlight beams slashing through the downpour.

'Garrickson,' said the voice on the other end of the line.

'It's me,' Heck shouted into his mobile, at the same time trying to follow his sat-nav to a place called Great Horton.

'Anything?' Garrickson asked.

Heck glanced at the witness statements. 'The crocodile woman's clothing has been identified by some of this missing girl's fellow sex-workers. I mean, black stockings, denim skirt, pink high heels . . . ten-a-penny stuff individually, but when all taken together it's a hell of a coincidence. I think this'll turn out to be our girl, which means the dead tramp is ours too.'

There was a brief silence as Garrickson took this in, no doubt wondering how the hell they could operate an incident room in Bradford as well. 'Shit . . . look, we need to be sure before we officially take charge.'

'We will be soon. Sir, there's something else.'

'Go on.'

'It may be too late for Chantelle Richards, but perhaps not for this other lass, Gracie Allen.'

'Something to suggest she's still alive?'

'Nothing to suggest anything. She hasn't shown up yet, but we can be damn sure she will at some point, and Christ knows what they'll have done to her. We've got to try anything we can to head that off.'

'I'm all ears.'

'The only thing I can think of is we get Claire Moody to put a false story out. Lie to the press that we've got a couple of perps in custody and that they're talking. It's a long-shot, but it may frighten the rest of the gang into running before they can do any more harm.'

Garrickson contemplated this. 'If we panic them, it might just make them kill the girl and dump her.'

'They're going to do that anyway.'

'Obviously, I'll need to run it by Detective Superintendent Piper first.'

'You'd better do it quick, sir. These guys are working to their own timetable.'

'I'll try and get her now.' Garrickson rang off.

Heck hadn't bothered to mention that if the gang killed their second hostage because they'd been panicked into thinking the law was onto them, at least they might kill her quickly, without ritual or torture. It wouldn't be much of an advantage to gain for the poor woman, but it would be better than the alternative.

Ten minutes later he arrived at the home of Irene Richards, the missing prostitute's mother. It was in a better-kept neighbourhood than the run-down slum where the two women had been abducted, but still comprised rows of old terraced housing, and under a leaden sky and lashing rain, looked dismal and decayed. The terrace in which Irene Richards lived fronted onto a small park, though even that was a storm-swept wilderness.

A narrow paved footway led along the front of the row. Irene Richards lived at number nine. Warm lighting was visible inside. Just as Heck tapped on the red-painted front door, his mobile rang.

'It's Kane,' said a distant, despondent voice.

'Yeah?'

'Just got that medical report. Those X-rays are a match.'

The front door opened.

'Did you hear me, Heck?' Kane said into his ear. 'The girl from the crocodile pool is definitely Chantelle Richards.'

Heck managed to focus on the person standing in the doorway. As Kane had forecast, she looked like a sweet old lady: probably just past sixty, wearing slippers and a cardigan over slacks and a sweater. She had neat white curls and wore a polite but enquiring smile. Two pretty children, a girl and a boy, perhaps two and three years old, stood one to either side of her, each holding their grandma's hand. The girl was in a flowered dress and buckled shoes; the boy wore a t-shirt with a print of Donald Duck on it.

Chapter 30

As Gemma descended the stairwell from Joe Wullerton's office at New Scotland Yard, she felt a tad more upbeat than she had done earlier. That meeting could actually have gone much worse. At least she still had a job and a team, though both still felt as if they were hanging by a thread. Outside, thunder rumbled; through every window she saw a London sky so grey it was almost green, the effect of which was to create an eerie, shadowy gloom inside the building. Jags of lightning sparked in the distance. Rain bounced from the encircling rooftops.

She'd now decided that Wullerton – who was in his fifties and of burly build, with a thick moustache, sleepy eyes and a preference for cardigans and open-collar shirts – wasn't pretending when he gave the impression he was a genial sort. But beneath the avuncular exterior, she'd always suspected there lurked a core of steel, and today he'd shown it.

'Let's analyse what's going on here, Gemma,' he'd said heatedly. 'The Serial Crimes Unit was specifically designed to provide intelligence and consultative back-up to regional investigations into major crime sprees. There is no one else more qualified than you and your team to tackle this kind of case. No one. You're our last line of defence. But how's that going to make the public feel if you can't pull it off? The truth is that none of us may stay in our posts after this. I'm Gold Command remember. In the eyes of many, I'm at fault too. The very existence of the National Crime Group may be on the line here – are we an elite crime-fighting outfit or an expensive luxury? It's your call, Gemma.'

When she reached the Serial Crimes Unit, it was virtually unmanned, which was understandable given that almost the entire crew was up north. In truth, that was a relief. She didn't feel like speaking to anyone as she trekked along the main corridor, took her keys from her coat pocket and let herself into her office, where she kicked her shoes off and slumped into her chair.

Joe Wullerton's parting words still echoed in her head.

'I'm not the sort of boss who says "I don't care how you do it" . . . we have a system we need to operate within, but use every means you have available, push every envelope, think outside every box. Just catch these psychos, Gemma . . . catch them now!'

She switched on the television in the corner, put the kettle on and threw a teabag and a few pinches of powdered milk into a mug. While the kettle bubbled, she sat back at her desk and channel-hopped, only stopping when she caught a news item regarding the case. Claire Moody was in the midst of chaotic reportage. Her hair was a mess and her cheeks ashen. It didn't look great, but it hardly mattered as long as she did her job.

'So are you able to tell us in which police station the two suspects are being held?' a reporter asked.

'For security reasons, no,' Claire replied.

If only they *did* have two suspects in custody, Gemma thought. Garrickson had rung earlier, catching her just before she went in to see Wullerton, with Heck's suggestion that they release a phony story in an effort to save the missing prostitute, Gracie Allen. Gemma had okayed it almost without thinking. It wasn't the best idea, but what other choice did they have? On screen, the tough line of questioning continued. Claire was indoors this time, making it into a proper, pre-prepared press conference. That was sensible. It would help create an impression the team were on top of things. That said, Claire was alone. At the very least, Garrickson should have been seated with her.

'Can we expect there to be more arrests?' someone asked.

'That's our hope, yes.'

'But is it your expectation?'

'It's too early to say.'

Gemma bit her lip. That hadn't been a convincing response. Claire should have said 'yes'. Why the hell not? They were already lying through their teeth. The idea had been to smoke the culprits out, not lull them into thinking they weren't in any danger.

'Which of these particular murders are these arrests in connection with?' another reporter asked.

'I believe the . . . erm . . .' Claire faltered. 'I believe the . . . Tara Greenwood murder.'

Gemma's heart sank.

There was a brief silence, and then an explosion of amazed questioning.

'Tara Greenwood was murdered in Lincolnshire back in 2009!' a TV crime editor said. 'Does that mean the enquiry's been widened?'

'Was Lorna Arkwright also a Desecrator victim?' another voice shouted.

'I'm sorry . . . I'm sorry,' Claire said hastily. 'I made a mistake. The suspect we currently have in custody is not being held in connection with Tara Greenwood.'

'The suspect? Earlier, you told us that *two* arrests had been made.'

'Yes of course . . .'

'Are the suspects being held in connection with different murders?'

'Yes, I believe they are.' Claire didn't look as if she believed any such thing. Her eyes were blank as they reflected the flash-bulbs.

'Is either of them being held in connection with Tara Greenwood?'

'No . . . forgive me. The Tara Greenwood homicide has nothing to do with this particular series.'

'So exactly which murders are the suspects being held for?' the crime editor asked.

'Our main suspect is being held on suspicion of murdering Ernest Shapiro.'

'Can we just clarify that there is another suspect?' someone else said. 'You don't seem very certain.'

'The other suspect was arrested in Manchester,' Claire said.

'There've been several murders on this side of the Pennines, Miss Moody. So in connection with which crime?'

'Tara Greenwood,' Claire said. 'Sorry no, she's not . . . the suspect, I mean. She's not being spoken to on that basis . . .'

'*She?* Does that mean the second suspect is female?'

'There is no . . . sorry, I meant Tara Greenwood. No, Ernest Shapiro. There is no second . . .'

'There is no second suspect?'

'No, I mean the second suspect is not female . . .'

Gemma hit the 'off' switch and slammed her mobile to her ear.

'Ma'am?' came Garrickson's distant voice. 'Everything alright?'

'No it bloody isn't! And you shouldn't even need to ask that question! Pull her out now!'

'In mid-conference?'

'Where are you, Mike? Hiding in the fucking toilets? Get her out of there before we look an even bigger set of tools! And when I get back up there, you'd better have a written explanation waiting on my desk as to why you weren't sitting at that conference table taking some of the heat off her!'

After she cut the call, she hurled her mobile on the floor.

As a rule, Gemma Piper didn't cry. There'd been many times during her career when she'd wanted to – for the grieving spouses, for the abused children, for the rape and robbery victims who'd wept and shivered as they'd tried to explain to her what had happened. But she'd always resisted crying for herself. Her late father, who'd never risen above the rank of inspector, had drummed this into her. 'This is a man's job, darling,' he'd said the day she told him, beaming, that she'd been accepted for interview. 'Always has been, always will be. So whatever happens out there, do not let them break you. You do, and they'll come down on you like a ton of horse poo. Whatever they say, whatever they do – don't blink, don't flinch, and don't you dare shed a single tear. Because that's all they'll need to tear you down.'

She'd clung on to those wise words many times, and now she clung on to them again – almost as tenaciously as she clung on to the edge of her desk.

Chapter 31

It was early evening when two female plain clothes from West Yorkshire, both trained in Family Liaison, turned up at the house in Great Horton, and Heck was able to leave. Outside, he stood for several minutes in the torrential rain, thinking that only this elemental fury could wash away the pain, horror and despair that he'd witnessed at such close hand for so many hours in the midst of that bereaved family.

'Hey, Heck!' Ben Kane approached under the shelter of a voluminous umbrella. 'Managed to get you someone in the end.'

'Couldn't you have left me in there a bit longer?' Heck said. 'I was really enjoying it.' He pushed past, heading for the cars.

'Where are you going now? We need a chat.'

Heck glanced back. 'About what?'

'About whether Barack Obama's wife wears knickers or goes commando. What do you mean "about what"? Are we opening another incident room here in Bradford, or am I going to have to work this crime as well? I'm already running one enquiry in Leeds.'

Heck shrugged. 'You go back to Leeds and deal with that one.'

'Yeah?'

'Yeah. Go and contemplate that broken chimney for a few days. While I catch the bastards who did it!'

Thunder still broke over the Pennine ridges as Heck drove west towards Lancashire. Tumultuous rain drowned the bleak landscape. His laptop was open on the passenger seat, and he clutched the wheel one-handed as he typed. He was descending the high moors towards Manchester by the time he'd finished. He closed his computer and dug his mobile from his pocket, placing a call to Jen Weeks. It was now after six of course. The unit's admin staff would no longer be on duty. Tough.

'Yeah, Jen . . . it's Heck,' he said. 'Sorry it's late. I know you ladies have finished for the day, but I need something. It's a special prison visit. Same as last time. Cameron Boyd. He's on the remand wing at Strangeways.' She droned out a few possible objections. 'No,' Heck replied, 'that's one thing we definitely don't need to worry about. Boyd will be well chuffed to know I'm coming.'

The tempest followed Heck all the way to Manchester. As he navigated the bustling streets, rain continued to hammer down. When he finally came in sight of the prison, its vast redbrick outline reared over everything like an industrial-gothic fortress, rain streaming down its windowless facade, spouting from its gutters. Even the short distance Heck had to cover from the visitors' car park left him sopping wet.

Cameron Boyd thought this hilarious.

'Oh fuck,' he chuckled, sitting down at the same table where Heck and Gemma had interviewed him the previous day. 'Caught in the rain, were we?'

Heck smiled. 'Not a problem you'll ever have, is it?'

'Smart arse.' Boyd glanced around the otherwise empty interview room. 'So . . . where's your sexy boss?'

'She's busy.'

'Too busy to see me? I'm a bit surprised. I wouldn't have thought a mere detective sergeant would have the authority to sort out the kind of deal I'm looking for.'

Heck placed his laptop on the table and switched it on. 'The only deal you're going to get, Cameron, is a kind prison governor giving you a slightly roomier cell . . . assuming you help us catch the Desecrator, that is.'

Boyd chuckled again. 'Still playing the heavy? It's your only tactic that, isn't it?'

'Who yanked out those clumps of hair that we found under Ernest Shapiro's fingernails?'

'Nothing's changed from last time. You know what you have to do.'

'I think, Cameron, you'll find that quite a bit has changed.' Heck turned his laptop around. 'See this?'

Despite himself, Boyd glanced down – seeing a mass of text on the screen.

'That's a witness statement,' Heck explained. 'From me. It'll be attached to my arrest report as a late addendum.'

'So fucking what?'

'According to this I've now remembered something relevant to your case. It concerns Detective Constable Gregson's attempt to apprehend you.'

Boyd's sneering smile faded. 'What happened to that rookie-pig was an accident.'

'I'm afraid not.' Heck shook his head. 'You were sat on top of that pile of bricks, and you started lobbing them down at him deliberately. You hit him four or five times . . . on the head obviously. The actual stack only collapsed when you saw me coming and tried to escape.'

'You're a sodding liar!'

Heck feigned hurt. 'You don't believe me? It's all here, see . . . it must be true.'

'You're a sodding, lying bastard!'

'At the end of the day, Cameron, it doesn't matter what you think. Because this statement is now attached to an email, and all I have to do is hit the "send" button, see?' Onscreen, he placed his cursor on the appropriate box; his thumb hovered dangerously above the keyboard. 'The moment I do that, it goes straight to DI Burgess, who's handling your case. That means you'll be rearrested in here and, on top of everything else, charged with attempting to murder a police officer.'

'You're full of shit!'

'Instead of getting fifteen years for aggravated burglary, Cameron, you'll be going down for life. It may get worse . . . Andy Gregson's not out of the woods yet.'

'You're full of fucking shit! You can't make this up now. No one'll believe it.'

'You wanna bet? I suffered a head trauma that night too . . . remember the ticket machine you threw in my face?' Heck indicated the fading mark on his temple. 'I got treated for that in the same hospital where they brought Gregson. It'll be on record. No one'll be surprised that my memories became clearer later on.'

'It was an accident, you pig bastard! My lawyers will have a field day with you.'

'You reckon? How many times do you think I've given evidence at crown court, Cameron? How many scrotes like you are rotting in jail because of me?'

'Fucking bastard, they'll tear you apart!'

'You want to take that chance? When all you have to do is tell me something that makes no difference to you anyway?'

Boyd's hands clutched the edge of the table so tightly that his knuckles turned white. He gazed at Heck malevolently, but words failed him.

'I've even brought the paperwork,' Heck added, whipping

an official form from under his coat and laying it down. Next, he produced a pen. 'You give me the witness statement I want, and the button I hit on here will read "erase", not "send".'

'You fucking . . .' Boyd was still choked with helpless anger.

'Your call, Cameron.'

Boyd clearly didn't want to talk. Cooperating with the police was against everything he'd ever stood for. But he was in deep enough shit without facing the possibility of life imprisonment as well.

'It . . . it was in The Moorside pub. Levenshulme.'

'When was this?' Heck asked.

'A few months ago.'

'Can you give me a date?'

'Sometime early November.'

'Tell me what happened.'

'This blonde came in with this bloke,' he said. 'I hadn't seen them before. Two bits of kids, really. Eighteen years old, tops. But she was fit as a butcher's dog and dressed like a right slapper.'

'Describe her.'

'Like I say . . . blonde, very long hair. Almost down to her arse. Clingy white top, denim miniskirt.'

'What about the bloke?'

Boyd shrugged. 'Didn't pay much attention to him. About the same age. Tall, six-two, six-three. Quite well built . . . like an athlete. Bit posh too.'

'How'd you mean?'

Boyd watched uncomfortably as Heck jotted all this down on the witness form. 'Look, if my name goes on this and it gets read out in court . . .'

'The Desecrator's going down for life, Cameron, or you are!' Heck retorted. 'Don't start fucking around now that we're getting somewhere! This bloke . . . posh, how?'

'I didn't hear him speak. But he looked wrong . . . for The Moorside, I mean. Refined, like.'

'Any distinguishing features on either of them?' Heck asked. 'Tattoos, piercings, birthmarks, scars?'

'Come on! It's five months ago.'

'Tell me exactly what happened.'

'They came in about eight in the evening. And at first they kept themselves to themselves. But then the lass starts tarting around with all the locals.'

'What do you mean?'

'Well . . . there's music playing, see. And she starts dancing. Real sexy. Giving everyone the come-on, trying to get all the old fellas to have a dance with her.'

'What was her boyfriend doing?'

'He was just sat there in the corner, sipping a Diet Coke. I remember that much, 'cos I thought what a fucking limpdick.'

'What was he wearing?'

'Donkey jacket, jeans, trainers.'

'He didn't say anything?'

'No. So then I starts thinking she might be a pro and he's her pimp.'

'A posh pimp?'

'Well, yeah . . . doesn't figure, does it? So then I thinks maybe she's one of these swingers, you know. She's shagging like a demon and he's sitting there having a wank. Anyway, she finally comes over and sits on my knee. Totally uninvited. Can't remember what she said, but she's getting all breathy like she's really turned on. Asks me where the action is, something like that.'

'Was she posh too?'

Boyd pondered. 'Sort of. Not a Manc lass. Course I'm not paying much attention to that, 'cos I've got a fucking boner in my keks.'

'Her bloke say anything to this?'

Boyd shook his head again. 'Just sits there. I remember thinking if this twonk steps in now, I'll twat him into the middle of next week . . . this bitch is begging for it. Anyway, next thing I'm spit-swapping with her. Eventually, she drags me outside by the belt, and I had her at the back of the pub, up against the bog wall.' Boyd smiled, reliving the lurid moment. 'I mean, she's got no undies on, I'm hard as a rock. My flies are down in a shot and I'm straight up her . . .'

'You can spare me that detail . . .'

'Hey, do you want to know what happened, or not?' Boyd gave Heck a challenging glare, as if it was all or nothing. 'Her hands are everywhere, right? She's gasping, squeaking. I shagged the guts out of her. I hadn't even taken my clothes off . . . but she's ripping at them. And she's ripping at my hair too.'

'Your hair?'

'Correct. She's that excited she's pulling my hair out in bloody handfuls. I'm excited too of course, so I don't really notice at the time, never mind object.'

Heck thought on this. 'What happened afterwards?'

'Well, when we'd finished I just slid down on my arse. I was totally knackered. She just saunters away . . . straightens her skirt, blows me a kiss. And that's it. The lad comes out of the pub and they walk around the corner together and they're gone.'

'Would you know her if you saw her again?'

'Yeah, but I never have.'

'What about the bloke?'

'I might remember him, I don't know.'

'Cameron . . . ten minutes ago you said I'd get ripped apart in court for telling lies. Now, seriously, how do you think *you're* going to sound offering that testimony?'

Boyd shrugged. 'If you don't believe me, there's proof.

263

A security camera at the back of The Moorside. It'll all be on film.'

'This happened back in November? What're the chances it still exists?'

Boyd leaned forward, as if to impart something confidential. 'One of the barmen there's a lad called Pete Dwyer. He lives upstairs. He's a porn addict. I've been in that bedsit of his . . . it's like a backroom in Bangkok. He also happens to be in charge of the security cameras, so if I know Dwyer, that blonde lass will now be a movie star. So . . . will that do you, or what?'

Heck sighed. 'Only an ignoramus would tell me a lie like that and expect to get away with it. And you *are* an ignoramus, Cameron. But at present, you don't leave me a lot of choice.' He dotted the final paragraph of the statement, then slid it across the table along with the pen. 'Read this and sign it.'

Boyd did so, but then sat there suspiciously while Heck folded the sheet and stuck it under his jacket, pocketing the pen and closing his laptop.

'Oi! You said you'd erase that phony witness statement.'

'Hold your horses.' Heck rose to his feet. 'I want to see what Pete Dwyer's got to say first.'

'He'll tell you I'm not lying.'

'If he does, good.' Heck moved to the door and knocked on it. 'But look, Cameron . . . I'd like to get you off that hook, but I can't lie to you that for the next fifteen years or so a prison snitch isn't going to be extremely useful to me.'

'You bastard!' Boyd whispered.

The door opened.

'That statement won't go anywhere,' Heck replied, 'so long as you keep delivering.'

Chapter 32

Heck trudged across the sparkling wet car park towards the Motel-With-No-Name. He wasn't sure how late in the evening it was, but he was so drained that all he wanted to do was strip off his damp clothes and fall into bed. Though he was hungry, he lacked the energy or inclination to look for food. His room was at the top of a half-stair leading up from the first floor. It was located at the end of a short passage, onto which only two other doors opened. Even though the entire SCU was billeted in this building, he'd never yet seen or heard anyone else on that level.

Until now.

Claire was sitting at the top of the half-stair, head bowed, arms wrapped around her knees. From her posture, he at first thought she was asleep. She was wearing a bathrobe and a pair of fluffy slippers; her hair was damp and stringy, as if she'd recently showered. But when she glanced up, she looked far from relaxed. Her eyes were red and puffy; her lips quivered.

'Hi,' he said.

'Hi,' she replied in a small voice. 'You're very late. I've been waiting ages.'

265

'Sorry. It's a job that won't rest. You okay?'

'Not really.' She chuckled at the thought. She clearly wasn't falling drunk, but he could smell alcohol. 'I really blew it today. At the press conference.'

'I heard a bit of it on the radio,' he said, feeling indifferent about it. Claire's honest confusion might now have dire consequences, but in truth he was too tired to be worried.

'What a performance, eh? No wonder DCI Garrickson tore such a strip off me afterwards. He was absolutely hideous. I've never had such a telling-off.'

'Ignore him.'

'I've let you all down.'

'I told you . . . headlines are a one-day wonder.'

'Perhaps it's one day too many?'

'Why are you sitting out here?'

'Why do you think?'

He glanced at his watch. 'It's nearly ten . . .'

'That prostitute's going to die because of me, isn't she?'

'Claire, that prostitute is going to die because she's in the hands of a bunch of sick weirdoes who get their kicks from hurting people.'

'I signed her death-warrant. That's what DCI Garrickson said.'

'The chance of saving that girl's life by lying that we were onto the bastards responsible was the longest of long-shots. There's absolutely no way in hell you should beat yourself up about it.'

She gave a brave but wry smile. 'Now . . . *that's* what I came here for. After a really shitty day . . . a bit of Mark Heckenburg wisdom. I thought if the man I was warned could sell STD cream in a nunnery can't show me how to put a positive spin on all this, no one can. And yes . . .' She half-stumbled as she stood up. 'I have had a couple of drinks, before you ask.'

'All I was going to ask was if you fancied another one? Little nightcap? I've got a bottle in my room.'

Such a suggestion might have seemed ultra presumptuous even as recently as a few days ago, but an awful lot of fire and water had passed under the bridge since then.

'Sure.' She sniffed and scratched at her brow. 'Why not?'

Heck's room in the Motel-With-No-Name was not much to write home about: whitewashed brick walls, felt carpet tiles, a desk, a chair, a single bed, a blind on the window (which gave a dull view over the M62), an insipid painting, and a small en-suite containing a shower so narrow that some men he knew would only be able to enter it sideways.

'Seriously, don't let the press conference bother you,' he said, closing the door behind them. 'None of us are bloody perfect, least of all our swaggering ape of a DCI.'

'You never let things get you down, do you?' she replied, slumping into the chair. It didn't sound entirely like a compliment.

He produced a bottle of Bushmills and two paper cups.

'Even in the middle of this bloody nightmare, you're somehow managing to keep your cool,' she said. 'Ploughing on, determined to crack the case.'

He shrugged as he poured them three fingers each. 'It's what I have to do.'

'All I had to do was keep a lid on this thing, and look what happened there.'

He handed her the drink, then sat on the bed. 'It's not your fault the word got out. It's a nasty game, this. Not all our enemies are on the other side. Even me and Gemma, who've been doing this for years, haven't totally learned that yet.'

'Nice speech.' She sipped disconsolately. 'But I know what you two think of me.'

'Garrickson doesn't speak for me or Gemma . . .'

'It doesn't matter what Garrickson said. He's just gobbing off because he's an oaf and an office bully. You two are more discreet but you all think the same.'

'How do you know?'

Claire took another long sip; her three fingers were gone already. 'Because I'd think it too, if I was you. I'm a complete liability . . . a weak link in the chain, and even one weak link can't be tolerated when you're trying to catch a bunch of murderers. Isn't that true? Everyone in this team needs to be on top of their game, and I'm way off that.'

'It was a ridiculously big job to give you in your first month.'

'Interesting.' She held out her cup for a refill; he duly obliged. 'You're not prepared to lie to me . . . to tell me that everything will be alright.'

'I wouldn't be doing you any favours if I lied to you.'

'Exactly. Which is why I'm tendering my resignation first thing in the morning.'

Heck had been expecting something like this, yet somehow it failed to move him. He'd grown to like Claire, and admire her spirit – his initial thought about her, that she was primarily a pretty face, now made him feel ashamed. But he'd also watched her wrestle to keep it together. If she found violence upsetting, which she clearly did despite her most strenuous efforts, she was in the wrong place here.

'I see you're not trying to talk me out of it,' she commented.

'It's your decision.'

'It wouldn't make any difference if you did.' She stood up, crossed the small room and plonked herself down next to him. In the process, her robe flopped open, revealing that she was naked underneath. It might have been an erotic moment, but she barely seemed to notice. She shuddered and leaned her head on his shoulder. 'I never knew such evil could exist in the world.'

He placed his arm around her; the peck he planted on her hair was gentle and platonic. 'It's not this bad all the time, you know.'

'I thought you weren't going to lie to me.'

'That's not a lie.'

'This department chases the worst of the worst. That's its purpose.'

'We also catch them; we protect society from them.'

'I agree, and maybe that gives you a boost from time to time. But don't try to sweeten something that can't be sweetened. Are you any closer to catching them?'

'We have a few new leads.'

'In other words "no". You see, Mark . . . even you have a skill for being economical with the truth. More than I do, and I'm the one who gets paid for it.'

'Claire, there's nothing to be ashamed of. Not everyone can stomach this kind of work.'

'They treated me like an enemy out there.' Fleetingly she didn't just look hurt by that memory, she looked stunned, dazed. 'I was trying to give them information, and . . . it was like *I* was the criminal . . . not the killers who are doing all this. *Me.*'

'No one responds well to horrific situations like this. Not the public, not the press . . . they lash out. If we're in the firing line, which we often are because we're usually the only ones there, we've just got to take it on the chin.'

'Well I haven't got as good a chin as yours, I'm afraid.' She turned her head as though to assess his physiognomy – and then kissed him on the side of the mouth.

'What are you doing?' he said warily.

Slowly, she twined her arms around him. 'Heck, we may not see each other again after today.' Her voice was breathy, husky. 'So why don't we end things on a high note, eh?'

'Claire, you're upset . . .'

'Come on, you want it as much as I do.'

'And you're drunk.'

'So what . . .'

Even as their lips met Heck knew this was a bad idea, but her curvaceous form melded against him, and though it might be slightly tainted by alcohol, the sweetness of her tongue was undeniable.

Chapter 33

Gracie wasn't sure when exactly it was that Chantelle had disappeared from the pit. Night and day no longer had meaning in this place of near-perpetual darkness. Every few hours the bucket was lowered containing water and food, the latter of which never varied much – bread, bacon, cheese – regardless of whether it was supposed to be breakfast, lunch or dinner. So she'd quickly lost all sense of how long she'd actually been down here. If she hazarded a guess, it was maybe a week ago when she'd woken to find herself alone. At the time it had seemed impossible that someone could come down and snatch one of them away without the other being disturbed. Surely Chantelle would have tried to resist them? That should have been sufficient to wake Gracie from her tormented sleep. But she remembered nothing of the sort.

It had occurred to her in the lonely hours following that maybe she'd been drugged. She'd felt nauseous and shivery, her head splitting – though it was difficult to pin the cause of this down with any certainty because incarceration in this dungeon was hardly likely to be good for her health. Despite the water she regularly drank, her throat was sore from her persistent pleading into the darkness above. On those few occasions when the light was lowered so that she could see into the bucket, her eyes stung from lack of use. As there were no seats to recline on, she was constantly on the floor, squatted or crouched against the wall, her joints aching, her limbs cramped. Then there was the smell of her own excrement; there was now a mountain of it on the other side of the pit, and its stench had become overwhelming. Sometimes it caused her to vomit, and, when there was nothing left inside, to dry-heave, which in itself was agony. God alone knew what kind of germs she was breathing down here.

'Whoever you are . . . whatever you've got planned for me, you'd better get it done soon,' she croaked up into the blackness. 'Because I'm pretty sure I'm going to die in this place . . .' Her head slumped backwards onto aching shoulders; the mere effort of raising her voice now exhausted her.

There was an echoing clunk of woodwork.

Gracie froze, her eyes snapping open and straining upward.

A light appeared, but it wasn't the light she'd seen before, the electric bulb attached to the bucket cable. This one had a reddish, wavering tint, and it swayed from side to side. An oil-lamp, she realised. It was maybe ten feet above her, but it was slowly descending. With a thump, something landed in the pit. The expanding glow revealed that it was the foot of a rope-ladder.

Gracie scuttled backwards until she struck the wall. Sweat prickled her face, her heart beating ten to the dozen. Was this it? Was this the moment?

A dark humped shape descended. The lamp she saw was swinging from its belt, the red light reflecting on the encircling brick walls. She could tell from the outline that the incomer was a man. When he alighted on the dungeon floor, he had his back to her, but he was tall, strongly built. He wore boots and waterproofs; the hood was pulled down, revealing a tousled thicket of black spiky hair. Even before he turned to face her, she knew who she was going to see – the young man who, along with the blonde girl, had first lured them into captivity.

On that occasion, though an impressive physical specimen, he'd seemed nervous and shy. He'd worn glasses and had smiled a little boy's smile, but he'd been handsome too – square jawed, with bright blue eyes, a firm red mouth and sharp, straight nose. He was still handsome now if she was honest, but in a cold, severe sort of way. When he took the lantern from his belt and held it up in his gloved fist, she realised – to her incredulity – how young he actually was. No more than eighteen.

With his other hand, he produced something from under his waterproofs: a flattish metallic device, about the size and shape of a small directory. When he dropped it on the ground, and she saw its rubberised upper plate and the neon numerals darting along its glass frontage, she realised that it was a set of weighing scales. So mundane an item was this that at first, perhaps absurdly, it had the effect of reducing her terror – though very quickly the increasing weirdness of this predicament struck her.

Weird could never be good.

'What . . . what do you want with me?' she stammered.

He didn't look at her, merely signalled her to stand. At the same time, he fished a roll of something from his pocket and unravelled it. It looked like a tape measure.

Slowly, nauseated, Gracie managed to get to her feet. 'Look, I . . . I don't know what this is about. If you'd just talk to me . . .'

But he remained silent, concentrating carefully as he extended the tape and dangled it alongside her, evidently taking note of her five feet, five inches. With a snap of his fingers, he indicated the scales.

'You want to weigh me?' She almost laughed at the craziness of it.

He snapped his fingers again, irritably, still not meeting her gaze though his eyes, whatever they were focused on, were suddenly bright, as if filled with intense but suppressed rage. Frightened again, though dizzy and awkward in her thigh-boots, Gracie stepped gingerly onto the horizontal scales and stood there, teetering; the whole thing would have been too ridiculous for words if she hadn't felt so sick with fear and exhaustion. A second later, he nudged her aside with his elbow, picked the implement up and shoved it back under his waterproofs.

'Look,' she pleaded. 'Just stop . . . stop this madness. I beg you . . . you've surely nothing to gain from it.' As he turned back to the ladder, her voice rose, becoming shrill. 'For God's sake, you're not leaving me here in the darkness again?'

She lurched forward, hooking her hands into his clothing, trying to cling on to him. He swung back to face her, and slowly and patiently, but with crushingly superior strength, took her wrists in his big, gloved paws and forcibly pulled her loose. Fleetingly, their faces were only inches apart – Gracie's scrawny and tear-stained, her captor's flawless, and icily indifferent. With a single shove, he sent her tottering backwards. She fell, landing hard on her bottom, though she barely felt the pain that jolted through her weakened body.

'Just . . . just don't,' she wept. 'Don't leave me down here. Please, I can't stand it, I can't stand it . . .'

'It won't be for long.'

These were the first words he'd spoken to her – the first that anyone had spoken to her since Chantelle had disappeared – and initially Gracie was so shocked that she clamped her lips together, gazing up at him with mute disbelief.

He smiled at her reaction, but it was the least warm, least enticing smile she'd ever seen. It wasn't even what she'd have called an evil smile – it was more an utterly blank smile. There was no emotion behind it at all.

'And . . . and what then?' she asked in a quavering voice, only too late realising what a mistake it might be to ask such a question.

He placed one foot on the rope-ladder, but paused as if to think, his head bowed. 'Do you know May Day?' He sounded educated; there was no accent there – but suddenly there was feeling. Tension maybe. Indignation.

'May Day?'

He glanced over his shoulder, eyes gleaming like polished buttons. 'A rancid political event in our time . . . espoused by those who've replaced our beloved religious and cultural ideology with a soulless humanist doctrine of their own manufacture, a doctrine which in practice has proved to be the most vicious in human history . . .'

Dear God, she wondered, ever more bewildered. *What is he talking about? He has to be insane.*

'I . . . I know May Day,' she ventured. 'I think.'

'Good.' He began to climb, the hellish glow rising around him, leaving only blackness below. 'We . . . or rather *you* will restore it to its former glory.'

'Wait please . . . tell me what you mean!'

But he said no more, and a few seconds later had vanished. Something heavy and wooden thudded into place overhead, and to Gracie's hopeless wails, the last vestige of crimson light was extinguished.

Chapter 34

The Moorside was a tall, narrow, redbrick building, located next to a humpbacked bridge and a disused station on the Manchester to Buxton railway line. A vast Victorian cemetery, complete with sooty sepulchres and crabby, moss-covered angels, lay to one side of it, while on the other was a sprawling council estate. No doubt this latter had once been the moor that The Moorside had overlooked.

Heck appraised it from his car. Without doubt, this was the dreariest-looking pub the investigation had brought him to thus far. Of course, the turbulent, rain-filled sky made a gloomy backdrop, and his own mood didn't help.

He'd woken that morning cold and alone.

The glimpses afforded to him last night through Claire's open bathrobe had aroused him the way they would any other red-blooded male, but she'd been drunk and vulnerable at the time. He'd kissed her long and deep, but had come to his senses before things had gone too far, and, despite her slurred protests – and a voice inside shouting hoarsely that desperate bastards like him couldn't afford to be so bloody ethical! – had tied the flaps of her robe together, and steered her back down the passages to her own room, laying her on the bed himself when they got there because she'd passed out in the doorway. It was the sort of gallant deed that might get him a reward in heaven but probably not on earth, he reflected morosely. Not only had he got up alone that morning, he'd then found a note pushed under his door from the lady in question, reiterating that she wasn't sticking with the job. It was just too much for her, she said, and though she expected that she'd probably get hardened to it eventually, all she could visualise at present was a future of being taken places where she didn't want to go. She hoped he understood and didn't think too much the less of her.

'Thanks for everything,' Claire's note had concluded.

Heck locked the door to his Volkswagen, and walked into the pub. Though a large building, only a fraction of the place was in use. Doors leading into other sections were closed and locked, chairs and tables stacked in front of them. The bar counter itself was small, eight feet long at the most, with a stack of well-thumbed newspapers at one end and a portable television at the other, on which the day's first race-meets were screening. It wasn't yet lunchtime, but several forlorn, unemployed drinkers were already gathered in there.

The barmaid was pleasant enough: young and pretty, wearing her blonde hair in a long ponytail. Her white t-shirt and tight jeans accentuated her buxom figure. When she spoke, it was in a Polish accent. 'Hi. What can I get you?'

Heck flashed his warrant card, and the welcome faded from her smile. 'DS Heckenburg,' he said. 'I understand you have a lad works here, name of Pete Dwyer?'

She nodded uncertainly. 'Yes . . . erm, Pete is not working today.'

'I understand he lives upstairs?'

She shrugged again.

'Well does he, or doesn't he?' Heck had long passed the stage where he was prepared to tolerate the runaround.

'I . . . erm . . .' Suddenly it seemed that she didn't understand English.

'Miss . . . if you expect me to believe that you don't know whether one of your co-workers lives on these premises, then you're taking me for a fool, and that's not something I appreciate. In fact, I so *don't* appreciate it that if you refuse to tell me exactly what I want to know right now, you could find yourself under arrest for obstructing an investigation. Pete Dwyer? Where is he?'

She glanced nervously at the other drinkers, though no one else was paying them much attention. Still not wanting to take chances, the barmaid produced a pen and scratched a number on a beer mat. It read '19'.

Heck nodded and moved away.

Access to the pub's upper floors was gained by a door to the left of the toilet passage. The stairwell was dingy and unlit, its paper mouldering, its carpet threadbare. He passed several other rooms on his way up. A couple stood open, their interiors dark and musty, smelling of stale beer. When he finally found number nineteen, it was at the very top of the building, on a narrow, creaky landing illuminated by a single, dust-covered skylight. From beyond the lone door came a low pulse of music: hard rock, accompanied by a repetitive gasping and grunting.

That bedsit of his is like a backroom in Bangkok, Cameron Boyd had said.

Heck knocked.

'Who is it?' came a gruff voice.

'Pete, I need a quick word.'

'I said who is it?'

'Can you just come out? Won't take a sec.'

There was a shuffling of feet on the other side of the door, and it opened a crack. The bloke peeking out was tall and thin. He had a bush of dark hair, a long, acne-scarred face and a lantern jaw. He was clad only in boxer shorts and mismatched socks.

Heck lunged forward, shouldering the door open and shoving him backwards. 'DS Heckenburg, Serial Crimes Unit. Can I come in? Oh . . . thanks.'

Dwyer hit the floor with such a bang that it sent a vibration across the room, flickers scurrying over the various computer screens. All were playing different types of kinky porn, but on the one directly facing Heck, a freckle-faced redhead in Swedish pigtails was frolicking with a Shetland pony in a manure-filled stable. Fascinated, he looked further afield. Jerry-built shelves sagged beneath the weight of DVDs, some of whose colourful plastic cases made them look legitimate, though others wore cardboard and had homemade labels affixed. In one corner, an open box spilled a host of foreign imports. Heck assumed they were foreign, as they all had photos of Japanese schoolgirls on the covers. Scruffy clothing littered the floor, alongside beer cans and unwashed plates and cutlery. The unmade bed looked damp and dirty.

'Caught you in mid-wank, did I?' Heck said. 'Or is this actually more of a business enterprise?'

Dwyer scrambled angrily to his feet – though he noticeably didn't approach. 'Hey . . . I don't know who the fuck you think you are . . .'

'I've told you who I am.' Heck showed his warrant card, but continued to glance from screen to screen. 'My, my . . . this is what you call the extreme end of the market, Pete. I guess the regular stuff is too easy to get hold of, eh? Blokes like you need to go the extra mile to make a profit these days?'

'It's for my own use,' Dwyer said defensively.

'Even so, I can't think what the Cyber Crimes Unit will make of all this.'

279

'I'm not doing anything wrong. There's nothing illegal here.'

'Maybe not, but they'll want to take a good look first. Ship everything back to the office – in sterile evidence sacks, obviously.' Heck pulled out a drawer. It was filled with unmarked computer disks and pen-drives. He shook his head. 'Got a lot of storage space here, Pete. Gonna take us a long time to trawl our way through this lot. But we have to be safe, you know what I mean?'

'You can't do this.' Dwyer pointed a shaking finger. 'This is an illegal search.'

'What would you say, Pete, if I told you that it's not you and your collection we're actually interested in?'

'I don't fucking care. You can't threaten me like this. I know my rights.'

Heck smiled. 'You don't have any rights. You're a dirty little parasite preying on people's inadequacies. So regardless of whether this is an illegal search or not, the next one won't be. And if there's anything in this room that shouldn't be you're going to prison. Your choice.'

Dwyer was still breathing hard. 'What . . . what do you want to know?'

'Cameron Boyd.'

'Oh, fuck . . .'

'Don't worry. He's in the slammer and he's likely to stay there for some time.'

'He's got mates.'

'In a round-about way you'll be saving Cameron's arse, so he'll probably be glad you've had a word.'

'What's he done this time?'

'He gave some blonde bird a knee-trembler outside this pub last November.'

Dwyer looked perplexed, but nodded. 'Yeah, I remember that.'

'Okay . . . so tell me what happened.'

'Well . . .' Dwyer still seemed surprised that he wasn't being asked about something more serious. 'It was a bit weird, I suppose. She came in the pub and started offering it. She wasn't charging, if that's what you're getting at . . . least, I don't think she was.'

'And she just picked Boyd out because she liked the look of him?'

'She picked him out for *some* reason. No one likes the look of him.'

'You obviously remember this well. Did you film it?'

'I didn't exactly film it. But we caught it on the outside security camera.'

'Let's have a look.'

Dwyer eyed him warily, before digging through another drawer and extricating a pen-drive. 'I copied what happened, and edited it, so I could put it on one of those compo things. You know . . . real security footage catches people at it?'

'No. I didn't know about that.'

'It's a niche interest.' Dwyer inserted the drive into a computer port. 'You can never see much. But even by those standards, this is crap quality.'

The image that came onscreen was black and white and pixellated constantly. Though it depicted two people against a brick wall, little else was clear. One of them might have been Boyd, while the other looked like a slim, blonde girl – though only the top of her head and part of her profile was visible. There was no facial detail.

'Has she been in since?' Heck asked.

'Not that I've noticed.'

'What about before?'

Dwyer shrugged. 'Never seen her once. But I'll tell you who might have. Mick the Muppet.'

Heck raised an eyebrow.

'One of our regulars. He's never out of here.'

Mick the Muppet was so regular a customer at The Moorside that he now had his own personalised seat. It was in a cubby-hole just to the left of the bar, and there was a wooden plaque over the top of it, bearing the legend:

Mick's Corner

He was somewhere in his late eighties, brown-skinned and incredibly wizened, but as per his nickname, he was spookily reminiscent of the TV character, Waldorf. Thick white sideburns grew down either cheek, he had a huge jaw, and his eyes were large, lugubrious and located either side of a bulbous nose covered in excrescences. Somewhat incongruously, he was wearing a bush hat and an age-old camouflaged combat jacket.

'I'm an ex-commando before you ask,' he grunted, as he finished his pint of mild.

'That's what I thought,' Heck said, pulling up a chair. 'Mind if I sit?'

'Free country. Thanks to people like me.'

'I'm a police officer.'

'You don't say.'

'Can we have a chat?'

'Throat's a bit dry.' Mick coughed. 'Never much of a conversationalist when my throat's dry.'

Heck turned to the bar, where Dwyer had appeared along-side the Polish barmaid and was watching nervously as he tucked his shirt flaps into a pair of jeans. 'Another pint of mild over here, please,' Heck shouted.

'Thank you kindly,' Mick said when the brimming glass was placed in front of him. 'Come about that slip of a tart, have you? That blonde piece from last November?'

'How did you guess?'

'Weird set-up, that. Pretty young lass doing what she did. Been murdered 'as she?'

'Not as far as we know.'

Mick looked vaguely surprised. 'Wouldn't have trusted that bugger who took her outside, I'll tell you.'

'Someone took her outside, did they?' Heck asked.

Mick nodded as he supped. 'Mean-looking young shithouse from down Longsight. Bad lot down there. Thieves and addicts. Turning this country into a craphole.'

'Do you know who she is, Mick? Because we need to contact her.'

Mick finished his mild and laid the empty down, smacking his lips.

'This is serious,' Heck said paiently.

'So's my thirst, son, so's my thirst.' Heck signalled for another pint of mild. When it arrived, Mick gazed down at it soulfully. 'I always think of pints of mild as being like buses.'

'You mean there's never one around when you need it?'

'Correct. And when there is, they've usually come in twos . . .'

'Bring him another,' Heck called. 'So . . . do you know who she is?'

'Can't help you with her name, son. She's not going to say it out loud, is she? Probably be a falsie, even if she did . . . coming to places like this to get dicks up her twat.'

'Would you recognise her again?'

'I might. Seen her before.'

Heck regarded him carefully. 'In this pub?'

Mick's lips quivered as he pondered. 'I visit so many pubs, you see. Can't recollect.' He nudged the glasses in front of him, even though one of them was still almost full.

'You've recollected okay up to now.'

'When you're my age, the brain needs oiling regular.'

'Pete!' Heck called to the bar. 'Another pint of mild please.'

'She wasn't in this pub as such,' Mick said. 'She was outside. Couple of weeks before that thing with the shithouse from Longsight. Saw her one lunchtime when I was coming in. She wasn't dressed for shagging that time. Had an anorak on, I think. Only saw the top bit because she was in the passenger seat of this flash motor. Just parked up, it was . . . like they were looking the place over.'

'Who was driving? The young fella who was with her the second time?'

'Don't think so.' Mick ruminated, then smiled with satisfaction as his next pint was placed in front of him. 'Older bloke, heavier. Couldn't see him properly. I'm eighty-eight, you know. You're doing well to get this much out of me.'

'Would you recognise this bloke again?'

'Think he had specs on – small ones, but I can't be sure.'

'What about the car? You said it was a flash job.'

Mick gazed down. The other empties had been removed. Only one pint glass remained, albeit a full one. 'Looks lonely that, doesn't it?'

'Keep drinking like this and you're genuinely not going to remember anything.'

'You make it to my age, son, you can lecture me about the perils of drink.'

'You know, Mick . . . your assistance here won't go unnoticed. You could be helping us solve a very serious crime, but you keeping stringing me along like this and that could be construed a crime in itself.'

Mick grinned. 'That's something else when you get to my age, son . . . *like I care.*'

'Another one please!' Heck called to the bar.

'I don't know what kind it was,' Mick said. 'Smoke-grey. Dead posh. Want me to draw it for you?'

Heck stared at him blankly.

Mick shrugged. 'Up to you, son, but it's the best you'll get. I once spent ten weeks at an observation post watching Jap troop movements up the Imphal road.'

Heck ambled to the bar. 'I need paper and a pencil.'

'This isn't a school-room, you know,' Dwyer said irritably.

'Just do as I ask, eh. Cameron'll thank you for it.'

'What about them five pints of mild?'

'Put them on *your* tab.'

'Eh?' Dwyer looked stunned.

'We don't get drink allowances in CID anymore. What decade you living in, Pete?'

Chapter 35

As evidence, the drawing in Heck's pocket was of limited value.

Mick the Muppet might once have been a dab hand at sketching Japanese tanks and artillery, but there had clearly been a significant deterioration in the last sixty-nine years. His crude picture, created entirely from memory, might – just conceivably *might* – be a Jaguar XF, but even if he'd produced the most vivid piece of art since Andy Warhol fulfilled his own fifteen minutes of fame, Mick the Muppet hadn't named it as such. By his own admission, he had no idea what make or model the car was, and without a VRM, even those details would be too vague. For the time being though, Heck decided he'd hang on to it – mainly because he couldn't bear thinking that the line of enquiry he'd been following for about three weeks had led precisely nowhere.

It was late afternoon when he got back to Manor Hill, but before he could even enter the building, he met Garrickson coming out, pulling an anorak over his suit. 'Where've *you* been?' the DCI asked.

'Chasing Boyd's DNA.'

'And?'

'Nothing so far.'

'Never mind that.' Garrickson strode across the car park, beckoning Heck to follow. 'You're coming with me to Preston.'

'Preston?'

'In your prolonged absence, there's been plenty going on.'

'Don't tell me we've got another body?'

'No, but we're not out of the woods yet . . . it's Beltane for another seven hours.'

'We shouldn't get too hung up on that,' Heck said. 'According to Eric's list, there are eighteen possible dates in May.'

'Not if we nip this thing in the bud.'

Gary Quinnell strolled out of the nick. He too was pulling on a waterproof.

'What's going on?' Heck asked as the big Welshman fell into step alongside him.

'We've got a new lead. A bloody good 'un.'

They piled into Garrickson's Ford Kuga and drove out through the barricade of journalists and press-vans. While not exactly jovial, the DCI seemed to be in a slightly more amicable mood than usual.

'You know Claire Moody's resigned?' he said.

'Yeah,' Heck replied.

'She's no fucking use anyway. We won't miss her, but I still gave her a bollocking.'

Heck strongly wanted to say something, but managed to confine himself to safer topics. 'What's the new lead?'

'Bit ironic actually.' Garrickon shook his head as he drove. 'The brass told us to keep our gobs shut, but if some fucker hadn't blabbed to the press, we'd never have got a break like this.'

'Don't follow.'

'Some bird called Tabby Touchstone. Apparently, she edits a horror magazine.'

'Horror magazine?'

'Yeah . . .' Garrickson chuckled without humour. 'These are the sort of dickheads we're having to rely on to break this fucking case. Anyway, she contacted us this afternoon. Apparently about six years ago something a bit weird happened to her. Some horror writer sent her a story called *Blood Feast*. It concerns a bunch of deranged killers who celebrate ancient festivals with human sacrifices. Ring any bells?'

'Who's the writer?' Heck asked.

'Name's Dan Tubbs. No, I've never heard of him either. But the main thing is this, this *Blood Feast* farrago . . . seems that some of the killings in it are a bit similar to the ones we're investigating.'

'What are we saying? This whole thing's a rip-off of some cheapjack horror story?'

'Funny, isn't it? Given the amount of grey matter we've expounded on it. I'd piss myself laughing if I didn't feel like crying. But get this . . . Tabby Touchstone rejected the story on the grounds that it was implausible. Like it couldn't happen in real life.'

'She was on the ball,' Quinnell remarked.

'In response, this bloke Tubbs turned nasty and sent her a threatening letter, in which he promised to show her otherwise.'

'Tell me this guy Tubbs is the one we're going to see now,' Heck said.

'Made a voter's roll check half an hour ago . . . he still lives in the same address he wrote to her from all those years ago. Ribbleton in Preston, only thirty miles north of here, but less than half a mile from the wasteland where Barry Butterfield got turned into a pig-roast last Bonfire Night.'

'We need that letter too,' Heck said.

'We're getting it. Tabby Touchstone's a bit on the meticulous side. Keeps records of everything. Brighton CID are taking a statement from her as we speak.'

They switched from the M62 to the M6, and entered Preston, Lancashire, about half an hour later. They drove through the inner suburb of Ribbleton, prowling one run-down neighbourhood after another, before parking up on the next street to Plumpton Brow, where the mysterious Dan Tubbs lived. Heck had expected that some of the team investigating the bonfire murder would have met them here, but apparently Garrickson hadn't sent word ahead. 'Everyone else is busy,' he explained as they climbed from the Kuga.

Heck glanced around. The drizzle had stopped, but the desolate streets were still wet. It was cold and breezy; it felt more like autumn than high spring. 'Okay . . . so why didn't we bring extra bods from Manor Hill?' he asked.

'They're busy too.'

This was almost certainly true. No one in Operation Festival was sitting around making paperclip chains, but though three of them ought to be enough to handle one prisoner, Gemma wouldn't have believed in taking such a chance, and would have made other forces available as back-up. Garrickson ought to have felt the same way too, but for some reason had decided against it. Heck wondered if the DCI was on Gemma's shit-list for leaving Claire to twist in the wind at the press conference, and was now trying to improve his position by casting himself as the guy who cracked the case. He'd brought Heck and Quinnell along as muscle, but he wouldn't want too many extra hands because he wouldn't want to share the credit. It didn't seem the best reason to go in under-strength.

They followed a connecting ginnel, ankle-deep in trash. When they reached Plumpton Brow, they waited at the end of the alley, watching number thirty-six, Tubbs's home address. It was about three houses away. Like all the others, it was in a poor state: sooty, scabrous brickwork, the front door scuffed and dented, but a thin curtain was drawn across the upstairs window, a light visible behind it.

'We just going blundering in, locking this guy up?' Quinnell asked, increasingly sharing Heck's reservations. Gemma had spent considerable time teaching her SCU protégés caution. There was something to be said for that, but by the same token, Garrickson's reply that they'd wasted too much time already watching suspects and not apprehending them also rang true. They needed to start making ground.

They hung on a moment, spying out the land. Still there was nobody around.

'Heck, you're coming with me to the front door,' Garrickson said. 'Gary . . . round to the rear. Don't let anyone see you.'

Quinnell nodded and withdrew along the ginnel.

Heck and Garrickson waited. The street was no longer bare of life. A figure appeared at the far end, walking slowly towards them. They stepped back a couple of paces. It was an old woman in a shabby mac and slippers, her lank grey hair in rollers. She let herself into one of the houses. Its door closed with an echoing *thump*.

Still they waited.

'Why don't you say something if you think I'm going about this the wrong way?' Garrickson said.

Heck shrugged. 'This is your show, sir. You're the one who'll live or die by it. But for what it's worth, I think we should be making arrests too.'

Garrickson focused on the house again. 'It's a good lead. You must admit that.'

'Best we've had so far . . . which is what worries me. This bloke Tubbs tells someone he's going to start committing a series of crimes he invented in a work of fiction? And then he actually *does*? I thought we'd be dealing with someone a bit smarter.'

'Well, if nothing else it meets your stipulation. What was it you said . . . that he'd either be a scholar or a writer?'

Heck had to agree with that. Garrickson's phone rang. It was Quinnell, letting them know he was in place at the rear.

'Okay.' Garrickson zipped his anorak up. 'Let's do it.'

As they walked across the street towards the house, Heck glanced again at the upstairs window. He could have sworn the curtain had just twitched.

'We'll talk to him at first,' Garrickson said. 'But if he doesn't want to play ball, we go at him hard. Whatever the bastard says, he's coming with us.'

As soon as they knocked on the front door, they heard the clump of heavy feet on an internal flight of stairs. The door banged inward to the length of its security chain, and a brutish visage peered out. He was a couple of inches taller than either of the two cops, with a bloated, bearded face and staring, bloodshot eyes. A huge beer belly pushed against his knitted sweater, and yet he couldn't have been more than twenty-eight.

'Yeah?' he said suspiciously.

'Daniel Tubbs?' Garrickson asked.

'Who wants to know?' Now that he'd had a few seconds to look them over properly, and not liking what he saw, the householder's tone was shifting from suspicion towards naked aggression. His hairy cheeks slowly reddened.

Garrickson displayed his warrant card, only for the door to slam in his face with such force that dust spurted down from the bricks over the lintel. Even Heck was caught on the hop, but fortuitously the door didn't catch; it bounced back from its latch and when Garrickson put his shoulder to it, the chain tore from its mooring.

They found themselves in a dim entry hall, minus wallpaper, with only cruddy lino on its floor; it led all the way through the house to the rear, where it seemed likely the back door would now be open and Tubbs in the process of vacating the premises.

But he wasn't.

He was waiting for them about ten feet away.

What was more, a huge Doberman Pinscher stood in front of him, ears pricked, sabre-like fangs bared as it snarled and drooled.

'Kill 'em, Toby!' Tubbs commanded.

'We're police officers!' Garrickson tried to shout. But the dog was already upon them, slashing and tearing. Before Heck could dodge backward, it sank its teeth through his trousers into his left thigh.

'Christ almighty!' He slammed both fists down on top of its long, narrow skull, initially to no effect – its jaws remained locked into his flesh.

Garrickson kicked and punched at it as well. *'Call your dog off, you lunatic . . . I told you, we're cops!'*

'Never mind me . . .' Heck gasped, 'get the bastard!'

Garrickson fought his way past the brute. A few yards away, Dan Tubbs waited for him, grinning through his tangled beard.

'You're in more trouble than you ever imagined, pal!' Garrickson shouted.

'So are you.' Tubbs produced a baseball bat from behind his back, and howling like a madman, swung it down over his head. Garrickson could do nothing but raise his left arm. The impact was sickening. Heck felt certain the splintering crunch of bone could have been heard out back by Gary Quinnell, who, by the sounds of crashing and banging at the rear of the house, was already trying to force his way inside.

'Gary, get a move on!' Heck bellowed. *'Shit!'*

The Doberman had loosened its jaws, only to slam them closed around his left knee, applying crushing force. He tried to hop backwards, but without success; blood was already

292

streaming through the many rents in his trouser-leg. Garrickson had crumpled down to his knees, left forearm hanging at a grisly angle. Tubbs, eyes bugged like discoloured marbles in a face hued purple, stood over him triumphantly. Heck had no choice – he went for the dog's eyes, both fore-fingers at the same time. Squealing, the Doberman shied backwards. Heck followed it, swinging his foot into its throat; knocking it down in a senseless heap.

'*BASTARD!*' Tubbs screamed, launching himself forward, bat in hand. But Garrickson was still in the way and managed to wrap his one good arm around Tubbs's legs. The giant fell full-length onto the linoleum floor. Garrickson shrieked as his shattered limb twisted in the process.

Heck rushed at Tubbs as he tried to get back to his feet, grappling with him, but was still hoisted upward and thrown sideways onto a radiator. From the back of the house the frenzied banging continued, until the rear door burst inwards, frosted glass flying, as Quinnell finally forced his way through. Tubbs, who now had Heck against the wall by the scruff of the neck and was about to brain him with the bat, was distracted by this – Heck rammed his good leg down, grinding the heel on his assailant's toes. Tubbs danced backward. He still aimed a blow with the bat, but Heck was able to duck, and a chunk of plaster was gouged from the wall.

At last Quinnell joined the fight. He was more Tubbs's size, only fitter. They wrestled savagely, Quinnell soon getting the better of it and landing a sufficiently meaty punch on Tubbs's jaw to knock him dazed to his knees, where Heck was able to cuff his wrists behind his back.

'You stupid psycho pillock!' Heck panted into his ear. 'You may not even be the bloke we came here looking for . . . but you'll be inside till you're sixty for this.'

Chapter 36

'Look . . . I have rage issues,' Tubbs protested.

'You mean you've got a filthy temper?' Quinnell said, one hand clamping his handcuffed wrist.

'It's a form of depression. I'm on prescription tranquillisers for it.'

'Doesn't surprise me much. You belong in the nuthouse, boyo. But you'll be lucky if you get off as easy as that.'

They were standing on the pavement outside thirty-six, Plumpton Brow. A couple of local police units were also parked there, one of them a van for prisoner transport. Neighbours stood outside their front doors, muttering quietly.

Tubbs, watching mournfully as the ambulance containing Garrickson receded down the darkened street, seemed genuinely sorry for what he'd done. This was only part of the personality change he'd undergone during the last fifteen minutes. The anger had drained out of him like water from a sieve, and he'd become almost child-like in his demeanour. He seemed bewildered by the flashing blue lights reflecting on the front of his house.

Heck, whose wound had been cleaned by one of the paramedics, and whose trouser-leg was now held together by safety-pins, was standing a few yards away with a uniformed sergeant.

'Hey, wait!' Tubbs shouted as two PCs began hustling him away. 'Wait . . . *please*!'

Heck raised his hand and they halted.

'Look, I'll . . . I'll come clean, okay!' Tubbs jabbered. 'I'll come clean!'

'You understand that you're still under caution?' Heck told him.

'Yeah, yeah . . . course. Look, it was about two months ago when I did it! I'll cooperate. Tell you everything. I just want this over and done with.'

'Did what?' Heck asked him.

'Used that credit card. Bought some stuff with it. I know it was a brain-dead thing to do, but I'm skint you see.'

Heck and Quinnell glanced at each other. 'What credit card is this?' Heck asked.

'Les Atkinson's,' Tubbs said. 'This bloke down the pub. Always pissed as a fart. It was easy doing it. He only noticed it had gone a few days later. Thought he'd bloody lost it. I felt bad about that . . . so I only used it once. I know I'm a dipstick, but it's the only crime I've ever committed. I've been sitting here ever since, crapping myself, waiting for you lot to show up. That's why I panicked.'

Heck felt as if he wanted to lie down. 'What's your *real* story, Dan? Who are you exactly and what do you get up to every day?'

'I'm an author.'

'That your full-time job?'

'I used to be a porter for the Health Authority, but I got made redundant a few years ago. Thought it was a good thing at the time . . . thought I could concentrate on my writing. But I've had next to nothing published.'

'What about *Blood Feast*?' Quinnell asked.

Tubbs looked startled. 'Eh?'

Heck took up the question. 'Didn't you write a story called *Blood Feast*?'

'A novella . . . yeah. How'd you know about that?'

'What did it involve?'

'Erm . . .' Tubbs still looked gobsmacked. 'A pagan cult. They sacrificed their victims on special holidays. Have a look at it, yourself. I've got a load of spare copies upstairs.'

Heck and Quinnell went upstairs in the house, while Tubbs was kept down in the hall by the local uniforms. His shouted directions sent them into a back bedroom, which was empty of furnishings aside from a few shelves piled with splotchy, printed sheets. At one end of the middle shelf lay a neater stack of fifty or so booklets – at first glance little more than rag-mags, crudely stapled, but each bearing the same cover illustration: a severed head and two severed hands mounted on spikes. Over the top, the title read:

BLOOD FEAST

Heck flicked through, stopping several pages in to read.

'Listen to this . . . Valentine's Day. Two lovers are caught shagging in a car. Their hearts are cut out and pinned to a tree with an arrow.'

'Not quite the same,' Quinnell said.

'Close though. How about this . . . Good Friday? A priest gets nailed to a cross made from pews in his own church. Two local toe-rags who were trying to pinch lead from the church roof get crucified alongside him.'

Quinnell regarded him with amazement. No words were needed.

Tubbs watched, baffled, as they came clumping down the narrow stair.

'You said you've been sitting here, crapping yourself, Dan,'

Heck said, slapping one of the booklets against the prisoner's chest. 'You've bloody good reason to.'

'Who are you, the fucking fiction police? It's just a story. No one even wanted it. I only sent it to one editor, and she rejected it . . . said it was totally unrealistic.'

'We know,' Quinnell said. 'But didn't you then threaten to "show her otherwise"?'

'Hang on . . . hang on a mo'!' An expression of dull horror was dawning on Tubbs's brutish face. 'You're not talking about these Desecrator murders? *Jesus H. Christ, you've got to be kidding!*'

'Did you or did you not write a threatening letter to Tabby Touchstone?'

'Yeah, yeah!' Tubbs nodded frantically. 'But it was bullshit. You've seen what I'm like. I lose my rag and do all sorts of stuff I don't mean.'

Even though a heated denial was only to be expected, Heck couldn't ignore a wearisome gut feeling that this wasn't their man. A cursory look around the place revealed dishes so unwashed there were cultures growing on them, carpets impacted with the crumbs of decades, a mantelpiece in the living room chocka with pills. On top of that, Tubbs was a total buffoon – big enough and crazy enough to hammer someone senseless on the spur of the moment, but lacking the organisational skills to run his own life effectively, let alone arrange a series of clever, preplanned murders.

'When the Desecrator crimes actually began,' Heck said, 'you never once thought "Hold on, there's a connection here? Has someone taken my ideas on board?"'

Tubbs groaned aloud. 'I told you . . . no one ever bought the story. I only sent it to one editor, and never again after she told me what a pile of fucking dogshit it was!' Slowly, convulsively, he began struggling, and it took Quinnell and a couple of uniforms to restrain him again, though this time there was no kicking out, no shouting or screaming. He slumped in their grasp, breathing heavily. Tears, possibly born more of sorrow than rage, seeped onto his cheeks.

'So Tabby Touchstone is the only other person who's seen this story?' Heck asked.

'Yeah. She said it was so daft I didn't dare send it anywhere else.'

'And what did you mean when you told her you were going to prove otherwise?'

'For Christ's sake, I meant I was going to rewrite it, then publish it myself. Make a mint out of it without having to pay some useless middle-man. And as you saw upstairs, I never sold a fucking one. It's cost me more than I've earned from it.'

'You're absolutely sure nobody else has ever seen this story?'

'Not a single person wanted to buy it . . . oh!' Tubbs's expression rapidly changed. 'Oh . . . *fuck*!'

'What?' Heck asked.

'Six years ago . . . the British Horror Convention in Bristol. I took it down there. Oh shit, any fucker could have picked it up.'

'What are you talking about?'

'I couldn't sell it, so I thought I'd give it away . . . you know, use it as a marketing gimmick to get me better known. So I left it on tables around the hotel. Only about twenty copies though.'

'How many were picked up?'

'Dunno. . . . I never went round to see.'

Heck pinched the bridge of his nose to check that he was still alive, before turning to the uniformed sergeant. 'If your lads can take him down to Preston Central, that'd be great. He's arrested on suspicion of stealing a credit card, obtaining property by deception, causing grievous bodily harm to a police officer and anything else I can think of regarding that dog. I'll be down to sort it in ten.'

Tubbs was wheeled away, still protesting, and placed in the caged section at the rear of the prisoner transport. It disappeared in a swirl of exhaust.

Quinnell leaned against the splintered door-jamb. 'What do you think?'

'It isn't him.' Heck rubbed at his mauled thigh, which throbbed horribly as the damaged flesh tightened. 'I wish it was, but it isn't.'

'What about this Tabby Touchstone? Sounds . . . I dunno, a bit witchy.'

'So she should. She edits a horror magazine. Probably only a pen-name anyway. We'll see what Brighton think of her . . . but I wouldn't hold out much hope.'

Chapter 37

It seemed ridiculous for a woman of her age, but Claire had never attempted to drive such a distance late at night before; not on her own.

At first, a midnight departure had seemed a sensible idea. The roads would be deserted; she'd be home in under three hours. And what if she *was* being tortured by worry and uncertainty at having suddenly run away? Maybe a few hours at the wheel, eyes glued on the spooled-out ribbon of empty blacktop, would help put things into perspective. She hadn't expected the roads to be quite this empty, though.

The surrounding woods and fields were an unlit void. Cars occasionally flipped by in the opposite direction, but she'd seen only one other vehicle on her side of the carriageway since joining the M62 – and that in itself had been a little unnerving. Because it was still there, behind her by a distance of about sixty yards; indistinguishable of course, nothing more than a pair of unblinking luminous eyes, but travelling at a steady seventy mph – as she was. At first she'd fancied that it might have come down the slip road from the motel in pursuit of her; had wondered if maybe it was one of the officers on the team who'd twigged what she was up to and was now tailing her. But it wasn't long before she'd dismissed that notion as guilt-fuelled paranoia.

Okay, it wasn't the done thing to sneak off in the middle of an investigation, even if you were a civvie; it could well be deemed an abrogation of duty. But she didn't see how anyone could have suspected that this was what she'd been planning – mainly because she hadn't been. It had been a spur of the moment decision, even if it hadn't been an easy one (despite yet another terrible tongue-lashing from DCI Garrickson). She didn't like what she was doing; she hated herself for it – but she genuinely didn't see what purpose would be served by hanging around at Manor Hill. She'd let everyone down, including herself. She patently couldn't do the job and was nothing more than a laughing stock.

Not that she'd put these exact thoughts in the resignation letter she'd emailed to Superintendent Piper. She'd said no more to Gemma than she had to Heck the night before: that she wasn't right for this post, and the sooner she was out of it the better for all of them. She'd had no response as yet.

She glanced again into her rear-view mirror. The other car had drifted further behind; it wasn't far off vanishing altogether – which was a bit of a relief, she supposed. Its failure to overtake her on an empty road, when she was only doing seventy, had perhaps seemed a little suspicious – but it really made no sense to assume that someone else on the team was watching her. At present they had vastly bigger fish to fry. She glanced at the mirror again; the car was now at the extreme end of her rear-view vision, and still receding.

But Christ . . . sneaking off at midnight looked a desperate ploy.

Again, Claire was torn by doubt. How would this appear? Even those of a charitable disposition would say that she was fleeing her responsibilities, and there'd be no way to deny that. She genuinely believed that she'd messed things up for everyone else and didn't know how she could face them, and if, as Garrickson had aggressively told her, the second kidnapped prostitute died 'because of her fucking inefficiency', she couldn't possibly stick around and be forced to gaze upon the crime scene glossies that would prove it. But there was no point pretending she wasn't deeply ashamed by what felt like rank cowardice. Claire had always prided herself on loyalty and stoicism. True, she'd never come up against a horror of this magnitude, but by nature she wasn't a quitter, and the more she thought about this, the more it hurt her.

She checked the mirror again – the other car had drawn a little nearer, but was still a good hundred yards behind. Then something else distracted her: a warning light next to the steering column.

It was the fuel gauge.

Claire's first reaction was shock; she'd filled up with petrol only a couple of days earlier, and had barely used her vehicle since. Her second reaction was further self-denigration; Christ, how ludicrous was it to have got so wrapped in other things that she hadn't noticed this before now? Her third reaction was panic, because the needle on the gauge was actually below the red, and according to her sat-nav, the next services were at Burtonwood, which was a good ten miles away. She shifted over into the slow lane, trying to calculate her chances of making it, but suspecting the worst. According to the fuel gauge, she was already running on fumes.

A turn-off appeared ahead, connecting with 'Clock Face' and 'Bold Heath', two localities she'd never even heard of before. That hardly mattered of course, if there was a petrol station nearby. She veered onto the exit road. Just getting off the M62 was probably a good thing if she was about to run out of fuel.

The slip road ended a hundred yards later at a T-junction.

302

Claire slowed as she approached, but didn't dare stop in case she wasn't able to start again. She swung left, cruising onto what looked like a deserted B-road. There was no sign of a petrol station yet, but it surely couldn't be long. Merseyside was a more rural county than outsiders might imagine, but it wasn't a wilderness – there were dollops of conurbation everywhere, even if at present only more moonlit fields and darkened woodland skimmed past her windows. She checked her gauge again; the needle was so low that it was beyond her understanding how she was still in motion. Even if she passed a pub or restaurant, it would be closed at this late hour . . . though its car park might still be accessible. She could at least exit the road.

And then what?

Could she call the AA? She didn't know if they'd turn out for someone who'd been dozy enough to run out of petrol. There had to be a local breakdown service, but the same question applied. The obvious thing to do was ring the MIR. That was manned round-the-clock. Someone would respond, though she'd feel like the biggest fool on Earth.

She peered ahead intently, doing her best to keep her foot off the pedal, trying to freewheel as much as she could to minimise fuel-use. She swerved around a hair-pin bend, the zigzag black and white flashes flickering through her head-lights. Beyond that there was more woodland – dense and leafy, enclosing the road from either side.

And then salvation – she rounded a second bend and saw what looked like a petrol station about thirty yards ahead on the left, complete with canopy and shop. No lights were visible, but that was hardly a surprise; nor did it really matter – at least she'd be in the right place to get refuelled in the morning. She made it over the final few yards without a hitch, the engine only conking out as she pulled up on the concrete forecourt alongside the pumps.

She slumped down with relief.

It was about a minute later when she finally glanced up again – and saw padlocked grilles on the shop's windows and doors, all eaten by rust. Some of the glass behind them was broken. When she looked across the forecourt, it was strewn with leaves and litter. The petrol pumps were thickly furred with dust.

Claire closed her eyes with disbelief. Her head sagged down, her chin hitting her chest. She now had no option but to call the AA. Well, that wasn't too bad. If nothing else, they could at least advise her. She groped in the handbag on the front passenger seat, rummaging for her mobile, but initially was unable to locate it. Frustrated, she switched the interior light on and peered into the bag, searching with both hands, but there was no sign of the phone among her toiletries and make-up. Puzzled, she climbed out and walked around the car, intending to search the passenger side footwell – and was shocked to see that the hinged flap covering the petrol-cap was open.

The cap itself was unscrewed, and hung by its plastic tag. At least the mystery of why she'd run out of fuel was solved. She obviously hadn't replaced the cap after filling up the day before yesterday, and had been driving around with the tank open. But no . . . that didn't ring true. Wasn't there a valve inside the average modern petrol tank, to prevent the liquid sloshing out?

Someone else had opened it, she realised with a chill.

There was no sign of damage around the cap, so it couldn't have been forced. Which meant only one thing; that someone had been inside her car and had used the lever under the steering column.

Slowly, the little hairs on her neck stiffened.

Had they forced the vehicle open? Again no – she could see no damage. Which meant they'd come upon it while it was unlocked, and the only possibility of that was back at the motel, when she'd brought her car around to the front and had gone inside the building to return her room-key. She hadn't initially been able to find the night-porter, so it had taken her a good twenty minutes at least. But would that be long enough? She supposed it was conceivable, but how likely was it that an opportunist petrol thief, out there in the middle of nowhere . . .

Good Lord, had they taken her mobile at the same time?

She yanked open the passenger door and checked the foot-well and the space underneath the seat. There was no sign of it. She rooted through her bag again. It was definitely not there. But more worrying still, her purse *was* – containing at least fifty pounds in notes and change, and all her credit cards.

So an everyday thief had been into her car, searched her bag – and had taken her phone, but not her purse?

Yeah, sure.

Now tingling with fear, Claire glanced at the silent under-growth encroaching from all sides of the derelict station. She tried to tell herself that this was nothing but supposition. All that had happened was that she'd run out of petrol . . . but no, her petrol had been stolen. And so had her phone. Was it possible that whoever it was had been watching the motel, waiting to pounce in this way?

She already knew the answer of course. Something she'd overheard Sergeant Fisher say sounded in her ears again: '*Whatever these nutters' motivations, they are bloody well organised. The way they're selecting victims, luring them into traps . . . It wouldn't surprise me if they aren't following the investigation in order to improvise . . .*' She wondered again about the car on the motorway that had followed her – and as she did, she heard an approaching engine. She spun around. Headlights speared along the road in the direc-tion she'd come from.

Whoever it was, they were advancing slowly – as if looking for something.

Claire retreated across the forecourt. Even if she could find somewhere to hide, her Micra was out in the open. They'd know she was here.

It's insane, she tried to tell herself. *It can't be the same people.* But good God alive! Images of the victims – warped and mangled relics, human beings reduced to pulp and gristle – swam before her eyes. And how many times were they likely to have seen *her* on the television? *Good God, Jesus Christ, surely not this . . . not me!*

She turned and ran blindly. Aware of the engine volume increasing, the light intensifying, she threw herself against the shop door, tears of terror filling her eyes. She rammed both hands against the rotted metalwork – and to her disbelief, it swung inward.

Claire stood blinking on the threshold, gazing into a dark, musty interior.

She blundered forward, kicking through wads of grimy junk mail. The belly of the shop was crammed with obscure shapes only vaguely discernible in the blackness: racks of shelving, all now empty and skeletal and knocked askew. She stumbled among them, tripping, barking her shins. Pluming dust made her sneeze. Then bright light flooded through the grilled window. Twisting shadows travelled across the rear wall as headlamp beams spilled across the station forecourt. Claire twirled helplessly, unsure where she could go – and in the same instant the lights were gone again.

She hardly dared believe it. Had the vehicle driven past?

She held her ground, heart hammering her chest wall. The rumbling engine was audible, but slowly fading as the vehicle drew away. It was still several seconds before she let out a breath, and several minutes before she risked moving back to the door and peeking out at the forecourt.

The Micra sat alone at the derelict pumps.

She listened again. Silence.

She ventured outside, wandering warily towards her car.

She didn't even know for sure that she'd been robbed. Perhaps she *had* just been lax when she was last filling up? Perhaps she'd dropped her mobile phone? She leaned against the bodywork as her pulse slowly settled, before walking around it to the low wall separating the forecourt from the road. The spring night was so quiet – and, for the first time this year, so warm. There was a scent of blossom in the air, and chopped grass. The English countryside, she realised, cursing herself for a fool – where bad things tended *not* to happen. She glanced left along the narrow lane in the direction the trawling vehicle had just taken.

But it was still there.

Parked up about forty yards away.

Facing her.

Its headlights snapped on at full-beam.

It took everything Claire had to yank herself away and stumble back towards the station shop. Behind her, an engine came to life. Moaning, she blundered back inside, slamming the door closed. Her eyes had already attuned, so she was able to grab what looked like an old mop leaning nearby, bracing one end of it against the door's inner face and jamming the other against the nearest skirting board. She pivoted around, looking for somewhere to hide. As she did, searing light poured in behind her again. This time the shadows fled in different directions.

The vehicle was pulling onto the forecourt.

With a clunk, a handbrake was applied.

Claire tried to make her way across the room without bumping anything. It was still possible they wouldn't know where she had gone. They might – just *might* – think that the abandoned shop had been left locked.

307

Footfalls sounded outside.

She spun around again. She couldn't see clearly beyond the mesh-covered window, but a figure – a brief, blurred silhouette – moved past, heading towards the door.

She'd be safe in here, she whispered to herself. They wouldn't think she'd been able to get in. They'd search through the woods instead. She could now distinguish the service counter just ahead of her. Behind that stood a tall, slender oblong that was even blacker than the shadows around it. A door, she realised, standing ajar. She moved over there, only to kick something metallic, which might have clattered more loudly had it not rolled through matted heaps of fallen magazines.

Even so she froze, not daring to breathe.

There was a corresponding silence from outside, followed, seconds later, by a dull, prolonged creaking. Someone was applying their weight to the front door. Frantic, Claire scrambled over the counter. The space on the other side was filled with plastic bottles and empty crisp packets, which crunched and squeaked as she trod on them.

The creaking of the front door abruptly stopped.

Claire stopped too, face prickling with perspiration.

BANG! . . . the massive blow reverberated through the entire building.

Another one followed, and another.

Claire lurched forward, more terrified than she'd ever imagined it was possible to be without collapsing. She shoved at the half-open door, and it swung back. Beyond it was a second room that was almost completely dark, only dim moonlight filtering in through a high, frosted window. Claire scanned it at a glance, identifying what looked like another doorway at the other side – and went rigid at the sight of a human outline close beside it.

For a second she was so shaken that she couldn't even

whimper. But then she realised the truth: partly because of its stiff, inflexible posture, partly because of its hairless cranium and bland, featureless face.

A mannequin on a pedestal. An obvious thing, really, in a storeroom.

Another loud bang at the front of the small building sent her scurrying across the room towards the next door, which also stood ajar. Beyond this, a narrow passage led to a door standing open to the outside, where misty moonlight dappled a tarmac-covered parking bay and beyond that, a line of foliage. Claire hesitated. The way was lit for her. It was a straight passage out of here – but for some reason she delayed.

No one could be out there. Whoever had followed her here was still trying to get in through the front. Another heavy impact landed on the main door. That mop handle was proving sturdier than she'd expected, but it couldn't resist for much longer. She started forward along the passage, only to stop after four steps.

Movement.

Had the foliage twitched? No, it wasn't that . . . because now she saw the movement again.

It was a shadow on the tarmac. At first it had been difficult spotting one particular shadow lying among so many, but when she looked hard there was no mistake. It undeniably had the shape of a man: a head, arms, a torso; an incredibly broad torso, incredibly long, apelike arms. Claire backed along the passage into the storeroom. Another thunderous blow echoed through the building, accompanied by a splintering of wood as the mop began to sag. Helpless and mumbling, she turned and turned.

People walled up alive, nailed to crosses, fed to crocodiles for Christ's sake!

With tears streaming down her cheeks, she tucked herself into the dark, narrow space behind the mannequin. Who knew . . . perhaps they wouldn't look very hard? Or maybe they would, but would miss her here? There was another blow, followed by an explosive *crack* as the mop broke. From the passage leading to the rear, feet thudded on the tiles.

'There's still a chance,' she whimpered in a tiny voice. 'There's always a chance.'

'Not today,' someone whispered from the darkness behind. Before Claire could react, a slim but muscular arm hooked around her throat, locking the scream into her chest. Hot breath spilled across the back of her neck. 'Definitely not today.'

Heck and Quinnell were engaged for quite a few hours at Preston Central, interviewing Tubbs about his various offences.

With his anxieties wearing off and a more belligerent personality re-emerging, the prisoner wasn't inclined to be as compliant as he had been on his initial arrest, though only his denials about the Desecrator crimes rang true. Antecedent searches indicated that Tubbs had no known criminal associates and, up until this point at least, no criminal record of any sort, let alone form for sadistic or sexual crime. What was more, a search of his premises by Preston officers had turned up nothing suspicious, apart from a credit card bearing someone else's name.

In the end, Tubbs was charged with theft of the credit card, deception and the assault on DCI Garrickson, for which he was remanded in custody.

When all that was done, Heck and Quinnell travelled down to the Royal Preston Hospital, to find that Garrickson had suffered compound fractures to the radius and ulna. The DCI was seated alone in the A&E waiting area, naked from the waist up, his anorak draped over his back, his left arm plastered from the fingertips to the shoulder. Thanks to the painkillers pumped into him, he only looked half awake, his face grey and crumpled as soggy paper. Despite this, when Heck and Quinnell trooped in, his mouth hitched up sideways in an attempted smile.

'Did we charge him?' he asked drowsily.

'Not with murder, boss,' Heck said. 'It isn't him.'

Garrickson nodded, as if he'd suspected this all along. 'What a fucking balloon.'

'You got that right,' Quinnell agreed.

They helped him outside, where a blue-gold dawn was rising from the east and birds twittered in the hedges – at long last, spring seemed to have arrived. Garrickson was so groggy that he didn't ask for any further details about Tubbs. Within ten minutes of the journey back to the motel commencing, he was asleep in the rear seat. Quinnell nodded off in the front passenger seat five minutes after that. Heck yawned as he drove; he was aching and stiff all over, but frustration and disappointment were keeping him awake.

Then his mobile began bleeping.

He glanced at his dashboard clock – it was just after five a.m., which led him to suspect that this was going to be bad news. When he saw that the call was from Shawna McCluskey, he *knew* it was.

Chapter 38

The maypole had been erected in a place called Fiddler's Meadow, which was actually a farm field in rural Cheshire, midway between Whitchurch and Nantwich.

It was a maypole in name only. It comprised a tall timber post, painted white, with a pink twirl around it. A few ribbons had been dangled from it to indicate its purpose, but these were inconsequential. The most obvious item of interest was perched on top, about twelve feet in the air. When Heck, Shawna McCluskey and Gary Quinnell first spotted it from the nearby country lane, it initially resembled a doll that some deranged child had brutally disfigured. But when they got closer they saw that it was a human body. At least, that was what it once had been.

She was female, and the tip of the maypole must have been sharpened to a very slender point, because she'd been impaled upright on it, possibly through the vagina, but most likely, to keep her in a vertical position, through the anus. Her arms had been bound to her sides with what looked like garlands of briars, some kind of dark circlet encased her brow, and her face was charred beyond identification. A grim-faced medical examiner, who'd already been up there on a ladder, told them that the circlet was iron and that it had been red-hot when first placed on the victim's head. It had now cooled but at the time had burned clean through to the bone, which had probably been the cause of death.

'You can't have a May Queen without a crown,' Heck observed.

The figure was wearing one thigh-high leather boot, though the other had fallen off and lay at the foot of the pole; such items marked her out as a good-time girl of some sort. But over the top of her own tacky garb she'd been made to wear an extravagant light-blue frock, which, though it was now smeared with blood and fecal matter and hanging in ragged strips, was recognisable as a coronation gown. Somehow, this only added insult to the already grotesque injury; but not so much as the green spring grass, the pebble-blue sky and the pink, fluffy cherry blossoms in the trees bordering the field.

They'd known they were going to see something bad on the way there.

What other impression could they have gleaned while weaving their way through the labyrinth of police vehicles that closed off most of the adjoining roads? Some fifty yards up the line, they'd spotted two older Traffic men in flat hats and shirt-sleeves standing by the roadside, trying to offer words of comfort as a younger colleague leaned over a bramble bush, vomiting profusely. They'd even seen teary eyes among the more seasoned coppers. Those who weren't actually crying were granite-faced with a combination of anger and disbelief. Shawna was already asking questions among them, trying to ascertain a timeline of events, but getting little in response save dull shakes of the head.

'It's got to be witchcraft, hasn't it?' a wild-eyed young PC asked belligerently. He was so young he had to be a probationer, but that didn't stop him squaring up to Heck and Quinnell as they stood against the tape. 'Some kind of black magic?'

Heck was aware they weren't far from Alderley Edge, but didn't reply.

'We don't know,' Quinnell admitted.

'Do you know anything . . . anything at all?' the probationer shrieked. 'Because someone's got to catch these fucking madmen! You fuckers clearly can't!'

Two other local officers hustled the disturbed youngster away. Heck, who'd been trying without success to get through to Gemma, pocketed his mobile and glanced again at the pathetic figure atop the pole, the reddened rags of the coronation gown rippling in the May breeze.

Shawna returned to the tape. 'Seems a little old lady walking her two poodles found the body. Medical Examiner puts the time of death somewhere between eleven last night and one this morning. He isn't able to say yet how long she was up there first. The heated crown was applied near the end.'

'So she was alive when she was impaled?'

'Looks like it. Doctor thinks she probably kicked her right boot off while she was spasming in pain.'

'Christ . . .' Before Heck could give full vent to the revulsion this made him feel, the mobile began bleeping in his pocket.

It was Gemma, returning his call. He relayed everything to her, from Mike Garrickson's injury to the latest murder, stating that they had no ID on the victim yet, but that it was almost certainly Gracie Allen, the missing prostitute from Bradford. His voice slid into a dull, emotionless drone as he watched the crane that Cheshire had now brought into the field lower the broken body to the ground, where the force pathologist and his assistants were waiting.

314

When Gemma finally replied, she sounded tired and despondent. 'I won't ask if you're able to run the MIR in my absence, Heck, because I know you are . . . but I'll be back as soon as poss. I'm on the witness stand for at least another day yet . . .'

Before Heck could tell her not to worry about it, one of the medical staff waved to attract his attention. 'Gotta go, ma'am. Get back to you.'

As he pocketed the phone, one of the examiners brought something over to the tape. It was already installed inside a sterile plastic sack, but they could see that it was a scrap of bloodstained paper. A few characters looked to have been scribbled on it in pencil, though they were barely legible.

'This was inside her left boot,' the examiner, a young woman, said. 'The one she was still wearing.'

Heck snapped a pair of latex gloves on before holding it up to the light. The paper was dog-eared and flaky, and blood had obliterated some of the writing, but he thought he could ascertain one or two digits; they'd been scrawled in two vaguely straight lines, one on top of the other.

'This is a vehicle registration mark,' he said.

Quinnell looked puzzled. 'Why was it in her boot?'

'Some toms have started doing this,' Shawna replied. 'It's a kind of insurance policy.' She stepped aside as a pair of undertaker's men wheeled the body past, now enclosed in a temporary casket. 'Not much of one though.'

'It may be in her case,' Heck said. 'Albeit posthumously.'

'Can hardly read it, though,' Quinnell said. 'Can we X-ray it or something?'

'Might not help, it's written in pencil,' Heck said. 'But that may not matter.' He borrowed a radio from one of the uniforms nearby and ascertained the call-sign for the nearest Comms suite. 'Serial Crimes Unit at Fiddler's Meadow, to Foxtrot Zulu?'

The radio crackled. '*Foxtrot Zulu receiving, over.*'

'Yeah, this is DS Heckenburg. PNC check please.'

'*Go ahead.*'

'Anything on the following . . .?' He examined the slip of paper again. 'Full index unknown, exact order unknown, but contains these details: Tango or Yankee – unsure which exactly – zero – Golf – Charlie?'

'*Stand by.*'

'There's probably dozens of combinations,' Quinnell said.

Heck made no reply. He noticed that most other conversations nearby seemed to have ceased. The Cheshire officers watched with interest.

'*DS Heckenburg from Foxtrot Zulu?*' the radio chirped.

'Receiving, go ahead.'

'*Tango or Yankee – zero – Golf – Charlie. There are eight hundred and forty-three possibles, over.*'

Shawna groaned. Quinnell bared his teeth.

'Can we refine the search?' Heck replied. 'Narrow it down to Jaguar cars, over.'

They waited patiently, aware that everyone at the crime scene was waiting with them.

'*DS Heckenburg from Foxtrot Zulu?*'

'Go ahead.'

'*There are thirty-eight Jaguars on the list, over.*'

Heck's heart was thumping. 'How many of those would be smoke-grey, over?'

The response to this was immediate. '*One strike on a grey Jaguar XF.*' Heck clenched his right fist. '*Index . . . Bravo-Yankee-six-zero-Lima-Golf-Charlie. Owner . . . Leo Enwright, fifty-four years old, known not wanted. Last known address: St Bardolph's Academy, Riphall, Staffordshire, over.*'

'A school?' Quinnell said, nonplussed.

Shawna stared at Heck in a daze. 'You said it could be an academic. Jesus H, Heck . . . *we've got him*!'

'Wait!' Heck held up a hand. 'Let's not rush into anything.'
'But it all fits . . .'
'It looks like it fits,' he said. 'Before we make a move, let's find out everything we can about Leo Enwright.'

Chapter 39

Gemma was halfway up the M6 when a call came through on her mobile.

Spotting that it was from Shawna McCluskey, she didn't know whether to be hopeful or worried. The May Day murder had sent shockwaves through the country like nothing that had gone before it. That was one of the reasons she'd cut herself loose from the trial at the Old Bailey as soon as possible, and was now racing north.

She answered the call hands-free. 'Shawna?'

'Ma'am, whereabouts are you?'

'Just come off the toll road. Why?'

'You passed Stafford services yet, ma'am?'

'Not yet. Why?'

'Can you pull off there and meet a few of us?'

'What are you doing at Stafford services, Shawna?'

'Tell you as soon as you get here, ma'am . . .'

'Wait, Shawna. Have we . . . caught some kind of break?'

'I shouldn't say this, ma'am, for fear of putting the mockers on it, but . . . yes.'

*   *   *

As requested, Gemma pulled off the motorway at Stafford services and found Heck waiting by the station's entrance doors. Wearing a suit and tie, and having had a shave, he looked unusually dapper. He even had the nerve to affect frustration when he saw that she was dressed in her usual driving attire of tracksuit and trainers.

'Got a change of clothes with you, ma'am?' he asked.

'Why? What's going on?'

'Something smart and sexy, that'll make you look like the cool professional you are?'

'On the basis that I always have a grab-bag in the boot, because I never know when I might be called to the big house to explain why my team has fouled up, yeah . . . I have.'

He nodded, pleased, beckoning her inside the building. It was late morning and crammed with the usual throng of motorway travellers, but he led her through into the coffee lounge, where several of the team were seated around a table in the corner.

Shawna handed Gemma a coffee as she sat down.

'Okay,' she said. 'Would someone like to explain why you're all absent from your posts when we've just had another homicide?'

'That's being taken care of, ma'am,' Heck replied. 'We've got lots of new bodies in from Cheshire. Experienced detectives, plus uniforms to do the crappy work. DCI Garrickson is back in charge at the MIR.'

Gemma looked bewildered. 'I thought Garrickson had a broken arm?'

'He does,' Heck said. 'But he came in this morning voluntarily. He can't leave the office obviously, but he's directing operations.'

'Come the hour, come the man,' Gemma remarked, still not sounding like she believed it.

'All lines of enquiry on yesterday's maypole murder are

319

being followed as we speak,' Heck said. 'But none are as good as this one.' He pushed a print-out across the table towards her. It was a colour photograph, downloaded from a website. 'Meet Leo Enwright. *Doctor* Leo Enwright, no less.'

The man in the photo was aged in his early fifties, with plump, jowly cheeks and curly, grey 'wirewool' hair, which extended down into lush sideburns. The eyes behind his small, circular-lensed spectacles were bright green. He wore a corduroy jacket, a checked shirt and flower-patterned tie, and a sly, catlike smile.

'Who is he?' Gemma asked.

'First let me tell you how we got to him,' Heck said, and he explained about the partial VRM found in Gracie Allen's boot, and the smoke-grey Jaguar it probably belonged to, which was almost certainly the same Jaguar that took the blonde girl to the pub in Longsight – the same girl who removed the hair from Cameron Boyd's scalp.

'Enwright's a middle-aged widower,' Heck added. 'He teaches at St Bardolph's Academy, a private school near the village of Riphall, about ten miles from here. His doctorate is in anthropology, but as a teacher his specialist subjects are history, philosophy, English and drama. He's published several papers on – wait for this – folklore.'

Gemma regarded him carefully. 'So far so good.'

'It gets better. Enwright's got form. He had a difficult upbringing. As a child he was abandoned by his hippie parents and taken into care. That's the kind of trauma that some individuals never recover from. Not long afterwards, he came to the attention of the police – he was arrested several times for petty acts of theft and vandalism. At school and at the local church.'

'Violence?' Gemma asked.

'Some,' Shawna said. 'He also got arrested for cruelty to

animals. I don't need to tell you, ma'am . . . this is like the blueprint for a serial killer.'

'And there's something else,' Heck added. 'This guy is a teacher, so he has a ready-made bunch of acolytes who can assist him.'

For the first time Gemma looked shocked. 'You're not thinking pupils?'

'It's a boarding school. Okay, it's mainly for the well-heeled, but there are always outcasts – kids who are lonely, alienated. Those are the sort that go looking for mentors, and who better than the most charismatic teacher in school, because that's apparently what Enwright is.' Heck could tell that she still wasn't convinced; he leaned forward into her personal space. 'Ma'am . . . when Mike Garrickson first took the piss out of this theory, he mentioned Charles Manson. Well, actually that's not a bad analogy. It only took Manson two years to turn a bunch of clean-cut college kids into mass murderers. If Leo Enwright is our man, he's had six.'

'There's other stuff too,' Shawna said. 'One of the kids there is the son of DCI Eddie Stapleton in GMP. Which might explain how they had information about those Longsight criminals. Another one, name of Anthony Worthington, is a native of Bolton in Greater Manchester. For the last two summers, he's worked part-time as a cleaner and general dogsbody . . . at Horwich Zoo.'

Gemma remained calm, but her fingers had knotted together. Heck knew what she was thinking – that when things looked too good to be true, that was usually because they were. 'Why . . .?' she said. 'Why would Enwright start killing now? In middle-age?'

'His wife died seven years ago. In a road accident. That could have altered his psyche in some way.'

'Heck, you realise this is all circumstantial?'

'Yes I do. Which is why, this afternoon, my wife and I are calling at the school to have a look around.'

'Your wife?'

'Either you or Shawna, ma'am . . . depending on which of you fancies the job. We're going as prospective parents. I've already made the appointment. It's okay . . . I spoke to Joe Wullerton this morning. We're fully authorised.'

'Aren't you forgetting something? A week and a half ago you intruded on a television interview. You might be recognised.'

Heck smiled. 'I'm counting on it.'

Chapter 40

'So, who are we?' Gemma asked as she freshened her make-up.

'Mark and Gemma Heckenburg,' Heck said as he steered her BMW up the five-mile drive to St Bardolph's Academy. 'We're a professional couple from London. I'm an investment banker, very successful. I travel a lot, which means I haven't got much time for family life. You're in recruitment. You specialise in international banking.'

'Also successfully, I hope?' she said.

'You'll soon be opening an office in Dubai, so you must be pretty good at it. Our son, Thomas, is a gifted youngster who's just turned eleven,' Heck said. 'We're here to see if St Bardolph's is right for him.'

'Still think it'd be easier if I'd just got a warrant,' she replied, putting her make-up away and wiggling her bottom to get comfortable in her smart, tight skirt.

He shrugged. 'Up to you, but would you really want that? Raid a school during term-time? Turn it upside down? What if we're wrong? We'll have caused maximum disturbance to the school. Maximum distress to the kids. The brass'll come down on us like an avalanche. My way, we get a chance to suss the place out at close-quarters. If it turns out to be nothing, well . . . no one's been hurt. And if we're still suspicious, we can get a warrant afterwards. On top of that, the whole point in *me* doing this is to smoke them out. If they recognise me and run . . . it's as good as a confession.'

Gemma didn't argue. They'd had this conversation already, and he'd persuaded her.

They met no other cars as they followed the lengthy approach road. It was early May, but the sun shone from a pearl-blue vault, shimmering on the verdant Staffordshire countryside. The extensive grounds were a riot of blossoms and new leaves. The school, when they eventually reached it, was a collection of old stone buildings, very elegant and covered in layers of ivy, surrounded by expansive lawns.

'You're telling me a bunch of psychotic killers live in a place like this?' Gemma said when they parked on the gravel lot in front of the main building.

Heck was similarly fascinated. The place had an aura of the ancient and venerable; a quick assessment online had revealed its Elizabethan ancestry, and that among its various original features, it boasted 'green man' carvings, shadow clocks and even priest's holes – yet somehow such arcana seemed to match the extraordinary nature of these crimes. He spied a Latin motto inscribed on the lintel over the main entrance door:

Novit enim Dominus qui sunt eius

Heck thought it meant something like: 'The Lord knows His own'.. There was no particular reason why it should have chilled him, but it did.

When they climbed from the car, a woman came fussing out of the entrance to meet them. She was middle-aged, short and stocky, with a mass of orange hair which just had to be dyed. She wore sensible shoes, a tweed jacket and skirt, and a fluttering black cape. Her glasses hung over her voluminous bust on a lengthy chain.

'Wanda Clayley,' she said, beaming, offering a well-manicured hand. 'Deputy Head. You must be Mr and Mrs Heckenburg?'

Heck shook hands with Mrs Clayley. 'That's right . . . how nice to meet you.'

'Dr Harding, the Head, would have greeted you himself, but he has an important meeting today at the education authority.'

'Not a problem,' Heck replied, secretly pleased.

'So?' Mrs Clayley's beam never faltered. 'You're thinking of bringing your son, Thomas, to us?'

'Assuming everything's satisfactory,' Heck said.

'Of course.' Mrs Clayley peeked around. 'He isn't with you then?

'Half-term's finished, so he's back at school.'

'And whereabouts would that be?'

'St Lucien's, Bromley.'

'I must say . . . you're sending him a long way to come to middle school.'

'Not just *any* middle school, Mrs Clayley,' Gemma said.

'No, of course . . .' Mrs Clayley laughed as she led them inside. 'What I mean is . . . what attracted you to Staffordshire?'

'Well, St Bardolph's consistently boasts some of the best exam results in the country,' Heck replied, doing his best not to sound as though he'd memorised the school prospectus. 'Your list of famous former students is extensive, and you seem to place an awful lot of people at Oxbridge.'

'We do pride ourselves on that, I must admit,' Mrs Clayley agreed.

It was perhaps understandable that she'd covertly questioned them. At fifteen grand a term, she wouldn't want any time-wasters darkening St Bardolph's doors.

The entrance hall reminded them of a set from one of those old Ealing comedies obsessed with class and tradition. It had a black and white tiled parquet floor, and was airy and spacious; its walls and the overarching ceiling were clad with neatly-fitted wooden panels. More Latin inscriptions were chiselled along the cornices, painted in gold. School photographs hung on every pillar, while trophy cabinets were filled with engraved cups and shields. The air was pungent with the scent of polish. On one side there was a large glass-covered board, on which photo portraits of the school staff were displayed. Heck recognised the same image of Dr Enwright that he'd lifted from the school website. Mrs Clayley explained who each and every person was, listing their credentials in detail.

'Dr Enwright?' Heck said. 'That name sounds familiar.'

'It will do if you've been looking us up,' Mrs Clayley replied. 'Leo Enwright is our pride and joy. He's Head of History, but he's not just an excellent teacher, he's hugely active outside of school hours . . . he gives tirelessly, and never asks anything in return. To start with he has an official pastoral care role here, but he also runs the School History Society, which may not sound like much but it's an organisation we're very proud of at St Bardolph's. The number of activities it pursues is breathtaking. It's all non-syllabus stuff, of course, but it keeps our boarders very busy. Dr Enwright was the man behind it from the beginning, and he still runs it – almost single-handed.'

Only when they commenced 'the Grand Tour', to use Mrs Clayley's words, did they start to spot the aforementioned children. Their uniform was conventional, the boys in navy-blue sweaters and maroon ties, the girls in blue pinafores. All were polite and well-behaved, moving in orderly fashion between classes. It was a far cry from the 'Wild West' atmosphere in the Lancashire comprehensive where Heck had been educated.

326

'The Fifth Form and the Upper and Lower Sixth are in their dormitories and common rooms, on study-leave as they prepare for their exams,' Mrs Clayley explained as they moved along cloistered corridors decked with photographs depicting innumerable aspects of school life: holidays, field-trips, sporting events, theatrical productions. Lessons were in progress, but there were one or two empty classrooms, which they were able to glance into. These were austere in atmosphere, tall and narrow, filled with rigid rows of all-in-one desks and chairs.

Mrs Clayley talked tirelessly, extolling every virtue of St Bardolph's, but Heck wasn't paying a whole lot of attention. He was busy looking out for clues or oddities, something – anything! – that might strike a chord. Nothing initially came to light, but then Mrs Clayley took them into the school carpentry shops, which were currently between classes and where there was an enormous variety of wood-working tools and benches, plus piles of freshly sawn timber. Heck thought about the solidly made crosses on the slagheap off the M62.

After the carpentry shops, they entered the school's theatre, where Mrs Clayley led them backstage to the dressing rooms and costume department.

'All handmade here at the school,' she said, as they gazed along rows of steel racks hung with fanciful period garb. Heck cast his mind back to the Father Christmas outfit and the May Queen gown, neither of which had been traced to any known manufacturer.

Next, Mrs Clayley led them towards the Sports Hall. This was currently being used for PE, so they prowled the corridors adjoining it, and saw yet more photographs: successful, trophy-bearing teams dating from many decades and many disciplines. St Bardolph's, it seemed, did not just offer the usual rugby, football, cricket, netball and hockey, but also tennis, swimming, athletics – and archery.

Heck's heart missed a beat when the Deputy Head casually mentioned that the school had its own archery range outside, just beyond the playing fields. She drew their attention to a row of images. In one of them, Heck found himself staring at a sturdy-framed, blond-haired youth with what looked like a hi-tech bow in his hands, and a quiver full of arrows on his back. The bow was of particular interest. According to the ballistics report on the weapon that slew the young couple on the West Pennine Moors, it had been far more powerful than the average target bow – possibly a modern hunting bow adapted for competition use. This one in the picture was what Heck thought was called a compound bow: double-curved and fitted with a levering system – cables and pulleys – to bend the limbs and store massive energy.

The lad wielding it was smiling at the camera, but the smile did not reach his eyes.

'That's Doug Latimer,' Mrs Clayley said proudly. 'He's in our Sixth Form and will shortly be leaving, but he's also the under eighteens inter-county archery champion for the North Midlands region.'

Heck tried not to look at Gemma as they were led away along more passages, seeing different arrays of photographs. In one, a group of eight older pupils in jeans and sweatshirts smiled at the camera as they sat around a campfire, in front of an old wooden building. It caught Heck's eye because Dr Enwright was with them, as was archery champ, Doug Latimer. In addition, there was a girl with long, platinum-blonde hair. She was cherub-pretty, though there was something faintly aloof about her – as if, like Latimer, her distant smile was only a token gesture.

'The School History Society,' Mrs Clayley said. 'The one I mentioned to you before. You must meet Dr Enwright while you're here. If he can't convince you to send your son to us, no one can.'

'You clearly value his input,' Gemma said.

'It's unquantifiable, if I'm honest. The History Society is completely self-contained and self-governing. But they contribute so much. Organising special day activities, festivals, the school pageant and so on.'

'It's not just an educational thing, then?' Gemma asked.

'Well no, but it serves that purpose. They indulge in all kinds of detailed research.'

'The internet is a marvellous thing when you're hunting something down,' Heck said.

'My goodness, yes,' Mrs Clayley agreed. 'But they use our libraries as well. They go on regular field-trips and weekends away. All under Dr Enwright's guidance of course. When they're putting a project together, they leave no stone unturned.'

Heck's hair prickled at these words, and at the innocent faces in front of him. He noticed that the blonde girl was holding hands with a tall, sullen young man with spiky black hair. The caption beneath listed all their names: the blonde girl was Jasmine Sinclair; the boy holding her hand, Gareth Holker. He was handsome in a clean-cut 'public school' sort of way, but he wasn't smiling and looked unusually stern for someone so young. In one of the other photographs he appeared in a muddied rugby kit in the middle of a trampled pitch, holding aloft a silver plate. He wasn't smiling in that one either.

Heck pointed this out. Mrs Clayley nodded.

'Gareth is our school sports captain and Head Boy. It's a position of great responsibility here at St Bardolph's, and he takes it very seriously. Gareth is one of our great success stories.' She lowered her voice. 'This kind of information is personal, but I don't mind divulging it as it demonstrates the kind of hands-on services we offer here at St Bardolph's. Gareth came to us shortly after his parents were killed in a

329

plane crash. He was devastated, the poor child, totally with-drawn. He didn't have a relative left in the world, aside from a wealthy uncle whom he rarely ever saw. But Dr Enwright took him under his wing. They didn't just start the History Society together, which seemed to give Gareth a new lease of life, but in his role as pastoral care officer, Dr Enwright was like a replacement father – he slowly encouraged the boy to rediscover his strengths, both intellectually and on the sports field.'

'He unleashed the beast maybe?' Heck said.

Mrs Clayley frowned. 'Not a phrase I'd have chosen, but it isn't inaccurate.'

'What's the building?' Gemma asked, indicating the wooden structure in the campfire photo.

'That's called the Old Pavilion. The school cricket pitches were moved about ten years ago, and a new pavilion was built, so the old one was left empty. Dr Enwright asked permission to use it for the History Society's meetings, and the Head was happy to oblige. You really must meet Dr Enwright.' She beckoned them down an adjoining passage. 'If he's in his office I'm sure he'll spare a few minutes.'

Around the next corner, they passed two pupils whom Heck recognised from the campfire photo. The boy was short for his age, and thin, with a floppy mass of carroty-red locks. In contrast, the girl was of solid, athletic build; her raven-black hair was cut severely short. Both stopped dead at the sight of the two visitors.

Mrs Clayley nodded and smiled as she passed them by, leading her guests through an exit door onto a sunlit grassy quadrangle. Heck threw a casual glance backwards. The two pupils were openly staring after them.

There was clear recognition in their faces, which had to be good news.

Mrs Clayley was talking about the advantages of a rural

environment and how, once the summer term was underway, it was permissible for the older students to come outside and study in the open air. Heck made a pretence of listening and approving, but glanced back again when they reached the far side of the quadrangle. The two pupils had also come outside. A third figure had joined them; Heck recognised the fair hair and powerful build of archery hero, Doug Latimer. Thus far, none of them appeared to be running.

As Mrs Clayley went chattering into the next building, Heck sneaked a peek at Gemma. She showed him the text she'd just covertly sent to Shawna:

Stand by. But summon extra bods from Div. NB: firearms support.

Chapter 41

Dr Leo Enwright occupied a sumptuous and spacious study, filled with leather furniture and lined wall-to-wall with books dedicated to his pet subjects. The arched windows were of diamond-paned glass and overhung with ivy; they looked out through cricket nets onto a sunny pitch, where a man in gardening overalls was riding lazily up and down on a motorised roller.

Dr Enwright himself was shorter than they'd expected and quite overweight, but clad in the same rumpled corduroy jacket and flower-patterned tie they'd seen in his school photograph. There was a certain charisma about him, which they detected immediately. He rose from behind his desk as if they were old friends, pumping their hands and welcoming them in rich, booming tones. He quickly ascertained which type of tea they preferred – he had every brand under the sun – and brewed it for them in an ornate silver teapot.

Mrs Clayley sat to one side, smiling indulgently while Dr Enwright introduced himself, the school and its ethos animatedly and articulately, but Heck couldn't help wondering if he didn't seem to be trying a little too hard. Okay, it was very difficult to associate this jocular, well-spoken figure with the depraved individual known as the Desecrator, but Heck had looked many times into the empty eyes of killers. He'd met the masters of deceit and subterfuge – and he quickly came to suspect that the Dr Enwright they were seeing here was an act. However, there was one thing Heck felt sure about. Even if Enwright's minions had recognised them as cops, Enwright himself hadn't – not yet. And perhaps that wasn't too surprising. Somehow he couldn't picture the good doctor doing something as inane as watching television.

'We hear you have a busy timetable of extra-curricular activities here?' Heck said.

'Why yes.' Enwright smiled broadly. His small-lensed spectacles enlarged his eyes unnaturally, and there was all that unruly, grey wire-wool hair; Heck was reminded of Garrickson's mocking reference to a 'nutty professor'. 'Our sports set-up here at St Bardolph's is pretty well second to none. I can't claim to have anything to do with that, much as I would love to. My little kingdom is the History Society.'

'Which sounds very interesting,' Gemma said. She sat down while Heck remained on his feet. 'Thomas . . . that's our son, is particularly keen on history.'

'How splendid!' Enwright rubbed his hands together. 'Well . . . I should say straight away that we aren't strictly about history. At least, not the dry, dusty parts, if you know what I mean. We meet to discuss historical events certainly, usually on the anniversaries . . . as a kind of commemoration.'

'A commemoration?' Heck said.

'Commemoration is what the History Society is all about.'

Heck glanced sideways and noticed a small group of pupils – the original two who'd first spotted them, and now several others (all identifiable from the campfire photo) drifting along the edge of the cricket square, passing the history master's window, gazing casually in.

'We share a mutual grief,' Enwright said, 'that modern society has allowed knowledge of those events and people who made us to dwindle to such insignificance.'

The last of those passing the study window was Doug Latimer.

'Would you agree, Mr Heckenburg?'

Heck nodded. 'Absolutely.'

'I hear you put on shows?' Gemma said.

Enwright nodded. 'We do indeed. The History Society is in charge of the school pageant . . . in a nutshell, that means we organise assemblies, carnivals, fetes, parades, that kind of thing. And yes . . . shows and plays on special occasions. Some of them humorous or satirical, all designed to inform the audience at festive times of year, but also to entertain them.'

'In effect, you make these special events fun,' Heck said.

More pupils drifted past the window. If Enwright thought their behaviour odd, he didn't react.

'I like to think so,' he said. 'A lot of fun. For all involved.'

'Well . . .' Gemma stood up. 'It looks as if Thomas will be coming to the right place. He'll be twelve when he starts here. I take it that won't be too young to join your group?'

Enwright smiled again. 'We take all ages.'

I'll bet you do, Heck thought. *And the younger and more pliable, the better.*

Enwright was briefly distracted by the sound of an electronic cock-crow. He glanced down at his desk, and Heck realised that he'd just received a text. In the same moment, Heck's attention was caught by something else. At the end of a row of leather-bound volumes was a pile of A5 magazines. The top one, which was clumsily typed and stapled, bore a familiar title:

BLOOD FEAST

334

'Well . . .' Gemma collected her handbag. 'I think it's safe to say we've seen everything we came here to see.'

Mrs Clayley stood up as well, confident the school's star turn had yet again done his bit to attract a fee-paying student.

On the other side of his desk, Enwright was ramrod-straight as he perused the message on his phone. He glanced up at Gemma and smiled narrowly. 'So glad I've been of assistance.'

'You couldn't have been more helpful,' Heck said.

Enwright turned to face him. 'It's remarkably diligent of you, coming all this way to look us over.'

'It's always important to be absolutely sure what you're dealing with,' Heck said.

'And you're *absolutely* sure, are you?'

'We've seen more than we need to, Dr Enwright,' Gemma said. 'Thanks terribly. Darling, we need to make a move.'

Enwright nodded stiffly, and as they left his office, began keying in a hurried return message. Mrs Clayley chattered gaily as she led them back through the corridors towards the front of the main building. En route, Heck sensed that they had company. Over his shoulder, he saw two pupils strolling idly in pursuit, a boy and a girl. They looked younger than those they'd seen before, and neither was recognisable from the campfire photo, but maybe that was only the tip of the iceberg.

A few seconds later, the two pupils veered away along an adjoining passage and vanished. Heck glanced left and right. Tall, arched windows gave glimpses of more sunny quadrangles – no one was out there. The school seemed amazingly quiet, though he thought he heard a distant angry shout. No other voice responded to it, and Mrs Clayley didn't so much as flinch. When they reached the entrance hall, several more pupils were hanging around for no obvious reason. A couple of these might have been sixth-formers;

the rest were younger. Again, Heck couldn't immediately place their faces, though he hadn't memorised everyone on that picture.

'Are you people waiting to see someone?' Mrs Clayley asked, bustling forward, cape fluttering. There were low, incoherent replies. 'I can take care of that, Luke, thank you very much. The rest of you, shoo! If you're on study period that means you should be studying. Come on now!'

Disgruntled, the youngsters sloped away. It might have been Heck's imagination, but one of them cast a quick, venomous glance in his and Gemma's direction. Outside, walking to the car, he looked back. The ivy-hung casements were blank screens, yet he could sense that from some of them at least, hostile eyes were watching.

'How soon can we get that warrant?' he said, as he drove them away.

'I'm on it now,' Gemma replied, fiddling with her mobile.

They maintained a steady pace along the drive, strangely relieved to feel the school buildings falling behind.

'If nothing else, we can certify the competence of the History Society,' Heck remarked. 'We've seen for ourselves how thoroughly they prep.' He glanced at Gemma, who was still trying to get through but without success. 'No signal?'

'No bloody answer. There's always some damn reason . . .'

'Keep trying.'

'I intend to. Just drive, will you?'

Heck put his foot down, but several minutes later, when they were still at least a mile short of the main road, he hit the brakes and they skidded to a halt.

On their right, a small wooden signpost pointed down a side-road. It read:

Old Pavilion

The side-road was little more than a dirt track. Trees and thickets crowded its verges, but it rolled off to a considerable distance, following what was roughly a straight line until vanishing in a leafy, sun-spattered haze.

'We've already got more than enough to raid this place,' Gemma said. 'Why delay?'

'May help us remove any shadow of a doubt,' Heck replied.

'So we find their clubhouse. We can't enter it yet. What good will it do?'

'Probably none, but are we really going to ignore it? Drive past without looking?'

She glanced at her watch. 'Okay . . . five minutes tops, and then we're out of here.'

He swung the car right, and they drove for several minutes, deep green dells flitting past on either side, the dirt road spooling out ahead. Eventually it began meandering, swerving from side to side, and it continued in this vein for another mile or so until they emerged into an open glade that was large enough to once have contained at least a couple of cricket pitches, though all were now hidden under tides of fresh ferns and flowering thorns. The track ended abruptly, Heck applying the handbrake and turning the engine off. Silence followed. It was mid-afternoon and May sunshine bathed everything, yet there was an eerie stillness to this forgotten place.

Three buildings were arranged in a row along the western edge of the glade. Two, the ones at either end, were no more than dilapidated shacks nailed up with planks, but the central structure was the one they recognised from the campfire photo.

The Old Pavilion.

Clearly, it had once been handsome: built from white-washed wood, with a low, steeply tilted thatched roof, a central steeple in which a bell had hung, and a clock on the triangular gable overlooking the frontal verandah. Now, its paintwork had flaked, birds nested in its eaves and weeds grew from its thatch-work. The clock was missing fingers and its numerals were barely visible. The ground around it was deeply overgrown, though a footpath snaked through this to the foot of the verandah steps.

'Let's have a poke around, eh?' Heck said.

Gemma glanced across the open space where the pitches had been. On all sides of it stood a bulwark of trees and bushes, hints of green shadow visible among them.

'Gemma?' he said.

She nodded and they climbed out, the double-thump of their doors echoing through the encircling woods. They paused again, listening, still hearing nothing. Finally, they ventured along the footpath. It was wide enough for them to walk two abreast, the well-trodden grass flattened and brown. They noticed rut-marks in it, as if wheeled carts had been pushed back and forth, or bicycles.

'That explains how they get around the estate,' Gemma said. 'Not going to look good in court. That these heinous criminals toured the school grounds on their push-bikes, dingling their bells, with packed lunches in their baskets . . .'

There was a crackle of foliage.

Heck, now at the foot of the verandah steps, whipped around. Nothing stirred – either out in the deep grass or under the shadows of the watching trees. They glanced towards the car. Behind it, the shady track veered from sight.

They ascended the steps, their feet clumping on hollow, desiccated wood. The main door was closed and padlocked – but compared to everything else here, the padlock was shiny and new. Not that this made any difference. They couldn't have forced an entrance legally. There were windows to either side. The glass in these was dusty and yellow with age; difficult enough to gaze through, though as a further security measure both looked to have been covered on the other side with black crepe paper.

They strode along the verandah to its left-hand corner. Here, they followed a narrow path running between the Pavilion and the shack alongside it. They passed a couple more windows. These too had been covered on the inside, apart from the last one; in this case, the bottom right corner of the paper, having caught on the backrest of a chair, had shifted, creating a narrow aperture. Heck crouched and peered through, Gemma handing him a pen-light. The beam penetrated seven or eight feet into the gloomy interior. The first thing he saw was a pile of square-cut timber. It looked fresh and new. Beyond that stood a rack of colourful clothing.

'Theatrical costumes,' he said. 'With a Father Christmas suit noticeably absent. They've either been making their own here, or they've been lifting them from the drama department. Hang on . . . there's something else.'

He angled the light down, and in the near foreground, close to the window, he spied two paint pots. Both were open and empty, but drying emulsion had streaked down their sides. One of them was white, one of them pink.

Nice colours for a maypole, he thought. *The little bastards!*

'We're going to need that warrant quickly if we don't want all this stuff to disappear,' he said. Gemma didn't reply. He saw that she'd walked along the path to the rear of the Pavilion. He followed.

'What do you make of this?' she said.

An articulated lorry was parked close to the Pavilion's rear wall, its bodywork and that of its trailer grubby and dented. While Gemma grabbed her radio and made a PNC check, Heck circled around it, stopping every yard to snap pictures on his mobile. He paid particular attention to the tyre treads, which, though he couldn't be sure, looked eerily reminiscent of the marks left on the slagheap near the crucifixion site.

The doors at the back of it were closed and padlocked; again, the padlock was new. The lorry was parked at the convergence of two additional dirt tracks. One led around the far side of the three buildings onto the cricket pitches, but was long disused – its wheel-ruts deep in grass and nettles. The other led in the opposite direction; this too was rugged and unmade, enclosed by trees, but the lack of vegetation breaking its surface suggested that it was used regularly. Heck tried to recall the rough layout of the grounds from the map they'd studied before coming here. There were roads and tracks all over the estate, but only two exits and entrances: the main entrance/exit was on the south side, but there was also a gate on the west. This secondary road might connect with that, though it was impossible to tell from here.

His eyes now alighted on something else. Twenty yards along on the left, half concealed by foliage, stood a vehicle port. It was open at the front, but the walls at its back and sides were of aged brick. The roof, which was corrugated metal, was covered with moss, grime and several decades of autumn leaves. Six cars were stored in there: a Ford Fiesta, a Ford Focus, a Toyota Avensis, a Volkswagen Polo, a Peugeot Clio, and a bright orange MG convertible, its roof folded back.

'The HGV's a knocker,' Gemma said, coming up behind him. 'Stolen over a year ago, would you believe . . . from Humberside.'

'No doubt during a very educational History Society trip to see the wharfs and cranes,' Heck replied. 'What about these?'

She gazed at the clutch of half-hidden motors. 'Jesus . . .'

'The rest of the fleet,' he said.

'Time we got this ball rolling.'

'Agreed.'

They headed back along the path to the cricket pitches. Heck got onto his radio. 'All units from DS Heckenburg . . . be advised, no one is to leave the school grounds until I tell

340

you otherwise. Anyone tries, pull them over on the basis that persons here are suspected of committing serious criminal offences, and detain them until either Detective Superintendent Piper or I get there. That goes especially for Dr Leo Enwright. He is now our prime suspect in the Desecrator murders. I repeat *he is our prime suspect*. Over and out.'

As before, the vast open space in front of the Pavilion was deserted. The shadows under the trees lay still and silent. They moved back along the path to the car.

'You drive again,' Gemma said as they climbed in. 'I've got some calls to make.'

He glanced behind them as he switched the engine on and shifted the BMW into a reverse position – only for it to snag on something at the rear, and then sag downwards.

'What now?' Gemma groaned.

Heck jumped out and rounded the side of the vehicle – where an arrow was stuck diagonally through the rear near-side tyre.

'Get down!' he shouted, leaping back in. Gemma was too surprised to move. 'Down, I said!' He gunned the engine, only to freeze at the sight of another arrow winging across the open space towards them. With a jarring crunch, it punched through the windscreen. Gemma screamed in agony.

Chapter 42

Heck didn't even look to see how badly Gemma was hit, he just threw the car into reverse and revved it backwards along the track, mud and grit flying in front of it. A third arrow struck the vehicle, ripping through the bonnet, leaving a gouge the length of a human arm.

'Oh . . . my God,' Gemma stammered. 'Heck . . .'

The dirt road was perilous at this speed, especially in reverse and with a deflated tyre. The BMW was all over the track as Heck divided his attention between the rear-view mirror and his passenger. She sat rigid, shaking violently. The arrow had buried itself in her right shoulder; blood was pulsing out.

'This is Heck,' he bawled into his radio. 'Urgent message . . . we're under attack at the Old Pavilion! Gemma's suffered an arrow wound and is losing blood fast! All units get in here now, including Trojans . . . and get an ambulance!'

Every jolt and bounce was a hammer blow to Gemma. She tried not to cry out, but it was almost impossible. 'Oh my *Goood!*'

'Just hang on!' He kept his foot to the floor, rounding bend after bend, twigs and leaves crackling along the BMW's bodywork. They still had at least two miles to go to the main drive, but they ought to be out of arrow range by now, so he could stop and turn around – at which point another car appeared in front of them.

At first Heck spotted only a bright orange flash – they were accelerating around tight corners at breakneck speed – but then he saw it again; the MG convertible from the vehicle port. Astonishingly, it was being driven by the carrot-topped kid he'd seen at the school. Standing up in the back, his athletic legs braced wide apart, was archery champ, Doug Latimer. A packed quiver hung at his hip, and his hi-tech hunting bow was again at full stretch. Even as Heck gawked at him, Latimer loosed another arrow. It whistled at them with speed and accuracy, only missing because the BMW was in mid-manoeuvre. Again they rounded a bend, the car hitting the verge and almost tipping. Two hubcaps hurtled into the undergrowth; heavy branches threshed the vehicle's flank.

Gemma's breath was ragged and stuttering. She'd managed to claw a handkerchief from her jacket pocket, and clamp it to the base of the arrow, but the makeshift poultice was already a sopping, crimson mess.

'We need back-up now!' Heck howled into his radio. 'I repeat, we are under fire!'

The MG swept into sight again, just ahead. It was much closer, less than sixty yards away. Latimer loosed another arrow. His ride too was jolting, he swayed and tottered, but his aim was unerring. The missile hit the weakened windscreen square-on, passing clean through the interior, missing Heck's cheek by inches, thumping into the backrest in the rear.

Heck floored his pedal even though they were on another murderous curve. The suspension shrieked; a third hubcap went spinning away. But the next time the MG came in sight their problems would *really* begin. Only the turns in the

343

track had saved them up to now, but the last mile or so was a straight stretch. That was where the MG would catch up and where, for a marksman like Latimer, they'd be sitting ducks.

Heck risked another glance at Gemma. She was icy-pale, drenched with blood and sweat. Her eyelids fluttered, but he could see that she was doing everything in her power to resist fainting. One hand still clutched the crimson dressing to her wound; the other was jammed against the dashboard. It was an impressive feat of courage, but it wouldn't count for much if Heck didn't do something soon.

He made a desperate decision.

They swerved, screeching, around a final bend. The MG briefly fell out of sight – and Heck jammed his brakes on, the BMW shuddering to a slantwise halt.

'Get down,' he shouted at Gemma.' You've got to get down!'

'I'm . . . pinned to the damn seat!' she stammered.

She was telling the truth. Only half the feathered shaft was visible. The rest had gone straight through her into the upholstery behind.

'This is going to hurt,' he said, grabbing her collar and yanking her forwards. Gemma's cry went beyond pain into horror and anguish, but behind her, the embedded arrowhead was torn free, bringing out chunks of fabric and foam-rubber. 'Stay there!' he said, pushing her down across her lap, throwing the car into first and hitting the gas, before moving swiftly up into second, third and fourth.

The last thing the two schoolboys were probably expecting when they rounded that final bend was to find their prey barrelling towards them.

The collision was explosive.

The smashing impact hurled Heck and Gemma forward with incredible force, but their belts held them and their airbags cushioned them. Meanwhile, the car's crumple zones

344

collapsed; in the blink of an eye, the entire vehicle changed shape. But the smaller MG took the worst of it. It was crushed to pulp beneath its bigger adversary, hammered into mangled scrap.

Its two occupants only survived because the roof had been folded back, and both were thrown clear.

Heck, ears ringing and head spinning, loosened his belt, pivoted around on his backside and kicked with both feet at his door. It was so warped that at first it resisted, but a second blow sprang it open. He leapt out, wafting his way through clouds of escaping steam. Carrot-Top was still rolling in trackside leaves and mulch. He looked stunned by what had just happened – but when he saw Heck looming towards him, he found his feet and lurched away around the back of the MG, heading along the track towards the main drive.

Heck followed, only to find Latimer sprawled in his path. The archery champ had taken a harder fall than Carrot-Top – his nose was badly bloodied, though he too was conscious. He groped towards his bow a couple of feet away. But Heck had reached him in two strides and kicked him across the face, knocking him cold, before grabbing up the bow and twisting it out of shape. Carrot-Top had only made it twenty yards. He might be young, but he was limping. He glanced back as he staggered past the shattered BMW – and never noticed when Gemma kicked the passenger door open into his path. He caromed away from it and fell sideways into the foliage. A second later Heck was on him. The kid squirmed violently, clawing and kicking out. He left Heck no option but to drag him to his feet by the belt of his pants, ram him back against the trunk of a tree, and cuff his hands behind it.

'Alright!' came an aggressive voice. 'Everyone down! Hands where I can see them! Hey dipshit, you in the suit . . . I said get fucking down!'

Heck half-turned, sensing that a gun had been drawn on him.

A Trojan unit, a heavily-armoured police carrier, had arrived from the main drive, and stopped in front of the two wrecks. Specialist firearms officers, or 'shots' as most cops knew them, were spilling out. Kevlar body-armour was strapped over their black, flame-retardant coveralls; only the black and white flashes on their visored helms revealed who they were. Several had drawn pistols or MP5s, and were advancing warily. Behind their vehicle, an ambulance had also arrived, but was waiting there helplessly, its passage blocked. The SFO who'd spoken was the closest, and now sidled forward. He was an older but fit-looking, broad-shouldered man, wearing inspector's pips. He had Heck square in the sights of his Kurtz submachine-gun.

'Better late than never,' Heck told him.

'I said hit the deck! Are you fucking deaf?'

'Watch out, boss!' an SFO sergeant shouted. 'No clear shot!'

'I'm DS Heckenburg, you stupid bastard!' Heck retorted, hands spread. 'Look . . . I've just made an arrest!'

The SFO inspector only flicked the briefest glance at the manacled schoolboy. 'Don't know you or him!'

'If you let me reach for my pocket, I'll show you.'

'One-handed. And slowly . . . very fucking slowly.'

Heck reached gingerly into his inside jacket pocket, extracting his warrant card. On seeing that it wasn't a weapon, the firearms inspector lowered his Kurtz and came forward, lifting his visor. By his hard unimpressionable face, he still wasn't convinced they were dealing with one of the good guys. He all but snatched the card, determined to scrutinise it for any sign it might be a fake. When he handed the warrant card back, Heck decked him.

It was a swift right-hook to the jaw, and it dropped him

like a sack of spuds. 'Next time I say get a move on, get a fucking move on!'

'*You fucking slimy bastard!*' the sergeant bellowed.

Heck pointed at the troop carrier. 'Shift that pansy wagon so the ambulance can get through, you knuckle-dragging wankers!'

The firearms sergeant was about to retort in kind, when he caught sight of Gemma crawling along the verge on all fours. Her hair hung in a sweaty mop. She was covered front and back in bloody froth. Half a foot of aluminium arrow jutted at an angle from her right shoulder.

Even the hardened shot's mouth dropped open. 'Oh, shit . . .'

'Get over *here*!' Heck shouted past the troop-van to the paramedics in the ambulance. 'This area's safe . . .' He was interrupted by the growl of a heavy engine from the near-distance. He spun around. 'Bloody artic . . . *Jesus Christ, they're going to get away!*'

Instinctively, he started running along the track. A shout sounded behind him.

'Get those medics on the job!' Heck called over his shoulder. 'The rest follow me! The bastards are making a break for it!'

Running in leather-soled shoes was never easy. Heck tripped and slid, but somehow kept staggering forward. None of the shots followed him initially. He glanced back as he ran. A couple were aiding the medics as they tended to Gemma but, ridiculously, the rest were attempting to shove the two wrecked cars off the track, presumably so they could get their own vehicle past. Heck swore, but charged on.

If nothing else, the SFOs were super-fit. They soon gave up trying to move the cars and pursued him on foot, and had almost caught up by the time he'd reached the Old

Pavilion. He stumbled around to the rear, panting and soaked, but the HGV was missing.

'This is Heck!' he shouted into his radio. 'Tell me someone's covering the west gate?'

'*That'd be me, sarge,*' a voice replied. It was Gary Quinnell.

'Be advised, Gary . . . there may be an articulated wagon coming your way. Check with PNC for the index. Gemma ran it twenty minutes ago. But you can't miss the bloody thing. It'll probably stop for nothing, so no heroics, okay? Just follow it till it runs out of fuel. In the meantime, get an all-points on it. If Central Counties Air Operations have got a chopper spare, that would help as well.'

'*Roger that,*' came Quinnell's reply.

Heck was about to say more when he smelled smoke. The shots had noticed it too; they'd removed their ballistics helms and were glancing around, puzzled. Then there was a shout and fingers were stabbing. Fire writhed behind the grimy windows at the rear of the Pavilion.

'Fuck!' Heck shouted, galloping around to the front.

The shots joined him, and the front door, which had been locked, was smashed down under a hail of boots and shoulders. Intense heat *whooshed* out; acrid smoke billowed in their faces. Heck wafted his way forward, coughing, shielding his eyes. The entire rear wall of the Pavilion interior was already a sheet of flame. Other items were also blazing: piles of boxes, racks of garments. Windows cracked like gunshots. A set of shelves collapsed, numerous bits and pieces catching fire as they scattered away from it.

'Better get out of here!' the SFO sergeant shouted. 'Place is going up like a tinderbox.'

'We'll lose a treasure trove,' Heck replied, pushing forward. 'Over there! Look!'

On the left, a table had been pushed against the wall, flanked on either side by filing cabinets. A desktop computer and screen sat on top of it, alongside documents, books and other stationery, and even what looked like a pair of night-vision goggles. A huge diagram – a homemade map of some sort – was pinned to the wall above, covered in marker-pen. All were blackening in the face of the inferno.

'We've gotta save as much of that as we can!' Heck said. 'Especially the computer.'

All the way there, he fought gusts of oily smoke and clouds of sparks – halfway over, a portion of the smouldering timber floor collapsed. It was a flimsy trapdoor, and he found himself gazing down a cylindrical pit about twelve feet in depth, with bare brick walls. It might once have been a well of some sort, though by the stench it had more recently been used as a dungeon. At least there were no prisoners down there now.

Heck himself pulled the map down from the wall and folded it under his arm. One of the shots snagged the computer, and two others managed to lug a filing cabinet back towards the entrance, before the intensifying heat beat them back. Once outside, they could do nothing but stand back, agog, as roaring flames engulfed the ancient, sun-dried structure.

Heck's mobile began chirping.

'It's me!' Shawna said.

'What's happening?'

'We're at the school, and we've got it locked down.'

'Good girl . . .'

'Don't thank me yet. Most of the birds have flown.'

'What?'

'Seems that about half an hour ago several pupils – we haven't got an exact number – absented themselves from lessons without permission. When a teacher tried to remonstrate, she got a punch on the nose for her trouble.'

'What about Enwright?'

'He's still here. Locked himself into an antechamber at the back of his office.'

'Break the bloody door down!'

'We've tried, but he must have piled stuff against it.'

'Alright, hang fire . . . I'm en route.'

Heck glanced around. Some of the shots were still fixated on the blazing Pavilion. Others were mopping sweat and muttering together. He set off back down the dirt track at a jog. The ARV was where they'd left it. But various local uniforms and CID officers had now arrived and were in conflab with the SFO inspector, who looked bruised around the chops. Charlie Finnegan was also there; he'd taken custody of Carrot-Top, but was on the phone to somebody. None of them noticed as Heck veered towards the troop carrier, whose burly, bearded driver was standing on the road, smoking a cigarette.

'Need to get up to the school fast,' Heck said.

'Call a fucking taxi then.'

'Wrong answer.' Heck stepped around him and climbed nimbly into the cab.

'*Oi!*'

The key was still in the ignition. Heck twisted it and the engine rumbled to life. He swung the heavy vehicle around in a massive three-point turn, uniforms and plain clothes scattering on all sides. The driver in particular ran shouting alongside him, threatening everything under the sun, until Heck gunned the ARV ahead and he fell far behind.

Chapter 43

Pupils and teachers alike crowded every window. The entire school was a hive of police activity. Local plod was everywhere, as were plainclothes officers, not to mention more shots, who, as usual, were bustling around in muscular fashion as if this was really their show. The only civilian out of doors was Deputy Head Wanda Clayley, dashing about in her fluttery cape like a manic, black-garbed butterfly. She stumbled from one officer to the next, jabbering questions, but none of them were able or willing to help her. She latched on to Heck as soon as he climbed from the ARV, barely noticing that he was sweaty and blackened by smoke.

'Mr Heckenburg! Mr Heckenburg . . . apparently you're some kind of policeman!'

'Some kind, yes, Mrs Clayley,' Heck replied. 'Not much of one.'

'I was about to say the same thing.'

'Just as you aren't much of a teacher.'

'Excuse me?' Her cheeks turned bright pink. 'I devoted an hour of my time this afternoon to showing you around our premises. I had no idea I was being duped in this most deceitful way.'

'It's my earnest hope that you also had no idea you were harbouring in your school a bunch of extremely disturbed and dangerous individuals, who may be responsible for a number of sadistic murders.'

'But this is simply nonsense! There's no conceivable way Dr Enwright . . .'

Heck brushed past her. 'Save it, Mrs Clayley . . . for the enquiry that will inevitably be held into the running of this establishment and those supposedly in charge here.'

She tried to protest further, but he signalled to two uniforms and she was led away. He headed inside, where more uniforms were on guard at the doors to offices and classrooms. A local inspector approached him in the main lobby.

'Heckenburg, sir. Serial Crimes.' Heck flashed his ID. 'No one's to leave this building. The kids are not even to leave the classrooms. Firstly because some of them may still be suspects, but mainly for their own safety.'

He caught up with Shawna in Dr Enwright's office; she was standing with a bundle of buff folders under her arm. Eric Fisher was seated in front of a desktop computer; paperwork was heaped on the floor alongside him. A uniformed PC hung around uncertainly, looking like a spare part.

'I've just heard that Gemma's being taken straight through for emergency surgery,' Shawna said, on seeing Heck. 'The arrow severed her subclavian artery. It's touch and go whether she'll be able to use that arm again.'

Heck nodded stoically. 'Where's Enwright?' She indicated a closed door in the far corner. 'What's on the other side of that?'

'Apparently just a storeroom.'

'Window?'

'Too small for anyone to use.'

Heck kicked at the door. His foot rebounded from what

felt like solid oak. The impact didn't leave so much as a dent. 'Dr Enwright!' he called. 'This is Detective Sergeant Heckenburg. Look . . . you're only delaying the inevitable.' He pressed his ear to the panel, but heard nothing from the other side. He straightened up again, glancing distractedly at the folders under Shawna's arm. 'What's that lot?'

She picked through them. 'School files on the kids who've done a runner. Names are Doug Latimer, Anthony Worthington, Heather Greer, Arnold Wisby, Luke Stapleton – copper's son, worryingly – Susan Cavanagh, Gareth Holker . . . and the blondie, who I think is Holker's girlfriend, is that correct?'

Heck nodded, remembering. 'Her name's Jasmine Sinclair.' He glanced through the files, looking at the attached photos. 'We don't need to worry about Latimer and Worthington – they've both been nicked.' He swung back to the door. 'You say you've tried breaking this down?'

'It's defied all our efforts so far.' She pointed at the PC, a large, raw-boned young man, who rubbed at his shoulder with a pained expression.

'We've been told there are racks of steel shelving in there, sarge,' the PC explained. 'He may have used them to shore up the door.'

Heck hissed through clenched teeth. 'We haven't got time for this.'

'Hydraulic ram?' Shawna suggested.

'And how long until it gets here?'

She shrugged. 'He's not going anywhere.'

'But these acolytes of his are.'

'What do you mean?'

'You don't think they've gone running off looking for their mummies and daddies, do you?'

Shawna looked stunned. 'You think they're gonna do another job?'

'A grand finale.' Heck thumbed at the locked door. 'Of

353

course, we'll not know until we speak to the maladjusted freak in here . . .' He turned and left the office, shouting over his shoulder: 'Shift that desk, yeah?'

Shawna glanced at the nonplussed uniform. 'Better do as he says.'

Enwright's desk, which was large and rather grand and apparently made from mahogany, wasn't particularly easy to shift, but at length – with much grunting and cursing – they were finally able to push/drag it to one side of the room. And just in the nick of time, because from the passage adjoining the office there was a shattering of glass – which sounded distinctly like one of the outer doors, and then the deafening clank and clatter of an engine that had seen better days. When Heck reappeared in the doorway, he was saddled on a motorised lawn-roller, which pumped fumes as he drove it across the office at top speed.

Its heavy steel roller slammed full-on against the locked door, the jamb of which buckled and split. The other officers watched in disbelief, as Heck rearranged the gears, reversed the machine, and drove it forward again.

The second impact was the one.

Heck was almost thrown over the handlebars, but this time splinters flew as the door cracked across its middle, its jamb shattering and hinges catapulting in every direction. Heck jumped off, ramming his shoulder against the sagging door, which gradually gave way to a complex mass of disassembled steel shelves erected as a barricade.

'A little help, folks,' he said through gritted teeth.

Shawna and the uniform joined him, as he yanked and pulled at the twisted metal. Within seconds they'd worked their way through it, but long before then it was obvious that the room on the other side – a ten by six storage chamber – was empty. It was equally obvious how this had come about.

Its high, letterbox-narrow window was still closed. But below that, at the foot of the far wall, Enwright had torn away a few carpet tiles, revealing a square aperture in the stone floor. This would normally be covered by planks, but these had also been removed, and below them a narrow shaft dropped into darkness.

'I don't believe it,' Heck groaned.

'What the hell is it?' Shawna said.

'A priest's hole.'

She looked dumbfounded. 'Leading where?'

'There's only one way to find out.' He produced Gemma's pen-light from his pocket, knelt and shone its beam as far down the shaft as he could. A floor of beaten earth was visible about ten feet below. A descending series of small niches had been cut in the stone on the right-hand side as hand and footholds.

'Heck!' came Eric Fisher's voice from the office. 'There's all sorts of interesting stuff on this desktop.'

'We haven't got time for research, Eric!' Heck called back.

'This is important.'

'Bag the hard drive, then.' Heck seated himself on the edge of the aperture, and turned to the uniform. 'Let your gaffers know what's going on. Tell them the fugitive's making his way out via a subterranean tunnel. It can't lead too far, so the grounds need searching top to bottom.'

The uniform nodded and hurried away. Heck buttoned his suit jacket, winked at Shawna, and lowered himself down. The walls enclosed him tightly from either side and back to front, the air dank and stuffy, but at least he had full movement. When he alighted at the bottom, he shone the pen-light in front of him. Rather than a tunnel, it exposed a tight squeeze of an alleyway built from sweating, crumbling brickwork. It was less than five feet in height and so narrow that a man could only move along it sideways.

'Bloody spider hole,' Heck said to Shawna, who had stopped just above him.

'So how the hell did Enwright get through it?'

'He's probably had lots of practice.'

'Watch what you're doing,' Shawna said, as he advanced at a crouch, left shoulder thrust forward.

The air became steadily more difficult to breathe and water dripped on his head; the geometry of the passage seeming to contract the further along it he progressed. At first he thought this an optical illusion, but soon his clothing was snagging on jagged bricks. His scalp scraped along the ceiling, making it ever more difficult to ignore the tons of rock and soil above his head. If this thing extended to inordinate length – for hundreds of yards, maybe thousands – Heck knew that he was going to have trouble. Close behind, Shawna, who was of considerably smaller frame than he was, was already grunting and panting.

'How far do you think we've come?' she asked in a strained whimper.

'Not far enough. We can't even be clear of the school yet.'

'Bloody hell . . .'

They continued for several more minutes, cramped, sweating hard despite the chill. All the way of course, the thought that Enwright had done this before them was a motivator – it couldn't just bring them to a dead-end. Even so, Heck felt a surge of relief when he spied a pall of natural light about fifty yards ahead. They accelerated, unmindful about scuffing and tearing their clothing. When they reached the end, the dusty light revealed that a modern steel ladder had been erected in the exit shaft, the upper section of which had been reinforced with recent brickwork.

Heck scrambled up towards another square aperture, through which he could hear the chugging of an engine.

'The bastards are here to pick him up,' he said urgently. 'They haven't even left the school grounds yet.'

He emerged at the top via a purpose-made trapdoor, and found himself in what looked like an old cottage kitchen, gutted of furnishings and filled with rags and dirt. The broken rear window had been covered on the outside with planks, though beams of sunlight slanted through. On his right, an arched internal doorway connected with another area, probably a living room. He ventured forward, peeking in. The living room was equally derelict, consisting of dust, crumpled newspapers and a couple of sticks of abandoned, mouldy furniture. The windows in here, which opened to the front of the building, were also covered with boards, but the entrance door, only six yards to his left, stood ajar. By the sounds of the engine, the lorry was just the other side of this. Heck heard voices – he fancied one belonged to Enwright, but he hesitated to dash out there. The phrase 'this is too easy' was unpopular with experienced coppers for good reason.

He moved to the window, but Shawna now appeared behind him and headed straight for the door. 'Shawna, wait!' he hissed.

BOOM . . . the thunderous detonation blew the lower half of the door inwards, and the young policewoman's legs were swept from under her.

Heck flattened himself alongside the window. Through the chinks between the planks he glimpsed the lorry pulling away along a narrow, wooded lane, though a single person had remained behind. It was Gareth Holker, the tall, spike-haired youth from the school photographs; but he'd given up his uniform for a hooded sweatshirt and, over the top of that, camouflaged waterproofs. He was also armed, carrying an over-and-under shotgun sawn down to half its normal length.

'You want to save this soulless land, officers?' he shouted, laughing. 'You need to try a lot harder than that!'

Even with his restricted vision, Heck saw that the youth's face was white as milk, his eyes gleaming like black jewels.

'Heck . . .' Shawna gasped.

He gazed over to where she lay amid smoking, splintered wreckage. Her slacks were torn to ribbons, blood soaking through them.

'Don't move, darling,' he said quietly. 'Play dead, okay?'

'You dare call us desecrators!' came the deranged voice outside. 'You couldn't have been further from the truth! We were venerating these special days . . . making them holy again!'

BOOM . . . half the planking covering the window was blasted out. But that was the second barrel, so Heck chanced it and darted past the window, throwing a quick glance outside and seeing the youngster thumbing two fresh cartridges into the shotgun breech. Then he was down along-side Shawna, whose face was tinged an unhealthy green.

'First they pummelled my pretty face,' she whispered. 'Now I've lost my lovely legs.'

'You've not lost anything.' He took her pulse, which, not surprisingly, was racing.

'Bloody thick policemen! You dare complain that these festive occasions are being ruined, but what have we got at present?'

BOOM . . . the outer wall took the brunt of this one, the whole cottage shuddering.

'Vomit-inducing materialism all December! Pissheads falling out of pubs on St Patrick's Day! Supermarkets selling corsets and fishnet stockings in time for Halloween!'

Heck glanced towards the door. What remained of it hung from a single hinge – only this was masking Shawna from Holker. There was no option but to try and drag her further in. Heck got straight to it, lugging her by the armpits, despite her choked gasps of agony. Her shredded legs smeared trails of gore behind her.

BOOM . . . the remaining planking blew in through the window frame. Heck ducked as he pulled the casualty around

he corner and into the kitchen, where he fished the radio
from his pocket.

'This is DS Heckenburg . . . we're under fire again!'

'We've drawn a line in the sand, copper!' Holker shouted.
'We're marking these feast days properly . . . by taking out
the trash!'

BOOM . . .

'This is DS Heckenburg, any units to respond?' But all he
was getting was static. The air was probably jammed with
messages.

'Marking them indelibly . . .'

BOOM . . .

'So that no tin-pot entrepreneur will ever again stick
cartoon images of Santa all over the discount beer shelves
in his shop without someone jogging his memory that a man
died in a chimney precisely because of idiots like him!'

Heck dragged his phone out and stabbed in a quick
number.

'Heck?' came Eric Fisher's voice.

BOOM . . .

'So that no sleazy nightclub owner will ever again host a
wild party on New Year's Eve without someone mentioning
that, thanks to his attitude, a student was once forcibly
drowned in a tub of Scotch whisky . . . oh yes, Sergeant
Heckenburg, there's lots more to come!'

'Eric!' Heck jabbered. 'We're being shot to pieces here.
Shawna's down . . . severe gunshot wounds to both legs!'

'Where the hell are you?'

'I can't say . . . some kind of gamekeeper's cottage. But
we can't be too far from the main building. Tell everyone to
shut their bloody gobs and listen for the shooting. And get
another ambulance!'

BOOM . . .

He glanced into the living room. More splinters, more

smoke. Only fragments of the front door remained. Outside there was a clunk-clack as the shooter reloaded.

'It's a pity lives need to be lost!' Holker shouted. 'But that's always the way of it, eh? Blood must be shed if a point is to be made.'

Heck lurched to the kitchen window, glancing out between the planks. An old yard lay on the other side, hemmed in by a high brick wall, and filled with tyres, tangled weeds and corroded bicycle frames.

BOOM . . . more exploding timber, more shattering glass.

Heck kicked and punched at the planks in the kitchen window, until one by one they were knocked out.

'Hey,' Shawna moaned, 'hey . . . don't even think about leaving me in here . . .'

Heck didn't look back; there was nothing to be gained from hunkering down and waiting for the cavalry. If that nutcase Holker decided to come inside, they'd be easy meat. The last plank fell, and he clambered outside. The house was a free-standing structure – there was nothing even near to it, just woodland on all sides – and no way to slide around the front without being seen. He glanced upward, seeing that the eaves were low; no more than eight feet in the air.

'We may die too!' came Holker's voice from the other side of the building. 'We don't care. We're ready to sacrifice ourselves. Clearly you're not!'

Heck scrambled up onto the wall, and from there over a rotted guttering onto the lower slope of the roof, which was loose and mossy, especially difficult in his lace-up leather shoes. Slates broke and slid away as he yomped his way up.

'But we're going to save the soul of this sterile, chav-ridden country and remind them what made it great!' Holker bellowed. 'What made it one of the best and most pleasurable places in the world to live!'

BOOM . . .

Why he hadn't yet entered the cottage to finish his victims off, Heck couldn't imagine, but maybe his brief was not to kill the cops, just hold them at bay. He'd now reached the apex of the roof and peered down the other side.

The youth was in the same position where he'd been in before, but prowling a little to the left and then a little to the right. He pumped another shell into the building, more glass and woodwork erupting inwards. Somewhere below Heck's feet, Shawna was sobbing.

'We're going to shame this land into realising that life isn't just one fucking party,' Holker shouted. 'That prayers need to be said and offerings made. We're going to remind them what matters . . . by showing them the price of forgetting.'

He triggered his shotgun again, before breaking it and digging in his pockets for more ammo. Heck threw himself over the central ridge, and slid downward on his ankles and backside. Holker only sensed the danger and looked up when Heck was in free-fall. He had no time to raise the weapon before the cop had slammed on top of him, flattening him on the ground, the impact of which was enough to knock Heck sick never mind the schoolboy.

Heck jumped up first. The shotgun had come loose, so he grabbed it by the barrels and slung it, before swinging around. Holker got to his feet more shakily. He looked groggy; in fact his nose was bloodied – but the whiteness of his cheek and the glaze across his eyes owed to more than pain and shock. This was a seriously disturbed kid, Heck realised, who had finally reached the end of his tether.

Holker came at him with a wild right hook. Heck ducked and hacked a good one into his belly. Holker toppled forward, gagging. Heck followed it with a left to his kidneys, and then a karate blow to the nape of his neck.

Holker slumped to the ground, insensible. Heck landed

on him from behind, knees first. 'You don't have to say anything,' he intoned, fixing the lad in a no-nonsense wristlock. 'But it may harm your defence if you do not mention when questioned something which you later rely on in court. Anything you do say . . .' a local patrol car screeched to a halt alongside him; the blue flashing lights of an ambulance weren't far behind it, '. . . may be given in evidence.' Heck stood up as a clutch of uniforms spilled out of the car, dragging Holker up with him and pushing him into their hands. 'This one's locked up for attempting to murder two police officers. That shotgun needs making safe . . . better get the SFOs on it.' He turned to the paramedics hurrying from the rear of the ambulance with their tackle bags. 'The casualty's inside. Hurry please . . .' He grabbed his phone again, bashed in Gary Quinnell's number and banged it to his ear.

'You still on the west gate?' he shouted.

'Affirmative. What's happened with Shawna . . .?'

'She's being attended to. You haven't seen that HGV yet?'

'Nothing yet, sarge . . .' But in the background, Heck could hear a fast-approaching rumble. He went cold as he pictured the heavy wagon, all six or seven tons of it ploughing towards the lone CID car parked across the open entrance. 'Hey, it's here now!' Quinnell yelled. 'Jeeesu . . .'

The phone went dead.

'Gary!' Heck bellowed helplessly. 'Gary!'

A rasping chuckle drew his attention to the patrol car, where Holker was now leaning against its nearside flank as the uniforms searched him. He smiled at Heck, bloody-mouthed. 'Another one down, Sergeant Heckenburg? You're not doing very well today.'

Heck approached him. 'We've wrapped you bastards up, at least.'

'You reckon?'

'Your friends won't get far.'

362

'They won't need to.'

'We'll get them all.'

'I don't doubt it, but will you get them in time?'

Heck was distracted from this conversation – mainly by the sight of Shawna being brought from the cottage on a gurney, but now he realised what the prisoner had said, and something in the way he'd said it made Heck's sweat-soaked hair stiffen.

Holker's battered face was written with a kind of devilish glee; his eyes, dead and black as buttons, only enhanced the effect.

'Care to elaborate?' Heck said.

'Let me see, erm . . .' the prisoner's sickle grin broadened, '. . . no. Except to say good luck. Because, trust me, you're going to need it.'

'Get him out of here.'

The uniforms turned Holker around, and the patrol car's rear door swung open.

'Oh, there is one thing,' Holker said. 'This next one's going to be a good one. It always had to be . . . the tenth one, you see. A real celebration.'

Heck strode away. 'Try gloating when you're watching the world from a one-by-two window.'

'This time we're going to do something special . . . with a very special victim.'

Heck ignored him, heading towards the ambulance.

'Surprised you haven't already missed her, to be honest.'

Heck halted in mid-stride.

'She was on the telly often enough. Surely you haven't forgotten her already?'

Heck spun slowly round, staring at the prisoner in disbelief. And before he could stop himself, he'd lunged across the two or three yards between them, grabbing Holker by the collar and ramming him back against the patrol car.

'You'd better be lying to me!'

'Yeah, of course . . . I'm getting beaten up for nothing!'

'Where is she . . . *tell me now*!'

'Not telling you where, I'm afraid.' The demented youth cackled. 'I'll give you a clue, though . . . this next one's all about treason. And traitors . . . just like your girl, eh, Sergeant Heckenburg? Because she betrayed the entire nation, telling those lies about us. Not letting the people know what they had a right to . . .'

Heck tightened his grip on Holker's throat. 'What are you going to do to her, you little shit?'

'That's for me to know and you to find out . . . if you're good enough.'

Chapter 44

They watched Claire with strange fascination.

None of them spoke, even though they were fixating on her. There appeared to be four of them in total. She'd thought there'd be more, but one of them was presumably driving the vehicle, the steel floor of which juddered beneath her as they followed endless, winding roads. The lorry's sides, which enclosed them in sepulchral dimness, vibrated.

Still they said nothing.

Though they'd now removed her blindfold and gag, she was kneeling painfully upright, hands and ankles bound together behind her. Her captors knelt too, surrounding her in a perfect circle. The half-light rendered their features ghostly and indistinct, which was much the way she'd seen them the last time – in that derelict petrol station, where they'd come at her like spectres through the shadows and moonlight.

It still seemed incredible to Claire that they were teenagers – little more than children.

First there was the pretty blonde girl who'd clamped her in a choke-hold in the station storeroom. After her came the girl Claire thought of as 'the Tomboy'. She was stocky, with short, raven-black hair and a permanent pugnacious sneer, but she too was athletic and strong; Claire knew this for a fact because it was the Tomboy who'd dragged her around the most. Last in the command structure came two boys. One was short and dumpy, with curious rat-like features; she imagined he'd been the butt of many jokes. The other was taller and leaner; he had a head of tight brown curls and the angelic looks of a choirboy, yet there was something menacing about him – perhaps his frozen half-smile, which she belatedly realised was not a smile at all, but some kind of facial flaw.

'What are you staring at?' he asked quietly.

'Nothing,' Claire replied, half mesmerised. His gaze was so forceful that she fancied she could feel it on her skin. It was the same with all of them.

They didn't seem angry with her, though there was an undisguised urgency when they'd dragged her up from that pit. At the time, somewhere in the near-distance, she'd heard male voices shouting. She'd wondered if that was Heck and the rest of them, closing in . . . but ultimately it hadn't mattered. Her abductors had flung her into the trailer of the articulated lorry, climbing in with her, and closing and bolting the doors. The vehicle had then rumbled away, swerving, stopping and starting up again, and experiencing at least one road accident, but not letting that slow it down. It had been on the move ever since, and still was.

'Miss Moody?' came a voice from somewhere else in the lorry's interior.

This was an adult voice, and Claire knew immediately who it belonged to. She glanced left, to where a fifth figure emerged from the darkness. It was the older bespectacled man, the one with the grey frizzy hair, the one whose car had pulled up on the petrol station forecourt. He smiled at her as he shrugged his large frame into an oversize camouflage jacket.

'My apologies for the roughness of your experience so far,' he said. 'It's a necessary evil, I'm afraid . . . but at the very least we can be courteous. I am Dr Enwright, but you may call me Leo.' He indicated the blonde girl. 'This is Jasmine.' Jasmine neither smiled nor nodded. 'And this is Heather.' The Tomboy did smile, but it wasn't pleasant. 'And these two reprobates,' Leo indicated the rat-faced boy and the taller one with the leer, 'are Luke and Arnie.'

'What do you . . .' she stammered. 'What do you want with me?'

'You're here to pay your dues,' Enwright said simply.

'Why?' she pleaded. 'In heaven's name, what have I done to you?'

'Not to us. To the nation. You told them we were gangsters, criminals.'

'But you are!' She couldn't help saying that, even though her voice had diminished to little more than a whine. 'You kidnap people . . . you murder them.'

'You called us desecrators,' the boy called Arnie accused her. 'That was an insult.'

'But I didn't invent that name . . .'

'Nor did you deny it,' Heather said.

'Listen, please . . . stop this madness.'

'You transmitted a message to the nation that we are its enemies,' Enwright pointed out. 'That we seek only to damage, to hurt . . .'

'I think they can draw that conclusion for themselves,' she interrupted, fear and pain hardening her tone. This old crackpot . . . and these stupid kids, these stupid bits of bloody demented kids! The vibrating steel floor was agony under her knees. Her wrists and ankles ached in their bonds. 'And you're hardly likely to make them think differently with this kind of behaviour, are you!'

'Quite the opposite, actually.' Enwright took two items

from a haversack. One of them rattled – it sounded like a box of matches. 'Because of those offerings we've already made, yours, I think, will be the most appreciated.' He glanced at her with apparent interest in her viewpoint. 'The British are a sporting set, wouldn't you say?'

'I don't know what you mean . . .'

'But they're a contrary lot too. With the same cynicism that has enabled them to stand back and watch, even while disapproving, as the spiritual life of this land has turned to ashes – they'll enjoy the irony that the one most deserving of their vengeance, the traitor who lied and misled them, is to be given a chance the others never had.'

A match sparked to life, and he inserted it into an oil lamp, which he then lifted above his head, casting them all in a faint, flickering luminescence. They were clad for the outdoors; she saw green and black waterproofs and leggings, lace-up hiking boots, gloves, more camouflaged jackets. The girl Jasmine was equipped with a firearm; it was strapped to her back, its carved wooden hilt visible over her right shoulder.

'Are we all going hunting?' Claire said, trying to sound scornful.

Enwright smiled. 'Some of us.'

A heap of neatly folded garments was flung down: a white chemise with frill cuffs and collar; a buff, hook-fronted tunic complete with a broad belt to be worn across the shoulder; a pair of baggy maroon breeches, and some gauntlets. As an afterthought, a pair of heeled, leather thigh-boots were placed on top.

'It's unlikely to be a perfect fit,' Enwright said. 'But needs must. As long as you wear it with pride, the illusion will be complete.'

Claire gazed at the outfit, uncomprehending. She said nothing as the boy called Luke shuffled behind her. With a rasp of steel, he drew his knife and sawed through her bonds.

When both her hands and feet were free, she slumped down onto her hip, rubbing at the weals on her wrists and ankles.

'Take your clothes off,' Heather instructed her.

Claire glanced up at them. 'Forget it.' She indicated the costume. 'I'm not wearing that stuff, if that's what you mean. This insanity has gone far enough.'

'Take your clothes off,' Enwright reiterated, blank-faced.

'No. You're going to hurt me anyway, so why should I?'

With deliberate slowness, Jasmine drew the firearm from her back. Claire stared aghast as what looked like a sawn-off double-barrelled shotgun was levelled at her face.

'Why?' Jasmine said without emotion. 'I'll tell you . . . because the small chance you have – and it is exceedingly small – will disappear entirely if you fail to cooperate.'

'You wouldn't dare,' Claire said more boldly than she felt, because in truth she had no doubt that this girl would dare.

'The only thing I'd regret is the waste of good material.' Jasmine squinted along the barrels – as if she needed to from three feet away. 'But we can always find more of that. We've always been able to find more.'

The others watched, eyes shining, mouths wet with excitement. Jasmine smiled too, for the first time; it was a Satanic vision, her lips a crooked curve, her glassy eyes boring straight through Claire; it could have been anyone she was about to execute here – literally anyone – and it wouldn't have mattered to her one iota.

Hurriedly, Claire slid off her jacket and blouse, unfastening the button at the front of her trousers and turning slightly to wriggle them down her bruised legs. She sat shame-faced in knickers and bra, arms folded across her midriff in an attempt to cover herself.

They regarded her dispassionately.

'Everything,' Jasmine said.

'Why everything?' Claire said tearfully.

'Because, my dear, humiliation is part of the ritual,' Enwright explained.

'Everything,' Jasmine said again, nudging her shoulder with the gun.

'So you're perverts as well?' Claire wept as she unhooked her bra and raised her bottom to pull her knickers down. 'I might have guessed . . .'

'Defending your dignity will cut no ice here,' Enwright said. 'Jasmine had to give up far more than you.'

'Nice pussy,' Arnie commented, though a fierce glare from Enwright prevented further crudity from him.

'What are you waiting for?' Jasmine asked, gesturing at the pile of clothing.

Scarcely able to believe what was happening to her, Claire clambered into the garish costume. As Enwright had hinted, it wasn't a perfect fit – a little on the large side, but if she tightened the belt to its last notch, it just about held together. She looked around at them. Again they were watching her in silence, but now it was the silence of approval. Luke lifted something into view from the darkness behind him: a cardboard box, overflowing with greenery. He turned his eyes to Enwright, who nodded once, and then smiled, as, with hoots and gibbers, the rest of them fell upon her.

Shrieking, Claire was borne to the lorry floor. The box of greenery contained nettles and thistles. With exaggerated laughs, they grabbed up handfuls of these and began stuffing them inside her costume.

Chapter 45

By the time Heck got to the estate's west gate, local support units were on site in the shape of two Traffic Division Range Rovers. They'd already closed down the main road with cones and visi-flashers. Gary Quinnell's Hyundai lay in the far lane, upside down. Its front offside had imploded. A sparkling trail of shattered glass and metal splinters lay across the blacktop.

Quinnell himself was seated on the kerb, a Traffic PC in a white hat and fluorescent slicker crouched alongside him, taking notes. Quinnell's face, shirt and tie were stained with blood, which had dripped down from a nasty gash in his brow. When he saw Heck approaching, he shook his head. 'Sorry . . . came out of nowhere. Fifty plus. Like a bloody tank. Crashed straight through me.'

'They'll do that to anyone who gets in their way,' Heck said. 'You alright?'

'Bit shaken. Tried to stand up a minute ago, had a funny turn.'

'An ambulance is on its way,' the Traffic officer said.

'Good,' Heck replied. 'Get him down to A&E. See he gets treated quickly, eh? Meanwhile, we need a fix on that wagon.'

'Air Operations have been alerted,' the Traffic officer said. 'But it was heading west, and that's where the M6 is . . . and there are lots of heavies on the motorway.'

'*DS Fisher to DS Heckenburg?*' Heck's radio chirped.

'Go ahead, Eric.'

'*You need to get back here, Heck.*'

'Correction. I need to find this missing HGV before something very bad happens to Claire Moody.'

'*That's why you want to get back here. Enwright left a lot of stuff behind . . . it's the best lead we've got.*'

Heck pondered this for an agonised moment, before reaching a decision. 'On my way.'

'So what do we know?' Heck said, ripping off his jacket as he entered Enwright's office.

The motorised lawn-roller was still jammed in the shattered doorway to the storeroom. Enwright's expansive desk stood in the corner where they had dragged it, but now the singed map that Heck had saved from the Pavilion fire was spread on top of it. Eric Fisher was present, his attention divided between the map and the computer, which he was plugged into via a pair of earphones. Paperwork was scrolling out, sheet by sheet, from a fax machine in the corner.

'*I said, what we have got?!*' Heck repeated loudly, when Fisher didn't respond.

'Oh . . . sorry, Heck.' Fisher removed one of the earphones. 'Bits and bobs. First, have a gander at that map.'

Heck did but could only distinguish the outlines of woods, fields and narrow lanes, which were probably little more than farm tracks. The marker-pen squiggles were unreadable.

'I couldn't work out where it's supposed to be at first,' Fisher said. 'But I think I do now. Sale Green and Huddington are the giveaways.' He indicated the two obscure hamlets in the map's lower left and right corners. 'It's the open country between Worcester and Redditch. Doesn't tell us what they've got in mind, of course.'

Heck shook his head. 'Whatever it is, we've got to get down there. Worcester's only forty miles from Riphall. They could be there already.'

'It won't be a piece of piss going at it blind. That map covers a big area.'

'Okay, we'll need foot troops. Let's hope West Mercia can spare a few.'

'Nothing else in the Pavilion?' Fisher asked.

'Most of it got burned. No time to look through the rest.' Heck pointed at the fax. 'What's this?'

'Enwright's criminal record.'

'Good . . .' Heck snatched it, rolled it and crammed it under his jacket. He turned to the computer. 'What are you ear-wigging?'

'Going through his audio files.'

'They aren't encrypted?'

'Nope.'

'Didn't think we'd get near him, did he?'

'You ought to listen to some of this stuff.'

'There's no time . . .'

'It's important, Heck. At first I didn't think they were relevant. It's mostly academic . . . anthropological experiments, observations of social behaviour, that sort of stuff. But then I realised quite a few of them refer to these kids who've gone AWOL.' He indicated the school records lying on a nearby shelf. 'And it isn't what you'd call flattering.'

Reluctantly, Heck waited while Fisher unplugged the earphones. He heard Enwright's voice – smooth, unctuous, but talking idly to himself, as if giving voice to a stream of casual contemplation. The subject appeared to be Gareth Holker, St Bardolph's Head Boy and rugby captain, two achievements which Enwright, though vaguely contemptuous of them, was, in a roundabout way, taking the credit for.

'*They say you can't polish a turd, can't turn a pig's ear into a silk purse . . . such clichés, such typical conceit of the chattering classes. How do men with nothing in their lives become super-powered Special Forces soldiers? How do tea-boys ascend the ladder and finish up running multinationals? Latent power lurks in all of us, and we don't even know it. All one must do is unlock it. That boy could climb a cliff-face with a hundredweight of bricks on his back if conditioned properly. It's the mind, not the body . . . the young mind in particular. So easy to meld, to bend . . .*'

Heck glanced at Fisher. 'Is there more like this?'

Fisher moved the cursor slightly. 'Lots.'

'*The Hitler Youth were the perfect example. Give them a flag and they're yours. Even if they don't totally believe, one reaches the stage where it is more important to be accepted than to do the right thing . . .*'

'He's deranged,' Heck said. 'As if we didn't already know that.'

Fisher hit the 'off' switch. 'Makes it a bit more explainable perhaps.'

'If no more understandable. There's nothing in there about Worcester, nothing specific?'

'Nothing specific. Just stuff concerning the kids . . . going back months, years.'

'Can you edit the relevant bits together into a single MP3?'

Fisher raised a bushy eyebrow. 'I'm an intelligence officer, not a hacker.'

'You spend most of every day online.'

'How soon will you need it?'

'ASAP.' Heck rubbed his brow. 'In the meantime, I've no choice . . . I'll have to lean on the prisoners.'

'You won't get much out of Latimer,' Fisher said. 'He's been taken to hospital with a broken jaw.'

'My heart bleeds.'

'There may be trouble. His mum and dad are bigwigs in the film industry.'

'Are they based over here?'

'LA, as far as I know.'

'While their son languishes at boarding school in rainy England? That explains plenty.'

'Will Holker talk?'

Heck shook his head. 'He's hardcore. Enwright had *him* the longest. How about Worthington? Still on the premises?'

Fisher nodded at the office door – just as Charlie Finnegan sauntered through it.

'Worthington?' Heck said.

'Yep.' Finnegan checked his notes. 'Comes from Bolton . . . almost certainly our zoo insider. No previous. Apparently been a model pupil . . .'

'Is he still here?'

'Sitting in a patrol car outside.'

'Get him out again.' Heck dragged his jacket on. 'He's coming for a ride with us.'

'What . . . where?'

'We're going to Worcester. We'll talk to him on the way.'

'Eh?' Finnegan looked startled. 'Hang on, sarge, we . . . we can't do that.'

'He's still your prisoner, isn't he?'

'Officially, yeah.'

'Fine. If anyone asks, you're taking him to the nearest nick. Your superior – in more ways than one – has specifically instructed you.'

'But he's a minor . . .'

'So find an appropriate adult.'

'What about a legal rep . . .?'

375

'What about getting him a pet too?' Heck said. 'And an Xbox to keep him occupied? What do you not understand, Charlie, about someone's gonna die if we don't get our arses in gear? Now jump fucking to it!'

Chapter 46

'Surprised the lorry wasn't spotted on its way down here,' Charlie Finnegan remarked, noting yet another Traffic patrol parked on a motorway bridge as they sped beneath it.

'They're clever,' Heck muttered, distracted by Leo Enwright's crumpled rap sheet, which he'd now read through a couple of times. 'Wouldn't surprise me if they'd stopped and put new plates on it. That'd buy them enough time to make it forty miles.'

A passing signpost showed that they themselves were only fifteen miles from Worcester. The M5 was normally busy, but it was now edging towards mid-evening, so the rush-hour traffic was thinning out. Of course, the advantage of that was offset by the disadvantage of approaching dusk – like they didn't have problems enough when the area shown on the map was so large. Not that Heck was overly worried by this at present.

He glanced again at the rap sheet on his knee. It was disturbing by any standards, not to say a little amazing. If such things happened now, the mental health services would have been activated as a matter of course, but the late 1960s and early 1970s had been a rough-and-ready era, during which time 'care' was rarely to the fore, and a clip round the ear had often been deemed sufficient response to unacceptable behaviour.

Finnegan was seated behind the steering wheel of Heck's Volkswagen. Three other figures were crammed into the back seat. First, was the rangy young constable who'd unsuccessfully shoulder-charged Enwright's storeroom door; his name was PC Mapling. In the middle, handcuffed to Mapling, sat Anthony Worthington, still in school uniform and wearing a petulant frown – a combination that made him look more like a kids' TV brat than any sort of real criminal. Squashed against the nearside door was Wanda Clayley, the well-manicured Deputy Head, looking flustered and distraught. Her constant attempts to hold Worthington's hand, which efforts he repeatedly rebuffed, seemed designed to provide comfort for herself as much as her errant pupil.

'Does your school offer its pupils clay-pigeon shooting, Mrs Clayley?' Heck asked, turning to face her.

At first she didn't seem to hear. 'Oh, erm, yes. We always have. It isn't every child that excels at rugby or football . . .'

'Or archery,' Heck added.

Her cheek reddened even more. 'St Bardolph's is a boarding school, Sergeant Heckenburg. By necessity we need to offer as wide a range of non-curricular activities as possible. And as we're in the heart of the countryside . . .'

'Yeah, I hear that.' He rubbed at the back of his neck, which was now aching in response to his whiplash from earlier. 'Just do us a favour . . . make sure when you get back that your cache of shotguns is only one short, eh? I'm sure they cost someone a pretty penny.' His gaze roved to Worthington. 'And how are you doing, Anthony?'

Worthington yawned as if bored.

Heck showed him a small Dictaphone, which was now running on 'record'. He placed it on the dashboard. 'You realise you're still under caution?'

Worthington gazed through the window.

'Do you think your friends haven't talked?' Heck asked him. 'We know everything. You're an accomplice to nine torture-murders. Let me explain what that means . . . you're not going to walk free for a long, long time.'

Worthington gave another false yawn.

'Nice bit of bravado, son, but I know for a fact that you were worried about getting caught . . . otherwise why did you run away from me?'

Worthington glanced sideways, finally deigning to acknowledge that Mrs Clayley was present. 'Are they allowed to do this?' he asked.

Mrs Clayley seemed nonplussed by the entire experience, but inclined her head, indicating that she thought (or maybe *hoped*) the police were in the right.

'This is what's called an "urgent interview", Anthony,' Heck explained. 'It's covered under the Police and Criminal Evidence Act, and it permits any arrested person to be interviewed before being removed to a police station if such interview may prevent physical harm befalling somebody else. Now thanks to your mouthy pal, Gareth, I have more than a sneaking suspicion that if we were to waste time booking you in at the local nick and then waiting for your solicitor to bother showing up, Claire Moody's life would be forfeit. Am I wrong?'

Again, Worthington affected disinterest.

'Anthony,' Mrs Clayley hissed at him. 'Talk to the officer. Tell him what he wants to know. Show him this is a big mistake, and then we can all go home.'

Worthington shook his head as if he couldn't believe the dunces he was dealing with.

'Okay Anthony,' Heck said, 'if you don't want to talk about Claire Moody, tell us why we're going down to Worcester.' The lad didn't respond to that either, but Heck noted that his shoulders had tensed slightly. 'Come on, Anthony . . . you're part of the school History Club, and it's a famous old city. Surely you've heard of it?'

'Well of course he's heard of it,' Mrs Clayley interrupted, gazing at the pupil, perplexed. 'Dr Enwright took them all down there on a field-trip several months ago – to the battlefield. I was the one who approved it.'

'To the battlefield, eh?' Heck said, not knowing anything about a battlefield near Worcester, though Holker's words about 'treason' were now echoing in his memory.

'The battle of Worcester was fought in 1651,' Mrs Clayley added conveniently. 'It was the last battle of the English Civil War. I presumed they were planning to base one of their History Club productions around it.'

'Oh, they were planning something,' Heck agreed. 'But *you'd* never have got to see it, Mrs Clayley.' His eyes burned into the prisoner. 'You might as well talk to me, Anthony. We wouldn't be on our way down to Worcester right now if we didn't already know this stuff. You getting arrested isn't going to buy your pals any more time than they've already got. But you should be glad, because if they succeed in this, that's a tenth murder you'll be implicated in.'

Worthington curled his lip as if amused, but it wasn't as convincing as before.

'Look son, you're not daft. You know you're a drip. Even in juvenile prison, you're going to be white meat. And in a couple of years' time you'll be in with the big boys, and that's an entirely new level of viciousness you'll be exposed to . . .'

'Sergeant Heckenburg!' Mrs Clayley said. 'I really don't see . . .'

'It's important he knows this,' Heck interrupted her back. 'Because I'll tell you, Anthony, no one is going to help you avert this very nasty future you're now facing. Except, maybe . . . you.' He let that hang. 'I need to know exactly where your friends are, and what they're planning to do next. I've even brought a map, so you can show me. You do that, and it will strongly indicate that you're not only sorry for what you've done, but that you weren't totally behind it in the first place.'

Worthington's cheeks had visibly coloured. At last he spoke but in a sullen, childish tone; his eyes were downcast. 'Dr Enwright told us you'd try this. Try to make deals with us. He said there'll be nothing you can give us. It'll just be talk.'

'Anthony!' Mrs Clayley exclaimed. 'What on earth are you saying . . .?'

'Can you afford to take that chance?' Heck said. 'You need to talk to me. There's nothing else for you.'

'Yes there is,' Worthington said, still sullen. 'He told us they'll try to cure us, not punish us. Kids who kill are never kept in long.'

'You don't have to be in long to get your throat cut, son.'

'Sergeant, please!' Mrs Clayley objected.

'At seventeen, Anthony, you may not even be classified as a kid. But I'll tell you what I think . . . that you participated in these acts because Dr Enwright made you?'

'He didn't make us. We were all volunteers.'

'Stuck posters up in the school corridors, did he? "Anyone who wants to rip the world a new one by brutally murdering people, let's have a chat." Did he hold interviews, Anthony? How many interviewees did he reject?' Heck snorted. 'I'll tell you, son . . . none. Everyone he approached got the handshake. You want to know why? Because he picked you all deliberately. He spotted lonely, isolated people, those who'd been neglected, or bullied, or abused . . . and he stopped all that, didn't he?'

Worthington now shot Heck a dull glare that was filled with hatred, though it was more the hatred of embarrassment, of having been discovered.

'This created a bond of trust, didn't it?' Heck said. 'And over a period of years, he used this trust against you, to change you, to make you detest your enemies rather than fear them, to break down any moral resistance you might have left.'

'Sergeant Heckenburg . . .' Mrs Clayley shook her head. 'You are so wrong about Dr Enwright. This has got to be some kind of awful misunderstanding.'

'Mrs Clayley, let me tell you about Dr Enwright.' Heck pinned her with his most no-nonsense stare. 'At twelve years old, he was arrested for stealing "church bread".'

'He had a bad start in life, I'm aware of that . . .'

'Church bread, Mrs Clayley? Would that be the Communion host? The Body of Christ? Which he then broke up and fed to the pigeons on the church forecourt.'

'He was only a child. If we were all held to account for things we did . . .'

'Agreed, but it's a bit weird, wouldn't you say? Especially as a number of those pigeons then died because he'd rubbed the bread with rat poison. I mean . . . poisoning innocent animals with Communion wafers, and then . . . what else did he do?' He made a show of consulting his paperwork. 'Oh yeah . . . dumping the bodies in the baptismal font.' He glanced up at her again. 'Seems a determinedly *irreligious* act. Goes a bit beyond common blasphemy, wouldn't you agree?'

By her glazed expression, Mrs Clayley did.

Heck turned to Worthington again. 'Your mentor, Anthony. What a guy, eh?'

Worthington looked equally fascinated by what he'd just heard. But then he shook his head, as though in an effort to convince himself that it was lies. 'Dr Enwright said you'd make accusations. But we know what he's really like. He's a crusader. We knew from the beginning that people would get hurt. He said it was the only way. We had to shock the country into realising that holy days matter.'

382

'By desecrating them?' Heck asked.

'No!' Worthington shouted, his face now livid. 'By mocking those who've already *been* desecrating them . . .'

'And the dead birds in the church font? Who was Dr Enwright mocking that day?'

'That was to make him strong.'

'What are you talking about?'

'He had us doing it too . . . to rats and mice.'

There was a brief, astonished silence.

'Anthony,' Mrs Clayley whispered, 'what are you saying?'

Worthington was breathing hard and fast, his face still red, though his spittle-slathered lips had cracked into a stupid, defiant grin. 'And not with poison, with our bare hands.' He jutted his chin out as if he was proud of his achievements, but Heck detected tears glinting in the corners of his eyes. 'So we'd be ready for the coming fight . . . against the real vermin. The drug addicts and winos, the tarts and chavs who are ruining Britain, turning it into a soulless cesspool, where it's all about flashing your tits for a set of beads, or downing as many shots as you can because there's a promotion at the bar . . .'

'And that young couple on the West Pennine Moors?' Heck asked him. 'How were *they* contributing to the chav cesspool?'

'Perhaps with those two gone there'll be a few less used condoms lying around in public picnic areas.'

Charlie Finnegan chuckled. 'It's a muscular version of religion, I'll give you that.'

'It's not about religion,' Worthington snapped. 'Not the way you people know it. It's about spirituality, not dogma. Doesn't matter what gods or spirits you worship . . .'

'You swallowed every bit of nonsense he fed you, didn't you, son?' Heck said.

'We just have to remind people there's something else there . . .'

'And you'll remind them by killing them?' Mrs Clayley asked, in a tone of disbelief.

'It's a harsh lesson, I know,' Worthington said; tears now streamed down his cheeks. 'But it's for their own good. Dr Enwright called it "tough love" . . .'

'Tough love?' Heck couldn't listen to any more. 'What bollocks is this?'

'Sergeant!' Mrs Clayley protested feebly.

'Murder is murder, Anthony!'

'You don't understand . . .'

'I understand perfectly.' Heck leaned towards him. 'Because I've locked up more killers than you've had fish and chips. And Leo Enwright is no different to any of them. He's a disturbed narcissist who put on a show to shock the world purely because of the sick pleasure it gave him. But do you know what . . . he's not even the original bloody author of this disaster. Here . . .' He dug an object from inside his jacket pocket and held it up; it was a dog-eared booklet inserted into a plastic evidence sack. 'I'm showing the suspect Exhibit MH33. What does it say on that cover, Anthony? Come on!'

'Blood Feast!' Worthington said.

'That's correct . . . Blood Feast.' Heck took the booklet out of the bag and pushed it towards him. 'Go on, you can touch it. We've got lots of copies.'

Warily, Worthington accepted it.

'This work of horror fiction was written in 2005 by an author called Dan Tubbs,' Heck said. 'Another headcase as it happens, but not in the same league as your pal, Enwright. In it, a bunch of losers – just like you and your friends – celebrate special holidays by committing human sacrifices.'

Worthington switched his uncomprehending gaze from the book to Heck, and then back to the book again.

'The only difference between the loonies in this book and you lot is that they were honouring the old gods to try and awaken them. You weren't trying to do that, were you, Anthony? I don't know why I'm asking actually, because frankly I doubt you have the first idea what you were trying to do. Go on . . . exercise that immense cerebellum of yours. Read the bloody thing. Leo Enwright certainly did. He picked it up for free at a horror convention about six years ago.'

Worthington still looked as if he didn't believe what he was being told. Almost reluctantly, he began to leaf through the booklet.

'I bet that piece of tat was never part of your re-education programme, was it?' Heck said. 'You won't get through it all now, of course . . . so let me paraphrase. On Valentine's Day, the hearts of two lovers are transfixed together with an arrow. On Good Friday, a priest gets crucified. Not a pervy, paedo priest who some victim is trying to get even with. This one's a good guy. He cares for his flock and looks after the poor – that makes him more like Jesus, you see. Just like that poor girl, Kate Rickman.'

Worthington didn't reply. He was reading selected passages in the book, his face growing visibly stricken.

'I'll tell you what,' Heck said, 'I'd feel better about you Anthony, if I didn't suspect that what's upsetting you right now is not these atrocious crimes you've been party to, but the realisation that your guru hasn't got an original idea in his head. Even though you've been treating him like he's got the hotline to God . . . you little prat! You've given up your entire life for the depraved fantasies of an anorak!'

'Sergeant, that's quite enough!' Mrs Clayley asserted.

Heck glanced at her irritably, even though she was probably right. 'Sorry about the "prat", Anthony, but I think you can see where this is going.'

Worthington glanced up at him; he looked lost, confused.

'This guy pulled the wool over your eyes big time,' Heck added. 'Not just you, but all the others. He's guaranteed you're going to spend a long, long time in the criminal justice system, and why . . . because enough people haven't told him how wonderful and amazing and brilliant he is.'

Worthington stared at the book again. He turned more pages with stiff, crooked fingers. By his glazed expression, he wasn't even seeing what was written there.

'Sergeant Heckenburg,' Mrs Clayley said. 'I understand that you had no choice but to speak to Anthony like this. But I really think, given his emotional state, and the terrible things that have happened today . . .'

'Royal . . . Royal Oak Day,' Worthington stuttered.

Everyone in the car glanced round at him. Even Charlie Finnegan was briefly distracted from the wheel.

'What's that, Anthony?' Heck enquired.

'Royal Oak Day . . . that's the next feast we were going to venerate.'

'Royal Oak Day?' Heck said. 'Can you tell us a bit more?'

'May 29.' Worthington swallowed. 'It commemorates Charles II's escape from Cromwell . . . after the battle of Worcester. And the restoration of the English Monarchy in 1660.'

'May 29,' Finnegan said. 'Gives us a bit of breathing space.'

'No,' Worthington shook his head. 'This time it'll be different.'

'How?' Heck asked.

The boy worked his lips together, as if, despite everything he knew, the act of speaking out was still a massive betrayal. Fresh tears trickled down his cheeks. 'There was . . . there was an agreement all along that . . . that if any of us got caught, the others would bring the next celebration forward. Make the offering early, before anyone else got nabbed.'

'Okay, so . . . when?'

'Soon as possible. Tonight probably.'

'Tonight?'

'If they get there in time.'

'Get where? Presumably it's somewhere on the battlefield.'

'Dr Enwright found the perfect spot,' Worthington said. 'It's under an old oak tree.'

Mrs Clayley glanced at Heck. 'Charles II hid in an oak tree after the battle, when the Roundheads were searching for him.'

'The same tree?' Heck said. 'Is it a famous spot?'

'No, the original tree was cut down years ago.'

Heck glanced at Worthington again. 'What happens on Royal Oak Day?'

Worthington hung his head, but was breathing more steadily now – as if having started confessing, it suddenly felt easier. 'The Civil War was a religious war as well as a political one.'

'Okay . . .?'

'That's largely forgotten now, but at the time the return of the Stuarts was seen as one in the eye for fundamentalist Protestants. And it was a fun time. Got celebrated with parades, picnics, costume galas and that . . . it was also used as an excuse to take the piss out of anti-royalists, who were all branded as traitors.'

Again that word, *treason*, Heck thought.

'Sometimes this got out of hand,' Worthington added. 'Everyone had to wear a sprig of oak leaves as a sign of their allegiance to the Crown. Anyone who didn't risked getting pelted with eggs and whipped with ropes made of nettles.'

'Nice.'

'Someone would volunteer to dress up as a traitor, and they'd be paraded around and get stuff chucked at them. Sometimes a mock-manhunt would be staged . . . in commemoration of the real hunt for Charles II.'

'And when they got caught, they all got drunk, I suppose?'

Heck said. Worthington nodded. 'Only that's not going to happen this time, is it, Anthony?'

'No.'

'Go on . . .'

'Oliver . . .' Worthington shuddered – as if everything he'd been party to had suddenly come home to him. 'In killing Charles I and chasing Charles II, Oliver Cromwell and his regicides committed treason. The ones they caught got . . .' he glanced up with a haunted expression, '. . . hanged, drawn and quartered.'

Chapter 47

When they first fixed the mask to Claire's face, she panicked.

They forcibly held her down, which was an ordeal in itself given the prickly nettles crammed inside her clothing, but the sight of this hideous rubber visage brought a scream to her lips. It had grotesquely exaggerated features: heavy sloped brows with coarse black hair upon them, a protruding Punch-like nose and chin, a malevolent grin with a stringy black moustache over the top, but most abhorrent of all, huge, warty growths over every part of it.

'This is the face of the traitor whose demise is celebrated on Royal Oak Day,' Dr Enwright solemnly proclaimed.

An even louder scream tore from her throat when she saw Luke smearing the inside of the mask with superglue. She shook her head feverishly and began kicking out, but they restrained her brutally. The girl called Heather slapped her face with stinging force, and held her head firmly in place. When the mask was pressed down, Claire's vision was almost completely obscured; the eye-slits were too narrow and too high. The glue was slimy and cold, but already she could feel her skin tighten in its hardening grip.

'Once it's adhered, which it will do in seconds,' Dr

Enwright said, 'you'd be ill-advised to try and remove it. You'll succeed, but it'll take chunks of flesh with it.'

'My God, my God . . .' Claire jabbered.

'So spake this Puritan traitor when he slew the innocents at Wexford and Drogheda,' Enwright responded. 'One man's God, it seems, is another man's Devil. It doesn't matter. Our rituals celebrate the holy and the unholy – we take no sides in the eternal struggle.'

Claire lay there shivering, barely hearing his insane rambling, new sweat seeping through the already sodden vegetation under her costume.

There was a sudden crunching of gears and a thunder of brakes. The interior of the vehicle jolted as she felt it skid to a halt on rough ground. A metallic clanking signified that bolts were being removed. Dim daylight filled her narrow vision and a cool breeze assailed her as she was hoisted unceremoniously to her feet, carried along the length of the lorry's interior and lifted down onto what felt like a grassy verge.

She stumbled and fell to her knees; no one attempted to prevent it, or to help her up again. There was a clumping of feet as her captors scrambled back inside the vehicle. She listened in disbelief to the creaking of hinges as its heavy rear doors were closed, and then a series of echoing thuds as bolts were shot into place. With a shattering growl of engines, a *skitter* of gravel and a blast of warm, noxious exhaust, the vehicle pulled away.

Claire stayed on her knees, breathing hard, sweat soaking her entire body, unable to believe that she'd been left here. In only a few seconds, the sound of the lorry had receded until it was inaudible. Instead, she heard the twitter of birds, the faint hiss of a gentle breeze. With desperate urgency she began clawing at the rubber encasing her face, but the more she yanked on it, the more it tugged her skin. Her whimpers became yowls as that skin tore. Tiny rips in the mask became full-on breaches as she pulled and twisted. More of her skin was snagged, but at last large pieces of rubber had been peeled away. When the section over her nose and eyes had been removed, even if it had stripped off her eyebrows in the process, she saw that she was kneeling beside a beaten track running across empty heath-land dyed blood-red by the setting sun.

At first she couldn't take it in. To her left, the track meandered away for a hundred yards before vanishing into a copse of silver birch. Clumps of gorse were dotted around, glowing gold in their spring plumage. They'd really done it. They'd simply abandoned her. They'd made a mockery of her and were now releasing her – that was the only explanation.

She heard a low laugh from behind.

Though still on her knees, Claire spun around.

The sight of Arnie's permanent leer was like a blow from a mailed fist. To see that he was armed with an old-fashioned musketeer's sword – a rapier, she thought it was called – was even more of a shock. 'Thought you were getting off easy did you?' he said, swishing the blade back and forth. 'Traitor.'

'Don't you . . .' Claire tried to sound less like a terrified prisoner and more like a disapproving adult. 'Don't you think you're in enough trouble already without continuing this farce?'

'I look at it a different way. I'm in so much trouble now that nothing else I do will make much difference.'

'Where are your friends?'

'Oh, they're around . . . but they're not close.'

'Is this what Dr Enwright meant when he said I'd have a chance?'

'Yes.' If it was possible, Arnie's sardonic grin broadened. 'And you'd better take it, because you won't get another.'

Claire stumbled to her feet, turned and tried to stagger

away – but a stinging blow across the back of her legs knocked her down to her knees again.

The sword, she thought, stunned. *He's just hit me with a sword!*

'But first,' Arnie said, strolling around the front of her, unbuckling his belt, 'I'm going to have some fun.'

She gazed up at him, hollow-eyed. He was so young. He'd be so boyishly handsome if it wasn't for that horribly twisted mouth.

'I was in a car crash when I was nine,' he said. 'They rebuilt my face afterwards, but nothing's ever perfect, is it?'

'Stop,' she said. 'Please . . . just stop.'

'I'm not supposed to be doing this, you understand? It wasn't part of the plan, but as I say . . . nothing else will make much difference now.'

She tried to scrabble away, but he threw his sword aside, and leapt down on top of her, forcing her over onto her back and jamming his forearm across her throat, compressing her larynx. Claire's eyes bugged in their sockets until she thought they would burst. When he released her, she coughed and gagged.

'If I were you, I'd try to enjoy this . . . it's likely to be your last experience on earth.'

She spat in his face, so he punched her. Claire's two front teeth broke, her mouth filling with coppery blood.

'For that, you're going to get it front and back.' He knelt astride her, continuing unfastening his pants – and she rammed her left knee up, connecting hard with his groin. He choked and toppled sideways, hands clutched between his legs. Claire scrambled away from him, breathing hard, and jumped to her feet, turning every which way, expecting the rest of them to suddenly appear. But no one else was in sight. She looked for the sword as well, but couldn't immediately locate it, and there was no time to spread the search.

Arnie still lay curled on his side, but was already craning his neck around to glare at her.

Wearily, spitting blood, Claire stumbled off along the track.

Chapter 48

A helicopter sounded somewhere in the distance as Heck unfolded the fire-damaged map on the bonnet of his Volkswagen. He glanced up and around, but saw no sign of it yet. West Mercia had agreed to assist in any way they could, but they'd been caught unawares by his request, and though they'd put all officers on duty on 'Operation Response', it would clearly take some time to mobilise, especially as Heck hadn't really been able to tell them where they needed to deploy.

He had stopped the car at the side of a rural lane. Below them ran a tributary of the River Severn. Far to the west, the last vestige of sunlight was winking out on the horizon, throwing purple-grey shadows across a quiltwork landscape of coppice and meadow. Even with the aid of his pen-light, it was increasingly difficult to make out details on the map. Arrows made in marker pen indicated various locations, none of which were specific to recognisable grid-references.

Visually, the battlefield hadn't looked the way Heck had expected. There'd been plenty of signposts and route-markers, but the museum and visitor centre was apparently located in a place called 'The Commandery' in the middle of the town, several miles southeast of where they now stood, while the area of actual fighting wasn't just an open plain; it had occurred on several different sides of the city at once, and covered a broad landscape of woods, streams, narrow lanes and humpback bridges.

'Try to remember, Anthony,' Heck said impatiently.

The schoolboy was still handcuffed to PC Mapling, but pored over the map, squinting. 'I'm trying . . .'

'What were you doing out here, Anthony?' Mrs Clayley asked. She still spoke with a tone of disapproval, as if she was trying to understand a pupil who had bunked off school rather than a conspirator in a series of sadistic murders.

'Things,' he said, shrugging.

'What things?'

'I'm sure you don't want to know, Mrs Clayley,' Heck answered for him.

'There,' Worthington suddenly said, pointing out a single, unswerving line bisecting the upper right quadrant of the map. 'That one, maybe.'

'Any particular reason?' Charlie Finnegan asked.

'I remember we took the school minibus along this straight road with fields and hills on every side.' Worthington ran a grubby, chewed fingernail along the line in question, even though there were no distinguishing features at any part of it.

Finnegan glanced at Heck. 'This is bloody ridiculous. We need to wait for West Mercia.'

Heck folded the map. 'If we wait any longer it'll be pitch black out here . . . there aren't even any streetlights.'

'Heck, we've got two civvies with us.'

Heck paused, pondering this very real problem – but thoughts of Claire's tear-streaked face overrode it. He shook his head. 'They can stay in the car.'

'At least wait for the chopper . . .'

'I'm not waiting for anyone.' Heck ushered them towards the Volkswagen's doors. 'We can give Air Operations the location while we're en route. *Come on, move it!*'

Claire followed the track through the trees for about five hundred yards, before realising that it had never been intended for human passage. It crossed a small river by a stone bridge, and on the other side ended at a gate, beyond which lay a meadow filled with cattle.

She was already sick to her guts and faint from lack of food. But she knew that Arnie would not be far behind. She glanced over her shoulder. The track curved away into increasing dimness – and then something else caught her attention. A wooden stake had been hammered into the dirt on the verge. A sign fixed on top of it, painted in gold leaf, read:

The King's Way

It pointed down a side-path, running along the top of the river's embankment.

Was that the way they wanted her to go, she wondered . . . along the King's Way? Well, she wouldn't. She pivoted right. A mirror image of the path, minus the signpost, dwindled away through darkening thickets. She stumbled that way, constantly catching her outfit on thorns and other undergrowth. It had torn at some of its seams just because she'd been running in it. It was rubbish, little more than a carnival costume. She'd managed to pull out most of the nettles they'd stuffed it with, but her flesh underneath was raw, her puckered skin chafing every time it came in contact with the cheap, sweat-soaked material. The path veered away from the river, twisting and looping as the thickets turned to trees. This meant there was more space between them, less ground cover. She slowed down, struggling to get her breath – and in glancing left, spotted the dim shape of one of her captors watching from about a hundred yards away. She couldn't tell which one of them it was – he (or she) was wearing a dark hoodie top.

Whoever it was, they made no effort to follow as Claire ran frantically on.

Ahead of her, the trees thinned and open, grassy ground rose upwards. She continued forward, but she was so tired that she only managed to ascend the slope at a sideways stumble. When she reached the ridge at the top, she found another of those makeshift signposts.

Here, gallant Sir Edward Massie was wounded

She tottered past it, now on flat but rugged pasture, covered with clumps of gorse. A figure emerged into view about thirty yards ahead, also with hood drawn up. Sobbing, she veered left, but the ground sloped downward again. She halted on the edge of it, sensing open space in front of her. A pale margin of dying light lay along what had to be the western horizon, but everything else between here and there was turning black.

She glanced back across the pasture. There was no one in view now, but night had fallen like a cloak; they could be creeping right up on her and she wouldn't spot them.

Helpless, she lumbered down the slope, constantly stumbling in the damp, tussocky grass. Hot saliva seeped from her mouth; flaps of rubber slapped at the sides of her face. She descended onto flat ground, but again half-tripped, turning her ankle in the process. She yelped in agony.

A pillar of fire exploded upward maybe twenty yards in front.

Claire came to a staggering halt.

A huge pyramid of timber had simply exploded, gouts of flame roaring into the night, hot sparks cascading whichever way the wind blew them – as if petrol had perhaps been thrown upon it (which was almost certainly what had happened, she realised). Other, lesser bonfires erupted into life on various sides of her, throwing rippling orange light across the whole of the rugged meadow, revealing several other things at the same time: only twenty or so yards to her right, an ancient, rambling oak with a trunk as thick as three or four men and a colossal spread of branches; perhaps forty yards beyond that, more trees – a thick, dark belt – but in the middle of them a farm gate, and on the other side of that what looked like a road; a real road, made of tarmac. Claire's heart leapt at the sight of this, and she stumbled forward, heart pounding, only to come to another tottering halt when she spied something to the right of the farm gate.

At first she'd taken it for a stand of foliage, but now she saw that it was a lorry parked under a green tarpaulin, with camouflage netting thrown over the top. Even as she stared at this, three figures in hunting garb filed out from behind it. They were Heather, Jasmine and Dr Enwright, the latter's bespectacled eyes like two crimson blobs as they reflected the firelight.

'No,' Claire moaned, backing away, only for her boots to slide in the grass. 'Nooo!'

When she tried to run the other way, more figures were coming down the slope towards her: the boy called Luke and a tall, robust, long-faced girl, who she hadn't seen before. The driver, she realised. The one who'd driven the lorry here – to this fatal spot.

'The traitor rejected the King's Way,' Dr Enwright announced. 'Sure proof of guilt.'

Heather assisted the other two as they grabbed hold of Claire.

'You bloody mindless idiots!' she wept, but they ignored her, twisting her hands behind her back, lashing them together with ropes.

They frog-marched her around to the other side of the oak tree, where she saw several items so horrific that at first they didn't fall into place: a noose fashioned from what looked like orange silk dangled from a lower bough; a three-legged stool stood directly beneath this; to one side, a trestle-table had been set out and was arrayed with glittering implements – knives, shears and cleavers, a heavy mallet and, more terrifying still, upright against the table, a five-foot length of serrated steel with grip-handles at either end: a two-man saw.

Before Claire could vent the horror she felt at this sight, there came a shout of 'Dr Enwright!', and another figure hurtled around the tree. It was Arnie, blowing hard.

'What happened?' Enwright asked. 'She was expected fifteen minutes ago.'

Arnie scowled at Claire. 'She got away from me.'

'So it's only good fortune that she's here at all?'

'He tried to rape me,' Claire said. 'He's not interested in playing your stupid game.'

'If that was true, I wouldn't have come at all,' Arnie retorted. He turned back to his mentor. 'We've got a problem . . . a car's pulled up in a lay-by a few hundred yards away. I just saw it as I was on my way down here.'

There was silence as the group absorbed this. Enwright didn't look alarmed or frightened, as much as frustrated. 'Which direction?' he asked.

Arnie pointed.

Enwright snorted. 'Most likely a courting couple.'

'All the way out here?' Arnie said.

'It hardly matters. There's dense woodland between here and there. They won't see us.'

399

'What if it's the police?'

'Use your loaf, Arnold. How could it be the police?'

'What if one of the others talked?'

'Impossible.'

'Are you so sure?' Claire blurted out. 'These are children you've got doing your dirty work for you . . . you really trust them that much?'

Enwright smiled. 'Heather . . . gag this traitorous bitch!'

Claire squealed and struggled as the Tomboy slapped a sticking plaster across her mouth, then wrapped a scarf over the top of it, pulling it tight. But as she did, a distant repetitive thudding now intruded on them. They glanced skyward.

'Chopper!' Arnie said, darting towards the farm gate. 'Into the trees!'

'Stay where you are!' Enwright shouted, with such force that even Arnie came to a standstill. 'You bloody little fools . . . have you learned nothing!'

'You're right, we are fools,' the boy whined. 'We've lit bloody great fires to lead them right to us.'

'They'll have heat-seeking cameras . . . they'll find you anyway.'

'Let's just get away then!'

'No! We haven't come this far to run like rabbits.' Enwright turned to the rest of the team. 'We carry on as planned.'

Claire struggled again, but with her hands bound there was only so much she could do as her captors again descended on her, fastening a belt around her legs, buckling them together. Only Arnie played no part. He backed slowly away.

'Dr Enwright . . . we haven't got time for this! Look . . . I always said this plan was too ambitious . . . that we'd be lucky to get away afterwards!'

'Get away?' Enwright snorted. 'Surely you've realised by now, Arnold? This was only ever a one-way deal.'

The signpost was knee-high, so Heck had to crouch to examine it with his pen-light.

Here fell William, 2nd Duke of Hamilton

He straightened up again, none the wiser. A few yards away, though almost invisible in the darkness, Charlie Finnegan was on the phone to the Comms suite at Castle Street Police Station. 'Sorry sir, I can't give you the proper coordinates. Well . . . we haven't got a real map. Yeah, I can hear India 99. Haven't seen him yet . . .'

Heck walked back across the meadow to the shallow ditch, and stepped over this into the lay-by where his Volkswagen was waiting. Worthington was still in the rear seat, handcuffed to PC Mapling.

'You sure you parked here?' Heck asked him, leaning in at the window.

Worthington shrugged. 'We stopped in lots of different places, but I think this was one of them. We walked for miles, I know that. We were setting up signs and stuff. Not real ones, just pretend. Dr Enwright said they were stage dressing.'

Stage dressing, Heck thought sourly. It gave him no consolation to realise how close to the button he'd been in his very first assessment of these murders.

'Worcester think they know roughly where we are,' Finnegan said, also stepping over the ditch. 'They've got support units out, and dogs. So we just sit tight. Soon as the chopper spots us, the world and his brother will be here.'

Heck felt exasperated but helpless; as far as he could tell, the sound of the helicopter's rotor blades was diminishing. 'Sounds like he's going the wrong way.'

'He's circling. Apparently it's part of the search system they use.'

'So we're officially lost. Bloody great!'

Claire didn't have much strength left, but she fought with every inch of it as they carried her towards the makeshift gallows.

With hands and legs bound, all she could really do was squirm – but she managed to get free twice, dropping to the ground on each occasion. They yanked her back up with increasing anger and violence. Heather, Luke and Susan did most of the work, while Jasmine covered them with her firearm. Arnie still hung back, glancing nervously onto the meadows beyond the oak tree.

'If you open your ears, Arnold,' Enwright said, 'you'll note the helicopter has gone.'

'We should go too . . . while we still can. They'll be setting up roadblocks.'

'What does that matter?' Jasmine snapped at him. 'Gareth took a fall covering our backs. Are we going to waste that sacrifice?'

Enwright smiled at Arnie through the firelight, his gloved fingers laced together. His expression was almost fond, but again the flames writhed brightly in the lenses of his glasses. 'Even Jesus found a Doubting Thomas in his circle. But in the end that fearful saint came good. He died by lance at the hand of a godless potentate.'

'We're not saints,' Arnie said, retreating. 'And I'm not dying by anyone's hand.'

At which point a vehicle rumbled past on the nearby road. Everyone stopped what they were doing as they spotted it through the trees, catching fleeting glimpses of white bodywork, a thick black grille over its windows, the word POLICE stencilled in black lettering. The vehicle swept on up the narrow lane, the roar of its engine fading, but it was too much for Arnie.

'Shit!' he said. 'Shit, shit, shit . . . we've got to get out of here!' He wasn't so much edging away now, as taking long strides.

'Where are you going?' Jasmine demanded.

'You made me do this!' Arnie pointed at Enwright. 'You tricked me . . . I've had enough . . .'

He turned to run, but he stumbled first – and that slowed him down.

Fatally.

With a nod from Enwright, Jasmine fired.

Heck and Finnegan spun around alongside the car. Finnegan lowered his phone. He'd been about to contact Comms at Worcester again to tell them that a fast-moving unit had just passed them by in the dark without stopping and was now headed in completely the wrong direction, when both he and Heck had heard a gunshot – from fairly close by.

'Don't like the sound of that,' Finnegan muttered.

'Me neither,' Heck replied. He yanked open the driver's door, extracted the keys from the ignition and tossed them through into the back seat, where PC Mapling caught them. 'You're in charge of these two,' he said. 'If this thing cuts up, get them away from here as fast as you can.' Mapling nodded, though he looked distinctly unnerved by the prospect. 'In the meantime . . .' Heck extended an empty hand, 'I'll need to borrow your baton and your CS canister.'

'What are you doing?' Finnegan asked as Heck pocketed the CS spray and snapped open the extendable baton to its full one and a half feet.

'What are *we* doing, you mean.' Heck stepped back over the ditch.

'You can't be serious,' Finnegan said, reluctantly tagging along.

Heck struck off along the meadow. 'We're finding out what's going on.'

'But they're obviously armed . . .'

'Taking a look won't hurt anyone. But if it bothers you, here . . .'

Finnegan snatched the baton that Heck handed to him, and got quickly back on the blower to Worcester Comms. 'Tell those fucking hayseeds of yours to turn around and get back here!' he said gruffly. 'They're going the wrong way! No, I don't give a shit who I'm talking to . . . we need armed support pronto!'

'Knock that crap off, Charlie!' Heck said. 'You'll let the bastards know we're here.'

'They probably already know,' Finnegan muttered. 'What's that light?'

They'd advanced into a copse of thinly spread trees, and were knee-deep in young spring foliage. The reddish glow of what looked like a fire was now visible over the tops of the hawthorn thickets about a hundred yards ahead.

Heck didn't reply, simply filched his own phone from his pocket and punched in a quick number. 'Yeah . . . Eric,' he murmured. 'I can't speak any louder than this. I don't care if the Deputy Chief Constable's arrived, tell me where you're up to . . . quickly!'

They didn't bother to check if Arnie was dead. Even if he wasn't, it hardly mattered: he wasn't going anywhere. He lay face down, his back a jumble of mangled, smouldering meat. They were too busy lifting the struggling Claire onto the three-legged stool, finally planting her feet on top of it.

She still writhed in their grasp, though weakly, exhaustedly. It was astonishing how suddenly nothing else in her life mattered – all the usual worries: bills, mortgage payments, car insurance. None of that had significance any more; only the sweating and the grunting . . .

From somewhere close by came the sharp bleeping of a mobile phone.

Enwright and his acolytes froze, then gazed into the wooded area a few dozen yards to their left. It was all the distraction Claire needed; she jumped from the stool again, throwing herself full-length on the ground.

'Mr Stapleton!' Enwright snapped. 'Miss Cavanagh! See what that is! Fix it!'

As Luke and Susan scuttled out of view, the other two girls – Jasmine and Heather – grappled with Claire even as she lay flat. She tried to roll away. Heather swore, landed vicious blows on her. Overhead, the orange silk noose swung wildly.

If Heck and Finnegan hadn't been around twenty yards apart when Finnegan's phone rang again – at full volume – Heck would probably have taken a swing for him.

'Worcester Comms,' Finnegan said, still not moderating his tone.

'Turn the bastard thing off!' Heck hissed.

Finnegan complied, shoving the phone into his pocket. The ferns they were wading through were filled with briars, and a massive hindrance to progress. The blackness among the hawthorns was cloying it was so deep, though sparkles of flames were clearly visible among the meshed branches ahead. Heck could hear what sounded like suppressed voices. He wanted to hurry, to go charging forward, but instinct again made him wary. He glanced left to right, seeing more swathes of undergrowth, more thick clumps of hawthorn – and then spied a hooded figure rise silently from the ferns just behind Finnegan.

Before Heck could shout a warning, what looked like a two-handed mallet had slammed into the back of the detective constable's ribs; his knees buckled and he slumped forward, gasping. The second blow, a swinging underarm, struck the back of his head. Heck would have lurched over there to assist, but a second figure had now appeared – directly in front of him. Heck glimpsed camouflaged fatigues, a scarf over the lower face. The assailant was of slight build but this made him lithe; more important was the shiny steel cleaver he now struck with in a slashing backhand blow.

By combining muscle-power, Jasmine and Heather had finally scooped their victim up and placed her on top of the hanging-stool. Though it took all their strength, they held her in place there while Enwright fitted the silken noose around her neck.

He didn't respond to the sounds of combat in the woods nearby. 'Orange is your colour,' he said matter-of-factly, as he pulled the noose tight around her throat.

Claire could still breathe, but only just. Suddenly there could be no more struggling. She had to stand perfectly still and maintain her balance – which wasn't easy, because even as Heather and Jasmine stepped back, she could feel the stool shifting beneath her, as if the legs on one side were sinking into the meadow floor.

'You've fought hard,' Enwright said approvingly. 'You've earned your Parliamentarian sash . . .'

Heck had ducked both the first and second blows of the cleaver, but now his legs tangled in strands of briar and he toppled backwards, falling full-length into the ferns. The hooded figure dived down on top of him, determined to seize the advantage, pressing the cleaver's blade with both hands towards his throat. Only Heck's left elbow prevented him ramming the blade down with guillotine force. The assailant was wiry and strong, but young and inexperienced; though they were nose-to-nose for several seconds, grunting, covering each other in sweat and spittle, Heck still managed to free the CS canister from his pocket with his right hand, and ejected its entire contents into the glaring, fanatical eyes.

The youngster jerked backward, gasping and choking, then disentangled himself entirely and rolled away, gloved fingers raking at his face. Heck followed, scrambling to his feet and dealing him two swift blows; a left to the gut, a right to the side of the jaw, before spinning around – just in time. The other one came to a stumbling halt some ten yards away, mallet in one hand, baton in the other.

They watched each other across the darkened clearing, breathing hard.

Even in the dimness, Heck could tell that he was facing a female. She too was clad in bulky waterproof coveralls, but her hood had fallen back and straggles of long brown hair hung from under her woolly cap. A scarf covered her mouth, but though her eyes were wild and dangerous, her brow was damp with the sweat of fear.

'And which one are you?' Heck wondered. 'Heather or Susan? My name's Mark. But no, I'm not telling you that to try and humanise myself . . . to prevent you attacking me. I'm just letting you know who'll be clubbing you unconscious in one minute's time if you don't drop those fucking weapons.'

Her eyes widened even more – as if she couldn't believe she was being spoken to that way. Then she reached a decision, flinging the extendable baton at him before racing away. It spun through the air. Heck deflected it with his forearm, though it still stuck him a stinging *thwack*. He didn't give immediate chase, but lurched over to Finnegan's prone form, crouching and checking for vital signs. The idiot was out cold, but breathing.

With a groan, the lad whose face Heck had sprayed rolled over – and promptly began gasping again. 'Shit!' he groaned in a thick, mucus-laden voice. 'My eyes!'

'They'll be nothing compared to your arsehole after a year in the lifers' block,' Heck said, walking over there.

'I can't see . . .'

'Keep them closed and stop rubbing them.' He turned the incapacitated boy over and pinned him down with a knee, while twisting his left arm and his right leg behind his back, and cuffing them wrist to ankle. 'It'll wear off in an hour or so.'

'An hour . . . Jesus Christ!'

'That's only the start of your problems, pal.' Heck got back to his feet, dragging the phone from his pocket, and stabbed in a number. 'Eric . . . you ready?'

'I've done the best I can,' Fisher replied, having to shout to be heard over a clamour of voices.

'Let's hope it's good enough.' Heck pushed on through the thickets towards the firelight. 'And shut that racket down! I don't care if it's the Home Secretary himself. It'll bollocks up everything!' He lowered the phone as he emerged fully into the firelight. He'd been prepared for something shocking, though perhaps not quite as shocking as this, even after everything that had happened.

The corpse of a young man lay face-down several yards to his right, divots of flesh and muscle blown out of his back, exposing a mess of broken bones and shredded organs; but worse than this, perhaps thirty yards away, Claire was balanced on a tilted stool with an orange cord around her neck, pulled taut against the oak branch above. Her ragged, ritualistic costume only added to the immense horror of the scene.

Four figures stood alongside her, apparently awaiting him. Three were females, including the tall girl he'd just confronted, who was still wielding her two-handed mallet, and the blondie, Jasmine Sinclair, who carried yet another sawn-off shotgun. The fourth, of course, was Dr Enwright.

'I told you he was alone,' the tall girl said. She'd ripped away her scarf to reveal unusual elongated features. 'He's not armed either.'

'It's over, Enwright,' Heck said. 'You surely realise that?' He tried not to glance at Claire, though it was clear that she held her rigid posture out of sheer terror. Even from this distance, he could see that she hardly dared blink her eyes against the sweat streaming into them.

'Nice to see you again, sergeant,' Enwright said, with another of those catlike smiles.

'I may be alone now,' Heck advised him, 'but others are en route as we speak.'

Enwright shrugged. 'Arrest and capture were always part of this deal.'

'You can stop pretending. If you're not frightened, all that proves is how insane you really are. But I can see it in your face . . . you know the game's up and you're frightened to death.' Actually Heck could see no such thing. Enwright was still smiling; there wasn't so much as a dimple on his brow. But he was undoubtedly a deep pool. There could be a lot going on underneath. 'It may have been part of the deal that these kids would get captured, but I'd like to bet you've prepared yourself a bolt hole. Just out of interest, what brainwashing techniques did you use on them?'

'Drastic measures like brainwashing aren't necessary if the goal you strive for is a worthy one,' Enwright said. 'Upright people, particularly *young* upright people – whose sense of morality is unsullied by cynicism and self-interest, make great activists. You wouldn't understand that, sergeant.'

'Oh, I understand perfectly. You made them into killers. On purpose.'

'A means to an end . . .'

'The end in itself!' Heck switched his attention to the girls. 'You've been conned . . . you understand that, don't you?'

Their faces remained blank, but Jasmine raised the shotgun to her shoulder, aiming it directly at him.

Heck persisted. 'This masquerade of murder he's launched is nothing more than a hate campaign against a world that failed to indulge him.'

Enwright chuckled – he sounded genuinely amused. 'Let me guess, sergeant . . . the police made you take a degree in psychology? Well done, but there's no need to show off.'

'He doesn't care that British culture is vacuous. He enjoys that . . . because it means that deep down, people aren't happy. And this little war you've started is designed to make sure they'll never be happy again. But even that isn't his real purpose . . .'

'Enough of this playing for time,' Enwright interrupted, stepping up to Claire's stool. 'We intend to celebrate Royal Oak Day in grand fashion, even if we are twenty-six days early. You'll be privileged enough to witness it, sergeant. But try to interfere, and Jasmine will blow your head off . . .'

'Don't take my word for it, girls,' Heck said, raising his phone into the air and thumbing its loudspeaker button. 'Listen to the man himself.'

Jasmine's attention remained locked on him, even though the other two had turned to deal with their prisoner – and then they heard the voice.

It was tinny and distorted, but unmistakably it was Dr Enwright's, and it echoed across the meadow from Heck's mobile.

'*Arnold Wisby . . . his facial injuries have rendered him a ludicrous clown.*'

Susan and Heather's heads jerked around. Enwright himself looked briefly fascinated, as if he was witness to something that simply couldn't be happening. Only Jasmine remained unaffected, gazing at Heck along the shotgun's upper barrel.

'*Little wonder he has no self-esteem. He's been mocked wherever he's gone. It won't be difficult affecting a significant degree of control. A child traumatised by isolation is always so eager to please . . .*'

There was a burst of static, a scrambled dirge of electronic disruption. Eric Fisher had said that his editing skills weren't high-end.

Enwright now seemed to have regained his composure. He stepped forward, pausing, only to throw at Heck a look of such loathing that fleetingly, he seemed animalistic. 'Just shoot him, Jasmine. This meddling fool has had his chance . . .'

'*Jasmine is a naturally beautiful child,*' his electronic twin added. The pretty schoolgirl's icy gaze was still fixed on Heck, but suddenly she wasn't seeing him.

'*One would never have expected to find her an outcast . . .*'

'These are my private files, compiled in my capacity as school counsellor,' Enwright said hurriedly.

'*But her emotions are in ribbons. Raped repeatedly by her stepfather, she embraced her new life at boarding school as an escape . . . only to find difficulty associating with others. Her looks and femininity have become millstones around her neck. Abused women often seek to reduce their attractiveness, hacking off their hair, disdaining beauty products . . .*'

'If you won't do it, I will,' Enwright said, reaching for the gun – only for Jasmine to lurch away from him. Her attention was still riveted on Heck, but she was listening intently.

'*Jasmine closes herself off. Refuses to participate in any form of social life. But she is a human being, with human*

411

needs . . . it will be easier to target her through Gareth, the most handsome boy in the school. Of course, he won't lay a finger on her until she is ready . . . his is to be a caring role, not a sexual one. But the sex will come, and that will have a purpose too . . .'

There was another burst of static. Heck watched the muzzle of the shotgun tautly. Jasmine's expression was impossible to read, but Enwright's face gleamed with sweat.

'Those with a yearning to be wanted, a desperation to belong . . . one must include them, give them a sense of worth. Only then can one break their individuality . . .'

'Are you hearing this?' Heck shouted.

'Desensitising children to suffering is never easy, but these particular specimens . . .'

'Did you hear *that*?'

'. . . will be easier than most, because all they have ever known is suffering. Heather Greer is clearly a lesbian, though she doesn't yet suspect, or if she does she is in denial – a form of self-loathing enforced on her by her distant, archly-conservative family.'

'That's not true!' Heather blurted, unsure who she was supposed to be addressing.

'She doesn't understand why she isn't attracted to boys and subsequently is hostile to the endless game of tease and titillation. Likewise, Susan Cavanagh . . . an ugly, ungainly girl, nicknamed "Craptits" by her classmates. She reviles the culture of the female sexual icon, the glamour models, the Z-list celebrities with enhanced assets and the soulless society in which they are idolised . . .'

Susan stood stock-still, face frozen.

'I made these recordings in my role as carer,' Enwright insisted.

'Some carer,' Heck retorted.

But now Jasmine's finger tightened on the trigger again; her

412

face wore a grimace of rage. 'This,' she stammered, 'this is some sort of trick . . .'

'That's it,' Enwright agreed. 'It's a trick.'

'Really?' Heck wondered. 'They go all the way back through your time at St Bardolph's.'

'How easy to persuade such creatures that Britain, a land they have no investment in, is a spiritual desert where sin is rewarded and merit ignored. Religion will be a problem. "Thou shalt not kill", says the Bible . . .'

Heck advanced towards the blonde-haired girl. 'Why don't you give me the gun, eh?'

'Back off!' she snarled.

'But it has been circumnavigated before. Christians have launched homicidal attacks upon non-Christians. The same goes for Jews and Muslims. This happened because they regarded their targets as evil. Or as innocents who must perish in a greater cause . . .'

'Shoot him!' Enwright urged her. 'This man has come here to destroy us.'

'It's all about the cause. Any cause.'

'*Any* cause, Jasmine?' Heck said. 'What does that mean exactly?'

There was a further fizzing of static, and then the voice assumed the air and confidence of a commandant: '*We must remind the world that things were better in the past, that there was a golden age of faith . . . when community mattered, when people lived simple, healthy lives, enjoying innocent pleasures. Merrie England! The greatest threat to a restoration of which lies with our new heretics, the thoughtless godless who believe in nothing but their own pleasure . . .*' It relapsed into a sly, fluting chuckle. '*What babble! Merrie England . . . what tosh!*'

Heck watched the girls' reactions. Jasmine included, they listened incredulously.

'A faith of all faiths. Where the enemies are the party-goers . . . you couldn't make it up. But there is a serious side . . . this will be the greatest experiment in history. The Stanford Prison debacle will have nothing on this. That zealous belief can be drawn from the incoherent ramblings of a hack horror writer . . .' More static intruded, more devious chuckles. 'But they are ripe for it. They nod when I tell them we must make examples. No one wants to kill, I assure them, yet some, I can tell already, will kill more easily than others . . . the world despises them. Why not strike back?'*

'We were an experiment?' Jasmine said, turning slowly to face her leader.

'The outcome is the same, Miss Sinclair,' he replied. 'Together, we've struck mighty blows against a morally bankrupt world.'

'We were an *experiment*?!'

'Not even a real one,' Heck said, venturing forward. 'Just his crazy control fantasy. You surely see now that he's stark staring mad!'

'You shut up!' she screeched, her emotions breaking as she whirled back around, training the shotgun on Heck's midriff – and not noticing Enwright spin and hurl a heavy punch at her jaw.

Jasmine crumpled to the floor, and as she did, Enwright snatched the shotgun from her grasp, twirling to face Heck, who, at only twenty yards' distance, was well within range.

'Callow youth,' Enwright sighed. 'They promise so much and deliver so little.'

He took casual aim but, like Jasmine, never saw the blow coming from behind.

It was delivered with a two-handed mallet, and it struck him squarely between the shoulder-blades. The impact was gut-thumping, and Enwright turned grey in the cheek as he slumped forward to his knees, dropping the shotgun. Heck dived towards it. Susan, her face streaked with tears, stood over her fallen mentor, still hefting the mallet.

'You sodding, lying bastard!' she screamed down at him, only for Heather to snatch her by the collar, screaming equal obscenities.

Heck grabbed up the shotgun and rolled over, only to see the twosome struggling.

'Didn't you hear what he said?' Susan wailed, but Heather thrust her backwards, and she blundered against Claire. There was a splintering *crunch*. A stool leg collapsed, and Claire was left swinging between heaven and earth, face contorted.

'It's that copper who's lying!' Heather raved, drawing a blade from inside her coat, raising it high, and charging at Heck. 'He's the real liar!'

Heck, who was still on the floor, took aim. He only had one shot left; he would hit his assailant easily – but instead, he elevated the barrel and fired over Heather's head.

The orange cord was cleanly severed. Claire dropped.

Heather seemed to sense this. She shrieked like a banshee as she ran the last few yards, intent on hacking and slashing her enemy to death.

The shotgun was out of shells, but it was heavy, and Heather was less than three yards away when Heck threw it horizontally into her gut. It struck with a thumping impact, doubling the girl over. She fell to the ground, gagging. Heck stamped on her hand, the knife came loose and he kicked it away.

'You . . . you bastard,' she whimpered, in a combination of pain and frustration.

Heck glanced up, and saw that Susan was halfway towards the farm gate when the headlights of a vehicle blazed over her. She tottered to a standstill as the police carrier that had passed them earlier came wallowing to a halt on the other side.

Meanwhile, Claire lay motionless, the orange silk tight around her throat.

Heck lurched towards her, grabbed her in his arms and quickly worked the material loose. A horrific purple welt was visible underneath. She was alabaster white, and didn't even stir in his grasp. He called her name, slapped her cheeks, and then felt something warm against his face – his head sagged down with relief – her breath.

Chapter 49

A couple of days after her operation, Gemma woke up in a private room attached to the surgical recovery ward, to find sunshine streaming through the half-open blinds, bouquets of flowers at the end of her bed, and Heck sitting alongside her, popping seedless grapes into his mouth.

She eyed him for several moments. Moving anything else wasn't easy, as she was heavily patched and padded, her right arm and shoulder fastened in stiff orthopaedic supports. She was still attached to a drip, which was supposedly feeding her anaesthetic as well as nutrition, though it perhaps wasn't feeding it fast enough, because she ached from head to toe.

'Those grapes are mine, you know,' Gemma finally said, wincing.

'I know.' He popped another into his mouth. 'They're good too.' As usual, he looked like he'd just come in from a lengthy shift: tie loose, collar unbuttoned, jacket rumpled.

'Apparently, this time you're the only one who didn't get hurt?' she said.

'Give me a break. What about that dog bite?'

'Don't be so soft.'

'They went down fighting, that's for sure.'

She pondered that. 'We got all of them, yeah?'

'Yeah.'

'What about Enwright?'

Heck shrugged. 'Two fractured vertebrae, but he'll recover. That said, I'm not sure he'll ever be deemed fit to plead. He's not undergone any evaluation yet, but . . . I dunno, the guy's as mad as a hatter.'

'So long as he's locked away.'

'I don't think there's any danger there. He's got Broadmoor written all over him.'

'And what's the damage? I mean to us.'

'Oh . . . extensive.'

'Who's the worst?'

'You, probably.'

'Not Shawna?'

'Not as bad as first feared. Mainly it's splinters. She'll be off her feet for a few weeks.'

'How about Gary?'

'Headache.'

'Andy Gregson?'

'A worse headache, but getting better.'

'Garrickson and Finnegan?'

'Does it matter?'

'You're all heart, Heck. How's Claire?'

'Well . . .' He paused, lips pursed, trying not to look too saddened by the near-tragedy that had befallen their former press officer. 'She's hurt and she's shaken up . . . badly. But there's no lasting physical injury. She's a tougher lass than she looks.'

'Something to tell her grandkids about?' Gemma suggested.

'Yeah . . . sure. But we won't be seeing her again. I assume you know that?'

Gemma nodded, and grimaced with pain. 'I . . . I should never have brought her into this in the first place.'

'She'd probably have coped in almost any other circumstance.'

'Maybe.' She eyed him again. 'I know you said that you and her were just mates, but I kind of thought, if she'd stayed with us long term . . . that, well, things between you might have changed?'

'Thought or hoped?'

'Wondered.'

'Some chance.' He gave her his best wolfish smile. 'You know there's only ever been one woman for me.'

'Trying to catch me when I'm vulnerable?'

He regarded her thoughtfully. It could never be less than alarming to see Gemma in this condition. She was ghostly white; her eyes had circles underneath them so dark they looked like bruises. For someone who normally radiated strength and fire, she was listless, fragile, so feeble she could barely move. But it was important to remember the words of the senior surgeon who'd removed the arrow and at the same time had saved her right arm: 'I couldn't have done it without her. The shock alone would have killed most people. She's a battler, this one.'

'You're never vulnerable,' he said. 'Take this, for example . . .' He took a document from his pocket and unfolded it. 'It's a copy of a memo sent from NCG Director Joe Wullerton to the Home Office, dated yesterday.' He began to read: '"In light of the successful conclusion to this enquiry, but also with regard to the exceptional numbers of casualties incurred by the Serial Crimes Unit, the evidence would suggest that, far from being a waste of taxpayers' money, the SCU in actual fact provides a vital service, despite clear evidence that it is undermanned, under-resourced and lacking in logistical support. It is my firm recommendation that, instead of closing the department down or merging it, we take all necessary action to boost its strength and facilities so that it may continue its essential work . . ."'

'Nice,' Gemma replied, nodding, as if this was something she'd expected.

'Joe rang this morning to say it's too early to claim a result, but the signs are good.'

She nodded again, contented.

'I thought you'd be jumping around the room in paroxysms of glee,' he said.

'Sorry . . . bit under the weather for that.'

'Now who's being soft?'

'Heck, I've been thinking . . . as Des Palliser and Bob Hunter are gone, I'm in desperate need of a new DI.'

'No worries there. They'll be queuing up to work with you.'

Her tone remained patient. 'You know what I'm saying.'

'Course.' He smiled again. 'And the answer's no. I prefer my roving commission.'

'You know, Sergeant Heckenburg . . . you're never going to get close to me again unless you start climbing the ladder.'

'Wanna bet?' He leaned down and kissed her forehead. 'Got to go. Duty calls.'

'See you later,' she said, as he moved to the door.

Outside in the corridor, he met Gemma's mother. She was hanging her coat in an alcove. He'd once heard it said that if you wanted to see the future self of the girl in your life, you needed only to look at her mother. If that was true, the signs were good for anyone who finished up with Gemma Piper. Melanie Piper was as tall as her daughter, equally trim, equally handsome, equally blonde, though that blonde hair was running a little to silver. As usual, she was attractively dressed, in a flower-patterned frock and heeled sandals.

'Hello Mrs Piper,' Heck said.

'How many times have I told you, Mark?' she replied admonishingly. 'It's "Mel". Anyway, how's our girl today?'

'After a wound like that, most folk would be up and about in around six weeks. With Gemma, it'll be about six days.'

'I'll make sure she doesn't do anything silly, like go back to work early.'

'I doubt the insurance will cover her until she's seen out her doctor's note.'

'And how are you, Mark?'

'I'm okay . . . good.'

She eyed him critically. 'Quite a hair-raising case.'

'That's the job.'

'You and Gemma should be together, you know that? It would make you stronger.'

He shrugged, smiled. 'We're both pretty strong already.'

'I said stronger.'

'Maybe.'

'There are no maybes about it. See you soon . . . I hope.' She bustled past him into her daughter's private room.

Heck headed outside into the midday sun. He wasn't sure whether this merry month of May would ever seem quite the same again, though that had been at least part of the motive behind the recent desecrations, so he determined to put such depressing thoughts from his mind. As he climbed into his car, his mobile rang.

'Heckenburg,' he said, placing it to his ear.

'Hello,' came an uncertain voice. 'This is DI Strickand, Nottinghamshire. I understand you're the Serial Crimes Unit?'

Heck almost laughed. 'I am at the moment, yeah.'

'I've got something I'd like you to take a look at. But I warn you in advance . . . it's a weird one.'

'That's okay,' Heck said, getting a pen out. 'Weird is what we do.'

Hooked on Heck? Read on for a sneak peek of *Hunted*, where Heck takes on his biggest challenge yet . . .

Chapter 1

Dazzer and Deggsy didn't give a shit about anyone. At least, that was the sort of thing they said if they were bragging to mates in the pub, or if the coppers caught them and tried to lay a guilt-trip on them.

'We do what we do, innit? We don't go out looking to hurt people, but if they get in the way, tough fucking shit. We pinch motors and have a laugh in 'em. And we're gonna keep doing it, because it's the best laugh ever. No one's gonna stop us, and if they get, like, really pissed off because we've just wrecked their pride and joy, so what? We don't give a shit.'

Tonight was a particularly good night for it.

Alright, it wasn't perishing cold, which was a shame. Incredible though it seemed to Dazzer and Deggsy, some numbskulls actually came outside, saw a bit of ice and snow and left their motors running for five minutes with the key in the ignition, while they went back indoors for a cuppa; all you had to do was jump in the saddle and ride away, whooping. But if nothing else, it was dank and misty, and with it being the tail-end of January, it got dark early – so there weren't too many people around to interfere.

Not that folk tended to interfere with Dazzer and Deggsy. The former was tall for his age; just under six foot, with a broad build and a neatly layered patch of straw-blonde hair in the middle of his scalp, the rest of which was shaved to the bristles. If it hadn't been for the acne covering his brutish features, you'd have thought him eighteen, nineteen, maybe twenty – instead of sixteen, which was his true age, though of course even a sixteen-year-old might clobber you these days if you had the nerve to give some indication that his behaviour affronted you. As was often the way with juvenile duos, the second member of the tag-team, Deggsy, though he wasn't by any means the lesser in terms of villainy, looked more his age. He was shorter and thinner, weasel-faced and the proud owner of an unimpressively wispy moustache. His oily black thatch was usually covered by a grimy old baseball cap, the frontal logo of which had long been erased by time and had been replaced with letters written in dayglo orange highlighter, which read: *Fuck off*.

There wasn't thirty years of experience between them, yet they both affected the arrogant swagger and truculent sneer of guys who believed they knew what was what, and were absolutely confident they did what they did because the world had been a bastard to them and fully deserved whatever they gave it back.

It was just around nine o'clock that night when they spied their first and most obvious target: a Volkswagen estate hatchback. A-reg and in poor shape generally – grubby, rusted around the arches, occasional dents in the bodywork – but it ticked all the boxes.

Posh motors were almost impossible to steal these days. All that top-of-the-range stuff was the sole province of professionals who would make a fortune from ringing it and selling it on. No, if you were simply looking for a fun time, you had to settle for this lower quality merchandise. But that could also be an advantage, because if you went and smacked a bit of rubbish around on the streets, the coppers would tow it away afterwards but would rarely investigate. So, if they didn't catch you in the act, you were home free. In addition, this one's location was good. Leatherhead boasted several sprawling industrial estates with lots of service and retail parking, not to mention numerous supermarkets, pubs, clubs and restaurants in the town centre, which also had 'own risk' parking lots attached. Most of these were covered by cameras, which made the punters feel it was relatively safe to leave their motors overnight, and in many cases that was true – it was certainly safer in Leatherhead than it had been in the pre-CCTV era – but there were black spots as well, all of which Dazzer and Deggsy were intimately informed about. And lucky for them the old Volkswagen estate was sitting right in the middle of one.

They watched it from a corner, eyes peeled for any sign of movement, but the dim sodium glow of the sparsely located streetlamps illuminated only a rolling beer can and a few scraps of wastepaper flapping in the half-hearted breeze.

Still, they waited. They'd been successful several times on this patch – it was a one-lane access way running between the back doors of a row of old shops and a high brick wall, ending at three concrete bollards. No one was ever around here at night; there were no tenants in the flats above the shops, and even without the January miasma this was a dark, dingy place – but all that such apparent ease of opportunity did was to make Dazzer and Deggsy more suspicious than usual. The very fact that motors had been lifted from around here before made the presence of this one seem curious. Did people never learn? Maybe they didn't.

The lads ventured forth, walking boldly but stealthily, alert to the slightest unnatural sound – but no one called out, no one stepped from a darkened doorway.

The Volkswagen was locked of course, but Deggsy had his screwdriver with him, and in less than five seconds they'd forced the driver's door open. No alarm sounded, which was just what they'd expected given the ramshackle state of the thing; another advantage of pillaging the less well-off. With rasping laughs, they jumped inside, to find that the steering column had been attacked in the past – it was held together by wads of silvery duct-tape. A few slashes of Dazzer's Stanley knife and they were through it. Even in the pitch darkness, their gloved but nimble fingers found the necessary wiring, and the contact was made.

The car rumbled to life. Laughing loudly, they hit the gas.

It was Dazzer's turn to drive today, and Deggsy's to ride, though it didn't make much difference – they were both as crazy as each other when they got behind the wheel. They blistered recklessly along, swerving around bends with tyres screeching, racing through red lights and stop signs. There was no initial response from the other road-using public. Opposing traffic was scant – another good thing about January; most folk, having spent up over Christmas, would prefer to slump in front of the telly rather than go out on the town. They pulled a handbrake turn, pivoting sideways through what would ordinarily be a busy junction, the stink of burnt rubber engulfing them, hitting the gas again as they tore out of town along the A246. They had over half a tank of petrol and a very straight road in front of them. Maybe they'd make it all the way to Guildford, where they could pinch another motor to come home in. For the moment, though, it was fun fun fun. They'd probably veer off en route, and cause chaos on a few housing estates they knew, flaying the paint from any expensive jobs that unwise owners had left in plain view.

Some roadworks surged into sight just ahead. Dazzer howled as he gunned the Volkswagen through them, cones catapulting every which way – one struck the bay window of a roadside house, smashing through it. They mowed down a 'keep left' sign, and took out a set of temporary lights, which hit the deck with a detonation of sparks.

The blacktop continued to roll out ahead; they were doing eighty, ninety, almost a hundred, and were briefly mesmerised by their own fearlessness, their attention completely focused down the borehole of their headlights. When you were in that frame of mind – and Dazzer and Deggsy nearly always were – there were almost no limits. It would have taken something quite startling to distract them from their death-defying reverie – and that came approximately seven minutes into this, their last ever journey in a stolen vehicle.

They clipped a kerbstone at eighty-five. That in itself wasn't a problem, but Deggsy, who'd just filched his mobile from his jacket pocket to film this latest escapade, was jolted so hard that he dropped it into the footwell.

'Fuck!' he squawked, scrabbling around for it. At first he couldn't seem to locate it, so he ripped his glove off with his teeth and went groping bare-handed. This time he found the mobile, but when he pulled his hand back he saw that he'd found something else as well.

It was clamped to his exposed wrist. Initially he thought he must have brushed his arm against an old pair of boots, which had smeared him with oil or paint. But no, now he could feel the weight of it and the multiple pinprick sensation where it had apparently gripped him. He still didn't realise what the thing actually was, not even when he held it close to his face – but then Deggsy had only ever seen scorpions on the telly, so perhaps this was unsurprising. Mind you, even on the telly he'd never seen a scorpion with as pale and shiny a carapace as this one had – it glinted like polished leather in the flickering streetlights. Or one as big; it was at least eight inches from nose to tail, that tail now curled to strike, its menacing pair of pincers – they were the size of crab claws – extended upward in the classic defensive position.

It couldn't be real, he told himself distantly.

Was it a toy? It had to be toy.

But then it stung him.

At first it shocked rather than hurt; as though a red hot drawing pin had been driven full length into his flesh and into the bone underneath. But that minor pain quickly expanded, filling his suddenly frozen arm with a white fire, which in itself intensified, until Deggsy was screaming hysterically. By the time he'd knocked the eight-legged horror back into the footwell, he was writhing and thrashing in his seat, frothing at the mouth as he struggled to release his suddenly restrictive belt. At first, Dazzer thought his mate was play-acting, though he shouted warnings when Deggsy's convulsions threatened to interfere with his driving.

And then something alighted on Dazzer's shoulder.

Despite the wild swerving of the car, it had descended slowly, patiently – on a single silken thread, and when he turned his head to look at it, it tensed, clamping him like a hand. In the flickering hallucinogenic light, he caught brief glimpses of vivid, tiger-stripe colours and clustered demonic eyes peering at him from point-blank.

The bite it planted on his neck was like a punch from a fist.

Dazzer's foot jammed the accelerator to the floor as his entire body went into spasms. The actual wound quickly turned numb, but searing pain shot through the rest of his body in repeated lightning strokes.

Neither lad noticed as the car mounted an embankment, engine yowling, smoke and tattered grass pouring from its tyres. It smashed through the wooden palings at the top, and then crashed downward through shrubs and undergrowth, turning over and over in the process, and landing upside down in a deep-cut country lane.

For quite a few seconds there was almost no sound: the odd groan of twisted metal, steam hissing in spirals from numerous rents in mangled bodywork.

The two concussed shapes inside, while still breathing, were barely alive in any conventional sense: torn, bloodied and battered, locked in contorted paralysis. They were still aware of their surroundings, but unable to resist as various miniature forms, having ridden out the collision in niches and crevices, now re-emerged to scurry over their warm, tortured flesh. Deggsy's jaw was fixed rigid; he could voice no complaint – neither as a mumble nor a scream – when the pale-shelled scorpion re-acquainted itself with him, creeping slowly up his body on its jointed stick-legs and finally settling on his face, where, with great deliberation it seemed, it snared his nose and his left ear in its pincers, then arched its tail again – and embedded its stinger deep into his goggling eyeball.

Chapter 2

Heck raced out of the kebab shop with a half-eaten doner in one hand and a can of Coke in the other. There was a blaring of horns as Dave Strickland swung his distinctive maroon Astra out of the far carriageway, pulled a U-turn right through the middle of the bustling evening traffic, and ground to a halt at the kerb. Heck crammed another handful of lamb and bread into his mouth, took a last slurp of Coke and tossed his rubbish into a nearby bin, before leaping into the Astra's front passenger seat.

'Grinton putting an arrest team together?' he asked.

'As we speak,' Strickland said, shoving a load of documentation into Heck's grasp, and hitting the gas. More horns tooted despite the spinning blue beacon on the Astra's roof. 'We're hooking up with them at St Ann's Central.'

Heck nodded, leafing through the official Nottinghamshire Police paperwork. The text he'd just received from Strickland had consisted of thirteen words, but they'd been the most important thirteen words anyone had communicated to him in several months:

Hucknall murder a fit for Lady Killer
Chief suspect – Jimmy Hood
Whereabouts KNOWN

Heck, or Detective Sergeant Mark Heckenburg, as was his official title at Scotland Yard, felt a tremor of excitement as he flipped the light on and perused the documents. Even now, after seventeen years of investigations, during so many of which shocking twists and turns had been commonplace, it seemed incredible that a case that had defied all analysis, dragging on doggedly through eight months of mind-numbing frustration, could suddenly have blown itself wide open.

'Who's Jimmy Hood?' he asked.

'A nightmare on two legs,' Strickland replied.

Heck had only known Strickland for the duration of this enquiry, but they'd made a good connection on first meeting and had maintained it ever since. A local lad by birth, Dave Strickland was a slick, clean-cut, improbably handsome black guy; at thirty, a tad young for DI, but what he may have lacked in experience he more than made up for with his quick wits and sharp eye. After the stress of the last few months, even Strickland had started to fray around the edges; 'frazzled' would have been one way to describe him, but tonight he was back on form, collar unbuttoned and tie loose, careering through the chaotic traffic with skill and speed.

'He lived in Hucknall when he was a kid,' Strickland added. 'But he spent a lot of his time back then locked up.'

'Not just then either,' Heck said. 'According to this, he's only been out of Roundhall for the last six months.'

'Yeah, and what does that tell us?'

Heck didn't need to reply. Roundhall was a low security prison in the West Midlands. According to these antecedents, Jimmy Hood, now in his early thirties, had served a year and a half there before being released on license. However, he'd originally been held at Durham after drawing fourteen years for burglary and rape. As if the details of his original crimes weren't enough of a match for the case they were currently working, his time back in the community put him neatly in the frame for the activities of the so-called 'Lady Killer'.

'He's a bruiser now and he was a bruiser then,' Strickland said. 'Six-foot-three by the time he was seventeen, and burly with it. Scared the crap out of everyone who knew him. Got arrested once for chucking a kitten into a cement mixer. Him and his mates did time for bricking a couple of builders who'd given them grief for pinching tools. Both workmen were knocked cold; one needed his face reconstructing.'

Heck noted from the paperwork that Hood, whose mug-shot portrayed shaggy black hair fringing a broad, bearded face with a badly broken nose – a disturbingly similar visage to the e-fit they'd released a few days ago – had led a juvenile street-gang that had involved itself in serious crime in Hucknall, from the age of twelve. However, he'd only commenced sexually offending, usually during the course of burglary, when he was in his late teens.

'So he comes out of jail and immediately picks up where he left off?' Heck said.

'Except that this time he murders them,' Strickland replied.

Heck didn't find that much of a leap. Certain types of violent offender had no intention of rehabilitating. They were so set on their life's work that they regarded prison time – even prolonged prison time – as a hazard of their chosen vocation. He'd known plenty who'd gone away for a lengthy stretch, and had used it to get fit, mug up on all the latest criminal techniques, and gradually accumulate a head of steam that would erupt with devastating force once they were released, and he could easily imagine this scenario applying to Jimmy Hood. What was more, the evidence seemed to indicate it. All four of the recent murder victims had been elderly women living alone. Most of Hood's victims when he was a teenager had been elderly women. The cause of death in all the recent cases had been physical battery with a blunt instrument, after rape. As a youth, Hood had bludgeoned his victims after indecently assaulting them.

'Funny his name wasn't flagged up when he first ditched his probation officer,' Heck said.

Strickland shrugged as he drove. 'Easy to be wise after the event, pal.'

'Suppose so.' On reflection, Heck recalled numerous occasions in his career when it would have paid to have a crystal ball.

On this occasion, they'd caught their break courtesy of a sharp-eyed civvie.

The four home-invasion murders they were officially investigating were congregated in the St Ann's district, east of Nottingham city centre – an impoverished, densely populated area, which already suffered more than its fair share of crime. The only description of a suspect they'd had was that of a hulking, bearded man wearing a duffel coat over shabby sports gear, who 'smelt bad' – suggesting that he wasn't able to bathe or change his clothes very often and so was perhaps sleeping rough.

Only yesterday there had been a fifth murder in Hucknall, just north of the city, the details of which closely matched those in St Ann's. There'd been no description of the perpetrator on this occasion, though earlier today a long-term Hucknall resident – who remembered Jimmy Hood well, along with his crimes – reported seeing him eating chips near the bus station there, not long after the event. He'd been wearing a duffel coat over an old tracksuit, and though he didn't have a beard, fresh razor cuts suggested that he had recently shaved one off.

'And he's been lying low at this Alan Devlin's pad?' Heck asked.

'Part of the time maybe,' Strickland said. 'What do you think?'

'Well . . . I wouldn't have called it "whereabouts known." But it's a bloody good start.'

Alan Devlin, who had a long record of criminal activity as a juvenile, when he'd been part of Hood's gang, now lived in a council flat in St Ann's. These days he was Hood's only known associate in central Nottingham, and the proximity of his home address to the recent murders was too big a coincidence to ignore.

'What do we know about Devlin?' Heck said. 'I mean above and beyond what the paperwork says.'

'Not a player anymore, apparently. His son Wayne's a bit dodgy.'

'Dodgy how?'

'General purpose lowlife. Fighting at football matches, drunk and disorderly, robbery.'

'Robbery?'

'Took some other kid's bike off him after giving him a kicking. That was a few years ago.'

'Sounds like the apple didn't fall far from the tree.'

As part of the National Crime Group, specifically the Serial Crimes Unit, Mark Heckenburg had a remit to work on murder cases across all the police areas of England and Wales. He and the other detectives in SCU tended to have a consultative investigating role with regard to the pursuit of repeat violent offenders, and would bring specialist knowledge and training to regional forces grappling with large or complex cases. They were usually allocated to said forces in groups of four or five, sometimes more. On this occasion, as the Nottinghamshire Police already had access to experienced personnel from the East Midlands Special Operations Unit, Heck had been assigned here on his own.

SCU's presence wasn't always welcomed by the regional forces they were assisting, some viewing the attachment of outsiders as a slight on their own abilities – though in certain cases, such as this one, SCU's advice had been actively sought. At the outset, Heck had been personally contacted by Strickland on the orders of Taskforce SIO Detective Chief Superintendent Max Grinton, who had solved many crimes off his own bat, but was a keen student of those state-of-the-art investigations carried out by other bodies, SCU figuring highly on his list.

Grinton was a big man with silver hair, a distinguished young/old face and a penchant for sharp-cut suits, though his most distinctive feature was the patch he wore over his left eye socket, having lost the eye to flying glass during a drive-by shooting fifteen years earlier. He was now holding court under the hard halogen glow of the car park lights at the rear of St Ann's Central. Uniforms clad in full anti-riot gear, and detectives with stab vests under their jackets, stood around him in attentive groups.

'So that's the state of play,' Grinton said. 'We're moving on this quickly rather than waiting till the crack of dawn tomorrow, firstly because the obbo at Devlin's address tells us he's currently home, secondly because if Jimmy Hood is our man there's been a shorter cooling-off period between each attack, which in plain English means that he's going crazier by the minute. For all we know, he could have done two or three more by tomorrow morning. We've got to catch him tonight, and Alan Devlin is the best lead we've had thus far. Just remember . . . for all that he's a scrote from way back, Devlin is a witness, not a suspect. We're more likely to get his help if we go in as friends.'

There were nods of understanding. Mouths were set firm

435

as it dawned on the Taskforce members just how high the stakes now were. Every man and woman present knew their job, but it was vital that no one made an error.

'One thing, sir, if you don't mind,' Heck spoke up. 'I strongly recommend that we take anything Alan Devlin tells us with a pinch of salt.'

'Any particular reason?' Grinton asked.

Heck waved Devlin's sheet. 'He hasn't been convicted of any crime since he was a juvenile, but he wasn't shy about getting his hands dirty back in the day – he was Jimmy Hood's right-hand man when they were terrorising housing estates around Hucknall. His son Wayne is halfway to repeating that pattern here in St Ann's. Try as I may, I can't view Alan Devlin as an upstanding citizen.'

'You think he'd cover for a killer?' Strickland said doubtfully.

Heck shrugged. 'I don't know, sir. Assuming Hood is the killer – and from what we know, I think he probably is – I find it odd that Devlin, who knows him better than anyone, hasn't already come to the same conclusion and got in touch with us voluntarily.'

'Maybe he's scared?' someone suggested.

Heck tried not to look as skeptical about that as he felt. 'Hood's a thug, but he's in breach of license conditions that strictly prohibit him from returning to Nottingham. That means he's keeping his head down and moving from place to place. He's only got one change of clothes, he's on his own, he's cold, damp and dining on scraps in bus stations. Does he really pose much of a threat to a bloke like Devlin, who's got form for violence himself, has a grown-up hooligan for a son and is well ensconced on his own patch?'

The team pondered, taking this on board.

'We'll see what happens,' Grinton said, zipping up his anorak. 'If Devlin plays it dumb, we'll let him know that

Hood's mug shot is appearing on the ten o'clock news tonight, and all it's going to take is a couple of Devlin's neighbours to recognise him as someone they've seen hanging around. The Lady Killer is going down for the rest of this century, ladies and gents. Devlin may be the hardest bastard in Nottingham, but he won't want a piece of that action.'

They drove to the address in question in a bunch of unmarked vehicles; five cars, one of them Heck's metallic-blue Peugeot 306, and one plain-clothes APC. They did it discreetly and without fanfare. St Ann's wasn't an out of control neighbourhood, but it wasn't the sort of place where excessive police activity would go unnoticed, and mobs could form quickly if word got out that 'one of the boys' was in trouble. In physical terms, it was a rabbit warren of crumbling council blocks, networked with dingy footways, which, at night, were a mugger's paradise. To heighten its atmosphere of menace, a winter gloom had descended, filling the narrow passages with cloying vapour.

The address was 41 Lakeside View. It was a boxy, redbrick structure, accessible by a short cement ramp with a rusty wrought iron railing, and then a single corridor running through from one side to the other, to which various apartment doors – 41a, 41b, 41c and 41d – connected.

Heck, Grinton and Strickland regarded it from a short distance away. Only the arched entry was visible in the evening murk, illuminated at its apex by a single dull lamp; the rest of the building was a gaunt outline. A clutch of detectives and armour-clad uniforms were waiting a few yards behind them, while the troop-carrier with its complement of PSU reinforcements was about fifty yards further back, parked in the nearest cul-de-sac. Everyone observed a strict silence.

Grinton finally turned around, keeping his voice low. 'Okay . . . listen up. Roberts, Atherton . . . you're staying with us.

437

The rest of you . . . round the other side. Any ground floor windows, any fire-doors, block 'em off. Grab anyone who tries to come out.'

There were nods of understanding as the group, minus two uniforms, shuffled away into the mist. Grinton checked his watch to give them five minutes to get in place, then glanced at Heck and Strickland and nodded. They detached themselves from the alley mouth, ascended the ramp and entered the brick passage, which was poorly lit by two faltering bulbs and defaced end to end with obscene, spray-painted slogans, which also covered three of its four doors. The only one that hadn't been vandalised in this fashion was 41c – the home of Alan Devlin.

There was no bell, so Grinton rapped on the door with his fist. Several seconds passed, before there was a fumbling on the other side. The door opened as far as its short safety chain would allow. The face beyond was in its mid-thirties, but pudgy and pock-marked, one eyebrow bisected by an old scar. He was squat and pot-bellied, with a shaved head. He'd answered the door in a grubby t-shirt and purple Y-fronts, but even through the narrow gap they spotted neck-chains and cheap, tacky rings on nicotine-yellow fingers. He didn't look hostile so much as puzzled, probably because the first thing he saw was Grinton's eye-patch. He put on a pair of thick-lensed, steel-rimmed glasses, so that he could scrutinize it less myopically.

'Alan Devlin?' the chief superintendent asked.

'Who the fuck are you?'

Grinton introduced himself, displaying his warrant card. 'This is Detective Inspector Strickland and this is Detective Sergeant Heckenburg.'

'Suppose I'm honoured,' Devlin grunted, looking anything but.

'Can we come in?' Grinton said.

'What's it about?'

'You don't know?' Strickland asked him.

Devlin threw him an ironic glance. 'Yeah . . . I just wondered if *you* did.'

Heck observed the householder with interest. Though clearly irritated that his evening had been disturbed, his relaxed body language suggested that he wasn't overly concerned. Either Devlin had nothing to hide or he was a competent performer. The latter was easily possible, as he'd had plenty of opportunity to hone such a talent while still a youth.

'Jimmy Hood,' Grinton explained. 'That name ring a bell?'

Devlin continued to regard them indifferently, but for several seconds longer than was perhaps normal. Then he removed the safety chain and opened the door.

Heck glanced at the two uniforms. 'Wait out here, eh? No sense crowding him in his own pad.' They nodded and remained in the outer passage, while the three detectives entered a dimly-lit hall strewn with crumbs and cluttered with piles of musty, unwashed clothes. An internal door stood open on a lamp-lit room from which the sound of a television emanated. There was a strong, noxious odour of chips and ketchup.

Devlin faced them square-on, adjusting his bottle-lens specs. 'Suppose you want to know where he is?'

'Not only that,' Grinton said, 'we want to know where he's been.'

There was a sudden thunder of feet from overhead – the sound of someone running. Heck tensed by instinct. He spun to face the foot of a dark stairwell – just as a figure exploded down it. But it wasn't the brutish giant, Jimmy Hood; it was a kid – seventeen at the most, with a mop of mouse brown hair and a thin moustache. He was only clad in shorts, which revealed a lean, muscular torso sporting several lurid tattoos – and was carrying a baseball bat.

'What the fucking hell?' He advanced fiercely, closing down the officers' space.

'Easy, lad,' Devlin said, smiling. 'Just a few questions, then they'll be gone.'

'What fucking questions?'

Strickland pointed a finger. 'Put the bat down, sonny.'

'You gonna make me?' The youth's expression was taut, his gaze intense.

'You want to make this worse for your old fella than it already is?' Grinton asked calmly.

There was a short, breathless silence. The youth glanced from one to the other, determinedly unimpressed by the phalanx of officialdom, though clearly unused to folk not running when he came at them tooled up. 'There's more of these twats outside, Dad. Sneaking around, thinking no one can see 'em.'

His father snorted. 'All this coz Jimbo breached his parole?'

'It's a bit more serious than that, Mr. Devlin,' Strickland said. 'So serious that I really don't think you want to be obstructing us like this.'

'I'm not obstructing you . . . I've just invited you in.'

Which was quite a smart move, Heck realised.

'We'll see.' Grinton walked towards the living room. 'Let's talk.'

Devlin gave a sneering grim and followed. Strickland went too. Heck turned to Wayne Devlin. 'Your dad wants to make it look like he's cooperating, son. Wafting that offensive weapon around isn't going to help him.'

Scowling, though now looking a little helpless – as if having other men in here chucking their weight about was such a challenge to his masculinity that he knew no adequate way to respond – the lad finally slung the baseball bat against the stair-post, which it struck with a deafening *thwack*, before shouldering past Heck into the living room. When Heck got in there, it was no less a bombsite than the hall: magazines were scattered – one lay open on a gynaecological centre-spread; empty beer cans and dirty crockery cluttered the table tops; overflowing ashtrays teetered on the mantel. The stench of ketchup was enriched by the lingering aroma of stale cigarettes.

'Let's cut to the chase,' Grinton said. 'Is Hood staying here now?'

'No,' Devlin replied, still cool.

Too cool, Heck thought. *Way too cool.*

'So if I come back here with a search-warrant, and go through this place with a fine-tooth comb, Mr. Devlin, I definitely won't find him?'

Devlin shrugged. 'If you thought you had grounds you'd already have a warrant. But it doesn't matter. You've got my permission to search anyway.'

'In which case I'm guessing there's no need, but we might as well look.' Grinton nodded to Heck, who went back outside and brought the two uniforms in. Their heavy boots thudded on the stair treads as they lumbered to the upper floor.

'How often has Jimmy Hood stayed here?' Strickland asked. 'I mean recently?'

Devlin shrugged. 'On and off. Crashed on the couch.'

'And you didn't report it?'

'He's an old mate trying to get back on his feet. I'm not dobbing him in for that.'

'When did he last stay?' Heck asked.

'Few days ago.'

'What was he wearing?'

'What he always wears . . . trackie bottoms, sweat-top, duffel coat. Poor bastard's living out of a placky bag.'

The detectives avoided exchanging glances. They'd agreed beforehand that there'd be no disclosure of their real purpose here until Grinton deemed it necessary; if Devlin had known what was happening and had still harboured his old pal, that made him an accessory to these murders – and it would help them build a case against him if he revealed knowledge without being prompted.

'When do you expect him back?' Heck asked.

Devlin looked amused by the inanity of such a question (*again false*, Heck sensed). 'How do I know? I'm not his fucking keeper. He knows he can come here anytime, but he never wants to outstay his welcome.'

'Has he got a phone, so you can contact him?' Strickland wondered.

'He hasn't got anything.'

'Does he ever come here late at night?' Grinton said. 'As in . . . unusually late?'

'What sort of bullshit questions are these?' Wayne Devlin demanded, increasingly agitated by the sounds of violent activity upstairs.

Grinton eyed him. 'The sort that need straight answers, son . . . else you and your dad are going to find yourselves deeper in it than whale shit.' He glanced back at Devlin. 'So . . . any late-night calls?'

'Sometimes,' Devlin admitted.

'When?'

'I don't keep a fucking diary.'

'Did he ever look flustered?' Strickland asked.

'When didn't he? He's on the lam.'

'How about bloodstained?' Grinton said.

At first Devlin seemed puzzled, but now, slowly – very slowly – his face lengthened. 'You're not . . . you're not talking about this Lady Killer business?'

'You've got to be fucking kidding!' Wayne Devlin blurted, looking stunned.

'Interesting thought, Wayne?' Heck said to him. 'Is that *your* bat out there . . . or Jimmy Hood's?'

The lad's mouth dropped open. Suddenly he was less the teen tough-guy and more an alarmed kid. 'It's . . . it's mine, but that doesn't mean . . .'

'So if we confiscate it for forensic examination and find blood, it's *you* we need to come for, not Jimmy?'

'That won't work, copper,' the older Devlin said, though for the first time there was colour in his cheek – it perhaps hadn't occurred to him that his son might end up carrying the can for something. 'You're not scaring us.'

Despite that, the younger Devlin *did* look scared. 'You won't find any blood on it,' he stammered. 'It's been under my bed for months. Jimbo never touched it. Dad, tell 'em what they want to fucking know.'

'Like I said, Jimbo's only been here a couple of times,' Devlin drawled. (*Still playing it calm*, Heck thought). 'Never settles down for long.'

'And it didn't enter your head that he might be involved in these murders?' Grinton said.

'Or are you just in denial?' Strickland asked.

'He was a good mate . . .'

'So you *are* in denial? Can't see the judge being impressed by that.'

'It may have occurred to me once or twice,' Devlin retorted. 'But you don't want to believe it of a mate . . .'

'Even though he's done it before?' Grinton said.

'Nothing this bad.'

'Bad enough . . .'

'You should get over to his auntie's!' Wayne Devlin interjected.

That comment stopped them dead. They gazed at him curiously; he gazed back, flat-eyed, cheeks flaming.

'What are you talking about?' Heck asked.

'He was always ranting about his Auntie Mavis . . .'

'*Wayne!*' the older Devlin snapped.

443

'If Jimbo's up to something dodgy, Dad, we don't want any part in it . . .'

These two are good, Heck thought. *These two are really good.*

'Something you want to tell us, Mr Devlin?' Grinton asked.

Devlin averted his eyes to the floor, teeth bared. He yanked his glasses off and rubbed them vigorously on his grubby vest – as though torn with indecision, as though angry at having been put in this position, but not necessarily angry at the police.

'Wayne may be right,' he finally said. 'Perhaps you should get over there. Her name's Mavis Cutler. Before you ask, I don't know much else. She's not his real auntie. Some old bitch who fostered Jimbo when he was a kid. Seventy-odd now, at least. I don't know what went on – he never said, but I think she gave him a dog's life.'

So Hood was attacking his wicked auntie every time he attacked one of these other women, Heck reasoned, remembering his basic forensic psychology. *It's a plausible explanation. A tad too plausible, of course.*

'And why do we need to get over there quick?' Strickland wondered.

Devlin hung his head properly, his shoulders sagging as if he was suddenly glad to get a weight off them. 'When . . . when Jimbo first showed up a few months ago, he said he was back in Nottingham to see her. And when he said 'see her', I didn't get the feeling it was for a family reunion if you know what I mean.'

'So why's it taken him this long?' Strickland asked.

'He couldn't find her at first. I think he may have gone up to Hucknall yesterday, looking. That's where they lived when he was a kid.'

Cleverer and cleverer, Heck thought. *Devlin's using real events to make it believable.*

'Someone up there probably told him,' Devlin added.

'Told him what?'

'That she lives in Matlock now. I don't know where exactly.'

Matlock in Derbyshire. Twenty five miles away. Quite a diversion.

'How do you know all this?' Grinton sounded suspicious.

Devlin shrugged. 'He rang me today . . . from a payphone. Said he was leaving town tonight, and that I probably wouldn't be seeing him again.'

'And you still didn't inform us?' Strickland's voice was thick with disgust.

'I'm informing you now, aren't I?'

'It might be too late, you stupid moron!' Strickland dashed out into the hall, calling the two uniforms from upstairs.

'Look, he never specifically said he was going to do that old bird,' Devlin protested to Grinton. 'He might not even be going to Matlock. He might be fleeing the fucking country for all I know! This is just guesswork!'

And you can't be prosecuted for guessing, Heck thought. *You're a cute one.*

'Don't do anything stupid, Mr Devlin,' Grinton said, indicating to Heck that it was time to leave. 'Like warning Jimmy we're coming. Any phone we find on Hood with calls traceable back to you are all we'll need to nick you as an accomplice.'

Out in the entry passage, Strickland was already bawling into his radio. 'I don't care how indisposed they are . . . get them to check the voters' rolls and phone directories. Find every woman in Matlock called Mavis bloody Cutler . . . over and out!' He turned to Grinton and Heck. 'We should lock that bastard Devlin up . . .'

Grinton shook his head, ignoring the door to 41c as it slammed closed behind them. 'He might end up witnessing for us. Let's not chuck away what little leverage we've currently got.'

'What if he absconds?'

'We'll sit someone on him.'

'Excuse me, sir,' Heck said. 'But I won't be coming over to Matlock with you.'

'Okay . . . something on your mind?'

'Yeah. Alan Devlin. Good show he put on in there, but I don't think Hood has any intention of going to Derbyshire. I reckon we're being sent on a wild goose chase.'

Strickland looked puzzled. 'Why would Devlin do that?'

'It's a hunch, sir, but it's got legs. Despite the serious crimes Jimmy Hood was last convicted for, Alan Devlin let him sleep on his couch. Not once, but several times. This guy is not too picky to associate with sex offenders.'

'Come on, Heck,' Strickland said. 'Devlin's in enough hot water as it is . . . he's not going to aid and abet a multiple killer as well.'

'He's in lukewarm water, sir. Apart from assisting an offender, what else has he admitted to? Even if it turns out he's sending us the wrong way, he's covered. It's all "I'm not sure about this, I'm only guessing that" . . . there aren't even grounds to charge him with obstructing an enquiry.'

'We can't *not* act on what he's told us,' Grinton said.

'I agree, sir. But while you're off to Matlock, I'm going to chase a few leads of my own. If that's okay?'

'No problem . . . just make sure you log them all.'

While Grinton arranged for a couple of his plain clothes officers to maintain covert obs on Lakeside View, the rest of them returned to their vehicles and mounted up for a rapid ride over to the next county. Strickland was back on the blower again, putting Derbyshire Comms in the picture as he jumped into his car. Heck remained on the pavement while he too made a quick call – in his case it was to the

DIU at St Ann's Central. As intelligence offices went, this one was pretty efficient. It was regularly utilised by the East Midlands Special Operations Unit, so its functionaries tended to know what they were doing.

'Heck?' came the hearty voice of PC Marge Propper, a chunky uniformed lass, whose fast, accurate research capabilities had already proved invaluable to the Lady Killer Taskforce.

'Marge . . . am I right in thinking that apart from Alan Devlin, Jimmy Hood has no other known associates in the inner Nottingham area?'

'Correct.'

'Okay . . . I want to try something different. Can you contact Roundhall Prison in Coventry? Find out who's been visiting Hood this last year and a half. Any regular names that haven't already cropped up in this enquiry, I'd like to know about them.'

'Wilco, Heck . . . might take a few minutes to get a response at this hour.'

'No worries. Call me back when you can.'

He paused before climbing into his Peugeot. The other mobile units had driven away, leaving a dull, dead silence in their wake. The surrounding buildings were little more than blurred, angular outlines, broken by the odd faint square of window light, most of which leached into the gloom without making any impression. The passage leading towards Lakeside View was a black rectangle, which bade no one re-enter it.

Heck climbed into his car and switched the engine on.

It was impossible to say whether or not they were on the right track, but it *felt* right. He still didn't trust Alan Devlin, but the guy's partial admissions had revealed that Jimmy Hood had been in this district as well as Hucknall – which put Hood close to all the identified murder scenes and in roughly the right time-frame. Of course, with the knowledge of hindsight, it was all so predictable and sordid. As Heck drove out of the cul-de-sac, it struck him that this decayed environment, with its broken glass and graffiti-covered maze of soulless brick alleys, seemed painfully familiar. So many of his cases had brought him to blighted places like this.

His phone rang and he slammed it to his ear. 'Yes?'

'We could have something here, Heck,' Marge Propper said. 'In his last three years at Roundhall, Jimmy Hood was visited nine times by a certain Sian Collier.'

'That name doesn't ring a bell.'

'No . . . she hasn't been on our radar up to now, though she's got minor form for possession and shoplifting. She's white, thirty-two years old and a local by birth. Her last conviction was over five years ago, so she may have cleaned up her act.'

'Apart from the bit where she gets mixed up with sex killers?'

'Yeah . . .'

Heck fiddled with his sat-nav. 'Where does she live?'

'Mountjoy Height, number 18 . . . that's in Bulwell.'

'I know it.'

'Heck . . . if you're going over there, you might want to speak to Division first. It's a lively place.'

'Thanks for the warning, Marge. But I'm only spying out the land. Anyway, I've got my radio.'

The murkiness of the winter night was now to aid Heck – mainly because it meant the roads were empty of traffic, but also because, once he arrived in Bulwell, he was able to cruise its foggy, rundown streets without attracting attention.

When he finally located Mountjoy Height, it was a row of pebble-dashed two-storey maisonettes on raised ground overlooking yet another labyrinthine housing estate. First, he made a drive-by at the front, seeing patches of muddy grass serving as communal front gardens, with wheelie-bins dotted across them and litter strewn haphazardly. There were only a couple of other vehicles present, but lights were on in most of the maisonette windows. After that, he explored at the rear, working his way down into a lower, winding alley, which ran past several garages. Some of these stood open, some closed. The garage to number eighteen didn't have a door attached, but was of particular interest because a large, good-looking motorcycle was parked inside it.

Heck glided to a halt and turned his engine off.

He climbed out, listening carefully; somewhere close by voices bickered. They were muffled and indistinct, but it sounded like a couple of adults; he wasn't initially sure where it was coming from – possibly number eighteen itself, which towered behind the garage in the gloom and was accessible by a narrow flight of steps running upward.

He assessed the motorbike through the entrance, and despite the darkness was able to identify it as a new model Suzuki GSX, an expensive make for this neck of the woods.

'DS Heckenburg to Charlie Six,' he said into his radio. 'PNC check, please?'

'DS Heckenburg?' came the crackly response.

'Anything on a black Suzuki GSX motorcycle, index Juliet-Zulu-seven-three-Bravo-Foxtrot-Alpha, over?'

'Stand by.'

Heck moved to the side of the garage and glanced up the steps. The monolithic structure overhead was wreathed in vapour, but lights still burned inside it, and the argument raged on; in fact it sounded as if it it had intensified. Glass shattered, which wasn't necessarily a bad thing – it might grant him the right to force entry.

'DS Heckenburg from PNC?'

'Go ahead.'

'Black Suzuki GSX motorcycle, index Juliet-Zulu-seven-

three-Bravo-Foxtrot-Alpha, reported stolen from Hucknall late last night, over.'

'Received, thanks for that. What were the circumstances of the theft, over?'

'Fairly serious, sarge. It's being treated as robbery. A motorcycle courier got a bottle broken over his head outside a fish and chip shop, and then had his helmet stolen as well as his ride. He's currently in IC. No description of the offender as yet.'

Heck pondered. This sounded more like Jimmy Hood by the minute. On the basis that he was now looking to make an arrest for a serious offence, Heck had the power to enter the garage – which he duly did, finding masses of junk littered in its oily shadows: boxes crammed with bric-a-brac; broken, dirty household appliances; even a pile of chains, several of which were wrapped around an upright steel girder supporting the garage roof.

'DS Heckenburg . . . are you saying you've found this vehicle, over?'

'That's affirmative,' Heck replied, pulling his gloves on as he mooched around. 'In an open garage at the rear of eighteen, Mountjoy Height, Bulwell. The suspect, who I believe to be inside the address, is Jimmy Hood. White male, early thirties, six foot three inches and built like a brick shithouse. Hood, who has form for extreme violence, is also a suspect in the Lady Killer murders. So I need back-up ASAP. Silent approach, over.'

'Received sarge . . . support units en route. ETA five.'

Heck shoved his radio back into his jacket and worked his way through the garage to a rear door, which swung open at his touch. He followed a paved side-path along the base of a steep, muddy slope, eventually joining with the flight of steps leading up to the maisonette. When he ascended, he did so warily. Realistically, all he needed to do now was wait until the cavalry arrived – but then something else happened.

And it was a game-changer.

The shouting and screaming indoors had risen towards a crescendo. Household items exploded as they were flung around. This was just about tolerable, given that it probably wasn't an uncommon occurrence in this neighbourhood. Heck reasoned that he could still wait it out – until he got close to the rear of the building, and heard a baby crying.

Not just crying.

Howling.

Hysterical with pain or fear.

'DS Heckenburg to Charlie Six, urgent message!' He dashed up the remaining steps, and took an entry around to the front of the maisonette. 'Please expedite that support . . . I can hear violence inside the property and a child in distress, over!'

He halted under the stoop. Light shafted through the frosted panel in the front door, yet little was visible on the other side – except for brief flurries of indistinct movement. Angry shouts still echoed from within.

Heck zipped his jacket and knocked loudly. 'Police officer! Can you open up please?'

There was instantaneous silence – apart from the baby, whose sobbing had diminished to a low and feeble keening.

Heck knocked again. 'This is the police . . . I need you to open up!' He glimpsed further hurried motion behind the distorted glass.

When he next struck the door, he led with his shoulder.

It required three heavy buffets to crash the woodwork inward, splinters flying, bolts and hinges catapulting loose. As the door fell in front of him, Heck saw a narrow, wreckage-strewn corridor leading into a small kitchen, where a tall male in a duffel coat was in the process of exiting the property via a back door. Heck charged down the corridor. As he did, a woman emerged from a side-room, bruised and tear-stained, hair disorderly, mascara streaking her cheeks. She wore a ragged orange dressing-gown and clutched a baby to her breast, its face a livid, blotchy red.

'What do you want?' she screeched, blocking Heck's passage. 'You can't barge in here!'

Heck stepped around her. 'Out the way please, miss!'

'But he's done nothing!' She grabbed Heck's collar, her sharp fingernails raking the skin on his neck. '*Can't you bastards stop harassing him?*'

Heck had to pull hard to extricate himself. 'Hasn't he just beaten you up?'

'That's coz I didn't want him to leave . . .'

'He's a bloody nutter, love!'

'It's nothing . . . I don't mind it.'

'Others do!' Heck yanked himself free – to renewed wailing from the woman and child – and continued into the kitchen and then out through the back door, emerging onto a toy-strewn patio just as a burly outline loped down the steps towards the garage. The guy had something in his hand, which Heck at first took for a bag; then he realised that it was a motorbike helmet. 'Jimmy Hood!' he shouted, scrambling down. 'Police officer . . . stay where you are!'

Hood's response was to leap the remaining three or four steps, pulling the helmet on and battering his way through the garage's rear door. Heck jumped as well, sliding and tumbling on the earthen slope, but reaching the doorway only seconds behind his quarry. He shouldered it open, to find Hood seated on the Suzuki, kicking it to life. Its glaring headlight sprang across the alley. The roar of its engine filled the gutted structure.

'Don't be a bloody fool!' Heck cried.

Hood glanced around – just long enough to flip Heck the

finger. And then hit the gas, the Suzuki bucking forward, almost pulling a wheelie it accelerated with such speed.

But the fugitive only made it ten yards, at which point, with a terrific *BANG*, the bike's rear wheel was jerked backwards beneath him. He somersaulted over the handlebars, slamming upside down against another garage door, before flopping onto the cobblestones, where he lay twisted and groaning. The bike came to rest a few yards away, chugging loudly, smoke pouring from its shattered exhaust.

'Bit remiss of you, Jimmy,' Heck said, emerging into the alley, toeing at the length of chain still pulled taut between the buckled rear wheel and the upright girder inside. 'Not checking that something hadn't got mysteriously wrapped around your rear axle.'

Flickering blue lights now appeared as local patrol cars turned into view at either end of the alley, slowly wending their way forward. Hood managed to roll over onto his back, but could do nothing except lie there, glaring with glassy, soulless eyes through the aperture where his visor had been smashed away.

Heck dug handcuffs from his back pocket and suspended them in full view. 'Either way, pal, you don't have to say anything. But it may harm your defence . . .'

Want more? Read the rest of
Hunted
*when it hits the shelves in
February 2014.*

PAUL FINCH
Stalkers

Time's up. You're next.

"All he had to do was name the woman he wanted. It was that easy. They would do all the hard work."

Detective Sergeant Mark 'Heck' Heckenburg is investigating the disappearance of 38 different women. Each one was happy and successful until they vanished without a trace.

Desperate to find her missing sister, Lauren Wraxford seeks out Heck's help. Together they enter a seedy underworld of gangsters and organised crime.

But when they hear rumours about the so-called 'Nice Guys Club' they hit a brick wall. They're the gang that no one will talk about. Because the Nice Guys can arrange anything you want. Provided you pay the price…

Dark, terrifying and unforgettable. *Stalkers* will keep fans of Stuart MacBride and Katia Lief looking over their shoulder.

A V O N

Follow Avon on
Twitter@AvonBooksUK
and
Facebook@AvonBooksUK
For news, giveaways and
exclusive author extras

A V O N